To my friend

Alfred Keys.

on my return from

Norwalk Conn

J. B. Kimerly.

1/10 73

HELEN AND WASHINGTON.

[See Page 277.]

PEMBERTON;

OR,

ONE HUNDRED YEARS AGO.

By HENRY PETERSON,

Author of "The Modern Job," &c.

"There comes a voice that awakes my soul. It is the voice of years that are gone, they roll before me with their deeds." OSSIAN.

PHILADELPHIA.

J. B. LIPPINCOTT & CO.

1873.

CONTENTS.

PART I.

PART II.

PART III.

PART IV.

PEMBERTON.

PART I.

CHAPTER I.

THE SURPRISE.

> **Oh, peaceful earth—oh, patient, green-browed earth—**
> **Sad mother of the whirlwind and the storm.**

It is a morning in October, in the year 1777. Early morning—for the sun has not yet risen, though the heralds of his imperial coming are seen flushing with their crimson and purple banners the eastern sky. The earth, too, seems to respond with a regal pomp of banners. Crimson, melting at one place into a rich brown, flashing in another into a living flame, and harmoniously blending everywhere with the deep green of the cedar and the hemlock, is all around us. The glory of the earth rivals that of the sunlit sky. For, as we have said, it is October; and we are in Pennsylvania, the wooded land of Penn.

Two young ladies, arrayed in riding costume, are standing before an open window, in an upper chamber of a large stone mansion. Their room being open only to the north and the west, they have caught but faint glimpses of the glory of the sunrise—but the glory of the earth-rise from darkness into light, is spread widely before them. The coolness of the morning air, which, though a little raw to those of maturer years, comes pleasantly upon their faces, glowing with the rich, warm blood of youth, also is like wine unto their buoyant spirits. Let us listen to what they are saying.

"Do you know what first came into my mind, Bel, when that fierce 'rap, rap, rap,' sounded on our door this morning?" said the younger of the two, a maiden apparently of some twenty summers.

"Yes—that the enemy were upon us. That made you spring out of bed in such a fright," said the elder sister, mischievously.

"Fright! and I the daughter of a Scottish colonel! You are joking, Bella. No, I thought we were again schoolgirls, among the nuns of Bethlehem.

> "'Sing a song of sixpence,
> Pocket full of tow,
> Sixty single bedsteads
> All in a row.'

"Oh, but we had high old times in Bethlehem, Bel. I wish sometimes we were back again, among the simple-minded sisters."

"Well I cannot say, Helen, that I do."

"Of course not—Pemberton!"

"André."

"Nonsense, Bel—I have not seen Captain André more than a dozen or twenty times in my life. But let us take one look more, and then go down. Uncle must be waiting."

"This is a beautiful place to live in, Helen—is it not? See how finely the walks are laid out, with their marble vases and statues. And what a glorious view one has to the west, over the valley of the Wissahickon! Where are the Chews now?"

"I think the judge has been sent to Virginia—you

know he is no more sound in the faith than old 'Cousin' Pemberton; he cannot quite swallow the Independence declaration. He would not even give his parole to the rebels. I suppose the ladies are with him. They are brilliant girls."

"Had we not better go down now?"

"Stay—one moment. Do you see that gray mist—how curiously it sweeps down upon us from the north. One might almost take it for the sweeping onward of a hostile army. I am afraid we shall have a dull morning after all, for our ride to town. See, how rapidly it comes—before it all light and sunshine; behind it all darkness and gloom."

"Hark! did you hear that?" cried Isabella, excitedly.

A dull report was heard, as if of a pistol, or distant musket.

"It is an attack!" cried Helen, when this was followed by a loud report, as of a field-piece, and then by the distant roll of a drum, beating to arms.

"Girls!" called a deep voice at the door of the room; and then the door was pushed open, and, seeing them attired, an elderly man, in the uniform of a British colonel entered, and joined them at the window.

"What is it, uncle?" exclaimed both, almost in a breath.

"It is an attack—it may be in force. It is a bad business, girls, having you here."

"Do not be alarmed for us, uncle. We will give you no trouble," said Isabella, proudly.

"If it is in force, we must march at once," said Colonel Musgrave, as if communing with himself. "And it sounds so"—as volley after volley of musketry broke upon his ears. "But there comes one of Simcoe's dragoons," he exclaimed, as a horseman rode up in hot haste, sword flashing, and helmet glittering. "Come down, girls, we shall learn something definite now."

They hurried through the almost unfurnished house, and down to the front door-steps where the dragoon had reined up.

"Colonel—the rebels are on us. It was almost a surprise. They have our camp. But we are holding them back."

"How many? in force?"

"The whole of Washington's army, I was bid to tell you."

"Wait one moment, girls," cried the colonel, as he sprang around the house, in the rear of which his regiment was encamped. Soon the roll of the drum was heard, and the silence of an orderly encampment gave place to loud commands and the bustle of military preparation.

"I must lead the regiment at once to the support of the light infantry," said Colonel Musgrave, as he again joined his wards. "Can you risk riding to town alone—or how would it do to ride to headquarters! That is only about a couple of miles off."

"If it were not for this mist, which has closed upon us so quickly, we could easily do either," replied Isabella.

"Why cannot we remain here?" said Helen. "We shall be near you, uncle—and there may be wounded men to care for. We are not cowards."

"No; I know you are not. But I should feel far easier in my mind if I knew you were in safety, and not exposed to those perils which always hang around contending armies. As to this house, if the enemy is in force, it will not long be a place of safety. I have sent word to Howe—but the advance of the rebels must be delayed as long as possible, in order to give time for him to get in position; and this mansion will make a capital fort, if need be."

Colonel Musgrave spoke rapidly and excitedly—as if anxious to be at his post.

"Well, uncle, do not fear for us; we will mount and ride, either to town or to headquarters, as may seem best," said Isabella.

"Who shall I send with you?"

"Nobody—we can protect ourselves for that distance."

"Perhaps you are right. A British uniform would be as apt to draw as to ward off a rebel bullet. And, rebels though the colonists be, they are not given to shooting at women. But come in and take a cup of coffee to brace yourselves up with."

A cup of coffee and some slices of bread were hastily swallowed, and then the young ladies mounted their horses —the colonel at the same time springing on his horse.

"Girls, you know the way?"

"Very well," said Isabella—"even in this mist."

"You had better, it seems to me, not try to go down the Main road. It may by this time be sprinkled with the rebel troopers. I should advise you to strike over to the east, to the Limekiln road, and make your way down it. You know that, about a mile down, you can either strike into Germantown again, at the market place, or, if you hear firing in that direction, turn to the east once more, and follow the New York road to the city. If anything looks dangerous, take refuge in some private house—nobody will refuse protection to two lorn damsels in distress. But let me know at once, after the battle, where you are."

Colonel Musgrave had spoken rapidly—for his men had already left their encampment, with the exception of one company, which seemed to await further orders, and the roar of battle swelled louder and louder in his ears. Now he passed his hand rapidly over his eyes, and said in a slower, softer tone:

"And, girls, remember, if anything should happen to your old uncle, that he loved you very dearly, and, next to his king and country, would have died for you."

Touching her horse with the whip, Helen was in a moment by the colonel's side—bending from her saddle to throw an arm around his neck, and to kiss his lips. "Uncle, let me stay with you—to live or die with you!" exclaimed she.

"Yes, uncle—do not drive us away from you," chimed in Isabella. "Dearest and best of friends—heaven knows how good and kind you have always been to us."

"You quite make a child of me, my dear girls," said the colonel, wiping his eyes once more. "And how foolish it all is! This is not my first, nor my fifth battle, as you well know. I came out of the others safely, and I mean to come safely out of this. But, if you do not go, and at once, I shall fight this battle with a heavy and troubled heart. Hear how the roar of the battle deepens! It is coming nearer. If you go at once, I do not think there is any great amount of danger—but, if you stay, I know not what to do with you."

"We will go at once then," said Isabella, turning her horse's head to the south. "And may heaven preserve you—best of benefactors and friends!"

"Stay," said the colonel—taking a pistol from its holster, and half smiling, notwithstanding the seriousness of the occasion. "Will either of you have this?"

"No, I thank you," replied Isabella, smiling in turn. "I will trust to the usual womanly weapons, and to the chivalry of men."

"Give it to me, then," cried Helen, impulsively. "Would I were a man to go with you, uncle, and not be shipped off as an incumbrance in this fashion. Is it ready for use?"

"Be careful with it, Helen—my servant always sees to it every morning. It will not fail you, if required," replied the Colonel. "But I can stay no longer. May the all-seeing God guide and keep you!" Putting spurs to his horse, Colonel Musgrave rode rapidly to the rear of the house—gave orders to the captain of the company he had held in reserve, to occupy the mansion, to barricade the doors and lower windows, and arrange everything for a vigorous defence if such should be necessary—and then dashed off after his regiment.

By this time the mist had so closed around, as to render it impossible to see more than twenty or thirty yards distance, and that imperfectly. Judging from the noise of the conflict however—the continual rattle of musketry, the cries and shouts, and the occasional roar of field-pieces—the battle was rapidly rolling down toward the mansion. This proved that the British were still giving ground. Occasional musket shots were also beginning to be heard on the Main road or street of the village, upon which, at a distance of several hundred feet, the building fronted. And it was evident to the young ladies that the sooner they started, the greater was their chance of effecting their ride in safety.

CHAPTER II.

MOLL OF THE HATCHET.

> MORTON. This is a cruel hag!
> PIETRO. Indeed, my lord,
> You well may say so.

WELL acquainted with the roads, and with the lanes—as all the shorter and narrower roads were appropriately called in that section of the country—the young ladies rode as rapidly as the misty obscurity would permit, in a southern direction through a farm path, to a lane which is now called by the name of Washington, but which then doubtless had some local designation. Helen had concealed the pistol her uncle had given her, in one of the large pockets worn at that day, and notwithstanding the possible difficulties of their situation, the spirits of the sisters seemed to rise as their high mettled steeds chafed under the curb which it was necessary to hold upon them.

"Pshaw! would I were a man!" said Helen. "I should like to fire one good shot at least for my king—and stand by Uncle Musgrave in the thick of the battle. We are but an insignificant tribe, we women, Bella."

"Well, for one woman, I am quite satisfied with my natural position," replied Isabella. "Why did you take that pistol? I declare I am afraid you will shoot me with it yet. I am glad that you have it on the other side of you. Take care you do not pull the trigger without meaning to."

"Never fear, sister mine. I have shot off a pistol before this. Captain André gave me a whole hour's practice, down at Gray's Ferry, one afternoon. But here is the road, is it not? Yes, there is the gate, lying in the road. What would the Chews say if they were here, and could see their beautiful country-place now—gates and fences down in all directions."

"They are just as well off as their neighbors. I scarcely think there is a single farm fence standing in Germantown. What with the Hessian huts, and all the soldiers' fuel, the farms and country-seats seem to be pretty well stripped. But, as you say, we turn toward the east here."

"If it were not for this mist we could canter to headquarters in half an hour," said Helen.

"Yes, in less time—but do take care, Helen; the ground is boggy near that stream," said Isabella, as they were crossing one of the little so-called creeks with which that part of the country is favored—streams which are seldom dry, even in the greatest heats of summer.

Slowly the young ladies rode on, the noise of the battle growing fainter as they rode. But they had not gone much more than a mile, before the quick ear of Helen caught a noise in front of them. "What is that, Bel? Do you hear it?"

"Stop a minute," said her sister. They had just ridden through a piece of woods, and they now gazed and listened intently. "It is the tramp and clatter of a regiment," said Helen. "They are going down the Limekiln road. What does it mean?"

"It means they are the Americans—marching to attack the British right wing," replied Isabella, in a low voice, her face whitening a little.

"We do not want to travel in that company," said Helen, defiantly.

"No. We must turn back. And quickly, too. I vow some of them are coming this way. Perhaps they mean to attack the Fortieth."

Wheeling their horses the young ladies rode back upon their track, and more rapidly too than they had come.

"What shall we do, sis?" said Helen.

"Wait a moment—let us see first how things stand."

They could not see, but they could soon hear how things stood. The large stone house they had left, then sleeping peacefully in its gray curtains of mist, was now a fortress, belching forth shot and smoke. Colonel Musgrave was evidently doing his devoir bravely, as a soldier true to his king. And other men, equally brave and true, and wiser in their day and generation, evidently were doing their devoir also with ball and bullet.

Despite the peril, Helen's cheeks flushed. "The Fortieth is holding back the whole of Washington's army," cried she, exultingly. "Give me the Scottish blood after all, in the hour—"

Her sentence was suddenly cut short by a cannon-ball, which struck the trunk of a large chestnut-tree not twenty feet from them, and rolled on the ground at the feet of their horses. The spirited animals, already excited by the deepening roar of the battle, sprung and reared, until it required all the skill of the fair riders—practised horsewomen though they were—to reduce them to subjection.

"What shall we do, Bel? This is getting a little too exciting here. We cannot go back to the house—the Main road is evidently full of rebels—and behind us are more of the same sort. Speak quick."

"The fences are all down—let us take to the fields, and push through them to the British lines. Of course there is some risk—but there is more in staying here," replied Isabella.

The good sense of the suggestion was so evident, that at the word "fields," Helen had turned her horse's head to the south, and rode into the open fields—commons as they now seemed, in their desolation. They could still see only a very little distance around them—not more than sufficient to enable them to keep the general direction in which they wished to go—while on the Main road, which ran parallel with their course, they could hear scattering shots which told that the advance of the Americans had passed Chew's house, and was pressing down upon the British centre.

It was rather a trying position for young ladies who had been carefully and even elegantly nurtured; but, as the old proverb has it, "blood will tell," and these were Grahams—daughters of a race that had proved its courage and endurance on many a hard-fought field; and what is more, in the cottage of the exile, and on the scaffold of the proscribed and the outlawed.

It would have seemed less trying even could they have put their horses into a wild gallop—but now that they had left the road, the danger of stumbling in the mist over empty post-holes, and partially removed fences, necessitated the greatest watchfulness. And, therefore, although they could hear the rattle of buckshot occasionally in the leaves of the trees under which they passed, they had to make progress slowly.

"Don't ride over that wounded horse!" at length suddenly exclaimed Helen to her sister.

Isabella pulled up hastily—for directly before her the animal was lying—evidently the horse of a soldier from the military equipments.

"I wonder where the rider is?" said she, in a sympathizing tone.

"There—look there—what does that mean?" cried Helen.

A wounded officer, dressed in the Continental blue and buff, was lying on the ground, apparently interposing as much resistance as possible, to the plundering efforts of a brawny Irish woman, who with a bag by her side, and a hatchet in her hand, was tugging at his coat to get it off his shoulders, careless of the pain she inflicted. As the ladies rode up, they heard her say,

"Be aisy now, you ribil, or I'll split yer head with my hatchet—as I've sarved many a better looking lad nor you."

"Moll of the hatchet," said Isabella, in a low voice to her sister. "It must be she."

The woman, looking up, suddenly perceived them. "What are the likes of ye doin' here?" she exclaimed hoarsely. "This is a swate place for the gintry, sure."

"My good woman," said Isabella, "you certainly are not robbing or hurting that wounded soldier!"

"He isn't a wounded soger, he's a baste of a ribil. Ride on wid ye, or it'll be the wus for you. Ride on, I say."

Moll of the hatchet, for it was indeed she, whose bad fame as a cruel robber of the wounded had spread through both armies, now rose to her feet, and shaking her hatchet menacingly, again hoarsely bade them ride onward.

"Not a step!" indignantly exclaimed Isabella; "are you not ashamed of yourself, you, a woman, to maltreat a wounded and, perhaps, a dying man?"

"There's no use talking with such vile Irish trash," exclaimed Helen, her haughty blood flaming in her face, as she cut her horse with the whip, and forced him between Moll and the wounded man, nearly overturning the woman. Then flinging her whip to the ground, and pulling out her pistol, and cocking it, she presented it full at Moll's face, exclaiming, "Now, by the good Lord above us, if you do not at once drop that hatchet, and leave this place, I will blow your cruel brains out!"

Moll hesitated—though her face blanched, as her eyes looked down the muzzle of the pistol.

"Down with your hatchet, I say!" said Helen, in the suppressed tones of deep passion. "One moment more, and I shoot."

The hatchet fell to the ground.

"Now, leave this spot—at once!"

"By the holy Pathrick—she's the divil of an angel, or the angel of a divil," said Moll, in a half stupor, taking up her bag to depart.

"Put down that bag!" said Helen, the pistol again bearing on Moll.

The bag fell.

"Now go—and at once!"—the pistol still lowering—the light, firm finger on the trigger.

"By the holy divil!" muttered Moll to herself, as she tramped off—glancing occasionally behind, to see the pistol still following her, until the mist hid her from view.

"That pistol was a friend in need after all, sis," said Helen, demurely.

"You are my brave and noble sister; and your taking the pistol was an inspiration from heaven," replied Isabella, gazing admiringly upon her. "But what are we to do now? We cannot leave this rescued knight lying here, perhaps to be murdered by that vile hag, perhaps to die from want of proper attention to his wound. There must be some house near, into which he could be taken."

"There are plenty of houses, here and there, along the Main road; suppose you go and see if you cannot bring help from one of them, while I remain here on guard with my pistol."

"I hate to go and leave you alone."

"And I hate to see you go alone. But what can we do?"

The case was so clear, that Isabella turned her horse toward the Main road, in quest of a dwelling. She soon came to the rear of a medium-sized stone building, and riding up to the kitchen door, beat it lustily with the butt of her riding-whip. But no one seemed to be within. Dismounting, she fastened her horse to a part of the garden fence which remained standing, and pushed open the door. Entering, she nearly stumbled over a masculine form, lying extended just inside the threshold.

"Bress de Lord! Bress de Lord!" the white black lips of a prostrate negro were ejaculating.

"Where is your master?" demanded Isabella.

"Bress de Lord—he am down in de cellur," replied the negro.

Opening the cellar door, Isabella called aloud—

"Halloo—the house!"

A step was heard on the stairs, and soon a tall, gaunt form in Quaker costume, presented itself.

"What does thee want?" said the figure.

"Is the cellar the usual sitting-room in Germantown?" inquired Isabella, sarcastically.

"No, not the usual one. But thee sees when bullets come visiting unexpectedly, they are apt to put quiet housekeepers out"—and the Quaker, whose face denoted a fondness for quaint humor and sly jokes, gave a little laugh. "But what does thee wish—has thee come to spend a quiet day with Uncle Seth and Aunt Hannah?"

In a few words Isabella made known her errand. And to do Seth justice, now that good was to be done, he manifested very little fear either of cannon-ball or bullet. Raising the trembling negro to his feet, and giving him a good shaking to restore his mental and physical equilibrium, they both proceeded, led by Isabella, to the relief of the wounded officer.

"There are a good many Quakers about Germantown, I believe," said Isabella, as they walked on.

"Yes, and a good many quakers, just now, who do not belong to the Society of Friends," replied Seth. "Now, here's this darkey, Juba—he's been the worst kind of a quaker, ever since he heard the first gun fired. But there's another of you, is there?" added he, as they approached Helen, who had returned the pistol to her pocket, dismounted from her horse, and was now bending over the wounded man.

She said he had been apparently conscious for a moment, when she had unloosed the tie around his neck, but had soon sunk again into unconsciousness.

"Fainted from loss of blood," said Seth—and taking the wounded officer carefully by the shoulders, while the negro supported his feet, they carried him to the house. The sisters accompanied them—one leading her horse, the other carrying the hatchet and the partially filled bag, which the Irish woman had left behind her.

When they entered the house, Seth deposited his inanimate burden on a settee, and said briskly to a kind-looking woman of middle age, who had come up from her place of safety to see what was going on:

"Now, mother—here's a wounded soldier. Bring down some quilts, while I see where he is hurt. Was he thrown from his horse, at the time he was wounded?"

"Indeed I do not know—we were not present—he is a perfect stranger to us," replied Isabella.

The Quaker looked as astonished as one of his composed sect could be expected to.

"I thought he was your brother, or friend," said he.

"No, we came across him accidentally," rejoined Isabella—and then briefly narrated who they were, and how they had left their uncle to seek a place of safety, and their encounter with the female marauder—saying nothing of the pistol however.

"And so you persuaded Moll to give up her prey, and leave her hatchet and her plunder? Well, I never! But," and here his face brightened, "ah, I see—a little silver or gold will do a great deal. Money makes even such vicious mares as Moll go."

During his remarks however, Seth had not been idle. He had examined into the condition of the wounded man's shoulder, which was the injured place, and was now about pouring some Jamaica rum into a cup. While the officer, on his part, manifested symptoms of returning consciousness.

"It is not an artery," said Seth, "that seems certain. The blood has clotted and stopped itself—and I will not remove the linen which sticks to it, because I might set it going again. When he swallows a spoonful of this good liquor, I think he'll feel stronger."

As the officer's face assumed a more natural hue, Seth started, and looked at him earnestly. Then he exclaimed, "Why, mother, look here! Is not this our Stephen's friend, Lefttenant Morris of McLane's troop? It is, surely."

"Of course it is," said his wife, "I wonder thee did not see it was, at first."

"I suppose I ought to, but then my wits were wool-gathering in a very different direction."

"Now," said Isabella to her sister, "as the gentleman seems to be doing well, and is among his friends, perhaps we had better pursue our ride."

"What!" said the Quaker matron. "You do not mean to go out among those dreadful soldiers!"

Seth stepped outside of the kitchen door. "Come here," he said to Isabella. "Hear that!"

The noise of musketry, which had been only faintly heard for the past half-hour, was evidently swelling up again, not only to the north of them, at Chew's house, but to the south, in the direction of the British headquarters, and between themselves and Philadelphia.

"If you ride either north or south, you ride into the fire," said Seth. "Now take an old man's counsel. Remain here—in comparative safety. In perfect safety, if you choose to go below, into the cellar," he added slyly.

Helen shook her head to the last proposition, disdainfully.

"Well, in this back room, with the front of the house closed, you are comparatively safe; and near to your uncle besides. I will put your horses in the stable, where they will take their chances with my horse—the only one they've left me. Mother will manage to find us something to eat for dinner—if we're alive to eat it—and when this horrible affair comes to a conclusion, as I suppose it soon must, one way or the other, you can mount, and ride wherever you think best."

"Indeed you are very kind," said Isabella. "We dislike to trouble you—"

"Not a particle of trouble, my dear," interrupted Mrs. Williams. "Come up-stairs now; I know you would like to fix a little;" and she led the way, while the young ladies smilingly followed.

At this juncture, the wounded officer drew a deep breath and opened his eyes. Gazing around him for a moment, he said in a faint voice, "Why, Uncle Seth, I did reach here, after all. I was wounded down below, and thought I should never get to you. What a dream I have had! I thought I was dead, and a fiend and an angel were fighting over my body, to see which should have me!" and the young man smiled faintly.

"Hem! thee is all right—but thee had better not talk any more just now, but turn over and go to sleep. Mother is a splendid nurse, and I'm as good as a doctor; and, if thee minds what we say, thee'll get well before many weeks, I warrant."

The young man closed his eyes, and seemed to obey very easily the advice given him. While Seth turned his face toward Juba, who sat, observant of all that was going on, in the corner of the fireplace, and saw the latter's white ivories illuminating the blackness of his visage from ear to ear.

"What is thee grinning about?" said Seth, severely—"go out at once, and stable those horses."

Then he sat down in a chair, and seemed to enjoy something himself hugely, though in a very quiet, subdued and decorous Quaker fashion.

"Well, I suppose young men will be young men, to the end of the chapter," said he at length to himself, apparently as the result of his meditations

CHEW'S HOUSE.

CHAPTER III.

THE BATTLE IN THE MIST.

MORTON. How went the battle?
PIETRO. Excellent, my lord;
We did not all we set about to do,
But then we gave the braggart enemy
A most uncommon scare.

WE avail ourselves of this pause in our narrative, to sketch in a few words the main features of the battle which came so unexpectedly, like a summer thunderstorm, upon Col. Musgrave and his fair visitors.

Lying on the Germantown or Skippack road, at a distance of about six miles from Philadelphia, the village of Germantown extended in a line of scattered stone houses, for about two miles in a northwesterly direction.

Across the centre of the village, where the road was widened for the erection of a market-house, the British army lay stretched like some huge bird of prey—some vulture, or some condor of the desert — measuring about four miles from the tip of one huge wing on the New York road, to the tip of the other on the Schuylkill.

But the weight of the body lay in the centre, directly in and around the market place, where its iron beak and talons—in the shape of a splendid park of artillery—were lying ready to tear and rend whenever the occasion offered.

In front, to secure the army against surprise, were a detachment of light infantry at Mount Airy, and the Fortieth regiment, under Col. Musgrave, at Chew's House—with other detachments in equally available positions.

The British force had been weakened by the detaching of three thousand men, comprising the elite of the army, to garrison Philadelphia, and make glad the hearts of the loyal in that important city. Another force also had been detached against the American defences on the Delaware. And well aware of these movements, after having been himself reinforced by fresh troops from New Jersey and Maryland, Washington determined to strike a blow at Sir William Howe, even in the midst of his fancied security.

The plan of the American attack was well conceived and daring. It was to make a night march, to cut off the British sentries before daybreak at the advanced post at Mount Airy, so that they could not give the alarm—to break like a tornado upon the light infantry and Col. Musgrave's regiment, driving them as chaff before the wind—and thus fall upon the British main line at the centre of the town, while it was wholly or partially unprepared.

Gen. Greene was to co-operate with this movement, by marching down the Limekiln road, which led to the front of the British right wing, to take it also unprepared, and drive all before him to the same central point, the market-house. Thus the right wing would either be divided or broken, the centre overwhelmed by sheer weight of numbers, and the left wing thrown back against the Schuylkill river, with a victorious army between it and Philadelphia, and doomed to surrender at discretion.

The plan was an admirable one, and only needed good soldiers, good fortune and a rapid execution. But the night was dark, the roads were bad, and by the time the attack was to be begun, day had dawned, and the British encampments were awake and stirring. Captain McLane, to whose daring enterprise had been intrusted the duty of quietly capturing or killing the pickets, failed to effect his purpose. The alarm was given, and soon the three field pieces at Mount Airy communicated that alarm to the whole British camp. Wayne, hotter than ever from the shame of his recent midnight defeat, pressed on dauntlessly with his brigade of Pennsylvanians—his soldiers shouting to one another, "*Remember Paoli!*"—but they met men of the same stalwart race; and the British advance, with tenfold their number in front of them, knowing well the importance of time, maintained to the full the ancient reputation of their arms. Forced back upon Musgrave, after half an hour's hard fighting, the latter also soon yielded ground, but flung himself into the stone mansion of Judge Chew, barricading its lower doors and windows, and keeping up a heavy fire from the second story, the roof, and the outbuildings; while the remnant of the light infantry, pursued remorselessly by Wayne's maddened soldiery, fled down the road toward the main body.

To add to the difficulties of the assailants, a heavy mist had arisen, which, combined with the smoke of the battle, rendered all objects obscure at the distance of a few yards, and prevented the commanders from knowing the position of their various corps and regiments.

Wayne had pressed on after the British, down the main road toward the market-house; but when Conway's corps came up, it halted and joined those who were engaged in the assault upon Musgrave.

At this moment up rode Sullivan, at the head of his brigade, and with him the Commander-in-Chief and his staff, with General Knox, of the artillery.

"What is this?" asked Washington.

He might well ask, for nothing could be seen, though the bullets were whistling all around them, and a return fire, accompanied with shouts, could be heard from the other side of the stone wall which lined the road.

An officer of Conway's brigade answered. "A party

of British have thrown themselves into a large stone house, about a hundred yards from the road, and we are trying to dislodge them."

"Wait a moment till I bring up my cannon," said Gen. Knox, a very corpulent but withal active man, with an animated, resolute face.

"This is madness!" broke in one of Washington's aids, a small, handsome and fiery young man, called at that day by some "the little lion," but afterwards known as one of the wisest of statesmen and ablest of financiers—Hamilton the Immortal!

"It would be madness to leave a fort in our rear, to cut off our line of communication," replied Knox. "That is against one of the first maxims of military science."

"A fort!" echoed Hamilton, disdainfully. "Leave a regiment here to watch them, and drive them back if they attempt mischief—but our time is too precious to waste in battering down houses."

"Yes, but who knows that the British are not marching up through the fields on the other side, and in force, to their support," interposed Sullivan. "They would take us then in flank and rear."

All turned to the commander. "Perhaps," said he, "while we stand here considering, an earnest attack will capture the house, and settle the question to please all of us. We have to decide at a venture, for we can see nothing in this mist. Major White, cannot you take a party, and force the main door?"

"Or fire the doors and shutters?" suggested Hamilton.

Major White, reputed to be the handsomest man in the army, as he had been previously in the ball-rooms of Philadelphia, smiled proudly as he answered—

"I will try, general."

Knox rode off rapidly, notwithstanding, to bring up his cannon.

Major White dashed against the door, it was already riddled with musket bullets, but it had been strongly barricaded, and his men dropped off rapidly beneath the constant fire from the upper windows.

Then he had some pieces of rails and other light stuff collected, and darted forward again alone, with a fagot of these, a bundle of straw, and a lighted torch. Sheltered under the cornice of the doorway, while his men poured a steady rain of balls into the upper windows, he might have succeeded—but a shot from a cellar window struck him, and he staggered back off the steps, and fell mortally wounded upon the ground.

By this time Knox had got a field-piece in position—but his heaviest guns were six pounders, and while the balls went through the walls of the house, they made no opening by which a foe could enter.

A half hour had been wasted. Washington had sat quietly upon his horse, listening to the reports his aids had brought him, seemingly unconscious of the storm of bullets raging around, until in compliance with General Sullivan's repeated importunities, he shifted his position a little out of the range of the heaviest fire.

"Hamilton was right," said he at length, "as he is apt to be. But, as we have remained this long, suppose we try a summons to surrender. General"—to Sullivan—"have a parley beaten, and a flag of truce sent in."

Unfortunate order. The American advance, while this attack was going on, had dashed against the British centre, but had been met by a determined resistance. Wayne had penetrated to the Market Square; Greene, with the left wing, had forced his way nearly to the same point; but the British were recovering from the first shock, were bringing up regiments from the left and rear, the ammunition of Wayne's men had given out, a Virginia regiment had been surrounded and captured, it was difficult in the mist and smoke to distinguish friend from foe, and when the parley was beaten at Chew's, it was taken by many of the undisciplined Americans for the beating of a retreat. "We are surrounded!" cried some. "The retreat is beating!" cried others. And in spite of all the efforts of their officers, several of the regiments turned and fled.

As the confused mass came surging back, up the main street, breaking the lines of Sullivan's brigade, it was evident that all the chances of success had passed, and Washington reluctantly gave the order to retreat. And thus bad roads, and mist, and the mistaken delay as it proved at Chew's house, and the want of ammunition, and the misunderstanding of a drum-beat, lost the battle of Germantown.

WALNUT STREET FRONT OF THE STATE HOUSE IN 1776.

CHAPTER IV.

CAPTAIN ANDRE.

A handsome man, and, more, a lovable;
And, though an enemy, our honor bids
Due entertainment should be given him.

By eleven o'clock the battle was over. The mist and smoke alike had cleared away. The sounds of the conflict had subsided into the calm peace of a sunny Autumnal morning. And were it not for the holes and rents left in the walls and wood-work of the houses by the passage of bullets and cannon-balls, and the stark and ghastly bodies of the slain, and the convulsed limbs and suppressed groans of wounded men, no one would have supposed that the hurricane of war had so recently darkened and deafened the apparently careless and unconscious heavens.

Seth Williams and his visitors, standing at his front door, had seen Cornwallis dash on after the retreating Americans at the head of his cavalry, all wet with the sweat and foam of their rapid gallop from Philadelphia—had seen the grenadiers and Highlanders, panting and exhausted with their six miles run, flinging themselves down to rest upon the sides of the road, and on the steps of the houses—and then had gone in to partake of a country dinner, which Mrs. Williams had prepared for them. The young ladies ate with but a moderate appetite, for they felt anxious, not only for their uncle, but for other officers of the British army whom they knew intimately, although Mrs. Williams's food was of the best, and served on the cleanest of pewter platters. A batter pudding which she had boiled in a bag, and which was eaten with butter and West India molasses, was of itself enough to have tempted the appetite of an epicure—if any epicure ever had a real and genuine appetite. But it was in vain she pressed her viands upon her visitors—they were too anxious at heart to enjoy anything but good news.

"Now," said Seth, as he rose from the table, "I will travel up toward friend Chew's, and see if I can find your uncle, young women, and let him know where you are, and that you are safe and hearty."

The ladies looked their thanks.

"As for Morris, I'm glad we got him so soon up-stairs —for if any of those pesky soldiers should come peeking in here, they might make both him and us trouble."

Putting on his slouched hat, Seth left the house, and made his way up the street. Parties of soldiers were already engaged in carrying the wounded into the nearest barns and other buildings, where the surgeons were busily employed. Others assisted by the citizens were burying the dead, several of whom, as Seth saw, had been plundered to the very skin, and were lying livid to blackness, and almost naked, on the side of the road, where they had either crawled themselves, or been dragged by others.

"And these be Christian men, who rend and tear each other in this savage fashion!" muttered Seth. "For my part, I never could call myself a Christian, if I took part in such horrid doings."

A short distance brought him to Judge Chew's place. Everything looked indeed as if a tornado had passed through there. The pleasant paths were torn up, the marble statues and vases mutilated and overthrown, branches of the trees were broken off, and hanging over and strewing the walks—and the fair mansion itself, with its doors and shutters riddled with bullets, was torn with cannon-balls, and blackened with fire and smoke. Above, scarcely a pane of glass or an entire window-sash remained. Soldiers were moving about, looking as dirty and grimy as the house itself—their faces blackened with gunpowder, and their clothes torn and soiled.

"Where can I find the colonel?" asked Seth of one of them.

The soldier looked at him for a moment, and simply pointed to the front of the house.

"A d——d Quaker!" said he to a comrade, as Seth passed on.

Suddenly Colonel Musgrave turned, and perceived him. Advancing with rapid strides, he confronted him, saying—

"You bring me word of my nieces? Are they safe?"

"Safe—but mightily distressed to hear from thee," replied Seth.

"How far off are they? I will go to them this minute."

"What, so near?" said the colonel, when Seth told him. "Tell them I will come in a few moments, and ride with them to town as we had arranged. Poor girls, they must be anxious to reach home."

Seth returned. And in a few moments Colonel Musgrave was at the door—and in his nieces' arms. He had escaped without a scratch—and was highly elated with his share in the fight. "We met and rolled back the whole rebel army!" exclaimed he with pardonable exaggeration. "They dashed against our stone fort like waves against a rock—but they could make no impression on my gallant Fortieth!"

Helen smiled proudly, and kissed his bronzed cheek. "You are my own gallant uncle, my father's dearest friend; and the Fortieth is the bravest regiment in the service! But," continued she, "is any one hurt—any one that we know?"

A shadow settled on the colonel's face. "Alas, the greatest victory will have its sacrifices. The cruel Moloch of War always demands its living victims. Many of my best and bravest officers and men are dead—and others maimed for life. Captain Campbell is dead. Legrange is wounded. Simpson has lost his leg. Orville his arm. Oh, it is a long, cruel list!"

"May God's mercy be with the dead and with the living!" said Isabella, fervently, while the tears stood in her eyes.

"And outside of your own regiment? Have you heard from the main body?" inquired Helen eagerly.

"Only partially. General Agnew is dead—killed almost at the close of the battle, and not far from this spot."

"It must have been that last sudden volley," said Helen; "startling us with its nearness, when we thought all was over."

"A small body of rebels threw themselves in his frcnt from the side of the road; he was leading on his troops, but turned his horse to ride back as he saw them. They delivered a volley and fled, shooting him in the back. Alas, poor Agnew—he was a noble fellow!"

"Was General Grey's division in the action," pursued Helen, her cheek coloring a rather deeper red; "and is the general safe?"

"Yes, the general is unhurt; he brought up the left wing in good time, and did good service. Trust our 'No Flint' for that."

"Is Major Tarleton safe?" still queried Helen.

"And General Grey's aid, Captain André?" added Isabella, with a glance at her sister.

"Yes, I think Tarleton and André are both safe. I saw Grey for a moment, and he said nothing of André's being hurt, which he certainly would have done, if it had been so, for André is such a favorite of his—and of everybody's, for that matter."

Helen seemed at length satisfied. And the conversation then turned upon the young ladies and their adventures. Nothing was said however about "Moll of the hatchet," or the wounded American officer—the young ladies evidently not feeling quite certain of their ground, as their uncle, with all his kindness, had very little respect for rebels, and just at that moment especially, could not be expected to be in a very placable and forgiving mood. They introduced him formally, however, to Seth and his wife, and said how greatly they were indebted to their kindness. And the colonel testified his gratitude in a few simple and manly words, ending with an intimation to them to let him know if any of the British soldiers gave them trouble, as he might be able to set matters straight.

"And now, girls," cried he, "let us mount and ride."

The young ladies went up-stairs to get their riding caps, as they said—but also to say a few words doubtless to Lieutenant Morris, who, what with the rest and a little food, was already quite another man. He was still weak however from the loss of blood, though Seth said that his wound was by no means a serious one.

"I scarcely know how to thank you, ladies; you probably saved my life," said he with great earnestness, as they announced their intention of leaving.

"Oh, it was all Helen's doing," replied Isabella.

"Nonsense. I just happened to have the pistol, that was all."

"I suppose all such things just happen," said the officer, smiling. "Perhaps Heaven allows them to just happen—but not the less is it true that to you, Miss Helen, I probably owe my life. And therefore I am in honor bound to hold it at your service. And will pay the debt, whenever you or yours need it."

"Lieutenant Morris," replied Helen, "what I did for

you, I would just as freely have done for any other man—friend or enemy. And you pain me by talking as you do. You must not consider yourself under any such grievous burden of gratitude."

"Grievous! it is a pleasant burden!" replied the young man, enthusiastically.

"Girls! are you not ready? Time is flying while you are fixing," called the colonel up the stairway.

Isabella extended her hand—the young officer pressed it warmly. Helen extended hers—he took it and pressed it fervently to his lips. Snatching it away, and blushing crimson, Helen sprang after her sister, who was already descending the stairs.

"It takes you young ladies a terrible time to arrange your hair and put on your riding caps," exclaimed Colonel Musgrave, a little impatiently.

"Oh, Helen was dreaming, as usual, of the days of chivalry, and knights and ladies fair," replied Isabella, archly.

"Helen is a—"

But a fair, soft hand was pressed over his lips, and intercepted the rest of the colonel's sentence.

"Well, say good-bye, and let us be going," resumed he, laughing.

Taking a warm adieu of Seth and his wife, and promising to ride out and see them before many days, the young ladies mounted, and resumed their ride under more favorable auspices, attended by Colonel Musgrave and his orderly—who rode behind in a very stiff and imposing fashion. Just before Isabella mounted, however, she had contrived to say in a low tone to Seth, that if anything occurred of interest to himself or his wounded guest, to let them know at once, giving him their direction in the city. And Seth had replied that he expected to be in town in a day or two, and would call in any event, and let them know how affairs were going on.

The road was considerably thronged as they rode down toward the city—alike with soldiers and with the inhabitants, who were gazing with deep interest on all the sad traces of the combat. The wounded generally had been by this time removed, but parties were still employed in burying the dead. At one place, just inside a field, a large shallow grave had been dug, and fifteen or twenty of the American dead lay beside it, as Colonel Musgrave and his party rode up. Stopping their horses at the side of the road, they gazed pitifully upon the solemn scene. The British soldiers began to lift in the bodies, placing the faces upward. Suddenly the colonel spoke:

"Not so, my men; put them with their faces downward. Let us not cast the dirt into their faces, for they also are mothers' sons."

"What a queer compound man is," continued the colonel, half apologizing as they rode on. "Here am I, fresh from dashing steel and bullets into the faces of live rebels —and yet tender of flinging a little dirt into the faces of dead ones."

"And you would not be my own noble uncle, if you were not thus inconsistent," replied Isabella, while Helen warmly assented with her expressive eyes.

Soon they reached the market-place, where a number of officers were assembled, some on foot, some mounted, at General Grant's* headquarters. Many were the salutations, and more the looks of surprise, as the ladies rode by. Then a young officer followed, and riding up to the party,

* General Grant commanded the British right wing. He was probably of the same Scottish family that President Grant is descended from.

saluted the colonel, and reined in his horse by the side of Isabella.

"Surely, ladies, you have not been in the battle?" said he.

"Not exactly in it—and yet in the midst of it," replied Isabella.

"I suppose you, Miss Helen, acted as aid to Colonel Musgrave—and this explains why the Fortieth made such a splendid defence. How could they yield, when they were defending the ladies?"

"My nieces were not with me, Captain, I am happy to say," said the colonel. "I do not know where we could have stowed them safely—except perhaps in the wine cellar."

"We ingloriously fled the fight—though in obedience to our commander's peremptory orders," said Isabella; "and sought a harbor of safety in the house of a peace-loving Quaker."

"Well, I am glad you came safely through—and glad that I did not know of the perils you were exposed to."

"The battle was pretty well fought on both sides, I think, Captain André," said Colonel Musgrave. "Grey, I hear, brought up his brigade just at the right time."

"Yes—and if it had not been for the thick mist, which hid the enemy completely from view, I doubt much whether more than half of Washington's army would have got back to their old quarters."

"True, the mist was greatly to our disadvantage. And it is a shame that so audacious an attempt as this, should thus, by sheer good-luck, go almost unpunished."

"I am sorry I cannot ride on to Philadelphia with you, ladies," said André, "but this is of course a busy day at headquarters. How is Mr. Pemberton?"

"He was in excellent health and spirits, I believe, yesterday, when we left," said Isabella. "Have you any message for him?"

"Tell him I shall be in the city in a day or two, to see him—if he does not ride out to see me. Good-bye, Colonel. Good-bye, ladies—*au revoir.*"

Returning his adieus, they rode on.

"That's a fine fellow," said the colonel.

"Splendid!" replied Isabella. "He is, in the opinion of us ladies, the very Chevalier Bayard of the army—without fear and without reproach."

"A lucky fellow," continued the colonel, "to have both the young men and the young women crazy about him. What do you think of him, Helen?"

"Oh, I suppose he'll do."

"Why, I thought, Helen, that André would just be a man after your own heart," said the colonel, in a surprised tone.

"After Helen's heart? Why, uncle!" jested Isabella.

"Bella, there are some things which it is not pretty to jest about," said Helen, with offended dignity.

"Of course Helen understood what I meant," said the colonel, who was not a very keen appreciator of a joke. "But as for André, why even Arthur Pemberton, who, I believe, is your great admiration, Helen, admires him to the utmost, if one may judge by their great intimacy on so short an acquaintance."

"Arthur Pemberton is the most splendid man I know," said Helen, decidedly.

The colonel opened his honest eyes. "Well, Helen, all I have to say is, that I have no objection to Arthur Pemberton but one, and that is a very serious one—I do not believe he is more than half loyal."

"Oh, I have no intention of marrying him, uncle—nor

he of marrying me. When I fall in love, if I ever do, it shall be with a thoroughly loyal man."

"Arthur Pemberton is as true and honorable a man as the most loyal and devoted subject of the Crown!" exclaimed Isabella, her dark eyes kindling, and her cheeks flushing.

Helen gave a little laugh. "Of course he is, sis—uncle knows I allow no one to abuse Mr. Pemberton, but myself."

"And yet, Isabel, I would rather not hear you speak in that way," rejoined Colonel Musgrave. "It seems to undervalue the great virtue and merit of loyalty—and fall in thus with the hateful rebel fashion of talking."

Isabella made no reply. And soon she began a conversation with her uncle upon the beauty of the Autumnal woods, and the delightful temperature of the Autumnal season in that part of the country, which lasted until they arrived at the house of Mrs. Pemberton, with whom the young ladies were residing.

CHAPTER V.

A WOMAN'S WILL.

He shall not be molested. Mind, I say
He shall not! Tut—a foe! What care we women
For that?

MRS. PEMBERTON—or Rachel Pemberton, as she preferred to be called—was a widow of considerable means, and a member of the Society of Friends. She lived with her only son, Arthur Pemberton, in a large brick house, which stood at that time on Chestnut Street above Third—the grounds, pleasantly laid out, extending on the west and in the rear to Dock creek, which was large enough for boating and skating. Distantly related to the Grahams, and taking a warm liking to them on acquaintance, she had proposed to the young ladies to board with her so long as they should decide to remain in Philadelphia—a rather indefinite period. Brought from their school at Bethlehem before the war, by their father, who was an officer in the British service, and stationed temporarily in Philadelphia, they had eagerly embraced Mrs. Pemberton's offer. They had never known a mother's care, and in Mrs. Pemberton they seemed to find a mother. And at their father's death, which occurred at the breaking out of the war, they had felt the blow softened by the love and tenderness of the aged lady with whom their lot had been so opportunely cast.

Colonel Musgrave was an old friend of their father's, and had consented to act as their guardian. They soon learned to love him, and to call him uncle—though he really was not related to them. They had some property—not very much, but ample for their personal support—they were connected through their mother, not only, as we have said, with the Pembertons, but with other of the old Quaker families of the city, and were thus as advantageously situated as two orphaned girls could well be.

They were beautiful girls, or rather, women. Finely formed, clear-skinned, intelligent, gay, and high-spirited. Isabella with dark eyes and dark brown hair—Helen with blue eyes and gold-brown curls; the first calm, self-poised and equable; the latter more impulsive—more a creature of the emotions and the passions. The one might be called the more queenly and charming, the other the more spirited and fascinating. Both were among the most bewitching women of a city, whose belles an impartial judge, Mrs. John Adams, termed "a constellation of beauties."

A day or two after the scenes already described, the sisters were seated in a little sitting-room adjoining their chamber. Helen was tossing over a lot of old letters—reading a few lines here and there, and commenting on their contents. At last she broke out in a clear and ringing laugh.

"Just hear this, Bel! Now I want to read you what you wrote me about Arthur Pemberton, when I was at Bethlehem, and you here in Philadelphia on a visit."

"You need not trouble yourself to read it, Helen. I think I can remember it without a reading."

"Oh, but I must—in fact, I want to refresh my own memory," said the laughing tease. "Just listen, Bella:"

"'He is rather tall—but not too tall'—("not so tall that he cannot be conveniently kissed," interpolated Helen)—'his features are clearly cut—his eyes a bluish-gray—his chin dimpled—his mouth finely formed'—("just ripe and sweet enough," again interpolated Helen—) 'and then—'"

"Helen, you would greatly oblige me by giving me that letter," interrupted Isabella, holding out her hand.

"Indeed I could not think of such a thing. Why, it is the very treasure of all my collection. Let me proceed—where did I leave off? oh, yes—"

"'And to crown all'—("of course; that is very well said, to *crown* all; where should it be if not on his crown?")—'and, to crown all, the finest head of hair I ever saw—a light, shining auburn, negligently tied, and waving down the back. Loose flowed the soft redundance of his hair.'"

"Helen, you are too bad—it is shameful!" exclaimed her sister, her face a crimson, and making a successful dash for the letter, which she crammed into her bosom.

Helen made a counter-dash to recover it. Isabella ran around the room—getting behind chairs, jumping upon a sofa, and making a gallant running fight for the vexatious and precious document.

Knock! knock! knock!

"Are you not ashamed of yourself, Helen? You make so much noise that some one has been knocking at the door unheard for the last ten minutes."

"Who began it?" said Helen, defiantly—smoothing her ruffled plumage.

Knock! knock! knock!

"Coming!" cried Isabella, smoothing her hair with her hands, and going to the door.

Opening it, there stood Fox, the old negro of the house.

"Miss Bella, an old Quaker gemman of de Friendly persuasion is down in de parlor, waiting for to see de young wimmen by de name of Graham."

"It is Mr. Williams, Bel, by all that is good," said Helen, who was listening. "No use in fixing any more for him—let us go down at once. Tell him we are coming, Foxey."

They found Seth in the parlor. After their mutually

warm greetings, Seth entered at once on the object of his visit. Lieutenant Morris was doing very well indeed—but the British provost, Captain Cunningham, had ascertained, in some way, that an American officer was lying in the house, had visited him, declared that he was plenty well enough to move, and was about to carry him off—either to the hospital, or to that den of horrors, Walnut Street prison. It was only by threatening him with the indignation of Colonel Musgrave, Seth said, that he could obtain a respite until the afternoon.

"I did not like to mention your names," said Seth, "and yet I am afraid that Colonel Musgrave may hear of the matter from that brutal captain, and say he knows nothing about the lefttenant."

"Perhaps we had better write to uncle upon the subject," said Isabella to her sister; "and yet he will wonder that we said nothing about the lieutenant when he called for us at Mr. Williams's."

"Yes, it is awkward," replied Helen. "But 'in for a penny, in for a pound.' Cunningham shall not have him! Could you find Captain André, if I should give you a note to him?" turning to Seth.

"Is he not one of those they call aidecamps, and along with General Grey? I think I know the young man—rather good-looking, is he not? dark-complected? brown eyes? almost always smiling?"

"A pretty good description," laughed Isabella—"though" (in a whisper to her sister) "hardly up to your standard, I suppose, sis. Helen, will you write to him?"

For answer, Helen opened the writing-desk attached to a large mahogany book-case, and wrote as follows:—

"Helen Graham's compliments to Captain André, and would be grateful if the captain could do her a service. A rebel lieutenant, named Morris, is lying wounded in the house of Mr. Seth Williams, the bearer of this note, at Germantown. Mr. Morris is an acquaintance of Miss Graham's, and she wishes him paroled at once, and exchanged as soon as possible. The case is urgent, as Captain Cunningham insists upon taking him to prison. Explanations deferred till Captain André next visits the city."

"Cold and formal enough," said Isabella, after reading it; "but I guess it will work. To make all sure however, let me now write a note to Colonel Musgrave, to be delivered if necessary."

Isabella's note also written, both were confided to Seth, with instructions not to deliver the second unless Captain André could not be found, or his exertions should prove unavailing. Then Seth mounted his steed, and departed in high good humor. As he rode up Fourth Street, as rapidly as his old horse could well go, he murmured to himself—

"Now, them girls may be Britishers—but they're what I call clear grit. That Helen in particular, is one of those females which take a man—I mean a *young* man—clean off his feet. Let's see what this Captain Andry will say. As for the lefttenant, he's gone already, hook and line, rope and bucket—any fool can see that. But he's a rebel, and she's a Britisher—perhaps a tory. Ah, well, well, well!"

CHAPTER VI.

THE WISSAHICKON.

All noble souls are kindred. Through the bars
Of Country and of Sect they shake warm hands.
And even o'er the yawning chasms wide
Of intervening Centuries, they send
Their messages of friendship and of cheer.

Several weeks have elapsed since the events narrated in our last chapter, and the British army is no longer at Germantown. Seeing the danger of dividing his forces, and being anxious to put himself in a position where he could safely detach a large body to reduce the American fortifications on the Delaware, Sir William Howe had marched one fine morning to the outskirts of Philadelphia. There he had erected a line of fortifications, extending from the Delaware to what is now called Fairmount on the Schuylkill, and then felt himself perfectly secure from any further audacious attempts at surprisal.

The note borne by Seth to Captain André had worked like a charm. Lieutenant Morris had not only been paroled but at once exchanged. And as a few weeks had made a great difference in his condition, he had already rejoined his troop.

It was on the morning of one of those beautiful days which crown with a halo of glory the American Autumn, that a party of four equestrians were preparing to set out from the house of Mrs. Pemberton. The usual little crowd had collected around to see the ladies mount—for when will not everybody stop and turn to see a young lady on horseback?—and, amid laughter and gay jests, the cavaliers had made a knee for their fair companions, and placed them in the saddle. There were but two couples—Isabella and Arthur Pemberton, Helen and Captain André.

The riding attire of the ladies was not very unlike that which is worn at present. The gentlemen wore the long breeches reaching to the ankle and lined with broad stripes of leather, called Cherry Vallies, which were often used for riding at that day in order to dispense with the high boots, which were heavy and clumsy.

"Where is Prince?" said Helen, after gathering up her reins; and she blew a silver hunting whistle which hung around her neck.

"Now, Helen," said Isabella—"let me entreat you not to take that dog. Prince is growing old and heavy, and we shall have a pretty long ride to-day."

"Yes, Miss Helen," added Arthur Pemberton, "I agree with your sister. Prince, before the day is done, would thank you for letting him remain at home."

"Just as you say," replied Helen. "See how amiable I am, Captain."

"Oh, I know you are a perfect paragon of amiability," returned André, smiling.

"What a pity that none of the rest of the party could go," said Isabella, addressing André. "What is in the wind, Captain?"

"I see that Foxey's largest flag is, for one thing," replied André evasively, looking up at the top of Mrs. Pemberton's house, on which a large British flag was streaming from a flag-staff.

"Why, Foxey," continued he, turning to the negro, who stood on the sidewalk, "you have your largest flag out to-day."

"Yes, Massa Ander, old Foxey knowed you'uns were goin' horseback to-day. He allers hang out de big flag on de great occasums."

"You evaded Bella's question," said Helen, as they moved off at a gentle pace, or rack, as it is often termed.

"Yes, I did; there were so many standing by. But the officers could not go, as they happen to be on service today, and the ladies do not care to go without their escorts. Miss Franks threatened to go till the very last, but even her love of fun could not keep her up to it."

As they rode out Fourth street, then only sprinkled with houses, and unpaved like all of the streets at that time, a small crowd attracted their attention. It was gathered around one of the street musicians of the day—a negro with what was called a banjo, a kind of guitar made of a gourd, who was singing a popular song in his rude dialect, apparently to the great delight of the listeners.

It was the fashion at that time for the ladies to wear the hair very high, somewhat in the style of the pompadour rolls of the present day, though a great deal higher. The fashion began in fact with rolls, over which the hair was combed back, but these were superseded by cushions, and artificial curled work, which was often sent out to the barber to be dressed, like a wig, while the fair owner remained at home. The gentlemen of that time, like the gentlemen of this and all times, were much given to satirizing these extravagances of the more beautiful sex, and with just as much effect as at the present day; and some wit had composed the song which the negro was singing, and which, in good English, would read somewhat as follows:—

Give Chloe a bushel of horse-hair and wool,
  Of paste and pomatum a pound,
Ten yards of gay ribbon to deck her sweet skull,
  And gauze to encompass it round.

"Let her flags fly behind for a yard at the least,
  Let her curls meet just under her chin,
Let those curls be supported, to keep up the jest,
  With an hundred, instead of one pin.

"Let her gown be tucked up to the hip on each side,
 Shoes too high for to walk or to jump,
And to deck the sweet creature complete for a bride,
 Let the cork-cutter make her a hump.

"Thus finished in taste, while on Chloe you gaze,
 You may take the dear charmer for life;
But never undress her—for, out of her stays,
 You'll find you have lost half your wife!"*

As our party rode by, the gentlemen half-halted to listen, but Helen exclaimed impatiently, "It is only that odious song again. I wonder that any gentleman could write it, or that any gentleman can listen to it."

"What was that you were saying about amiability, a little while ago?" asked Pemberton, demurely.

"Amiability is one thing, and stupidity is another," said Helen.

"I quite agree with you as to that," replied Pemberton, smiling. "But what do you think of the sign on the tavern there," pointing to a representation of a man carrying his wife on his back.

"What does that mean?" inquired Isabella.

"Read the legend beneath," said Pemberton—"'*The man loaded with mischief.*'"

"It should read, '*The man in his proper place, as a beast of burden.*'" commented Helen, sarcastically. "For my part I think that all that men are good for, is to provide money and amusement for women. Don't you think so, Mr. André?"

"Yes, if you will allow me to add a sentence—and all that women are good for, is to provide homes and love for men."

"I agree with you fully," said Isabella over her shoulder—she and Pemberton were in advance.

* The reader will note how curiously the fashions, including high hair, high heels, bustles, paniers and hoops, have all come round again in the course of about a century.

"Oh, well, what is the use of quarrelling?" cried Helen. "I hate quarrelling, and like to have my own way. If that is not being thoroughly amiable, I don't know what is."

"There are the barracks," said Pemberton. "There are not as many lounging in front as usual, to-day. And I do not see the Hessians at their encampment either."

"Ah, that is where the officers have gone—with the soldiers," commented Helen. "I hope they will all get safely back again. I don't admire battles so much, since I saw those poor fellows huddled into the earth at Germantown."

"Ah, Helen is half a rebel now," said Pemberton; "that young lieutenant has done what I could never do, convince her that the rebels have some little good left in them."

"That is not surprising," replied Helen. "Mr. Morris is a gentleman and a scholar. I do not think I have seen so handsome a man, since—since, when shall I say, Bel?"

"Let me see. Since—since you had that flirtation with General Knyphausen at Mr. Bingham's."

"General Knyphausen indeed! I don't fancy gentlemen who spread their butter on their bread with their thumb nails. Besides, I never flirt. Did you ever see me flirt, Mr. Pemberton?"

"I never saw you do anything else," replied Pemberton, laughing.

"Arthur Pemberton!" exclaimed Helen, her face coloring to the temples.

"I think that is hardly fair, Arthur," said Isabella, gravely.

"I own up—beg forgiveness—plead guilty," replied Pemberton. "Indeed, Helen, I only said it because it came in so well. In fact, it a-kind of said itself. I know very well you do not flirt—not even with Major Tarleton."

"I detest Major Tarleton!" exclaimed Helen; "and you know it."

"Hush! hush!" said Isabella. "You know the old saying, 'Speak of Satan, and he will appear!'"

They were approaching, by this time, one of the British redoubts, which commanded the road. A number of dragoons were scattered around, while a rather short but somewhat heavily-built officer, with a swarthy complexion, was seated on his horse, and conversing with the commander of the outpost.

"Good-morning, ladies and gentlemen," cried he, as they rode up; "you are bound for a ride, I see."

After due salutations, Tarleton continued. "Why, André, where are your regimentals? Are you not a little afraid to venture beyond our lines without them?"

"I am a good deal more afraid to venture as far as we are going, with them," replied André, smiling. "Some of the colonists, you know, grow rabid at the sight of a red coat; and they might make it dangerous, not only for me, but for my company. I was a little puzzled, too, what color to substitute. Pemberton here can wear blue, but I don't like it. Green is the refugee, and also the French color. Brown is rather dull. And so I have chosen gray, as you see, which suits admirably in one respect, as I am in Grey's corps!"

"I hope, then, you either have a pass, or else will not meet any of Lee's or McLane's light horse, for they are the rabidest kind of rebels."

"Oh, we are all right in that respect, Major," said Pemberton. "Would you like to see the rebel pass?"

"I never object to seeing anything," replied Tarleton; "it may prove useful some day"—turning his small and piercing black eyes upon the paper. "That is a curiosity in the way of a pass." He read it aloud:

"Allow Miss Helen Graham, and not more than twelve of her friends, either in or out of military costume, to pass our patroles to the Wissahickon, in the neighborhood of Cresheim creek.

"GEORGE WASHINGTON,
"Commander-in-Chief."

"That is the first time I ever saw the old surveyor's signature," continued Tarleton. "Would not some of their other generals have done as well? Miss Helen, you seem to be a person of influence at the rebel headquarters."

"Miss Helen generally is, wherever she is known," replied André.

"But it puzzles me how she can be known there," continued Tarleton, as if nothing ought to puzzle him.

"I think you will have to stay puzzled a little while, Major," said Helen, rather coldly. "There is something for you to exercise your vaunted penetration upon. I thought you always knew pretty much everything."

"I think I shall be able when I see you next to tell you all about it," replied Tarleton, a little nettled. "Of course if I learn that Washington once happened to see you with his field glass, at twenty miles' distance, I shall understand it all. Valor always is the devoted servant of beauty."

"Come, gentlemen—if we stop to listen to Major Tarleton's flow of compliments, we shall never get to our journey's end. We all know the Major is famous as a lady-killer," rejoined Helen, giving her horse the whip.

"If you meet any of McLane's men near Germantown, tell them I am coming up that way in an hour or so," cried Tarleton, as they rode on.

"We shall do nothing of the kind," replied Isabella.

"Now for a sharp trot—or shall it be a fast canter?" cried Helen.

"Can these pacers trot?" asked André, of Pemberton.

"I see you have had to come to the pacers," laughed Isabella.

"Yes, indeed," replied André. "It is too much like torment to ride an English trotter at his slowest trot, in company with one of your American pacers. Besides, I admit there is no gait so favorable for conversation as the pace, when you wish to get along a little faster than a walk."

"A perfectly gaited horse, according to our Philadelphia ideas," said Pemberton, "should be a fast walker, a gentle pacer, a square, honest trotter, and easy at the canter and the run. Now here is Selim, who is perfect." He patted the neck of the beautiful chestnut he bestrode—gentle and quiet as a lamb, but, at the touch of the whip or spur, full of fire and spirit.

"Is that the horse that is fond of liquor?" inquired André.

"That is hardly a fair statement. He will turn off his single cup of beer or spirits with anybody—but if you hand him a second cup, he will let it fall, and place one of his forefeet upon it. He is quite a temperance horse, you see."

"Let us be off—let us have a canter," cried Isabella.

The road was good, the morning air bracing, and with Helen and André in the advance, the miles flew by in the ecstacy of rapid motion. When they pulled up, they were at the top of a long hill, and entering Germantown.

"Was not that glorious?" exclaimed Helen, wiping her heated face.

"I call that the poetry of motion—even more than dancing," replied André. "A good horse, a fine day, and a beautiful lady—what more does a man need to be perfectly happy?"

"Did you see, Helen, how ruined all the country-seats looked?" questioned Isabella, riding up with her companion. "Is it not shameful—fruit-trees cut down, fences and gates demolished, the beautiful grounds destroyed, and many of the houses themselves with their shutters torn off, and doors broken in. Captain André, why do you allow such things?"

"It is difficult to prevent it, Miss Graham. Our generals and their officers do what they can; but war is destruction, not peace, you know."

"And the rebels have brought it all upon themselves," added Helen.

"A truce," cried Pemberton. "You know that Captain André and myself never talk upon these questions, except upon grave, set occasions. To-day we have come out for a good time—and intending to have a little oasis of peace in the very midst of this cruel desert of war."

André's face beamed upon Pemberton. "Pemberton and I have agreed to disagree upon this question," he said. "We know we are both thoroughly honest and sincere in our convictions of duty. I count it among my sorrows, that I cannot convince him that loyalty is the truest policy for the colonies. But we can and do both of us agree in this—to do all that lies in our power to mitigate the bitterness and cruelty and horror of the war."

"What was that story Ferguson was telling you the other day?"

"Only that he could have shot Washington with his rifle, at the recent battle."

"Why did he not do it, then?" said Isabella. "That sounds like boasting."

"Ferguson is not a boaster," replied André; "he is the best shot in the army, if not in the world. He says that he did not know it was Washington—and either this, or because he dislikes the practice of singling out officers, or something else, he cannot now explain or understand what, kept him from doing it."

"I know," said Isabella. "It was the same reason that prevented that Indian chief from shooting him, when Braddock was defeated at Fort Duquesne."

"What nonsense!" exclaimed Helen. "Bella, I declare you are fast growing to be as bad a rebel as Pemberton. As if the Almighty, who has commanded us to obey the king and those in authority, would shield the bosom of a rebel."

Pemberton made haste to speak. "What of those breech-loaders that Ferguson has had his riflemen armed with? Do they work?"

"He says so," replied André. "He says his men can fire six shots in a minute. Some of the officers think that in a few years 'Brown Bess' will be thrown aside, and the whole army armed with these breech-loading rifles."

"Doubtful," said Pemberton; "you have too many martinets in the service for that."

Stopping for a moment, but not dismounting, at Seth Williams's door, and passing some kind words with the worthy dame—Seth himself not being at home—they cantered on, past Chew's house, in its blackened desolation, and up to Mount Airy, where the recent battle had begun.

"I guess we shall see somebody soon," said Pemberton slyly to Helen. "I have seen the hoof-prints of McLane's cavalry for the last mile or two."

"I'll bet you a sovereign you cannot tell the hoof-prints of one horse from another, to save your life. Can he, Captain?"

"I expect he can. A troop of horse leaves a number of prints together, and the English horses' hoofs are larger than the American. And as each company is apt to have its own shoer, and it is sometimes an object to make the shoe so that its print can be distinguished, you can easily see that Pemberton may be right. But here is Allen's lane—"

He was interrupted by the sudden appearance of a young American officer, who with half a dozen troopers emerged at this moment from the lane. A glance showed that it was Lieutenant Morris, still rather pale, and with his left arm in a sling, but seeming not much the worse for his recent wound.

"Good morning, ladies. Good morning, Cousin Arthur. Good morning, Captain. I am eternally indebted to you and to Miss Helen. You got the pass all safely, I see."

"Yes, and here is the precious document," replied Helen. "I take it as quite a compliment."

"I thought I would meet you, and ride up with you as far as Mr. Livezey's, if you have no objections," said the lieutenant.

"Indeed we shall all be very happy to have your company," replied Helen, while the rest gladly assented. "Come around, and ride on my right, Mr. Morris."

Giving a brief order to his men to await his coming, he spurred to the side of Helen, and they rode on.

"It is just the time to see the Wissahickon in its robes of glory, Miss Helen," said he, as they pulled up after a gay canter. "Have you ever been to Cresheim creek?"

"No, but I have been down near the Schuylkill."

"Stop," cried Isabella; "is not this view beautiful?"

Through a gap in the trees they looked down on the valley of the Wissahickon. It was Indian Summer, and a bluish haze was spread like a softening veil over the whole landscape. The trees were still full of foliage—though here and there the bright and glowing crimsons had deepened into rich browns. All was singularly quiet, as with the weird quiet of a dream—save, at intervals, was heard the accordant sound of a distant flail on some barn threshing-floor.

"See one such sight as this, and die!" enthusiastically exclaimed Isabella.

"I have a friend," said André, "he is in Lord Howe's fleet, who always hopes to die far out at sea. He is ever quoting—

"'And Death, whenever it comes to me,
In calm or storm, may I sink to rest,
Rocked by the waves of the great, strong sea,
And coffined for aye in his breast.'

"But for me when I die, I should like to have my last gaze rest on such dreamy skies, such a crimson and brown and purple earth as this."

"You make me melancholy, with all this talk about dying," broke in Helen. "Now, I say that, when I get married—"

But a general laugh spoiled Helen's speech.

"When you get married, I should like to be there as groom—'s man," said Pemberton.

"Please put your words a little closer together, Mr. Pemberton," returned Helen, with an air of mock dignity.

Soon they were descending a rough, rocky road into the valley of the Wissahickon, Lieutenant Morris manifesting great concern lest Helen's horse should stumble, while André smiled, and riding in advance in the narrow road, left the whole care of the young lady to her new escort.

"This is like the primeval forest," cried Helen, gazing with admiring awe into the giant woods of oak and chestnut and walnut and hickory and hemlock. "We might think ourselves out in the savage wilderness here."

"Yes, a hundred miles at least from any crowded city," echoed Isabella, enthusiastically.

"How soon do we come to your Cousin Livezey's, Mr. Morris?" asked Helen.

"There, look below you, over that piece of cleared land —do you see that chimney?"

"You surely are not going to take us down the chimney, in Santa Claus' fashion?"

Lieutenant Morris laughed, and soon a turn in the road brought them down a steep hill to the front of the house. It was, as usual in this section, of stone, two-storied and double-fronted; and with the customary covered porch, with its two short side benches, before the main door. A wall ran before the house, inclosing a little garden, and in the wall was an aperture, left for the convenience of riders, to aid them in mounting and dismounting. At the distance of about a hundred feet from the side of the dwelling, ran the Wissahickon, which here dashed and foamed over a dam, erected for milling purposes. And in front of the house stood the mill itself, with its first story on the level of the house, and its third on that of the hillside—

obviating the necessity of hoisting up the grain which was to be ground.

Dismounting and entering the house, Morris and Pemberton, who both claimed cousinship with the owner, introduced the party to Mr. Livezey and his wife. They also were "Friends"—or "Quakers," as the "world's people" irreverently call them—and of the usual hospitable and kindly Quaker type. The room into which the visitors were shown was simply furnished, but the thick walls below each window were fashioned into seats, and covered with cushions; and in a corner of the room was a large East India lounge, made of cane, also cushioned, which pulled out creaking to afford a full-length repose. Helen threw herself upon this immediately, for it was a new piece of furniture to her, and had a thought of Asian skies about it.

In a few moments a lunch was brought in by their kind hostess, and after doing this justice, Pemberton proposed they should start for a boat-ride and a ramble. As they emerged into the yard again, about a dozen colonial riflemen in their green and fringed hunting-shirts were lounging on the grass.

"Why, Morris, is there any danger?" inquired Pemberton.

"No—your pass will protect you from any of our scouting parties, but these riflemen of Morgan's have been detached to scour the woods between Chestnut Hill and the Schuylkill, in order to arrest some British deserters who are reported to be giving the farmers considerable trouble. Some think they are spies"—with a smile toward the British officer—"but the more reasonable opinion is that they are deserters. Spies or deserters, however, they are uncommonly fond of butter and milk and poultry, and occasionally even a cow or ox disappears, which, considering the condition of our own commissariat, is a thing not to be tolerated."

"Has Cousin Thomas been troubled?" inquired Pemberton.

"Not before a night or two ago, when they broke into his mill, and carried off some bags of flour.

"I do not suppose the fellows are at all dangerous," continued the lieutenant; "but as these rangers were about, I thought I might as well introduce you to them, and let them sweep through the woods in advance of you, as they go down."

"It was very kind of you, indeed," replied André. "Our pistols are in our holsters, had we not better take them with us?"

"I think there can be no need of that," said Isabella. "What horrible times these are, when we cannot take a little stroll without some dreadful weapon or other, putting you in fear of your life, lest it should go off, all the time."

"Of course, Miss Graham," said André, "we will not take them, if you object; besides, after what Mr. Morris has said, and following, as we shall, right in the track of these brave fellows, I see no necessity for doing so. Do you, Pemberton?"

"I am for risking that much to save Miss Graham from annoyance."

"Do you not, then, go along with us, Mr. Morris?" queried Helen.

"I regret very much that I cannot," replied he; "but I must rejoin my men." The "regret" and "must" being, in truth, mainly based upon the fact that Helen had a cavalier engaged already. He had hoped fervently—though, as he knew, rather foolishly—that it would be otherwise.

"I am very sorry, indeed," rejoined Helen. "Now, suppose I should be in danger," continued she, with a little touch of that coquetry which seemed a part of her very make and nature, "you would not be near to afford me any assistance. You know you are one of my knights."

Helen blamed herself at once, when the young officer replied, in a tone whose affected pleasantry could not conceal its undertone of deep feeling:—"Miss Helen, if I thought you were liable to the least shadow of danger, I would be the last to leave you."

"Well," said Helen, jestingly, "if danger appears, I shall blow this horn of mine with as loud and shrill a blast as that of Roland at Roncesvalles, and perhaps you will hear it all the way to Germantown." Saying this, she blew her hunting-whistle till Isabella clapped her hands over her ears, and the rough riflemen laughed heartily.

"Not one of us, Miss Helen," cried André, throwing himself into a theatrical attitude, "but will rush to your rescue when we hear the blast of that wondrous horn, as Charlemagne and his Paladins rushed—or should have rushed—to the rescue of the peerless Roland."

"But with rather better success, I hope," replied Helen, laughing.

Morris then remounted his horse, and, making him curvet a little—as is the manner of young gentlemen—cantered lightly up the slope, until a turn of the road concealed him from view. The riflemen, with a sergeant at their head, moved off Indian-file around to the back of the house, and up a wooded hill which rose immediately behind it, extending their line to sweep the forest. While the party in whom we are more immediately interested, turned, under Pemberton's guidance, to the water-side of the house, and passing through a neatly-kept flower-garden, prettily terraced, descended a flight of steps to a spot just above the dam, where a little skiff was moored.

Carefully seating themselves in the boat, Pemberton took the oars, and rowed gently up the pellucid stream. It was now about noon, and the sun shone down upon them with a soft but not unpleasant splendor. On each side the high, dark, wooded hills were draped with the magnificent hues of the Autumn season—amphitheatres of green and crimson, and brown and gold. And reflected in the still, glassy water, was all this pomp of variegated glory.

"This is magnificent!" exclaimed André, enthusiastically. "The old world has nothing to show like this. It is the gorgeous splendor of an Indian princess."

"It is fairy land!" cried Helen, enthusiastically.

"See that cedar!" said Isabella, "with its deep green lighted up by a single spot of blazing crimson."

"And the woods are full of purple grapes," exclaimed Helen. "Are they good to eat, Pemberton?"

"Try them," said Pemberton, bringing the boat near one of the banks. "Daughter of Eve, pluck and eat."

"Pshaw—these small ones are sour and full of seed."

"Those are Chicken grapes. The others are better, the Fox grapes."

"Yes, they will do tolerably well—they are sweet."

"One moment, Pemberton," cried André, extending his hand to grasp a pretty blue flower that grew along the margin. "What do you call this, ladies?"

"It is the Fringed Gentian," said Isabella.

"I don't know what it signifies, Miss Helen—I may be doing something very serious or shocking, indeed—but will you accept this blue Gentian from one of the very humblest of your devoted admirers?"

"Captain André, I do wish you would leave all that

style of speeches at the theatre down South Street," replied Helen, drawing back the hand she had involuntarily extended.

"I beg pardon, Miss Helen. Will you accept this flower in token of forgiveness, and as a pledge of my earnest friendship?"

"I am most happy to do so," replied Helen, mollified.

"What a delightful, tart, sweet, spirited and fascinating creature she is," thought André, as he leaned over the side of the boat, and dallied with the cool, clear water.

"Leap out, André, with the chain, and hold the boat," cried Pemberton, bringing the skiff up by the side of a rock, and at the entrance of a little cove. "This is Cresheim creek."

Fastening the boat, they made their way along the sloping, rugged side of a shallow and rocky stream, that emptied at that place into the Wissahickon. Soon they came to where it poured over and between huge rocks and boulders into a little pool.

"Now for a climb, girls," said Pemberton. "André, you take care of Miss Helen."

"Miss me no miss, among these rocks, Arthur. It is out of place," cried Helen. "Here I am simply Helen Graham. These old rocks do not like such courtly titles. This huge one is my father."

"Let me help you up on your father's shoulders, then," laughed André, in response to the ardent girl. Without much help from the gentlemen, for both were supple-limbed and sure-footed, the ladies made their way to the top of a huge moss-covered rock, and gazed down the cleft where the stream was pouring.

"That is the Devil's pool," said Pemberton, pointing to the still water below. "The fall is rather quiet now, but after a rain it is quite a roaring cascade, I assure you."

"Is the pool deep?" asked Helen.

"The devil is said to be very deep," replied André; "and of course his pool must be, or else it would not hold him."

"Ah, you have caught it—you have caught it at last," cried Pemberton, shaking his head mournfully.

"Caught what?"

"The vile habit of punning. It is said to be in the Philadelphia atmosphere. I believe that even Washington would pun were he to live here for six months."

"Oh, nonsense," said Helen—"how deep is it?"

'I will give you two authorities, and you may take your choice. I know, of course, which you will prefer. When Morris and I were boys, he one day, as he says, took a line, and attaching a weight to it, lowered it down, and down, into the pool; but he could find no bottom. Not long after, I thought I would try; and I took a long fishing pole, and pushed it down, and down, until I could push it no farther; and thus very easily found the bottom."

"Of course I accept Mr. Morris's statement as the most reasonable and reliable," replied Helen. "And I think your father, Pemberton, ought to have taken that same long fishing pole and broken it into very little pieces over your naughty back. You are by far too skeptical, Arthur. I hate skepticism. It is that which makes men rebels."

"Hush! hush! hush!" cried André, "you know that subject is tabooed."

"Well," said Pemberton, "it may be that there is a cleft somewhere between the rocks, which will let a stone down a good ways. I thought myself that there was a hidden passage somewhere below, letting the water flow underground into the creek."

"Ah, now you begin to talk a little more sensibly," said Helen. "You could not persuade me that there is not something mysterious and uncanny about this pool—why the whole place bears witness to it."

"If you ladies are sufficiently satisfied," said Pemberton, "suppose we stroll up the Wissahickon for half a mile or so—though we shall have to return again of course this way. Come, Bella."

"Wait one moment more," said Helen to André, as their companions left them; "I can hardly tear myself away from this romantic spot."

"Allow me to assist your beautiful self down this rugged descent, Miss Helen," said André, in the courtly phrase he was rather too fond of, as she rose from the rock on which she had been sitting, a few minutes afterwards.

"John André," exclaimed Helen, pausing and facing him, "I would beg of you to forget for a while the theatre, and the formal language of polite society, and so long as we are in the presence of these old gray Quaker rocks and these solemn pines, to be simply a sincere and earnest man."

André's brown face colored to the forehead.

"I thought that with you, Helen, I always had been both sincere and earnest."

Helen made no reply—but accepted his assistance in making her way over and around the precipitous rocks and boulders. That she was not very greatly displeased, he could easily infer—though there was nothing of the coxcomb in his nature—by the freedom with which she allowed her hand to remain in his grasp, and the readiness with which she placed it upon his shoulder when necessary.

"Ah me, I am tired—let us rest a moment," said she,

when they had reached the Wissahickon again, after a short but rugged tramp, and gone up the stream a little further. "Here is a mossy seat, made on purpose."

It was a low ledge of stone, moss-covered, at the base of a little cliff which rose behind it in a wall of rock some ten or fifteen feet high.

"You have made no reply yet, Helen, to that last remark of mine. When was I other than earnest and truthful with you? You know that of all the women in the world, I think of no one more highly than of you."

"Are you sincere and truthful now? I was told by a friend of yours, only yesterday, that you always wore upon your breast the miniature of a young and beautiful woman. If so, you ought to think of her more highly than you think of me."

André had been standing before her. Now he sat down by her side.

"It is true, Helen, that I wear upon my breast the likeness of Honora Sneyd; but it is also true that there is no woman in the world I care for more than for you." The tones of the young officer, always soft and mellow, grew softer with that suppressed tenderness which women love.

"You give me a riddle," replied she, with studied coldness. "I am not good at guessing riddles. Do you no longer love this Miss Honora Sneyd? Then why wear her likeness?"

"Honora Sneyd is now Honora Edgeworth—has been so for years. Helen, I loved, or thought I loved her, passionately. She thought she loved me. But it seems she was mistaken; and when another came, and offered his hand, she accepted it. If I did not care for you greatly, would I thus lay bare my inmost heart before you?"

André started from his seat and for a few moments paced

up and down the leaf-covered ground before her. Then he resumed—

"I could not give her up, married though she was. When I was taken prisoner two years ago at St. Johns, the only thing I saved from my capturers was her likeness—and saving that, I thought myself happy. Still my passion, thus denied and hopeless, must have been gradually wearing itself out. For the last month, I have scarcely thought a moment of Honora Sneyd—and yet, so powerful is the force of habit, I have continued to wear her image."

He resumed his seat by Helen's side; and then said, in a still lower tone, "Do you think that a noble-hearted woman could ever esteem a man's second love, as if it had been his first? Do you think it possible that I, who loved so devotedly then, can love another even more passionately and truly now?"

"I, for one woman, would rather have the second love, which is the man's, than the first love, which was the boy's"—and Helen paused, and seemed listening. "I thought I heard Pemberton and Isabella returning."

"It was nothing but a squirrel dropping his nut," said André.

"I thought it sounded like a footstep," rejoined Helen. "Had we not better go on, and see what has become of them?"

"In one moment,' replied André. The woman was already satisfied, for the time; the man, man-like, would have his conclusions made doubly sure, and leave no room for doubt. "Helen," continued he in a low but impassioned tone, "I love you better than ever I loved Honora Sneyd."

"Dear John, I have loved you since that first hour two years ago," whispered Helen, looking up into his brown eyes with a look that he had never seen in that spirited face before.

He put his arm around her for the first time—he pressed his glowing cheek to hers. She submitted for a moment —then she widened the distance between them.

"Was Honora Sneyd so very pretty then?" she said.

He took a small miniature from his bosom. "See, she also has blue eyes and golden hair."

"My hair is not golden."

"It is golden, in the sun. I like your hair the best. It is the richer looking."

"She is very beautiful," said Helen; but there was a proud satisfaction in the tone. It was as if she had said, what she really would have scorned herself for even consciously thinking, much less saying—"but I am more beautiful."

"And she is now Mrs. Edgeworth?" continued she.

"Yes, and the mother of two children, living what she so greatly loves, a quiet and happy domestic life. I think," continued André, his face flushing, "that that really was the bar fate set between us. She is not the least ambitious—she must have felt, even almost without perceiving it, that I am very different—caring not so much for peace and quiet, as for a proud and brilliant career. She never could have sympathized with me as you can, and will, Helen."

The eyes of the girl shone like two stars; her cheeks flushed; her proud bosom heaved. "You are my king of men—you long for the station which is your natural right. And I am fit to be your queen."

"Now, Pemberton," continued André, "fine fellow as he is, has no ambition—scoffs at it. He would be satisfied, he says, with a quiet life among his books, at such a place as Woodland—or even in some little cottage on the Schuylkill."

"Isabella fully agrees with him in that," replied Helen. "Think of such a glorious woman as Bella, such a perfect queen, passing her whole life sequestered in some little cottage in the neighborhood of Philadelphia. I believe that both she and Pemberton, when they marry, will abandon even our little provincial society, and play Darby and Joan in the most approved fashion."

"I think I see a career before me," continued André, proudly. "If I fail, it shall not be for want of effort and daring. I am simply a captain now. In one year I mean to be major, in another colonel—in another, perhaps, general. See how rapidly Churchill rose. I have given you my heart, Helen; when I give you my hand it shall have something in it."

"I am in no hurry," said the girl, with a lofty look in her eyes. "I am ready to wait for you, André—forever, if need be! And I know I can often assist you in mounting the steeps of fortune and fame. I would scorn to be an incumbrance to you. Trust me entirely and utterly with all your plans and schemes—let me be one with you in heart and life. You shall never have cause to blush at any weakness or indiscretion of mine."

"I shall trust you—entirely! utterly! And when I have won my coveted honors, we shall have the happiness of knowing that we have planned and toiled for each other."

But we must leave these young lovers together for a while, rapt in their blissful dreams of a glorious future, and give a fragment of another conversation, taking place at the same time, not a quarter of a mile off.

These, sitting on this fallen trunk, within the solemn

shade of this dark grove of hemlocks—sitting so closely, and toying with each other's hands and hair, and gazing proudly and fondly into each other's eyes—have evidently been acknowledged lovers for some time—to themselves, if not to the world. Pemberton is speaking.

"I am not, as you know, Bella, in the least ambitious—and I dislike and abhor the soldier's bloody trade—but I confess I can hardly endure to remain quietly at home, when the great Cause is in such peril."

"I really think it would break your mother's heart, Arthur, if you should join the army. To go out to war would be a sad blow of itself; but to join those whom she considers rebels, would be something almost unendurable to her."

"That is what I have said to myself all along," replied he. "But it looks as if I were a coward, to stay at home for any reason whatever."

"But you know, yourself, that it is not cowardice. Why regard then what others may think or say? Besides, are you not really affording more valuable aid to the Colonial cause, than you could give in any other manner?"

"They all say so. Washington himself says I must not leave the city. But I hate this kind of service."

"You do not deceive anybody. You pry into no person's confidence. You let every one know that you are not thoroughly loyal. You merely avail yourself of outside means of obtaining information," said Isabella in a low voice, and glancing around her, as if remembering the old adage that "trees have ears."

"I know it," replied he, in the same low, cautious tone. "I would not do it in any other way. But if I am discovered, notwithstanding, my name will suffer reproach and I may suffer the fate of a spy."

"A spy—what, you, in your own city—your own house?"—and Bella whispered the dangerous words.

"Military men are not much given to nice legal distinctions, Bella. You see I am not acting in the dark. I know my position and its dangers. And I have taken this opportunity to let you know them, thinking it your right. Besides, I have been myself a little puzzled; and I have great confidence in your sound judgment and noble instincts, my sweet love."

"I never dreamed of this terrible view of your conduct. I shall never see that flag waving again, without a flutter at my heart," said Isabella huskily.

Pemberton was too much occupied with his own thoughts, to note how seriously his fair companion was affected. Else perhaps he would not have continued.

"What shall I do, Bella? Shall I go on with this dangerous business, or shall I give it up?"

The color fled from her face, and left it like marble. She put out her hands before her, as if pressing away from her some hideous thing. She tried to speak, but the words gurgled in her throat. Suddenly she threw her arms around his neck, and burst into uncontrollable tears.

"Forgive me, Bella! I thought not it would move you thus. You are usually so calm and self-possessed, you know. Cheer up, my sweet, there is no danger yet—and probably will be none."

"You asked me a question, Arthur," said Bella, regaining her composure with a strong effort. "It came upon me so suddenly, you see, that it unwomaned me a little." She paused a moment, and twined the beautiful bright hair she admired so much around her fingers. "You have taught me—a British soldier's daughter—to love the cause of the Colonies as I love you, to revere it as a religion, to hesitate at nothing lawful that will hasten its triumph. I would give my own life this day, if I could ensure its success—but I am a woman, and do not ask me to decide that you shall thus peril yours. Decide for yourself, and I will submit to your decision, as a woman should—and then leave the event to the good God."

"Did you hear André questioning old Foxey this morning?" continued she, after a pause.

"It meant nothing, and Foxey is well named—that old negro, stupid as he looks and talks, is wider awake than most white men."

"There is only one man that I am really afraid of," continued Isabella. "It is that Tarleton, with those small, snaky eyes of his. Promise me one thing, Arthur."

"What is it?"

"If Tarleton ever begins to question and suspect, that you will escape at once."

"Thank you for the hint, Bella. I will, you may depend upon it, if I have the chance. But with Tarleton it generally is a word and a blow, and the blow first."

"Where can Helen and André be? I thought they would have overtaken us by this time," said Isabella, rising to her feet.

"I imagine that Helen and André are having a very pleasant time by themselves," replied Pemberton, smiling. "André is terribly smitten, or I never had the complaint."

"Helen ditto," said her sister, smiling.

"Well, they are a splendid couple—but what then is to become of my poor cousin, Morris? He is over head and hair in love also with Helen, ever since she saved his life, as he is pleased to term it."

"Poor fellow!" sighed Isabella. "It cannot be helped though; for Helen is terribly loyal, and besides, thinks André a Chevalier Bayard and an Admirable Crichton both in one."

"I do not wonder at it. I love John André, loyal as he is, more than I ever expected to love mortal man. He is a noble fellow—true to the core. He has only one fault—he is too ambitious. 'By that sin fell the angels.'"

During this latter conversation they had been retracing their steps, and soon came upon Helen and André, who were seated about three feet apart, and appeared to be carrying on a brisk conversation, in a light tone of badinage.

"We were just wondering if you *never* were coming back," cried Helen, as she saw them—though the crimson of her cheeks was richer and more widely spread than usual, as her sister saw at a glance.

But she was a good and discreet sister, and knew when to talk, and when to be silent. So she simply said that she thought it was about time they were returning home, and passed on with Pemberton, while Helen and André demurely followed.

"It is not late, let us climb up that rock above the pool once more," cried Helen.

The others assenting, they were soon grouped again on the top of the huge oblong rock or boulder overlooking the Devil's pool.

Suddenly a heavy stone fell splashing into the stream above them, and the whole party almost involuntarily turned their heads, to see where the stone had come from.

CHAPTER VII.

THE DESERTERS.

Offscourings of the war—a mutinous crew—
They roam the woods at will, and know no law
Save their own wicked pleasure.

"Stir not a step, for your lives!"

Such was the rude command which came from one of four men, dressed in torn and faded British uniforms, who stood with muskets in their hands, not more than thirty or forty yards in a direct air line from them.

Our party were grouped, as we have said, on the top of the rock. They were overshadowed by huge hemlocks, but perfectly exposed to view, as there were no low branches. Behind them, on the brow of a lofty precipice, formed by the jutting out of a narrow ridge from the higher portion of the hill, and about fifty feet above their level, stood the deserters—one of them wearing the chevrons of a corporal. Between the two parties was a deep chasm or ravine—but the muskets of the deserters commanded the entire position.

André took in the aspect of affairs at a glance with a soldier's eye. Stepping back on the rock, a little out of the roar of the waterfall, he cried sternly—

"What mean you?"

What the reply would have been, we know not, for at that instant Helen placed her whistle to her lips, and blew a shrill and prolonged note, which pierced through every nook and cranny of the ravine.

With a volley of fearful oaths, the deserters raised their muskets to their shoulders, and one of them, a vile-looking wretch, fired. André had sprung in an instant in front of Helen; but if the villain's left foot had not slipped on the dry leaves, as he threw it out when taking aim, Helen probably would have paid for her daring with her life. As it was, the ball whistled just over her head.

"How dare you fire without orders," cried the leader of the deserters—"do you mean to bring the riflemen on us?"

"They are fur enough away," angrily responded the ruffian; "they are down below the Falls by this time."

"Then, what harm could that silly whistle do us? But," raising his voice, "if you try that again, my lassie, the next bullet will be surer aimed."

"What do you mean by this ruffian-like conduct?" exclaimed Pemberton. "If you fire another shot, I'll have you all hung for it."

"Aye, aye, I suppose you will," replied the deserter. "But you must first catch your hare before you skin him —mustn't he, boys?"

His comrades laughed recklessly and defiantly. "Ask Captain Andry what he's done with his red coat," said one of them. "Has he gone over to the rebs?"

"Don't get off that rock!" exclaimed their leader, savagely, and levelling his musket again, as Isabella, her eyes flashing, made a movement as if designing to leave their perilous position.

"Do you want money?" cried Pemberton.

"Aye! money, and watches, and rings—everything! We'll send a man down to search you."

"We will not submit to be searched," exclaimed both the young men in a breath.

"You cannot help yourselves."

"We cannot?—come on and see!" cried André, putting his hand in his breast pocket.

The deserters talked together in low tones for a few moments. They could kill them all from that distance; but, if they did, they would themselves be hunted down like wolves. To attempt to overpower the young men in a close struggle would be attended with danger, for they might have dirks or pistols. At last their leader, the corporal, again spoke in a loud voice.

"Put down your purses, your watches and your rings on the top of the rock; and then go, and be d—d to you."

"You will not molest us further?" cried Pemberton.

"No—curse you."

"What security have we for that?" asked André.

"The only security you can have, the honor of a British soldier," scoffed the leader.

"In the sacred name of God, and of the Virgin Mother?" continued André; adding, in a low voice to Pemberton, "I know that man; he was the only English Roman Catholic in our regiment."

"In the name of God and the holy Virgin Mother!" repeated the man, lifting his hat, while one of the others imitated his example. "But hurry with you—we're not going to stay here all day."

The young men took out their gold watches—worn more unfrequently at that time than now, even silver ones being not very common—and laid them with their purses on the moss-covered portion of the rock.

"Now for the ladies—come, hurry!" cried the deserter.

Helen threw down her purse disdainfully; Isabella calmly placed hers with the rest. They did not seem very heavy; but ladies' purses are expected to be lighter than gentlemen's—besides, they had both taken the precaution of undoing the clasps, and emptying them as far as possible, before taking them out of their pockets. Each laid down a ring or two also—none showing afterward on either fair hand.

"Stay" cried the head deserter, as they were about leaving the rock. "Captain, I think you have a small gold case, with a picture inside it, on a blue ribbon around your neck."

"Sneak and spy!" cried Helen, her woman's heart excited beyond endurance—"disgrace alike to the name of soldier and of man! if you ever had loved a wife, a sister, or a mother, you would scorn to make a demand like that."

Wretch as the deserter was, he evidently was shamed a little. "Some keepsake from the young lady herself, I suppose," cried he. "Well, we won't be too hard on the captain. He shall keep his love picture. But you must put down that silver whistle and its chain, young lady. That's not a love-gift, too, I suppose?"

Helen was about to lay down her whistle, when a commotion was evident among the deserters. They had faced about, and were now standing with their muskets levelled, apparently peering into the foliage in front of them.

"What does it all mean?" exclaimed Helen.

"I hope it means that the riflemen have found them," replied Pemberton.

"Fire!" was at this moment called out—apparently at a considerable distance. A scattering report followed—as of a dozen rifles—from parties too intent upon their aim, to care much about firing closely together. Three of the deserters fell at once to the ground, as if stone-dead. Their leader, however, flung back a yell of defiance, fired his own musket, and then snatched the muskets of his comrades in turn from the earth, and discharged them at the advancing assailants. With a shout, when the last barrel was emptied, the riflemen rushed upon him. Clubbing his musket, the deserter struck out savagely right and left, backing sometimes to the very verge of the cliff.

"Take him alive, men—shooting is too good for him!" shouted a stern voice.

"Never! never! you cursed Yankees!" howled the deserter—desperately keeping his assailants at bay, even on the utmost verge of the precipice.

"Then die, like a dog!" shouted a stalwart ranger, bringing the butt of his rifle full upon the ruffian's temple. The deserter reeled, staggered for a moment, and crashed down the side of the precipice a hundred feet to the sharp rocks below.

The young ladies turned their eyes away from the horrid sight. Then Helen started forward involuntarily, as if to assist him.

"It is useless," said Pemberton. "He is past help."

"He has died the death of a deserter and a thief!" exclaimed André, with compressed lips. "They are not worth thinking of—this world has had enough of them."

"I suppose so," said Isabella. "Poor fellows!"

"Here come our gallant rescuers," exclaimed Helen, as the riflemen began to file down into the glen. "I suppose we may take up our treasures now."

We need scarcely describe the enthusiastic welcome with which the rangers were received. Even the roughest of these hardy sons of the frontier, felt rejoiced that he was one of the party which had come so opportunely to their aid. For both the ladies shook hands with every man at least once, and thanked him personally for his share in the fight. And one of the rangers, who had received a slight bullet wound in the arm, was envied the hurt by all his comrades. For Helen would bandage the wound with her own handkerchief, and both she and Isabella made as much ado about it, as if the wounded man were injured for life.

"Simon lets on to be a great deal more hurt than he is," laughed one of the riflemen to another.

"Thet's so—but I would too, under the same aggravatin' carcumstances," replied his comrade. At which there was a general grunt of assent.

"It was a lucky thing you came up when you did," said Pemberton, to the sergeant commanding the party.

"Wall, there wasn't much of what you call luck in it," replied the sergeant. "The fact is, we shouldn't a been hyere at all, hadn't it been for Lefttenant Morris?"

"What is that about Lieutenant Morris?" cried Helen.

"The sergeant says," replied André, "that the lieutenant sent him here."

"Wall," continued the sergeant, "we had got down to the mouth of the crick, and were coming out of the woods on the Ridge, when who should dash up but the lefttenant. 'I'm not asy in my mind, sargeant,' says he. 'Thim desarters may be paceable characters, mere hen-roost thieves, or they may not. I wish,' says he, 'you'd just tarn back, and go up to Luseley's agen. I wouldn't like any harm to come to them ladies.'"

"Spoken like a gentleman and a soldier," said André.

"'Wall, lefttenant, it's all the same to me,' says I. And so we tarned back, lookin' a little closer arter the varments. Soon we cum on a trail. Bless your hearts ef they hadn't hollered out a cave under some rocks—and we had gone clean by them; and Simon there a half-Injun too! Drat it but we were mad. All of a sudden Simon sed—'I heered the lady's whissel.' 'No?' says I. 'Yes,' says he. 'Git out,' says I. 'I am sure,' says he. But we all heered the gun plain enough. 'Ah,' says I, 'that's your little game is it?' We tore along, sending Simon fust; he's half-Injun, you know. Then we heered them talking—and closed in all roun' them. Jist in time too, I s'pect. I reckon the ladies were gittin' a little skeart."

"Not much more scared than the gentlemen," replied

Pemberton, smiling. "I am free to admit that I, for one, felt very uneasy. But it is time now we were making our way back to Mr. Livezey's."

Some of the riflemen had already investigated the condition of the deserters, and finding life extinct in all of them, had gone off to procure spades to bury them with. The others divided into two parties, one to await their return, the other to continue on their way to Mr. Livezey's.

And in a very sober and thoughtful mood indeed, the gay party of the morning sought their boat, while Pemberton rowed slowly back.

At the landing stood Lieutenant Morris. "Welcome back!" cried he. "I hope you have had a pleasant excursion to Cresheim."

"Here we are, all safe," answered Helen, to whom his eyes seemed more particularly turned.

"I am heartily glad of it, I confess," ejaculated Morris, fervently. "To tell the truth, my wound seems to have enfeebled my mind a little, for a more foolishly anxious three hours I never passed. Why, if the Indians had been upon you, and scalping you, as they did poor Jane McCrea, I could not have felt worse."

"Well, Mr. Morris, we came about as near being scalped as I ever want to come," said Helen, impressively. "But I whistled, as I said I would, and you sent help."

"I sent help!"

"Yes, the riflemen—they came just in the nick of time."

"Are you in earnest? Were you in danger, then?"

By this time they were on the porch; and, taking a seat, Helen recounted, with frequent interruptions from the rest of the party, all that had taken place.

"And now, Lieutenant Morris," said she, holding out

her hand, "I think we are fully even—only the balance is a good deal in your favor."

Morris took the fair hand, but seemed a little puzzled what to do with it. It was not a very small hand, one of those you can hardly feel, but the proper hand to belong to a rather tall, finely-developed woman. It was well-shaped, soft, somewhat plump, and glowing with vitality. Such a hand, in short, as thrills a lover through and through. But the Lieutenant, as we said, did not seem to know exactly what to do with it. If it had been a man's hand, he would have given it a hearty grasp, and this was what Helen expected; but, after gently fumbling with the fair, soft fingers a little in his embarrassment, he bent down his head, raised it to his lips, and, before the whole party, as he had done once before in private, fervently but reverently kissed it.

"Fie, Mr. Morris!" cried Helen, flushing. "You must not do that."

To save embarrassment, Pemberton interposed—"It is full time we were going, I think. Morris, will you have the horses brought up, while we go in and bid adieu to our Cousin Livezeys?"

CHAPTER VIII.

PHIL MORRIS.

> "For indeed I know
> Of no more subtle master under Heaven
> Than is the maiden passion for a maid,
> Not only to keep down the base in man,
> But teach high thoughts and amiable words,
> And courtliness, and the desire of fame,
> And love of truth, and all that makes a man."
>
> *Tennyson.*

As our party emerged from the valley of the Wissahickon, on their homeward ride, the sound of a distant but heavy cannonade was heard. Helen looked inquiringly at André.

"It is no secret now," said he; "a corps, mainly of Hessians, under Count Donop, is attacking Fort Mercer, while the fleet is bombarding Fort Mifflin."

An anxious look passed over the faces of Pemberton and his cousin. "God defend the right!" exclaimed Morris, fervently.

"God defend the right!" repeated André, with equal fervor.

The serious events of the day, and the continued noise of the cannonade, naturally had a sobering influence on the spirits of all. They could not laugh and jest when their fellow beings, many of whom on both sides were personally known to them, were hazarding their lives at the musket and cannon's mouth. And they rode rapidly forward, almost in perfect silence.

As they turned into Germantown, Lieutenant Morris bade them good-bye, with many mutually expressed kindly wishes. The others kept down the road, at a rapid canter —the noise of the cannon growing louder and louder as they neared the city.

"I never saw Morris like he was to-day," said Pemberton to Isabella, as they drew up into a walk at the three-mile run to breathe their horses a little. "Phil is generally so overflowing with reckless gayety and good-humor. He really did not seem the same man."

"His wound, in weakening him, has probably affected his spirits. Did you observe how pale he was, when not excited by the conversation?"

"Of course I did. By the way, it was a little curious, Bella, that you and Helen should have had the opportunity of doing so great a service to a cousin of mine."

"Yes, and that shows the necessity of helping every one when you can, no matter how great a stranger he may be," replied Isabella. "I had no idea when I heard him called Lieutenant Morris, that it was your old crony, whom you had so often spoken about."

"But you have not seen Phil Morris, even yet," rejoined Pemberton. "This grave and sentimental young man we saw to-day, is very different from the Phil of whose pranks at old Benezet's school, I have so often told you—the best mimic, and most reckless and daring fellow in the whole school. Did I ever tell you about the negro boy?"

"Not that I remember."

"You know Benezet is the kindest-hearted and most benevolent man in the whole world."

"I think he must be, if that story I heard you tell about his feeding the rats down in the area is true."

"It is sober truth, Bell. He used to feed the rats regularly every morning. He did it to keep them honest. He said that rats only stole because they were forced to do so from necessity, and that his rats never stole anything. And he will not eat poultry—he says it is like eating his neighbors."

"What a comical old fellow!"

"He is a saint—if goodness ever made a man a saint. And Phil knew it, and would have fought for him any time—but what will not a boy do for a joke?"

"What did he do?"

"Blackened his face and hands, and passed himself off for a poor little negro runaway from Virginia, in the sight of the whole school. Benezet is a great hater of slavery, you know. Oh, but the whoppers that Phil told of the way he had been abused down South—while we, boys, knowing the joke, roared with laughter."

"I should think that Mr. Benezet would have suspected something from your merriment."

"He is too sincere and guileless for that. He was inexpressibly shocked by it however—though he could hardly credit such boyish heartlessness, save by imputing it to the hardening effect of 'the wicked system' upon our youthful minds."

"Did he find out the deception?"

"Never—to this day. Though he could not account for the sudden disappearance of the injured negro, save by supposing he had been seized by some minion of his master, and carried back into slavery."

"I confess I should never have accused Mr. Morris of any such prank as that," said Isabella. "He seemed to-day as sober as a judge. But there is a great difference between being sick and well. 'A little blood in the veins more or less,' I once heard my father say, 'often makes the difference between the saint and the sinner.'"

"I fear," replied Pemberton, smiling, "however true that saying may be in a general way, that in Phil's case, his unusual seriousness is owing quite as much to Cupid's arrow in his heart, as to the British ball in his shoulder."

"If so, you had better warn him at once," replied Isabella, earnestly. "Helen could never love a rebel; and, besides—you have eyes, Arthur."

'I shall take the first opportunity to enlighten Phil," said Pemberton. "I love him too well to have him suffer with heartache."

"And I will caution Helen. She does not mean to flirt, and she does not exactly flirt; but to fling about the bright sparkles of her eyes, and to captivate men with the tones of her voice, and the thrilling touches of her hand, seems to come as natural to her as breathing. You know it is natural to her, Arthur."

"Of course I do. You might as well blame a rose for flinging around its fragrance, or a star for twinkling. But it's a pity she couldn't carry a badge on her breast, labelled 'hands off, this property is not for sale.' And yet I suppose it would make no difference—every moth still would fly right into the bright fire of her eyes, and get his foolish wings scorched."

"Hush!" said Isabella, "they are coming up to us."

8

CHAPTER IX.

THE DREAM OF ANDRE.

> "There is no doubt that there exist such voices—
> Yet would I not call those
> Voices of *warning*, that announce to us
> Only the inevitable. As the sun,
> Ere it is risen, sometimes paints its image
> In the atmosphere, so often do the spirits
> Of great events stride on before the events,
> And in to-day already walks to-morrow."
>
> *Schiller's Wallenstein.*

A HALF-HOUR'S gentle canter, and our party drew up once more at Mrs. Pemberton's. Giving their horses in charge of the servants they entered and made ready for dinner—five o'clock being then as now, a common hour with the wealthier classes of the citizens. André remained at Pemberton's invitation.

The dinner was an abundant and substantial, but simple affair. Two courses; at the first a round of roast beef, and the vegetables and stewed fruits of the season—potatoes, sweet and white, turnips, stewed cranberries, apple sauce and cole-slaw; for the second course, dried-peach pies and a rice-pudding, ending with nuts, and a cup of coffee for those who desired it. For drink, there was good water—rather a scarce article in the world—home-brewed beer, and claret and Madeira wines. These last were very sparingly partaken of—for fifty years before, the evils of intemperance had been strongly portrayed at public meetings held throughout the province—a prohibitory law in relation to *distilled* liquors had been warmly urged—and the "Friends" had many a solemn testimony uttered by their preachers against the danger of over-indulgence in intoxicating drinks.

Mrs. Pemberton presided at the head of the table. She was a rather large, and, for her years, quite a comely woman, with something of the air of a queen about her, notwithstanding the severe simplicity of her Quaker attire. The smooth and unruffled serenity of her face told of feelings habitually kept under control. It was doubtful that she could be easily wounded by any assault of fate that did not touch the weak point in her smooth-shining armor—her love for Arthur, her only remaining child.

Mrs. Pemberton, like a large proportion of the sect to which she belonged, was intensely loyal in her feelings—so much so that when the British entered the city, she had sent to Sir William Howe her carriage and horses for his own use while he remained. This she could do conscientiously; but to contribute in aid of warlike measures, even to benefit the cause she deemed just, she would not do, under any pretence whatever. The royal commander might take from her what he pleased for such purposes, and she would submit—but she would not aid voluntarily in any way or manner in the shedding of blood. Her opposition in fact to the Colonial cause was based upon this very thing—when the Colonies took ground that involved a resort to violence and war, she no longer sympathized with them.

Her residence was called by many the Flag House, as it was the only one belonging to a citizen which displayed the British flag. But this flag had been run up at first entirely without Mrs. Pemberton's knowledge. It was apparently the work of old Fox. The late Mr. Pemberton had been a large ship-owner, and in the attic of the house Foxey had found a collection of flags, of various sizes. One of these he had run up on a tall but rude flag-staff of his own manufacture, when the British army entered the city, greatly to the disgust of that portion of the citizens who were Whigs.

Mrs. Pemberton was not, by any means, a bigoted "Friend," but still she disliked this particular exhibition of loyalty, as not being in accordance with what she termed "Friends' testimonies." But, as it had been done, and seemed to please General Howe very greatly, and as her son represented to her that it really was a matter of very little importance, the flag was allowed to remain.

And Fox was permitted to fly his flags at his pleasure, substituting one for another, sometimes a small one, sometimes a large one, and sometimes the very largest he could lay his hands on, according apparently to his own African notions of what was suitable and proper. That he should fly his largest flags upon what he deemed the greatest occasions, seemed to be only in accordance with what might naturally be expected. But to return to our company.

After the removal of the first course, which you may be sure all parties did ample justice to—though the noise of the cannonade still continued at intervals, not however so constant and heavy as at first—Mrs. Pemberton was informed by her son of the particulars of their day's ride, including the adventure with the deserters. She was of course greatly affected. "Poor, misguided men!" was her comment upon hearing of the tragical fate of the deserters. "If the riflemen only could have captured them, or driven them off, without killing them, how much better it would have been."

While Arthur had been telling his story, André had turned around to a little desk behind him, on which stood writing materials, and seemed to be sketching something with a pen. As Pemberton concluded, he turned back again, smiling.

"Here we are, Mrs. Pemberton," cried he, gayly handing her a sheet of paper, on which he had made a rude but highly artistic sketch. "Here is the rock. That is Helen—you would know her by her defiant expression and attitude—she has just blown the whistle. That is poor me—half scared to death. That is Pemberton, looking as grave as a Quaker preacher in meeting. That's Isabella, standing erect, like a queen. And there up on the brow of the precipice, are the horrible deserters."

The sketch was handed around, and greatly commended for its accuracy and spirit; Helen, in the end, appropriating it as her own, without a word, and apparently in the most unconscious manner.

"My dear children," said Mrs. Pemberton, "we should thank the kind Father for bringing you assistance at so critical a moment. Philip Morris was but the instrument in His holy hand."

"It seems to me though, it can easily be accounted for in a natural way," said Arthur in a low voice to André, who was sitting opposite to him.

But his mother caught the words. "Arthur, I do not like to hear thee say that. History is full of such Providential interpositions—especially the history of the early Friends."

"In your own family, Friend Pemberton," said Isabella, "you have frequently had such cases, have you not?"

"Yes, indeed," replied Mrs. Pemberton, evidently embarked on a favorite subject; "hand down that tureen, Arthur, from the sideboard."

Arthur did so. It was a silver tureen, and on it was engraved the device of a cat bearing off a rabbit. The others had frequently seen it, but it was new to André, and the story connected with it was new to all but her son.

"When the first settlers came to Philadelphia," Mrs. Pemberton resumed, "many of them made caves in the high bank, on the river's edge, to live in, until they had time to build more comfortable homes. An ancestor of ours and of Philip Morris's, when the dinner hour came one day, found she had nothing left in the house to eat, except a little biscuit and cheese, and with no immediate prospect of getting anything more. Then she gave way to despondency, and began to wish she had remained among the flesh-pots of the English Egypt. But suddenly a voice within seemed to say: 'Didst thou not come for liberty of conscience—and hast thou not got it? Neither hast thou suffered greatly thus far.' Then she fell on her knees, and prayed to be forgiven, and for a greater measure of faith."

"That was just like you would have done, my dear Aunt Rachel," exclaimed Isabella.

"Well," continued Mrs. Pemberton, not displeased with the compliment from her favorite of the two girls, "when she rose from her knees, and was going to seek for other food, her cat darted into the cave with a fine large rabbit which it had caught. And thus our Heavenly Father answered her humble petition, and gave her a lesson which she never forgot. For when, in after days, they became prosperous and wealthy, she had this tureen made, and engraved as you see it, in order that none of her descendants might forget the rock of their strength, to the latest generation.

"And many other such incidents have occurred in the history of our family," continued Mrs. Pemberton, "both here and in the old world, which I could mention, if it were necessary."

"Mother," said Pemberton slyly, "how do you explain the flash of lightning last June, which melted the crown on Christ Church steeple? Do you think that it meant God's displeasure with the course of the mother country toward these colonies?"

"I think it may have been intended as a warning to the king," replied she, "that unless he reigned with greater justice, his kingdom in this part of the world would be taken from him.

"Pretty well answered, I think, Master Arthur," said Isabella.

"And then again," continued Mrs. Pemberton, "we all know what happened at Birmingham meeting-house. Years before the bloody conflict at Brandywine—yes, years before the beginning of the war, one of our most gifted ministers, enlightened by the Word, predicted not only the coming on of the contest, but how that very place would be the scene of frightful carnage, how the blood would be spattered red on the horses' bridles and housings, and that very house itself be filled with the wounded and the slain!"

"He did?" said Helen, her face glowing with her interest in the subject.

"Yes, I believe that is so," responded Arthur. "But I also remember how another very eloquent minister, the Rev. Morgan Edwards—"

"He is not a Friend," interrupted his mother; "he is a hireling minister. It is a different case entirely."

"But, mother, let me go on," said Arthur, laughing. "I admit that he is not a Friend—but he was always considered a very worthy, conscientious and sincere man. The Rev. Morgan Edwards was persuaded that he had received a warning from above—a kind of inward monition, mother—that he was about to die, and on a certain day, at a certain hour. He felt so sure of it that he announced it from his pulpit. It made a great sensation, of course.

When the fateful day came his house was crowded. He breathed slowly. Everybody was expectant. You could hear the big clock tick. The minutes wore on. He breathed slower and slower. Every moment, he thought, would be his last. But he could not die! And, greatly to his own vexation and disappointment, and the vexation and disappointment of his numerous friends and admirers, the dreaded minutes passed on; the hour passed over; the day passed over—and here twenty years are gone, and the reverend gentleman is still alive and frisky."

"If I had been he, I would have taken laudanum," said Helen, in a mortified tone.

"Of course it killed him, in one sense, if not in another," continued Pemberton. "His congregation lost all faith in his spiritual discernment; and he left the city in disgust. Now, that he was earnest and sincere, is proven by the whole course of the affair. What have you to say about these matters, André? you have not spoken a word for the last half hour. Are you a believer or a disbeliever?"

"Captain André is not a disbeliever, I will warrant," said Helen. "Aunt Rachel, you must take Arthur to meeting with you more regularly. He is getting quite Frenchified."

André had been sitting very quietly, as Pemberton had said, but was evidently an attentive listener to the conversation. Now he took a sip of wine, and said in a low and musing tone:

"I know not what to say. There is so much evidence on both sides. But I will also tell a story—an anecdote of what happened to young Percy, the very day he was killed at Brandywine. I had it from his servant, after the battle.

"You may have heard what a splendid fellow Percy was," continued André; "so kind, so noble, so generous! I knew him well—and many a pleasant talk we had together on our way from the head of Elk. He was a volunteer, you know; and rode with whom it pleased him. He wore a handsome uniform, and looked and rode as a descendant of Harry Hotspur should. He was in Cornwallis's division, and that long, well-planned march of the general's brought them to the flank of Washington's army about two in the afternoon. They absolutely stopped and took a comfortable dinner about two miles from the Americans; only the rise of a hill concealing the two armies from each other's view."

"I should think that was not very wise nor prudent," said Isabella.

"Perhaps not—but it is hard fighting on an empty stomach—and the result justified it," replied André.

"At four o'clock," continued he, sadly, "the British column ascended the intervening hill, and came in sight of the American position, their troops all in line, and awaiting the onset."

"Oh, it is horrible!" exclaimed Mrs. Pemberton—"brothers thirsting for brothers' blood. Where was your religion—where your common humanity?"

"As Percy came to the brow of the hill, he suddenly reined in his steed, and gazed with a curious, questioning eye over the scene before him. There was a gentle hill and dale, interspersed with dark patches of wood, green pastures and low, gray farm-houses; and, just seen in a little opening on the right, the glittering waters of the Brandywine, flowing peacefully and quietly in the glorious sunshine. I stood afterward in the very same spot, Miss Helen."

"Well?" said Helen, breathlessly.

"Calling his servant to his side, Percy took his gold watch from his pocket, and gave it to him. 'Take this, David,' said he, 'and give it to my sister in far Northumberland. I have seen this hill and stream and landscape before; in a dream, in England. Here I shall die! And'—taking his purse from his pocket—'take this for yourself.' That was all he said—every word. Then he rode on. In the midst of the fight, in that fierce contest for the possession of the graveyard and Birmingham meeting-house, Percy fell. That is all," said André, passing his hand over his forehead.

"May he sleep in peace amid the quiet hills of Brandywine!" said Pemberton, solemnly.

"And God comfort his sister, in far Northumberland, when the sad news comes," said Isabella.

"It reminds me of my own dream—one that I have dreamed twice, once in England, and again nearly two years ago in Lancaster," resumed André, with a touch of sadness in his tones, and a dreamy look in his dark eyes. "It was a very vivid dream, and I awakened on both occasions feeling intensely sorrowful. And yet there was nothing very sorrowful in it. I thought I was riding alone, along a country road. At length I came to a gentle declivity, at the foot of which seemed to flow a little stream. The landscape was beautiful and quite peculiar, and I should know it at once if I ever really saw such a scene. On one side of the road, a little distance from it, towered a majestic tree. At the north, they call them Whitewood; you call them Tulip Poplars. But this was immense; its trunk I should think nearly thirty feet around; and its boughs the size of ordinary trees. But the great peculiarity of the tree was its gnarled and fantastic branches, which twisted down in places almost to the earth, and then rose again. While I was gazing at it, a soldier in British uniform suddenly stepped out from the side of the road, presented his musket at my breast, and cried 'Halt!' At the sound, on both occasions, I awoke. If I ever see that spot, that tree, and hear that voice, I shall feel as Percy felt at Brandywine."

André leaned his head upon his hand. He evidently had been deeply impressed by the prophetic vision, as he deemed it. Helen rose from the table to conceal her sympathetic agitation.

"Come now, André," cried Pemberton in a cheery voice, "you are giving us all the dismals. That dream is susceptible of two explanations. Your tree was the great tree of Life, Ygdrasil, which you had probably been reading about in some old Norse fable; and the soldier was Death, who is certain to start out even from under the very giant and twisted branches of the tree of life, and cry 'Halt' to all of us—and this is the most reasonable explanation, and does credit to your involuntary powers of fancy and invention, making me think you even more of a poet and artist than I thought you before. Or, if you will have the dream more literally fulfilled—here is our adventure of to-day, with big trees enough, and soldiers wearing British uniforms too, and crying 'halt' into the bargain. Your dream came to-day as near an accurate fulfilment as dreams are apt to come, I fancy."

Helen's face brightened. "Yes, Mr. André, Mr. Pemberton has explained all in the most satisfactory manner. Why, Arthur, you are a second Daniel; and here is a kiss for your reward"—tossing him one of those sweet little compositions, so appropriately named, out of the cake-basket.

"I shall try to think so, at least," said André, rousing himself to gayety, as with an effort, "for such forebodings are not inspiriting to a soldier. And, apropos to all this, would you not, ladies, like to visit the famous witch, conjurer, sorceress, astrologess, and fortune-teller, Madame Dumont, who has been making so much talk lately? Tarleton has been there, and even he, who believes in nothing he cannot see and hear, is puzzled. Miss Shippen says she predicts the most curious career for her. Miss Franks says she is the—bad one. While Miss Vining keeps a silence which is more significant than words. Let us all go."

"Suppose we do," said Pemberton.

"I do not approve of such tampering with sacred things, John," said Mrs. Pemberton. "If the spirit wants to speak, it will speak; but I think it wicked, and even dangerous, to have anything to do with witches and those who have familiar spirits.

"But, Aunt Rachel, we should not have the least faith in her; and it would be such rare fun," remonstrated Helen.

"Well, we can decide about it another time," said André, who did not wish needlessly to controvert Mrs. Pemberton's strong religious convictions upon the subject. "I still hear the cannon booming at intervals, and think I had better go up to headquarters to learn what has been going on to-day."

"I will go along," said Pemberton. "I also feel anxious to hear; and even the ladies, doubtless, would like to know that all their friends are safe, before retiring."

The gentlemen left. But in half an hour Pemberton returned, with a face in which joy and grief blended. He brought back word that the Hessians, under Count Donop, had been repulsed in their attack on Fort Mercer, with great slaughter. The British ships, also, had been able to make no impression on Fort Mifflin, while two of the vessels, the Merlin and Augusta, were aground, and might have to be abandoned. None of their immediate friends, on either side, were injured.

Pemberton's face glowed as he told this; while Isabella's eyes shone triumphantly in sympathy. Helen threw herself on a sofa and shed tears, while Mrs. Pemberton gave a deep sigh. Nothing was said, however, on the one side of exultation, on the other of anger or regret—they all loved and respected each other too much for that.

"I also was deeply pained to learn," continued Pemberton, "that Count Donop, who commanded the expedition, now lies mortally wounded, and a prisoner. One of his officers had just brought the news to General Howe. He had obtained permission to visit the count, after the contest. The latter lay dying, in a neighboring farm-house. He seemed to feel ashamed and mortified at this sad close of a brilliant life. He said, bitterly, to the officer, "And here ends, early and ingloriously, my proud and ambitious career. I have moved in half the courts of Europe, and am now dying here ignobly, in the house of an obscure Quaker."

Weary with their ride and the exciting events of the day, the ladies retired early to rest—thankful that they had no visitors. Whenever they awakened through the night they could still hear at intervals the sad booming of the cannon. And the next morning the whole city was startled by a tremendous explosion. A red-hot shot from the fort had set the Augusta, a large 64-gun ship, on fire, and she had blown up!

CHAPTER X.

THE FORTUNE TELLER.

We hear the slow and solemn steps of Doom
Approaching through the corridors of Time.
They echo through our dreams.

THE young people persevered in their projected visit to Madame Dumont, notwithstanding Mrs. Pemberton's sensible objection. For Helen and André, anything of the kind had a peculiar fascination; while Pemberton regarded divination as a curious study, and worthy of sufficient investigation to ascertain whether there was even a single spark of light-giving fire among such thick volumes of smoke. Isabella was very much of Mrs. Pemberton's opinion—but, if the others went, she would go also.

They went by appointment. And Pemberton had taken great care that the alleged sorceress should not have the slightest intimation as to who would constitute the party. He had even loaned André one of his own coats in order that it might not be known that he was a soldier.

The night was dark and gusty when they set forth, with some indications in the west of an approaching storm. But as all the arrangements had been made, and as the ladies had arrayed themselves in their oldest and commonest dresses, in order to conceal even their social rank, they cared comparatively little for a drenching.

Philadelphia, at that time, though the largest and wealthiest city in the colonies, contained only about thirty thousand inhabitants. It was built up with tolerable compactness along the Delaware, from South to Callowhill Street, and as far west as Fourth Street; beyond Fourth—the houses were few and scattered. The State House and Walnut Street jail were on the outskirts. The streets were generally unpaved, and to a great degree unlighted—lanterns being carried at night by the citizens when necessary. Dock creek ran up into and through the heart of the city, requiring numerous bridges. At one time there were as many as a dozen of them. It was a totally different place from the well-paved, well-lighted, immense city of to-day.

Madame Dumont had taken a house out Walnut Street, several squares beyond the inclosure of the State House. Whether she had chosen it purposely or not, it was a house of evil repute, inasmuch as it had the reputation of being haunted. It had been the residence of a man whose wife had been murdered—by whom, no one knew. He said, by robbers. He was himself suspected, but the case never came to trial, for want of proof. The fortune-teller obtained it cheaply, for no one else would live in it. Probably its reputation was also an inducement to her. It was calculated to surround her with an atmosphere of the supernatural.

It was after eight o'clock when our party set out. The evening, as we have said, was dark and gusty; and they made their way over the uneven side-paths, up Chestnut Street, over the Dock creek bridge, and then along Fourth to Walnut. Turning up Walnut, they entered into almost the open country. Passing along the high stone wall of the State House yard—then full of cedar bushes, its stately elms and other noble trees as yet unplanted—they came opposite the Walnut Street Prison. Occasional lights were flickering through its grated windows; but, in the main, its huge front was dark and stern and cheerless.

"That is Cunningham's little hell!" exclaimed Pemberton, bitterly, turning his head back toward André, who followed with Helen. "Sir William Howe looks and talks like a generous, genial man, but how such a man can allow a foul den like that, and tolerate such a monster as Cunningham, is a mystery to me."

"Between you and me, Pemberton, it is a mystery to me also," replied André. "If I had the power, or if General Grey, stern as he is, had it, Cunningham would not retain his place an hour. He knows it too—he would have cursed me only yesterday, to my face, had he dared."

"Did you offend him?" queried Helen.

"Yes, for common humanity always offends him. I was passing the prison, when who should come along but Captain Cunningham, with a party of prisoners. One of them, I declare, Pemberton, was not more than fifteen—a mere boy! He was crying bitterly. He had accompanied the detachment in a boyish love of sport and excitement—and here he was."

"Of course you interfered?" said Isabella. "I know you did it."

"It was mere common humanity," replied André. "The boy told me of his father and his poor mother at home, who did not know where he was; and I told him to be of good cheer, I would see what I could do for him. The little fellow was comforted, and hushed his crying—while Cunningham looked on, black as night. I've no doubt," continued André, laughing, "the Provost would have helped to hang me at that moment, with the greatest satisfaction."

"Did you get the boy released?" inquired Helen.

"Of course—at once. General Howe said he would give Cunningham a talking to for such doings—but I am afraid that that will be the end of it. Sir William has but one fault, as a soldier and a man, he loves his ease rather too much."

Helen clasped closer the arm she held. Perhaps it was

owing to the darkness of the night, and the increasing roughness of the way; but André thought not.

"Take care at this gulley—go slowly," cried Pemberton. "It runs down through the Potter's Field.* You cannot see the newly-turned earth by this light, and the long line of pits. Hundreds of American prisoners are being carried weekly out of the hospitals, and out of that hideous jail, and crowded like dead dogs into those holes."

"See! what is that?" whispered Isabella, as a tall, ghostly-looking figure in white rose up from among the graves.

They all were startled. It was evidently coming toward them. Then Pemberton laughed. "It is only crazy Leah," said he. "She has a habit of sleeping there at times—she says, to keep off the doctors."

"It would drive me crazy to meet her here alone, on such a night as this," said Helen. "I should think it was the ghost of that Miss Carpenter who committed suicide."

"You should be above that," replied Pemberton. "I like the spirit shown by her relatives, the Carpenters and the Storys. When they found she could not, poor unfortunate! be buried in consecrated earth, they walled in that little inclosure for a family ground—and there she, and many others of her family, lie buried."

"That was noble!" exclaimed André. "I have often wondered what that little walled inclosure in the centre of the field meant. There is something grand about that."

"Yes, I suppose there is," said Helen; "but what with all this talk about graves and suicide, and this dismal

* Now Washington Square.

night, I am half-frightened already. How much further is it, Arthur?"

"We are nearly there. Now, not a word as to who we are, or that will give her the slightest clue in any direction."

Pushing back a gate, Pemberton led the way up to the house. He knocked at the door. There was no response. He knocked again.

"Why don't she come?" said Helen, in a whisper. "This is an awfully ghostly place. And hear how the wind whistles."

A step, at last, was heard inside, approaching the door. A light gleamed, and the door opened. A tall negress received them, and led the way into a medium-sized room, hung with alternate breadths of some blue and crimson stuff, and from the ceiling of which a large silver lamp depended. Under the lamp, which seemed fed with some kind of aromatic oil, judging from the heavy perfume, as of mock-orange, which pervaded the apartment, stood a round table covered with a crimson cloth. On the table were several richly-bound volumes, and what seemed a brass triangle, whose flat sides were marked with various cabalistic figures. At the end of the room stood what appeared to be an altar, with three unlighted wax candles upon it.

After requesting them, more by a motion than by words, to seat themselves on a richly-draped settee or lounge, the negress left them.

"Well," said Pemberton, in a low but amused voice, "this is the thing exactly. This is just what I wanted to see—a regular witch's den of these modern days. Let me see what these books are," continued he, stepping to the table. "Oh, yes, the genuine articles—'Hidon's Temple of Wisdom,' 'Scot's Discovery of Witchcraft,' and 'Cornelius Agrippa on Necromancy,' of course. Now for the witch herself. I hope—"

His remarks were cut short by a most unearthly shriek, which caused the ladies, and even André, to start from their seats in horror, followed, as it was, by the terrible cry of—

"Help! help! murder! mur—der! Oh! oh!"

Isabella grew pale, Helen almost shrieked herself, and André laid his hand where he was accustomed to find the hilt of his sword. Hearing a slight rustle, Pemberton turned his eyes toward one of the windows from near which the cry had seemed to come, and then walking to it, drew aside the heavy fold of a curtain.

"Do not be alarmed, ladies; it is only a cockatoo," said he, smiling.

They gathered around him, while the cockatoo, having displayed his powers to his satisfaction, gave vent to his delight by a low chuckle. It was a beautiful bird—large, with dove-colored feathers and white crest—but singular withal, as its breast and shoulders were a bright crimson, as if stained by a gush of blood.

Gazing at the bird, they had for the moment forgotten the object of their visit, when a rich, deep voice caused them to turn, and Madame Dumont evidently stood before them.

Tall and dignified, apparently of about fifty years of age, and judging from her brunette complexion a French or Spanish Creole, with dark, burning eyes—a richly-colored shawl drawn around her shoulders, and a handkerchief, equally richly colored, worn as a turban upon her head—Madame Dumont evidently was no vulgar fortune-teller, but one of the mistresses of her solemn and imposing art.

"Welcome, fair flowers of Scotia! welcome to my

humble dwelling. Welcome, true lover of woman; welcome, faithful son of a woman, to the home of the unloved and the desolate. What would you of the daughter of the Tropics?"

"We would," replied Isabella, with a little of a tremor, "learn of our Future. We would read the pages of destiny."

"And why read the Future? Why not dwell contented in the happy Present?"

"How dost thou know that it is the happy present?" interposed Helen.

"When one sees the glory of youth in the eyes, the beauty of youth on the cheeks, it requires no deep divination to read the Present. But thou wouldst know of the Future. Give me thy hand."

Helen stretched forth her hand. The sorceress gazed into the soft palm, holding it to reflect the light.

"All the lines are fortunate, save one," said she quietly. "Canst thou not be happy with one thing denied?"

"I should think," replied Pemberton, smiling, "that it would depend very much upon what that one thing was."

"What is to be denied me?" said Helen quickly.

"All the lines are fortunate and straight and full save one—only the line of love, though straight and full, is suddenly broken."

"Only the line of love!" repeated Helen. "Then I suppose my fate will be to lead apes hereafter, instead of here."

"This palmistry—this hand-divination, is very imperfect, lady," replied the fortune-teller. "It is the lowest branch of my art. And even that says not thou shalt live a maiden. I have not said so."

André made a step forward. "Why is it so often the

case, good mother, that the oracies of Fate will bear a double interpretation?"

"The oracles of Fate! Would you then really hear them?" exclaimed the woman, in a solemn, somewhat sad voice. "Hark! do you hear the wind rushing through the branches? It portends the tempest. And that low roaring of the thunder—it foretells that the storm is rolling nearer and nearer. I feel in my spirit the rushing of the wind. I hear the low roaring of the thunder. The storm will burst full soon."

"Yes," said Isabella to Pemberton, anxiously, "a storm is indeed coming up. Had we not better return home at once?"

"It would be on us before we had gone a square. Ha! there it is—" as a sharp peal rang through the air, and seemed to shake the building, while they heard outside the rushing of the rain. "It may all be over in an hour or so—it is the way with our thunder storms."

"Of course we will stay," said Helen. "And now that matter is settled, let us learn something of those spiritual tempests which we have been told of. Can you not be a little more precise in your readings of the dark page of the Future? If the reading of the hand be imperfect, let us witness some of the higher evidences of your power."

The fortune-teller appeared to hesitate—her manner seemed for the moment irresolute.

"If money be an object with you—" interposed Arthur.

"Thy money perish with thee!" cried the fortune-teller, her eyes and face glowing. "Know, young man, that I, like the called and anointed of thy father's faith, neither preach for hire, nor divine for money. All my offerings are free-will offerings—and I never even look at what each man gives."

"Pardon me, good mother! I erred through ignorance. I both understand and honor the feeling you manifest."

"I hesitated only," said the woman, "because I fear my own art. When the curtain is raised, is it wonderful that I also should sometimes start and shudder? Can I see a pit in your onward path, all black and yawning before you—and you, young hopefuls, hastening gayly and cheerfully on—and not myself suffer? and suffer more, because that I have faith!"

"But," interrupted André, "is it not better that in such a case the reckless gayety should yield a little to more serious and befitting thoughts? Would not the wayfarer be thus better prepared for the pit?"

"It may be so—and that comforts me," replied the fortune-teller.

"And moreover," continued André, "forewarned, are we not somewhat forearmed? Is the future thou seest, inevitable?"

"It is inevitable—so far as the natural order of things and events is concerned. Only he who rules this world, be he the Great Supreme, or some wise archangel or angel under him, can interpose to save the menaced one."

"Does he ever interpose?" questioned André, earnestly. "Is his workmanship so poor, as ever to need the helping hand of alteration or correction?"

"In making man a free agent," replied the sibyl, "he has himself necessarily made his workmanship imperfect. Allow for the workings of a free agent, and not even infinite intelligence can exactly perceive and provide for the infinite future. And thus what I term, in one sense, the inevitable, *may* never come to pass. But let no one calculate upon this—for in ninety and nine cases in the hundred, the inevitable, as I see it, will come to pass. I never knew but of one case in which it did not.

"But we waste time," she continued. "You at least," addressing André, "may confidently hope for a happy future. You have the eye and voice which captivate alike men and women. You have in that the key to all success. Give me your hand."

There were two seats drawn into the middle of the room, near the table. To one of these the sibyl led André, while she herself took the other. She sat for several minutes in perfect silence—then she spoke:

"Prince of the Powers of the Air! thou that seest and knowest from thy exalted height the ways of men—make my inward mind pure, my inward sight clear, that I may see and understand the destiny of this man now before me!"

She rose and lighted with a taper the three candles on the altar, and then returned to her seat.

Taking the right hand of André in her own, and sitting in perfect silence, soon her head fell forward, her eyes partly closed, and she seemed to sink into a kind of trance. A low sweet strain of music, the source of which it was impossible to fix, floated through the room. Then, after a long, deep breath, she spoke in a rapid but clear tone, audible to all, though scarcely louder than a whisper:—

'I see a great crowd. There is a high hill. I see you—yes, it is certainly you. You are in a military uniform. It is red—it is a British uniform. The crowd is very sorrowful—some are weeping. There are generals and other officers. You are standing on a wagon—on a coffin. It is a scaffold. A rope is around your neck. Oh—oh—oh!"

With a wild wail the sibyl sprang to her feet—dashing

her hands over her brow and eyes, as if to wipe away the memory of a fearful dream.

The young ladies also had sprung to their feet, greatly excited—Helen fairly trembling with the excitement and terror.

André's face was pale, but he said, calmly:—

"Good mother, you have given the ladies a great fright."

"It is terrible, terrible!" exclaimed Helen. "How could you conjure up such a scene?"

"Pardon, sweet lady!" said the sybil. "When I go into these trances, I know not what I shall say. But those that are fearful of heart, should never seek to explore the future."

"I am not fearful! I am startled and excited—not fearful! I am not afraid to hear or see any fate, true or false, that you may call before me," replied Helen, the blue eyes of her father flashing above the cheeks into which the blood had returned in a torrent. "Sit down again, John, and let us have it out."

"Yes," added Isabella proudly, "we are a soldier's daughters, and not such cowards as to be frightened by mere words."

"Well," said Pemberton, "you are the ones to decide, ladies. I suppose we gentlemen can endure anything that you can."

André smiled, and again took his seat.

"See if you cannot give me something more pleasant than that; or, if you cannot, give me that over again, that I may not forget it."

"The spirit never repeats itself—and you will never forget it!" said the sibyl solemnly, taking her seat and his hand anew.

Again the silence—then the low, sweet æolian tones of

music as before, but in a wilder, more triumphant strain.

"I see a glorious building. It is in England. Yes, it is Westminster Abbey. A new monument has been erected. Men—the titled and high-born—and beautiful women, are gazing upon it. Stay—I can read the name. 'Sacred to the memory of John André.'

"That is all—it passes from before me. Ask me no more of thy destiny."

"It is enough!" proudly exclaimed André, rising. "A tomb in Westminster Abbey, amid the noblest and best of England, might well content the ambition of a prouder man than I am. Good mother, thy second prediction, though it seems to give the lie to the first, is quite sufficient for me. No man that lived the life of a felon, no man that dies the death of a felon, shall ever lie in the Abbey of Westminster."

The sibyl smiled. "I am well pleased that it is so. But it grows late—and I begin to feel exhausted. Will not this serve for one evening?"

"You have done so well on the second trial for our friend, can you not do as well by me?" said Helen. "This sending one home to bed, to dream of hopeless love, is hardly the right thing, mother."

"You call me 'mother'—would to God that you had a mother!" said the sibyl fondly but sadly. "But I have not predicted the hardest fate—better be unhappy in thy love, than unloved and unloving."

Helen took her seat in the chair of divination, and in the wilful manner which became her so well, held out her hand. The sibyl shook her head sadly, but took her usual seat, kissing the beautiful throbbing hand as she laid it in her own.

Then ensued the deep silence, followed by a very faint,

yet sad strain of music. A shudder ran through the frame of the sibyl. She spoke.

"I see a maiden. She wanders along the shore. It is a dark night. I see high cliffs. She tosses her hands wildly. She—"

"No," exclaimed the sibyl, breaking through her trance with a strong effort—"I will not! I can not! I am weak and faint. I am not certain of my power. The lower spirits may delude me. Lucifer is cunning. The book is closed and sealed. Live thou in the happy Present."

"But I *must* know!" exclaimed Helen, imperiously. "I am not a child—I am a woman! What a man fears not to do or to hear, I fear not to do or to hear.

"Then, not to-night," replied the sibyl earnestly. "Can you not imagine the strain this divination must be upon my spirit? I am exhausted."

"Help! help! murder, mur—" again began the cockatoo; but ceased at a hasty gesture from his mistress. "Cease, Goblin!" cried she.

"It is a horrid bird!" exclaimed Helen. "How can you bear to have it about the house?"

"He belonged to the lady who once lived here—and died here," replied the sibyl, her voice sinking—"yes, in this very room! They say that Goblin was once a great talker—but ever since that time, he utters but this one cry; caught perhaps from his terrified mistress in her hour of agony, and driving out from his memory every other. They also say his plumage was changed at the same time, and that this crimson stain like blood, was never seen on his breast before the murder. This, however, may be a mere unfounded superstition. But you have heard yourselves his only cry."

"Poor, poor bird!" said Helen in a sympathizing voice.

"Ladies," said Pemberton, "do you know that it grows late?"

"I am ready to depart," replied Isabella.

"And I suppose I must be," said Helen—"though I never like to hear a tale half-told."

"You are a little unreasonable, sometimes, *ma belle Helene*," rejoined Isabella, as she threw Helen's shawl over her shoulders. "Let us make our adieus and depart."

But the sibyl had disappeared, probably through some concealed passage, as suddenly as she had entered—and the negress was at the door of the room, waiting to show them out. The young men exchanged a few words, and then each deposited a gold piece upon the table.

As they left the house, the sky was covered with broken masses of cloud; but the storm had passed over, the full moon had risen, and all nature slept calmly in its silvery light.

Isabella drew a deep breath. "That is the first and last time you ever catch me at a fortune-teller's," exclaimed she. "How peaceful and heavenly this moonlight is, after that awesome room."

"Bella, I do believe you are a coward," replied Helen.

"Coward or not, Helen, I am content for one to take things as they come, not seeking to penetrate the future. I think it well to have a pleasant time as I go along, even if I am to be hung, or sent wandering like a maniac along the seashore, some twenty or fifty years hence."

"I think you are more than half right," said Pemberton. "But that woman impressed me greatly. She is evidently a superior person, and deeply and enthusiastically sincere. Of course that proves nothing for the truth of her predictions."

"I should think it did," said Helen.

"Not at all, Helen. Mr. Edwards was just as sincere

in predicting his own death, as Madame Dumont is in her predictions. He fully expected to die. But he did not."

"And yet sometimes these predictions come true," said Isabella. "I have heard of several cases—and doubtless your mother could tell us of more."

"Doubtless mother could," replied Pemberton, laughing. "She has not all that Welsh blood in her veins for nothing."

"I think it would be a good thing for you, Arthur," said Helen, "if you had a little more of that Welsh blood in yours."

"I know you do, Helen; but I am very well satisfied with my share."

"Of course. I never saw a man who was not almost absolutely perfect in his own estimation." André pressed the hand on his arm, and smiled. "I admit there are a few brilliant exceptions," she added,

"I suppose those are the cases in which you consider that the gentlemen are almost absolutely perfect," replied Pemberton, gayly. "But apropos of fortune-telling, I will tell you an anecdote which my mother never told me, but my father did. A friend of his, a military gentleman, like André here, had been told by a gypsy in whose predictions he had great faith, that he need never fear bullet nor ball, but to beware of cold steel. Of course in battle he never felt the least fear of anything that gunpowder could do, but he disliked mightily to hear the order to charge bayonets."

"Oh, I know the rest; he died safely and soundly in his bed," interrupted Helen saucily.

"Not so fast, *ma belle Helene*. He did die in his bed, but my father always contended that he died of cold steel —for the doctors, Sangrado like, absolutely bled him, and bled him, till it was impossible for him to recover. Nature gave up the contest in despair, and he died. So you see you must always allow a wide margin in the interpretation of these predictions. As your favorite Shakspeare says, André, they often 'palter with us in a double sense.'"

André had been very quiet, and continued so all the way home. Was he thinking of that terrible scene which the sibyl had conjured up—or of that far different one in Westminster Abbey? Whichever it was that occupied his thoughts—or whether his mind was brooding over far different themes—he gave no clue to judge by words. Declining Pemberton's formal invitation to enter, when they arrived at Mrs. Pemberton's, and only lingering a moment on the step to exchange a few loving words with his betrothed, he took his way to his own lodgings.

CHAPTER XI.

THE QUAKER PREACHER.

"And things are not what they seem."—*Longfellow.*

As Pemberton sat in the parlor one morning, a week or two after the evening at Madame Dumont's, he heard a loud, peculiar knock at the front door, and shortly afterward old Fox entered, ushering in a gentleman of rather singular appearance. The visitor was apparently an aged member of the Society of Friends. His hair was silver white—evidently with age, not with powder—and hung low over his forehead, while it straggled, untied and queueless, down the sides of his face, and behind over his neck. His dress was not that of the Quaker aristocracy of the period, but of the more simple and austere class of Friends who inhabited the distant country neighborhoods. It was a complete suit of homespun drab—from his drab hat to his worn and drab buckskin shoes. Despite his age, he seemed erect and vigorous; his eye seemed not deficient in fire, and his face was rather ruddy than otherwise—appearances not unusual in the aged members of his temperate and moderate sect. For it is excess which dims the lustre of the eye; and passion which bends the frame, ploughs furrows in the face, and spreads a pallor over the once ruddy surface of the skin.

"Art thou Arthur Pemberton?"

"Such is my name," politely replied Pemberton—wondering who the stranger could be.

The visitor's face took a more solemn aspect. "My name is Joshua Parsley. Thou hast heard thy late father speak of his old friend, and humble minister of the word, Joshua Parsley?"

"I regret to say that I never heard my father speak of you. But any old friend of his is always welcome."

"It is strange! Peradventure he did not take thee into his inmost confidence—thou wast rather young when he died. But he left me a solemn message for thee. I have refrained thus long from delivering that message. But I have felt of late that I must no longer refrain. I have felt a moving, yea an urging, yea a—"

The sentence was suddenly interrupted by Major Tarleton, who threw the door of the room open excitedly, having entered the house, as was not uncommon in those days, without knocking.

"Pemberton—have you seen André this morning? I thought perhaps I might find him with you. That rascal, McLane, has been at some more of his tricks. But I have his trail this time—and if I can once get sight of him, I'll tree him, or my name's not Banastre Tarleton."

"And dost thou really wish to see that man of violence and blood, my son?" spoke the solemn tones of the Quaker from the sofa, where he sat, concealed by the half opened door from the view of Tarleton, who had not entered, but continued standing in the doorway.

"Satan! who have you got here, Pemberton? I thought you were alone."

"Not Satan, my son—but an humble opponent of Satan, and follower of the lamb."

"Of the Fox, you mean," laughed Tarleton, disrespectfully. "Curse me, if some of the slipperiest fellows I have met around here have not been you same Quakers."

"Courtesy, if you please, Major," said Pemberton, a little haughtily. "This is an old friend of my father's. You asked about Captain André; I have not seen him this morning."

"Well, I must find him," replied Tarleton, coolly, turning on his heel.

"Stay, my young friend," said the Quaker. "Thou spakest of him whom the men of Belial call Captain McLane, and said thou wished to meet with him."

"Aye, that I do. I'd tan his hide for him—the rebellious rascal."

"Well, my son, I happened to be visiting a brother in Germantown, the other morning, when the men of sin were contending together—yea, verily! And I looked out of the cellar window—for we had all gone down into the cellar; yea, and also into the spiritual cellar, into the dark depths of affliction—and there was a confused noise, the thunder of the captains and the shouting—and, as I said, I looked twice out of the cellar window. And first I beheld a horseman, at the head of other horsemen, riding down the road furiously—and then, the second time I looked, I beheld another horseman, at the head of other horsemen, and he also was riding down the road furiously, yea, like the riding of Jehu, the son of Nimshi—and my friend said the second horseman was pursuing the first horseman—yea, verily! And my friend said the name of the first horseman was Tarleton, and that the name of the second horseman was McLane. Now, if thou wast the first horseman, and thou really wished to meet the second horseman, why didst thou not halt and wait for his coming?"

The Quaker had run on in his discourse, in the kind of rapid sing-song peculiar to certain of the preachers of his sect, heeding not the impatient mutterings and startings of the British officer. But, as he paused, Tarleton took a step forward, and put his hand to his sword in his anger.

"It *was* McLane, then! You know well, you sly and malicious old Thee-and-Thou, that my troop ran, not from

McLane, but from the whole rebel army. Of course he will brag how *he* chased Tarleton through Germantown. But Tarleton led the advance which chased the cursed rebel horde of tatterdemalions back to their holes again. By the—"

"Swear not, young man!" interrupted the Quaker solemnly, rising to his feet. "Take not the name of thy Creator in vain! Ah, I feel the spirit moving within me—it moves to the word of exhortation, to the word of warning, to the word of—"

"Go to the devil with your canting! Good-day, Pemberton," exclaimed Tarleton, as he flung himself through the door, slamming it violently behind him.

"The young man seems rather excited," said the Quaker, calmly resuming his seat. "I trust he will not continue long in that angry frame of mind—he might hurt somebody."

"He undoubtedly *will* hurt somebody," replied Pemberton, who had been greatly amused—though he managed to keep all traces of mirth from his countenance—at the conversation between Tarleton and the preacher. "But you said you had a message from my father for me."

"Yes, my son, I have a message, an earnest and important message; but it is one which I would rather confide to thee in the secresy of thy chamber than here, where we may be interrupted by other children of the flesh."

"Just as you please," replied Pemberton, rising. "My chamber is one of the upper rooms."

Pemberton noticed that the Quaker, notwithstanding his age, seemed to experience no difficulty in ascending the stairs; and he felt proud of the country which could produce such staunch and enduring sons.

"I think thou hadst better bolt the door," said the preacher, taking a seat.

Pemberton smiled—but did as requested.

"My son," began the Quaker, "the message which thy father entrusted to me was this. He had observed with sorrow that even before his death, thou hadst utterly, and I may say entirely, and even altogetherly, given up the use of the plain language."

"What!" cried Pemberton, impetuously. "You do not mean that this is the message you were intrusted with by my father?"

The Quaker seemed to be suddenly taken with a fit of convulsions—he bent his head nearly to his lap, while his frame shook with emotion. At length it broke forth in an apparently uncontrollable burst of laughter—not loud but deep—and all the more convulsive from his evident efforts to moderate and subdue it.

"I—shall—burst!" at length exclaimed a voice, entirely different from that which had before spoken.

Pemberton looked on in amazement. He thought the venerable preacher must be losing his senses.

"I cannot keep up the farce any longer—I cannot, to save my life," said the Quaker, in a low voice that seemed strangely familiar. At the same time he removed his hat, then his long silver hair—which proved to be a wig—composed his countenance to its natural and not quite so sanctimonious expression, and the gay, undaunted face of Lieutenant Morris was revealed to his astonished cousin.

"Why, Arthur, you stare as if you never saw me before," said the Lieutenant. "I think that is a pretty good disguise, to deceive even you."

"Philip—this is a tremendous risk. How you puzzled me. I thought at the last you must be crazy," replied Pemberton, half laughing, half alarmed at his cousin's temerity.

"You *looked* puzzled. Oh, I shall die just thinking of

it," rejoined Morris, going off into fresh convulsions of subdued laughter. "And—didn't—I—give—Tarleton—fits?"

"You were bold to recklessness. Tarleton is not the man to trifle with in that way, I assure you. Had you not passed as a guest of mine, I am not certain that even your assumed age and Quaker garb would have protected you."

"Oh, of course I calculated the chances. I knew the weazel could not help himself."

"But the risk—the great risk of this disguise, Phil. You know it is death if they discover you."

"I know all that," replied his cousin, coolly; "but do I not look death in the face almost every day of my life?"

"But the dishonorable death of a spy—and on the gallows!"

"Pshaw! mere words. Dying for one's country is the death of a patriot, whatever men say, and be it by rope or steel or bullet. If I can do tenfold the good to my country by coming here disguised, that I can in the field as a soldier, why I should be a selfish coward not to run the risk. But all this is not to the purpose. Here I am. Now what is the news?"

"Nothing is stirring, to my knowledge—save what I infer from Tarleton's words of an expedition this afternoon. I shall signal a small attack. I will move about a little this evening, and pick up what I can. Of course you will not pass the night in the city?"

"No. I have some friends to see—some of the leading ministers and elders of the flock," replied Morris, smiling. "My market wagon, well-loaded, is hitched at your door. It is well that Howe and the others are so fond of good dinners. How is auntie?"

"In good health, as usual."

"Loyal, as ever?"

"Loyal as ever."

"You do not forget the flag? Do not let Foxey oversleep himself. The other night we came near being surprised—the flag had said nothing. And we heard nothing either through Captain Fanny. That is the reason I am here."

"Foxey does the best he can. But we cannot obtain information of every movement. You know I will not play a double-handed game. I will not profess to be a devoted royalist, and worm myself into the confidence of the British officers, in order to betray it. That is not my style, Phil."

"They say that you and André are devoted friends, and I believe so from what I saw at Wissahickon. Who is the deceived one?"

"Neither."

"He must give you many important pieces of information."

"No. I will not let him. I always shut his mouth, when the confidence of friendship opens it too widely."

"Some of our officers are beginning to doubt you. They ask, how can he be a true patriot, and yet be hand and glove with a British officer?"

"I cannot help it," replied Pemberton, while his face glowed with his earnestness; "I will go thus far to aid my country and her cause—as far as I can go in honor. Not to serve myself, or her, will I go further. I will betray no one. If your superiors doubt me—fear I will purposely mislead them—let them set at naught my signals and my messengers, and pay no further attention to them."

"Well, Arthur, you know what *I* think. I trust you to the uttermost; trust you with my own life, as I am doing now, but that is nothing; would trust you with my country's life, which is everything."

"What does Washington say?"

"He says that he fully understands you, respects you, believes in you. The trouble is not with him, you may be assured. It is with a commoner order of men."

"What do you think of the General, Phil? The British officers used to express a great deal of contempt for him, giving to Lee, the Englishman, the credit of every able movement; but since Lee's capture, and the splendid dash on Colonel Rahl at Trenton, they do not seem quite so certain that Lee was our 'palladium'!"

"A fig for Lee," exclaimed Morris. "Washington is not only the ablest commander we have, but by all odds the noblest and most glorious man. Notwithstanding the calumnies of Lee and his friends, for Lee wished to have Washington's place, you know, he manifests no irritability, always speaks of Lee with courtesy, admits his brilliant abilities, and laughs not, while all the camp is laughing, at his ridiculous capture. You have not heard, perhaps, Arthur, how it all happened; it is, as the old saying goes, as good as a farce."

"I have heard nothing, save that Lee ventured too far from his army, and was betrayed by a tory."

"Oh, it is a capital joke. Major Wilkinson tells it. He sought out Lee with a letter from Gates; Gates was up Jersey, in a deuce of a quandary, you know, fearing he might stumble with his little reinforcement on the British. Wilkinson finds Lee in bed at a tavern at Baskinridge, three miles off from his troops, that much nearer the British at New Brunswick, and with only a small guard. Well, Wilkinson throws himself on the floor in his blanket among Lee's suite, and sleeps till daylight next morning. About eight o'clock Lee comes down half-dressed, in his slippers and blanket coat, collar wide open, and dirty linen, a regular sloven. I don't believe in slovens; a slouch in one thing, a slouch in everything. Washington is always dressed like a gentleman. Not till ten o'clock was Lee ready for breakfast!

"Rather late that, I confess," said Pemberton; "he was not the early bird that catches the worm."

"No, indeed, he was the foolish bird that the fowler caught. He wasted full two hours in quarrelling with some Connecticut privates, then, after breakfast, he sits down to write to Gates. Was barely through with the letter, had just signed his name at the bottom, when Wilkinson, looking out of the window, sees a party of British dragoons dashing up the lane. 'The British are on you!' shouts Wilkinson. 'Where's the guard? D—n the guard, why don't they fire?' cried Lee."

"Where were the guards?"

"Like master like man, slovenly general, slovenly discipline; the guards had stacked their arms, and gone off to sun themselves. Before they knew, the red coats were upon them, and they scattering in all directions. Then a voice shouted, 'Come out, General, or we'll burn you out.' And again, 'Come out at once, curse you, we've no time to lose.' The General walked out, they knew their man, in slippers and blanket-coat and bareheaded; they mounted him as he was, on Wilkinson's horse, which stood saddled and bridled at the door, and clattered off triumphantly to New Brunswick."

"They did not stay then to make the General's suite prisoners!"

"They were in too much of a hurry for that. But the cream of the joke is yet to come. When they first galloped up, Wilkinson had possessed himself of Lee's letter to Gates, which was lying on the table. And I know not whether he read it then and there, or whether Gates showed it to him afterward, but he says the letter was full of sarcastic comments on Washington's want of generalship. One sentence in particular he remembers, where Lee said that, between himself and Gates, 'a certain great man was most damnably deficient in military ability.' The ink was hardly dry before the red-coats galloped up the lane, and proved Lee 'most damnably deficient,' I think. It's a splendid joke, is it not? All the army is laughing at it."*

"Retribution came soon in that case," replied Pemberton. "But, Phil, it sounds very odd to hear you talking in so loose a strain, with that Quaker coat on. I should think that you could not utter an oath in that garb."

"I do find it difficult," laughed Morris; "but, then, on the other hand, I feel an almost irresistible propensity toward lying."

"Hush, hush, Phil, don't catch up the slang of the streets. You know that that is false. And, by the way, I fear you rather overdo your part as a Quaker preacher."

"Of course; you suspected who it was, all along! Undoubtedly! Oh, Arthur!"

"No, I own up frankly that you deceived me entirely,

---

*General Charles Lee, who was thought of so highly at the opening of the war, after his court-martial and sentence of one year's suspension, for his conduct at Monmouth, sank somewhat into disrepute. His animadversions upon Washington led to a duel with Col. Laurens, one of Washington's Aids, in which Lee was wounded. He died from an attack of chills and fever in Philadelphia in 1782, and was buried in Christ-church ground, notwithstanding the following curious passage in his will:—"I desire most earnestly that I may not be buried n any church or churchyard, or within a mile of any Presbyterian or Anabaptist meet ng house; for since I have resided in this country have kept so much bad compan wh le living, that I do not choose to continue it when dead." That he was still c u te popular, is proven by the fact that he was buried with military honors, while h s funeral was attended by the highest civic and military characters, and a large concourse of citizens. He was a man of undoubted military ability, and, as Washington Irving says, "there was nothing crafty or mean in his character, but he was a disappointed and embittered man, and the gall of bitterness overflowed his generous qualities." He died unmarried.

at the time; but I think my suspicions would have arisen after reflection."

"That is because you know the genuine article. But these red-coats do not. I must act up—or down—to their conceptions of the character. If I were simply to give them nature, they would suspect me. A country Quaker preacher, who was not something of a crazy bigot, would make them open their eyes suspiciously. But I give them what they will consider the genuine article."

"I think we have talked quite long enough together," said Pemberton, rising. "Do not forget yourself, outside of that door."

"Trust me for that, my son," replied Morris, resuming his hat and wig, casting his countenance into a cold, cast-iron mould, and speaking as with a new voice, which proved his wonderful power of mimicry. "And now, having delivered the message with which I was sent, I will cry aloud as one did formerly—yea, as David did, when he was a wanderer, and peradventure in deep affliction—no doubt alluding to the spiritual horse—'a horse, a horse, my kingdom for a horse!'"

"That's stolen, Phil," said Pemberton laughing.

"My young friend, thou art wrong, and slanderous, and presumptuous! A man cannot steal what has no owner—therefore I have not stolen; nay, verily, I have only appropriated."

"Well, grow serious, Phil. I am about to unbolt the door."

"One word first," said Morris, pulling off his hat and wig again. "How is that beautiful Miss Graham?"

"Miss Isabella is as well and beautiful as ever," replied Pemberton, gravely.

"Pshaw—I mean the other, Miss Helen. Isabella is

too cold and stately for me. But Helen Graham is certainly the most beautiful and fascinating woman the good Lord ever made."

"I disagree entirely with you, Phil—I think Miss Isabella the most charming and beautiful woman the good Lord ever made—but I hope you are not growing foolish over Helen Graham. I thought perhaps it was your wound and the loss of blood that made you act so funnily the other day at Germantown. Really I could hardly believe that that serious, sentimental youth, kissing a lady's rosy fingers, was the same old laughing, reckless Phil I used to know, and whom I see here to-day."

"Be merciful, Arth!" replied Phil, with a lugubrious expression of countenance. "But really that Miss Helen fascinates me so, that I am no longer myself in her presence."

"And you a good Whig, too! Why Helen is as rank and bitter a Tory as you can find in the State."

"I don't care if she is—we don't fight with women."

"And cares more for the little finger of a certain British officer, than for your whole body."

"Do you mean Captain André?"

"I do."

"Well, he is a handsome fellow—for an Englishman, but she has seen him fifty times to where she has seen me once."

"I wish she could see you with that hat and wig on—and yet it would be dangerous, for she has sharp eyes, and she might think it her duty to give you to the halter."

"Let us try her," replied Morris, rising. "Of course she would know me; but if she would betray me—well, I would be ready to die then."

"Phil—in one word, and it is better said now at once, Helen Graham is entirely beyond your reach. She loves another—and would not love you, a Whig, if she were fancy free. Think no more of her."

"Arthur Pemberton—did I ever give up anything because it was difficult?"

"No," laughed Arthur, "I will say that for such a rattlecap, you were always the most pertinacious and obstinate of created beings!"

"Others may doubt and despond as to the success of our arms, I never doubt it. If we persevere to the end, we shall win. The eye that never blenches, the cheek that never pales, the hand that never falters—these, in the end, win the victory! What I am in war, old fellow," and he laid his hand affectionately upon Arthur's shoulder, "I am in love. I mean to win Helen Graham."

Pemberton shook his head.

"I mean to win her! As to loving her, I cannot help myself. The thought of her puts me in a ferment—the sight of her, as you saw, makes a different man of me."

"This is folly, Phil," said Arthur, in a low voice—"that folly which leads to bitterness and heart-break. I tell you as a secret, trusting it to your honor—because I would save you and her needless pain—that I have the best of reasons for believing that Helen is betrothed to Captain André."

Philip gasped as if he had received a stab. "Be it so," he said, after a pause; "I still love her, and shall never cease to love her."

Then, resuming some of his former defiant recklessness of manner, he added—"Arth, when I see her the wife of another man, and half-a-dozen children around her knees, I will give up my case as hopeless. But not till then. You know my motto—which has brought me through so many desperate places—'Never despair!' I *will* win Helen Graham!"

'A wilful man will have his way; and if you ever get

Helen Graham, there will be two wilful people, that is all," replied Pemberton.

"I hope that won't be *all*, Arth," replied Phil, laughing. "But as you find I am, as of old, utterly unpersuadable and unconvertible from anything that I have made up my mind to, suppose I resume the costume of the sect of whose stubbornness and obstinacy I have inherited such a distinguished share, and visit some more of the brethren."

"One word further," said Pemberton in a low voice. "I intend to change our plan as to showing flags. Some one may grow suspicious. After the first of next month, we will show the largest flag while all the royal troops remain in the city. If they should all march out—or nearly all—we will haul down the flag entirely. How does it strike you?"

"It is an excellent plan to throw suspicion off the scent—that is, if Foxey can be made to understand the change, and does not blunder."

"Oh, I'll see to that. Have you any difficulty in making the signals out?"

"None in the least—especially with field glasses. We have three excellent points of observation—a house on the Ridge, one on the other side of the Schuylkill, and one in Jersey. They all notify headquarters—and the Jersey station the forts also. But I really must go now. Somebody may steal my poultry."

Morris resumed his disguise, and, as Pemberton unbolted and opened the door, his face grew almost severe in its solemnity.

At the bottom of the flight of stairs they encountered Fox. The apparent Quaker paused before him.

"Art thou a son of Ham? then art thou still in the bondage of sin and the mire of corruption!"

"What's yer say, Mas'? O' course I'se fon' of ham, I's berry fon' of ham, so's Dinah, so's the pickaninnies."

"I am fearful this is a degenerate son of perdition. Negro, what is thy name?"

"Foxey—Mas'. Fox—George Fox—Mas'. Ain't dat yer a good name?"

Deigning no reply, the seeming Quaker placed one of his hands on the negro's head.

"Foxey, Fox, George Fox—mind the light, mind the light! dost understand? mind the light!"

"Yes, Mas', I 'tend to mind all de lights—missis am berry particuler about dat," said the negro, as the seeming Quaker passed on to the front door; ana then, shaking hands solemnly with Pemberton, got into his wagon, and drove off.

"Dat's a mighty queer ole gemman, Mas' Arthur," said Fox, as Pemberton closed the door. "Fon' of ham—of course I is fon' of ham. Ha, ha, Mas' Arthur, a berry funny ole gemman."

"How about the flags, Foxey? Does the proud ensign of Britain still flout the air?"

"Say dat agin, Mas' Arthur."

"Does the proud ensign of Britain still flout the air?" repeated Pemberton, smiling.

"Dat's berry purty. Does de proud ensime of Britain flog de air! I mus' recommember dat."

"How about the flags, Foxey? I have only seen that smallest one for some time now."

"De berry littlest one, Mas' Arthur," said the negro, his eye lighting with a little extra intelligence.

"How would it do to give that one a rest, and fly a rather larger one—say the next size larger, Foxey?"

"De berry ting, Mas' Arth. I'll run him up, dis berry subjunctive moment."

As the negro mounted the stairs, he might be heard trying to repeat the phrase which had so charmed him—especially the "proud ensime," and "flog de air," which latter he evidently thought a most happy conception.

That afternoon Pemberton strolled around but heard nothing of interest, save that Tarleton had gone off, as he threatened, on the track of Captain McLane. But late in the evening Tarleton's party returned, tired and disheartened. Tarleton himself gave the curious questioners no satisfaction; but his men could not keep so careful a guard over their tongues. They had got on the trail of McLane near Frankford—had found him alone, and hemmed him in. When they came in sight of the noted partisan, he was riding quietly along, and seemed to meditate no resistance. Two of Tarleton's men had spurred up to capture him, one on each side, and as they neared him, let their swords fall in their slings to have their right hands free to grasp his shoulders. But McLane, at the last moment, had rapidly drawn a heavy pistol, shot one trooper through the head, knocked the other senseless from his saddle with the discharged weapon, leaped the fence, and escaped into an adjacent woods. Tarleton was angry enough to have shot a dozen men, but his mortification was so great that he did not utter even a single oath, after the first fiery, tremendous imprecation. His dragoons joked about it, when well out of hearing, saying that if McLane went on, he would end in making the Major quite a religious character.

CHAPTER XII.

PRO AND CON.

Men have two eyes and power of mental motion
That they may see all sides of everything;
And learn sweet Charity and Christian Love
Even for those they earnestly oppose.
None are entirely right, and none all wrong.

ANDRE and Pemberton, though they had become the warmest of friends, seldom conversed upon the great and absorbing question of the day. At first they had often argued the matter; but at length, each finding the other firm as a rock in his own opinions, they had by a kind of tacit understanding agreed to differ. But on one pleasant Sunday afternoon, as the two took a stroll out through the woods to Centre Square—then a natural forest of oaks and hickories—and further on to the banks of the beautiful Schuylkill, André renewed the subject. In truth, the Colonial cause, with its loss of Philadelphia, followed by the loss of the forts which commanded the Delaware—for a second attack by Lord Cornwallis had proved more successful than the Hessian attack under Count Donop—the destitute condition of the army at Whitemarsh, owing in a great degree to a badly managed commissariat, and the rapid depreciation of the Continental paper money, looked discouraging enough just then, notwithstanding the defeat and capture of Burgoyne.

As we calmly and dispassionately gaze back upon the field from this distance of time, the game seemed up—the queen and castles taken, and the king with but a few moves left upon the board before encountering the inevitable checkmate. If Franklin had not succeeded in negotiating the French Alliance, it is very difficult to avoid the conclusion that the Revolution would have failed, and Independence have been put off for fifty or even a hundred years.

But your "ifs" are pregnant things. The persuasive philosopher did not fail—and the sword of Charlemagne was thrown into the scale of Destiny.

"Pemberton," said André, as they stood in the warm sun of that November day, and looked up and down the graceful windings of the "hidden river," "this is too bright and beautiful a world to be the abode of hatred and contention—especially the hatred and contention of brothers. Why cannot this unnatural war be ended?"

"It can, very easily. Let Sir William Howe and his soldiers embark for home, and the land will be at peace."

"Would it be at peace? Would there not begin at once a hunting down and hanging of all its sons who had proven their loyalty to their king?"

"I think not, if it were agreed that the lives and property of the Tories should be held sacred, as the price of peace and independence."

"Independence; what a delusive word that is. I wonder, Pemberton, that a man of your fine sense can be deluded by it. Do you not see that you cannot be independent? That you are not strong enough to be so? In the very nature of the case, you must lean upon and be protected by one of the great European Powers, you must be the child or ward either of France or of England. Are you not already seeking the protection of France, conscious that you cannot stand alone? The only real and practical question, therefore, is, shall these Colonies belong to England or to France? To Protestant England, or to Roman Catholic France? Shall they strengthen the great European bulwark of the Protestant cause, or shall they strengthen the favorite son of Rome? I, as a child of the Huguenots—those hunted exiles from the Papal scourge—wonder that any man with English blood in his veins, and with Protestant blood in his veins, can give other than one indignant answer."

"André, my dear friend," replied Pemberton, "looking at the question from your point of view, I might answer as you do. But if I know the temper of my countrymen, and of our leading classes—and you know this Revolution was made by our best and ablest men, our Colonial aristocracy, if I may use the word; men who rebelled not so much against despotic and grievous measures, as against despotic and unjust principles, seeing to what in practice they would ultimately lead—if I understand the temper and feelings of these men, we intend just as little to be the tool and puppet of Roman Catholic France as of Protestant England."

"I suppose, of course, you do not intend it—but my argument is that you cannot avoid it; that you will inevitably be compelled, by the pressure of circumstances, to lean upon one or the other nation for guidance and support."

"And I hold that the Colonies are no longer children—that they have become of age, and are entitled to the rank of States, with the liberty of acting for themselves."

"Parson Duché, your eloquent divine, does not think so. Have you heard that he has written to Washington, advising him to give up the struggle. He was heartily with you, the lauded chaplain of your Congress, until the Declaration of Independence was adopted; then he saw the folly of the thing, as I do. Have you heard of his letter?"

"Yes, and that Washington instantly sent it on to Congress for their information. If Duché thinks he is doing right, if he is acting according to his sincerest and best judgment—you know I am not a fanatic, if I am a Whig—I do not blame him."

"Judge Chew, Beverly Robinson, Mr. Galloway, your cousin James, and the dozen other leading gentlemen that your Congress banished to Virginia, and thousands of others whom they represent, and who went with you so long as it was a mere question of your rights as Englishmen, see this matter almost as I do. Why even that clever Mr. Dickinson, who wrote your famous 'Farmer's Letters' against the foolish course of the Ministry—you know I am with you on that question—is opposed to the notion of independence. The brave and intelligent Governor Franklin, too, takes sides against his father in this matter."

"All very worthy and estimable gentlemen, doubtless," replied Pemberton, smiling. "But you know, André, my dear fellow, I always do my own thinking."

"And Lord Chatham too, who has stood your friend in Parliament, through thick and thin, till now, he says he never will consent to sever so wide a region from the dominion of the British crown."

"I admire and respect Lord Chatham, and, in common with the rest of my countrymen, thank him most deeply for his many noble and generous efforts in our behalf. But André, it is natural that a born Englishman, who expects to live and die in England, should see this matter from a point of view very different from ours."

"And I suppose," commented André, a little ironically, for he was in great earnest, and deeply moved, "that as you colonists hold that all men are created equal, the opinion of the Earl of Chatham has no more weight with you than the opinion of your old negro Foxie."

"Do you not think, upon consideration, that you are a little unjust in saying that?" responded Pemberton, in a warmer tone than he had hitherto used.

André paused a moment before he replied. "Indeed, Pemberton, it seems to me that I am not in the least unjust. That is, if you adhere to and support the Independence declaration. It says, as I well remember, because it struck me as such a piece of absurdity for a respectable body like your Congress to put forth, 'We hold it to be self-evident that all men are created equal.' If that does not put Lord Chatham and old Foxie on a level, then I do not understand the meaning of words."

"In one sense I hold they are on a level; that Foxie has just as clear a right to the enjoyment of his life and liberty, and to pursue his happiness as he sees fit, as Lord Chatham has."

"Then why do you hold Foxie as a slave?"

"I do not; Foxie is a free man."

"That is simply because of your Quaker principles; but the great body of your countrymen have no such scruples, and I find negro slaves, and sometimes thousands of them, in every one of your colonies. Washington holds slaves, and your Mr. Jefferson, who penned, I believe, that fine saying about equality, holds slaves himself."

"That only proves our laws and ourselves inconsistent, not that the principle is false. And if we establish the principle, it will, slowly perhaps, but surely, work out the extirpation of all laws and customs that are opposed to it. We are even now taking steps to do away with slavery in Pennsylvania."

"But, according to your own statement, if you establish a false principle it will be continually evolving mischief. Now, granting, for the moment, that all men are equal in the sense you mention, your assertion of equality is an absolute one. You make no mention of the natural inequality between men. Depend upon it that if you succeed in establishing a Republic, with that Declaration as its corner-stone, you will find the great masses of the people—even the most ignorant and vicious of them—continually asserting their belief that they, being equal, are fully as capable of managing all governmental affairs as the wisest and best men among you. You will become the prey of vulgar and unprincipled demagogues. Why, even your leading classes themselves—or those who should be the leading classes—will learn to doubt their own ability and fitness to rule, and, in thus doubting, will lose the ability itself. A majority—a mere majority of numbers, without regard to intellect or culture—will think itself authorized to settle all questions, alike of politics, religion and morals, and you, and other intelligent men like you, will find the little finger of this legal mob misrule thicker than the King of England's loins."

"You draw a terrible picture," said Pemberton smiling, "and I might admit its truth, if I could imagine that the great fact of the natural inequality of men, could ever be obliterated from the minds of a people by any amount of false teaching."

"You admit then," said André, in a surprised tone, "that your vaunted doctrine of Equality has a flaw in it?"

"I admit this—that all men are created equal. And I assert, also, that all men are created unequal."

"Are you not rather inconsistent, my friend Arthur?"

"I think not," replied Pemberton. "You know how earnestly all we colonists have studied this matter of government, within the last ten years. Now, this is the conclusion that I for one have come to. There are two great facts or truths of human existence. 1. That all men are Equal, inasmuch as they have a common manhood, and are equally entitled to the enjoyment of life and liberty, and to pursue their own happiness in their own way—of course not interfering with the rights or happiness of others. 2. That men are created with Unequal powers and capacities. If you base a form of government upon the first of these facts alone, you have, as the ultimate result, a vulgar, unprincipled, mobocratic government—a government in which demagogues become for selfish ends the flatterers of the people—telling them, (as courtiers tell despotic monarchs) that they are the sole source of power, and can do no wrong; and thus you finally uprear a huge colossus of brass and clay, which it ultimately becomes the solemn duty of all wise and able men to dash to pieces."

"That is what you will come to, if you succeed," exclaimed André warmly. "Your famous Liberty bell at your State House, was flawed before it was put up—and I warrant it will crack again, before a hundred peals have been rung upon it."

"We shall see," replied Pemberton, calmly. "But you interrupted me before I had finished. On the other hand, if you base a form of government upon the fact of Inequality alone, you have some kind of an Aristocracy—in which the masses of the people are looked upon as mere beasts of burden—mere hewers of wood and drawers of water; such as Europe was in the feudal ages, and, in a great degree, is now."

"There is at least something noble, refined and glorious in Aristocracies, the governments of the best, even with all their faults," replied André enthusiastically. "Give me such a government a hundred times over, rather than a government of the ignorant and uncultivated multitude, led by a set of selfish and unscrupulous demagogues, who pander to their prejudices and passions to promote their own unworthy ends."

"I might perhaps agree with you," said Pemberton, "for my instincts, I confess, are all that way—but it seems to me there is a government better than either. It is a government based upon both of those great facts—Equality and Inequality. A government which shall recognize natural leadership, and yet also recognize that the masses of men come into the world for their own purposes, and not merely to be the tools and slaves of those who are more gifted. A government which shall hold that while all men have an equal right to be governed fairly and justly, shall also hold that all have not an equal right to be legislators and governors—that no man has a right to fill any office, legislative, judicial or executive, unless he has the intelligence, culture and character to perform its duties efficiently. And shall be thus a real Aristocracy, or government of the best, not for the mere selfish interests of that ablest class alone, but for the promotion of the great interests of all the nation. And I should call this not a Democracy, but a Republic."

"Pemberton, my dear friend—you do not suppose that I, of all men, would object to such a government!"

"Perhaps not—but you are fighting against it."

"What a dear, delightful visionary you are, Arthur. Now to come down to common sense—not Tom Paine's, but that of ordinary mortals. Did you ever find a man who would accept that view of yours of what your government should be!"

"I think I could find a good many; but just now, thanks to General Howe and his regiments, we have more pressing business on hand than discussing how our turkey shall be cooked. The first thing is to catch our turkey."

"Well, to leave these theoretical questions, and come back again to the great practical question—how shall this unholy war be stopped?"

"Oh, I suppose by embracing Sir William's modest offer; the rebels all to come in on bended knees, with halters around their necks, and say they repent; and Sir William in return to give them absolution; and everything to go on in the same delightful manner as before," replied Pemberton ironically.

"Would your leaders not accept a settlement on the basis of Galloway's proposition? That came within one vote of a majority in Congress, a year or two ago. A General Council to be established for the Colonies—and no law to be considered passed that does not meet the approbation both of your Council and of Parliament."

'Two years ago that might have been accepted if it had been generously offered," said Pemberton musingly. "I have not the least idea that it would be accepted now."

"Pemberton," said André, in a lower and more confidential tone, "I do not deny that I am ambitious—but I trust it is a high and generous ambition that I cherish. It would be a feather in any man's cap to settle this unnatural difficulty without further bloodshed. Why cannot you and I settle it here. I feel sure that I know the terms on which England will settle it; and probably you are equally well informed as to the ultimatum of your countrymen. I never have sought to penetrate your secrets, any more than you have mine; but I know that you are in correspondence with all their leading men. What say you?"

"I think you over-estimate my standing and importance, though not my knowledge of the feelings of my countrymen. But what would you propose?"

"In one word, what you choose; so it is not Independence. The claim to taxation shall be given up. I think it only fair that the Colonies should agree to contribute something toward the general expenses of the kingdom, for the army and navy are maintained for the defence of all. But we will not even stand upon that. Everything shall be granted but Independence."

"For myself," said Pemberton, grasping André warmly by the hand, "I believe I would at once, if I had the power, accept such a proposition. I am, by education and constitutionally, so utterly averse to war, so conscious that even its triumphs contain the fruitful seeds of other wars, which ripen generally in about a generation. But I must answer you for others, not for myself. I do not think that anything short of Independence would be accepted."

"If there even is a probability of such a proposition being accepted, it might be offered."

"I do not think there is at present the slightest probability. Two years ago—perhaps one year ago—and it would have been hailed with joy, with bonfires and acclamations. But the keen sword of war cuts national bonds quickly. When a man has been fired at half-a-dozen times, and tried to shoot another as often, it confuses the natural ties of relationship," added Pemberton, smiling.

"But they are willing to welcome the French with open arms, against whom, with their Indian allies, they have been fighting at our sides for the last fifty years."

"The Indian allies are now with you, however."

"Not all of them, by any means. Did you not hear Lord Cathcart tell how he was startled by their yells, during his recent consultation with McLane. But you do not think there is any use in agitating this liberal plan of settlement?"

"Not the least. Of course, if the Continental arms should meet with a great reverse, it might be different. But at present things look tolerably fair—and a French alliance would render the success of the States almost certain."

"No, indeed!" exclaimed André proudly. "Even despite a French alliance, we should conquer. But I would save the useless spilling of human blood. For, come what may, France shall never add this wide and beautiful land to her crown."

"I agree with you heartily in that—never! But we shall win our Independence; and then, when the heat and bitterness of the contest have passed by, be always and ever your faithful friend and ally."

"We have come back to where we started from, Pemberton. It cannot be! I know you mean well, but the Colonies must belong either to France or to England. Knowing this, I shall hope to urge this plan, which you think it would be useless to urge now, at a more propitious season—when some great turn of the tide shall prove to the most sanguine among your leaders the folly of further resistance."

"It is getting late, let us return," said Pemberton.

And the young men walked slowly homeward, saying little on the way, for each was considering whether he had said what was wisest in answer to the other. And Pemberton was further considering and wondering how far André had authority for his proposition of settlement, and how far it was merely the result of his own views as to the temper of the English Ministry.

THE LOXLEY HOUSE.

CHAPTER XIII.

PLOTS AND COUNTERPLOTS.

Great kings by humble means are set at naught.
Great fishes are in tiny meshes caught.
Great lakes by little leaks do melt away.
Great fortunes vanish 'twixt the eve and day.

EARLY on a December morning, two British officers sat talking to each other in what was then called the Loxley House, on Second Street, near Dock creek. One was Major—afterward Colonel—Tarleton, and the other the Adjutant-General of the British army. The Loxley House was the quarters of the latter, who had been billeted upon the family of a Mrs. Lydia Darrach, who occupied the premises.

"We shall have rather a cold march, Major Tarleton, if the present weather holds; but we intend this time to make it a surprise. Not a man whose loyalty is the least doubtful, must be allowed to leave the city, to give the rebels warning of our approach."

"I never saw such a sieve for letting out news as this place is," replied Tarleton. "Why even I can hardly stir out with my troop, but the rebels seem to know all about it, and McLane or Harry Lee is ready to receive me. There must be an infernal lot of spies about."

"No matter," said his superior, in a low voice, as if fearful that the very walls had ears, "this time I think we shall be too many for them. The movement was only determined upon last night; and to-night we move. I wish you in the interim to exercise your utmost vigilance, to prevent word from being carried to the enemy. Sir William considers you one of the most vigilant and active officers in the service."

"What man can do I will do; but the long lines of this city are very difficult to watch. I should like to call your attention to one thing, however. You know that flag which nearly always floats from Pemberton's?"

"Of course; the flag-house."

"Perhaps I am rather over-suspicious, but I confess I do not understand why the old nigger, who seems to manage that flag, makes so many changes in it. He has, I believe, a large stock on hand; for the Pembertons used to be, they say, great shipping merchants; and sometimes he flies a large one, sometimes smaller ones, sometimes none at all."

"Does there seem to be any regularity in his changes?"

"Yes; and that is why I have grown suspicious," rejoined Tarleton, his small black eyes assuming a puzzled expression. "When our whole army is in the city he flies a small flag; but the other day, for instance, when Cornwallis marched out to take the forts, he flew his largest flag."

"That looks a little suspicious, I confess, and it behooves us to be very watchful. But Mrs. Pemberton cannot be suspected of being a party to any treachery. Her sentiments and those of her family are too well known. Why, her cousin James is now under rebel arrest down in Virginia."

"Very true—but her son Arthur scarcely makes a secret of his disloyal principles—and, for myself, I believe that were it not for the pain it would give his mother, he would be this day in Washington's camp."

"Let me see," said the Adjutant General, pulling out a manuscript book. "Yes, here is the name. 'Pemberton, Arthur, son of Rachel. Disloyal, but not to be dreaded; a visionary young man. Sometimes even writes poetry. Honest and truthful; rather timid.' I think that a character like this would not expose himself to the dangers of playing the spy. Besides, is he not a warm friend of Captain André's."

"Yes; André is just such another," replied Tarleton, with a little disdain. "But I do not think either of them is wanting in courage."

"Can the negro be doing anything on his own account?"

"It is not improbable, though he seems very stupid."

"But how could he procure the information?"

"Oh, that is not difficult; every General and Colonel almost has now a darkey servant, and they soon find out pretty much all their masters know about the contemplated movements. And darkeys always like to air their knowledge to one another; it gives them consequence."

"I should not like to take any step that would prove unpleasant to so loyal a citizen as Mrs. Pemberton; why she loaned Sir William her carriage and horses; and, besides, the raising of that very flag has brought on her a perfect torrent of rebel abuse; but keep your eyes open, Major."

"Suppose that nigger attempts to run up his largest flag to-day, had I not better prevent him at once? If that be a signal, what is the use of stopping all passes, and letting that be shown?"

"Very true; and to-day will afford a pretty good test as to whether there is any reality in your suspicions. Suppose that as it snowed last night, not a flag should be raised all day, what would you think then?"

"Either that my suspicions were entirely groundless, or that Foxey had no information," replied Tarleton.

"But he could hardly help knowing that something was going on by afternoon, if he has means of information at all."

"That is true. And I will own myself entirely mistaken, if no flag is raised. But I'll bet a bottle of brandy that you'll see that nigger's very largest flag waving in the wind within three hours; that is, if one of my men was not on hand to prevent it."

"Perhaps you are right, Major."

"I am so sure of it, that I'm in a hurry to put myself as soon as possible in a position to keep it down. I guess a musket-ball at Foxey's head, will give him a speedy hint not to raise it."

"Do not hurt him," said the adjutant.

"You cannot hurt a nigger by shooting him in the head," replied Tarleton, as he hurriedly left the room.

—

While this conversation was going on in Mrs. Darrach's house, another conversation upon a similar subject, was being held at Mrs. Pemberton's.

An hour or so before, Mrs. Darrach had taken a bag and basket, and left her residence with the avowed intention of procuring some meal and groceries for that day's dinner. Making her way up the path that led along the border of Dock creek, she had entered the large and well-kept grounds attached to Mrs. Pemberton's mansion, and walking up to the kitchen, asked Dinah, the colored cook, whether her young master was at home.

Dinah was Foxey's better half, in two senses, both the spiritual and the material, and one of those truly efficient cooks who were the wonder of a former generation, and seem to be the despair of ours. Dinah knew, if not consciously, then unconsciously, which is a higher sort of knowledge—what common people describe as "feeling a thing in their bones"—that the Almighty had created her to be a cook. She felt as we have said in her very bones —for she had bones, though they were not perceivable—

that she had been created not to be a missionary, or a female politician, or even a lady, so far as that word implies culture, but simply what she was. And she stood there in her rotundity, as she had stood in the same kitchen for at least twenty years, with never a thought of changing places, a living, weighty refutation of the truth of the old maxim that "the Lord sends victuals, but the devil sends cooks." Black and shiny, but neat and cleanly in her attire, with a gay turban on her head, and evidently constructed on the same principle that boys use when they construct snow men—a small ball on the top of a large ball, upheld by two stout upright sticks—or as she herself might have constructed a human being out of apple dumplings, or doughnuts, or gingerbread—Dinah stood there, before Mrs. Darrach, the very model cook of the period.

"Des, Miss Lyddy, Mas' Arthur's to hom'—shill I call de missis?"

"Oh, no. I only wish to see Arthur about a little business. Is he in the breakfast-room?"

"Breakfas'! we-uns had breakfas' a hour ago. I reckun you'll find him in de libr'y."

Going to the library, Mrs. Darrach knocked at the door, and was told to enter. Arthur was alone.

"Why, Friend Darrach, is that thee?" said Pemberton, using his Friendly language. "Take a chair by the fire, it is cold this morning."

"Yes, it is quite cold," replied she, taking a seat near the fire, and near him.

"Is the snow deep?—I have not been out yet."

"No, not very—only some three or four inches."

"Any news?" asked he, in a lower tone, and with a peculiar glance.

"Yes, and very important," replied she, in the same tone. "There is no danger of interruption?"

Arthur disappeared, but in a few moments returned. He had stationed Foxey in the entry, with directions to see that all inquirers for him were shown into the front parlor.

"This room is my sanctum, you remember," said he, again taking his seat. "It has a dead-latch, and no one can open the door from the outside, when it is shut, without the key."

"It is best, thee knows, to avoid all danger of suspicion," said his visitor—"especially to-day."

"They had then a council of war last night, as I supposed they would?"

"Yes. I knew what was coming—for I was warned to have all the family in bed early. And I did. But I got up again, and putting something around me, stole to the door of the room. Thee knows the house is an old one, and the doors not of the closest."

"And you could hear distinctly?" said Pemberton, forgetting his Friendly language in his interest.

"Almost as plain as I hear thee now."

"Is it to be an attack in force?"

"Yes, the whole army."

"When? Could you hear that?"

"This very night they are to march."

"That is soon—are you certain as to the time?"

"I am positive."

"It is rapid work—I must get word to the camp at once."

"That is what I want most to speak about. Can thee do it?"

"I can signal them—but I must also send a messenger. I would that old Abram were in town," continued Pemberton, musingly.

"They agreed that not a pass should be granted to a single man to leave the city."

"That is bad," replied Arthur in a puzzle. "My messengers *can* get out without passes, but it is a much longer route, and they run the risk besides of capture."

"I have a plan," said his visitor, while a gentle radiance lit up her pale but expressive face.

"Ah! what is it?"

"I will go."

"You, Lydia?"

"Yes, to save life, the lives of my countrymen, perhaps the life of my country; I will go."

"How?"

"As thee knows, there is very little flour in the city, and most of what we get comes from Frankford. I went there about a month ago for flour, and I will go again to-day, if I can get a pass."

"But it is cold, and snow on the ground. And a walk of ten miles, half the way with a sack of flour, is a great task for one so frail as you are."

"It is no harder than walking barefoot over the frozen ground, as so many of our poor soldiers are doing. Not one-tenth as hard as dying with camp-fever or small-pox in the hospitals, as so many poor prisoners are doing. If I could save one man's life I would do it. I may save hundreds of lives, and the life of my country, too."

"You have always refused to take any reward heretofore, Lydia. This news is of the utmost importance. You are poor, and it is only right the country should compensate you."

"Not a farthing, not a single farthing!" exclaimed she with great earnestness. "It would seem to me like the price of blood. Only one thing," and the pale face was suffused with crimson, "it is a weakness, but we all have our little weaknesses, I suppose; if I should succeed in my errand, and the army should be forewarned, let Washington know that this was the work of a woman, of one who honored and revered him, and loved her struggling country, and that her name was Lydia Darrach."

"He shall know it! And the country, at some safe future time shall know it!" exclaimed Pemberton with enthusiasm. "And your name shall be held in reverence by our children, and our children's children, to the latest generation."

"But how am I to get the pass?" said his visitor, relapsing into her usual quiet and thoughtful manner. "They may refuse to give me one, and it is important not to lose time."

"I think I can arrange that," replied Pemberton, reflecting for a moment; "come with me."

Leaving the room he went forward to the door of the back parlor, and saw that Isabella was there reading.

"Miss Graham," said he, "Mrs. Lydia Darrach, whom I think you have met before"—Isabella bowed—"is anxious to obtain a pass to go to Frankford to purchase some flour for her family. I told her I thought you would be able to get her one from General Howe. The Adjutant General, you know, boards with her, and therefore, you see, it is rather important," continued Pemberton, smiling.

"I do not care much for the Adjutant General's dinner," replied Isabella, "soldiers, of course, can rough it, but I do feel, Mrs. Darrach, for you and the children. And yet, I confess it, I do not like much the idea of going around to headquarters for a pass. Perhaps if I gave Mrs. Darrach a note to Colonel Musgrave, he could get her one."

"That would not do, Bella," said Arthur, a little impatiently. "I should be very much obliged to you, if you would put on your cloak and go at once."

Isabella looked at him in surprise. There was no mistake—curious as it seemed to her, he was evidently very much in earnest.

She hesitated not a moment longer. "Wait a minute," said she to Mrs. Darrach.

While she was gone, Pemberton instructed Mrs. Darrach as to whom she might safely apply in Frankford. "At Friend Evans's—Joshua Evans, you know, the tanner's—you will probably find either Captain McLane, Lieutenant Morris, or Colonel Meigs, one of whom doubtless will be there in the course of the day. If Joshua should happen to be out, go to his brother Samuel's."

Here Isabella appeared, equipped for walking; and the two left for the headquarters of General Howe in Market Street.

Arrived at the dignified mansion—one of the best in the city—which the British commander had appropriated for his own use, and passing the sentry at the door, they entered. One of the lower rooms was occupied as an office for the granting of passes and other official matters, and opening the door of this, Isabella perceived Sir William himself, while his Aid and Secretary, Captain Munchausen, sat at a desk before the window.

Sir William arose in a moment. He was a tall, handsome, dignified-looking man—bearing considerable personal resemblance, as was often noted, to Washington; a genial, kindly man, greatly beloved both by his officers and men. An admirable general, moreover, when in the field—though failing perhaps in pushing his enemy's defeats into routs—but too much given to taking his ease when the battle was over. Some of his own officers averred that Philadelphia was his Capua; and Doctor

Franklin said that instead of his taking Philadelphia, that city had taken General Howe.

Rising, as we have said, Sir William addressed Miss Graham—

"I am happy to see you, Miss Graham. Be seated, ladies—what can I do for you this snowy morning?"

"Sir William," said Isabella, "I have a favor to ask of you."

"Which you know will be granted if I can possibly do it," replied the General gallantly. "To oblige so fair a lady is in itself a pleasure—and when that lady is the ward of Colonel Musgrave, who did us such admirable service at Germantown, the pleasure becomes almost a duty."

"I know you would oblige me, if you possibly could, had I something important to ask of you," replied Isabella, smiling pleasantly. "But this is nothing—it is merely to give my Quaker friend here, Mrs. Darrach, who keeps the house where your Adjutant boards, a pass to go to Frankford, to buy a little flour to make his pies and puddings with."

"It is but a trifle, of course," said the General, a little confused; "but the fact is, my dear Miss Graham, we are not issuing any passes at all to-day."

Isabella's manner instantly grew colder. "I suppose though, like other army orders, it is liable to exceptions, and to be overruled at the pleasure of the commanding general."

"But I have directed in the orders of the day, Miss Graham, that not a pass shall be issued to a single man—does not the order read in those words. Captain Munchausen?—and you must admit it would hardly look well for me to be the first to break my own orders."

Now this would have had to be enough for a man, but

a woman, and moreover a young and beautiful woman, is a very different person to deal with. Isabella was a very sensible as well as beautiful woman; but she had a beautiful woman's wilfulness and dislike to being foiled in anything she undertook. She would not have stirred from home on an errand like this, except at her lover's earnest request, but having done so, she would not easily take a refusal. And she had already had an advantage, in that Sir William had complimented her. Although a veteran, he had not yet fully realized the bad policy of complimenting a lady who wants a favor of you. It is like giving the enemy in a battle the choice of ground; and Sir William had the sun in his eyes all through the remainder of the interview, and Isabella knew it.

Captain Munchausen, at the desk, tumbled over some papers, and then perusing one, made answer:

"Those are the very words, your Excellency."

"I see nothing in that order to prevent my having a pass for Mrs. Darrach," said Isabella coolly. "It says, 'not to a single *man*,' and that may be, for all I know, reasonable enough; but Mrs. Darrach is a woman."

The General smiled.

"You are a keen reasoner, Miss Graham, but do you not see that women are supposed to be included in the prohibition?"

"And children then, too, I suppose? No, I see nothing of the kind. And a pass to Mrs. Darrach will be both for a woman and her children, who cannot have bread to eat if they cannot get flour. But if the safety of the city, and of the British army and its General, is to be endangered in some way by giving a pass to Mrs. Darrach, of course she must submit," and Isabella laughed a very pretty, but still slightly ironical laugh.

Now we suppose it is only human nature, but it is a little

curious to a philosophical mind, to see with what dislike a gentleman even in high authority, will run counter to the wishes of a lady who stands high in the circles in which he himself moves. Sir William evidently felt embarrassed. The color of the good wine he was so fond of deepened upon his face, and turning to his secretary, he said:

"Perhaps it would not be a very serious infraction of orders, Munchausen, to give Miss Graham the pass for her friend. We all know that the 'Friends,' to their honor, are nearly universally loyal."

"We are all opposed to war and the shedding of blood," replied Mrs. Darrach.

"Yes, I know," said Sir William; "and to the rebels, because they made the war."

Lydia said nothing. She did not feel bound to contradict the General's assumption.

The secretary, who had taken up his pen at once, in answer to his General's suggestion, handed the pass to Isabella, who perused it, and finding it all correct, gave it to Mrs. Darrach.

And she, saying she had but scant time as it was, immediately left on her patriotic expedition.

"I am very much obliged to you, Sir William," said Isabella, in a tone that also seemed to say, and I would have been still more obliged if you had granted the favor at once.

"You are very welcome, Miss Graham. You know that we soldiers are sometimes compelled by a sense of duty to refuse what it otherwise would be our greatest pleasure to grant."

"I know that all men are very perverse and troublesome beings," replied Isabella, with something still left of the tone of offended bellehood.

The General thought he had better change the subject.

Glancing to his secretary, "Are you acquainted with Captain Munchausen, Miss Graham? I took it for granted you were acquainted. Captain Munchausen, Miss Graham."

The Captain rose and bowed deeply. The lady bowed, but not very deeply.

"Captain Munchausen assists, I suppose, in writing your dispatches; your accounts of your victories, and things of that kind," said Isabella with apparent innocence.

Some of the wits among the rebels had said the same thing—though not very innocently—but Sir William had never had it said before to his very face. Again the claret deepened on his cheeks; but the lady looked as serene and smiling as possible.

"Yes, the Captain generally copies them out for me. He is my secretary, you know."

"I thought I occasionally recognized the touches of his pen," rejoined Isabella, smiling very benignantly upon both of them.

"All I do, Miss Graham, I assure you, is simply to transcribe; or else to write out what Sir William dictates," replied the Captain with frank sincerity.

"Ah, you are too modest by half, Captain. Is he not, Sir William? But I detain you, no doubt, from your important duties. Good-morning, General; good-morning, Captain Munchausen,"—and Isabella, with her usual graceful dignity, left the office, being accompanied by the Captain to the front door.

"That's a d——d unfortunate name you have, Captain," cried Sir William, as gruffly as he was ever in the habit of speaking to his officers, when Munchausen re-entered the room.

"I am ready, Sir William, at any moment, to relieve

you of the unpleasantness of it," replied the Captain, with gentlemanly dignity.

"Pshaw, my boy, don't get offended. I'll keep you in spite of all the wits, of both sexes, in the universe. But just see how unreasonable these pretty women are. Because I did not, at once, and without consideration, do as that magnificent Miss Graham wished, she would not entirely forgive me. I warrant she'll let me feel that I have displeased her, every time she meets me in society for the next month."

The Captain laughed. It was not entirely respectful, but he could not help laughing.

"If she were not so splendid a woman," continued his chief—"some say that she and her sister are the two very finest women in Philadelphia—I should not care. But I really like the girl—in a fatherly way, of course—and old Musgrave, her guardian, is one of my best officers."

Here the entrance of half-a-dozen colonels interrupted Sir William's commentary on what had passed.

GENERAL HOWE'S HEADQUARTERS.

CHAPTER XIV.

PARTING.

After Isabella left the house with Mrs. Darrach, Pemberton had sought out old Foxey.

"Any flag flying to-day, Foxey?"

"Oh, no, Massa Arth—no flag to-day. Snow heavy dis las' night, you know," with a grin.

"You must not forget what I said the other day," continued Arthur, in a low tone. "It would be foolish to fly a big flag when there are no soldiers in the city. Now I have an idea that the whole of them, pretty much, will be marching out of town some time to-day, and of course it would be ridiculous to hoist any flag."

"Werry dick'lous, Mas' Arth—Old Foxey not gwine to spile his flags by gittin' them snow'd on—no, no, hi! hi! hi!"

Having done the best he could, Pemberton sat down to await the return of Miss Graham. In about half-an-hour she came back, her face all glowing with excitement and success; and, finding Pemberton in the parlor, she gave him an account of her mission.

"It was lucky you were about, Bella," said he. "I would not have failed in getting that pass," he continued in a whisper, "for a thousand pounds."

"Then what are you going to give me?" asked Isabella archly.

He put his hand in his pocket, jestingly, as if to take out his purse; but she laughed and blushed, and said—"Oh, you stupid man!"

In an instant his arm was around her waist, his lips pressed to hers. "My own sweet, precious love!" he exclaimed in a low but passionate tone, still enfolding her queenly, yielding form; "only my country in her peril can rival you in my heart."

"Arthur—my prince, my king, my country, my all!" she murmured.

Suddenly she started from him. It was nothing but a noise in the street—but she resumed her seat at a more decorous distance.

"I did not want to be under any obligations to Sir William Howe," said she smiling.

"I am sorry, but indeed it could not be helped, Bella," replied Pemberton.

"Oh, it is all right. He refused my request at first—and so I left him under a sense of obligation to me, instead of the obligation being the other way. I could not have managed the matter better had I planned it all from the beginning."

"That is curious," said Pemberton, his man's wit at fault; and it required a detailed account of the whole conversation, to show him how it was possible for a lady to accept a favor, and yet leave the burden of obligation resting upon the broad shoulders of the poor masculine who had, in one sense, conferred it.

—

The day rolled on. Mrs. Darrach, after trudging five miles through the snow, reached Frankford safely, saw Colonel Craig (who had been sent by Washington expressly to pick up information), and trudged back again with her sack of flour, feeling that she had done a life's work in that one day.

Major Tarleton's sentries, stationed in the garret of a neighboring dwelling, and armed with muskets, had kept a strict watch over Foxey's doings, but had seen no traces of any suspicious movements. As Tarleton himself rode in from the outposts, about 4 o'clock in the afternoon, he saw Foxey standing very unsuspiciously in front of the Pemberton mansion, talking with one of his sable brethren. Stopping his horse, and glancing up at the flag-staff, Tarleton said—

"Why, Foxey, you are not flying any flag to-day?"

"No, no, Massa Captin—Foxey no fly de flag in de snow—spile de nice flags, Massa Captin."

As Tarleton rode on, he heard Foxey say to the other negro—

"I s'pose you go to-night, Sam, wid all de rest of de sogers, hi! hi! hi!"

"Foxey evidently knows of the movement, and yet his flag—even the smallest one—is not flying," thought Tarleton. "I must be getting too suspicious. I would have bet fifty pounds to one, that either Foxey or his master, or both, were playing traitor."

Shortly after Tarleton had passed, Captain André knocked at the door, and inquired for the ladies. Colonel Musgrave had already been there, and taken an affectionate parting from his wards—for who could tell whether all who should leave the city that night, would return? With sad faces the two ladies entered the parlor into which André had been shown, for the parting with their much-loved guardian had deeply affected them.

"I came to bid you good-bye for a day or two," said André, with forced gayety. "We start to-night, to pay General Washington a visit. We design it for a kind of surprise party, you know."

But his listeners looked more like crying than laughing.

"Oh, that this awful war were over!" said Isabella, with a deep sigh.

"None can wish that more heartily than I do," responded André. "But I see no other means of stopping it, than just this kind of one we are now pursuing. One

14

good beating, and the colonists, I think, would be ready to treat for peace."

"Good-bye, Captain," said Isabella, rising, and holding out her hand, which André pressed warmly within his own—"I shall pray God daily and nightly for your safe return. And do be prudent, for the sake of those that love you."

"Good-bye, my dear Miss Graham; and I know if prayers can aught avail me, I shall return safely from this conflict. Remember me to Mr. Pemberton and his mother, please. I do not care to have too many of these partings—they take the soldier out of a man's heart."

Isabella left the room, discreetly closing the door behind her, and André reseated himself by Helen's side. So far she had said nothing; but now she flung her arms around his neck, and kissed him repeatedly, saying, between her kisses and her sobbings,

"Oh, John, I can hardly bear it! I cannot risk so soon the losing you!"

He comforted her as many another soldier had done in similar case before—and has done since—with embraces, with kisses, with honeyed words, with loving misrepresentations of the extent of the danger, with loving assurances of his faith that he should return unscathed—all those things which the sincerest man will say in such an hour, to the woman he dearly loves.

At last she grew more calm, and he ventured to say:

"I cannot linger, Helen; I have many duties yet to perform. Remember that you are the daughter of a soldier—and are to be a soldier's wife."

The crimson flush spread to her fair forehead at that last word, but it seemed to fill her veins with a more exalted life.

"Forgive me this weakness, sweet! The news came

upon me so suddenly to-day. But I *am* a soldier's daughter—and I am strong enough to be a soldier's wife."

So saying, she sat up erect, and wiped the tears from her cheeks, and looked as her father may have looked perhaps, when he gazed right into the eyes of battle.

"Now, indeed, you are my own Helen, my proud one, my queen!" exclaimed her lover. "One kiss before I go. Remember, in life or in death, I am yours—yours only!"

"Yes, in life or in death, always mine, as I am always yours—always! always!"

They flung their arms around one another for a last embrace. They pressed their warm, palpitating lips together. They clung heart to heart. Then André tore himself from the arms of his mistress, opened the door, and left the house.

She sprang to the window, caught and returned one last loving glance, and flinging herself down upon the sofa, buried her face in her hands.

CHAPTER XV.

A DARING RAID.

Rash is no word for such a reckless youth!
And were it not the goddess Fortune loves
Those who trust all to her, and guards them well,
His body and soul had long since broken troth.

At eight o'clock that evening, leaving a small garrison in Philadelphia, the British army marched out to surprise Washington in his fortified camp at Whitemarsh. But their coming was fully expected. Captain McLane met their advance about three miles from the city, and retired before it, disputing the passage at every available spot.

For three days Sir William Howe tried to find an opening where he could successfully make an attack—first on the right, then on the left. But Washington would neither show a good opening, nor advance himself into the field. He evidently deemed it his policy not to fight, unless at a great advantage. It was the old Roman story over again:

"If you are the able general you claim to be," said Howe, "come out from your intrenchments and fight me."

"And if you are the able general you claim to be," replied Washington, "make me come out and fight you."

After various ineffectual attempts to do the latter, General Howe ingloriously marched back to Philadelphia, taking with him forty wagon-loads of wounded men, and a considerable number of cattle. His army, not in the best of humors, burned and pillaged to no small extent—especially on the road the Hessians travelled—as they marched. Of course, without orders, as so many things of the kind get done in war, and which makes of war even a more cruel and horrible thing than it necessarily must be.

It was evening before the rear of the British army

reached the city. The larger portion resumed their old encampments on the northern outskirts of the town; but others, including of course the principal officers and their staffs, marched into the heart of the city.

The citizens generally came out to their doors as they passed, and Mr. Pemberton, with the Misses Graham, imitated the general example. All felt gay and joyful, either at the failure of the British movement, or at the safe return of their friends, or for both reasons. Colonel Musgrave had passed, well splashed with mud, but looking as active as ever, and had pulled up to speak a word of greeting to his wards. And then André, in like plight, but with his brown face and eyes glowing handsomer than ever in the light which shone from the windows, also had halted to accost the young ladies, and to exchange a loving glance with Helen.

The ladies still lingered at the door, although thinking that all the military which were coming that way had passed, when another body of horsemen were seen trotting down the street. There seemed to be about twenty or thirty dragoons, for they were equipped like Tarleton's men, and in the rear three or four led saddled but unridden horses.

"I thought at first that was Tarleton," said Pemberton; "but it is not he. I believe I do not know them, though there is something familiar in the appearance of that second rider."

As he spoke, the rider in question left the ranks, and spurring up to the side of the street—and even inside the posts which then marked the line, instead of curbs—tossed a rose to the party in the porch, saying, very plainly, "With my best compliments to Miss Helen."

"Who is that, Helen?" asked her sister, eagerly, as Pemberton stooped and picked up the rose, evidently plucked from some green-house, or other sheltered nook, for it was too late for out-door roses.

Helen's face grew white. "I am not certain," said she. "But I fear—" here she paused.

"It cannot be," replied Pemberton, in a low voice; "it would be madness."

"What are you two whispering about?" inquired Isabella.

"It is cruel in him!" exclaimed Helen. "He has no right to put me to such a test."

"What do you both mean?" again asked Isabella, in a low but earnest voice, as Pemberton left them, and darted after the troopers, down the street.

"Sis," said Helen in a whisper, giving a cautious glance around her, to see that she was not in danger of being overheard, "it was Lieutenant Morris!

"He knows I will not betray him," continued Helen, excitedly, when they were seated again in the parlor; "but he has no right to put me to such a cruel test."

"Probably you are mistaken, Helen. It may have really been some English officer."

"What one is there, presumptuous enough to fling me a rose thus publicly?" said Helen. "None but a rebel would venture to do so—especially on so short an acquaintance."

"Oh, he is but a mere boy," replied Isabella, "and probably a little demented, since his wound. Do you not think so? I see him now, kissing your hand the other day"—and she laughed.

"Bella, I think you speak rather unkindly, considering that Mr. Morris, if he is but a mere boy, did us such a great service," exclaimed Helen, with flashing eyes. "And, for my part, I saw nothing the least ridiculous in what he did at Mr. Livezey's. He felt embarrassed, doubtless, and it was rather awkward all round—but remember he thinks that I saved his life."

"Oh, I have no doubt that he is a very fine young fellow," rejoined her sister, not very consistently, but very sagaciously; "and I only wish that Arthur would come back, and let us know what it all means. Perhaps he has been converted, repented of his sins, and turned Tory."

"I wish he may get safely out of the city—without doing any mischief," said Helen.

After waiting with only a moderate degree of patience for about two hours, Pemberton returned.

"Was it he?" cried Helen.

"What does it all mean?" said Isabella.

"Did he get off safely?" added Helen.

"Did you hear anything about it?—do speak, Arthur!" exclaimed Isabella.

Arthur behaved as most men do, when met by a volley of excited questions—took his time to answer them. It is a failing which few, even of the noblest and best of their sex, are superior to. Adam doubtless thus plagued Eve.

"Ladies, if you will allow me just one moment in which to breathe, and collect my scattered thoughts, I will answer all your questions *seriatim*."

They waited, not patiently, but expectantly.

"It was he. It all means mischief. He did get off safely. And I did hear something about it. Any more questions?"

Helen raised her hand to box his ears. Isabella posed her graceful form before him—

"Mr. Arthur Pemberton, will you be kind enough to tell us what we want to know, without further delay, circumlocution, or needless aggravation?"

Pemberton smiled. "It was McLane and a party of

his men, disguised as British troopers. They came in on the rear of the British. When they passed here, they continued on down Chestnut to Second — turning down Second. The Adjutant-General had just dismounted and entered his house with his papers before they came up. Good luck for him. On Second Street bridge they overtook Captain Sandford on horseback, and carried him off with them. They then turned up Walnut Street, and on the bridge there, captured Varnum, one of Cunningham's jail-keepers. Going out Walnut Street they just missed Sir William Howe and several colonels. They then pushed out to the Ridge Road, dashed boldly past the block house, where the guards, seeing their uniforms, supposed it was all right, and so on, I infer, to the wilds of the Wissahickon. Tarleton will probably know about that—for he is after them in hot indignation. But as they have full fifteen minutes start, I *guess*, as our Yankee friends say, he will only see the tails of their horses."

"I hope he catches them," exclaimed Helen. "It was a great piece of impertinence. And I wish you would inform Mr. Morris the next time you have a chance, that I consider his conduct very audacious. He ought to know that I am loyal to the heart's core, and have no sympathy with rebels."

"I think myself it was a very silly piece of business to fling you that rose," said Pemberton, pointing to the rose, which was a very pretty one—half blown and a deep red —and which Helen had placed, perhaps unconsciously, in her bosom.

"I do not see anything particularly silly in it," replied Helen. "I think it was audacious and reckless."

"Helen is very hard to please where Lieutenant Morris is concerned," said Isabella, a little slyly.

"Bella, you know better. I think Mr. Morris very

much to blame indeed—very reckless and audacious—but I do not like to hear one who has done me, and all of us, so much service, ridiculed and called silly."

"I said his action was silly—not himself," rejoined Pemberton.

"It is the same thing," replied Helen, as she left the room, not caring apparently to have the matter discussed further.

When she came to disrobe in her chamber that evening, she opened a little casket in which she kept, under lock and key, her most precious souvenirs of love and friendship, and put Philip's rose among them.

Was Helen rather inconsistent? You may think so—but it is because you do not look upon her from the right point of view. Her actions and words might appear inconsistent with each other, but they were not inconsistent with herself. For she who acts and speaks naturally and impulsively, must, perforce, upon a subtle cord of harmony, as on a fine gold thread, string all her apparent inconsistencies of word and action.

CHAPTER XVI.

HAIL TO THE CHIEF.

Oh! a soldier's life for me,
With its strife and its jollity—
  A banquet to-night,
  To-morrow a fight,
And the shouts of victory.

The Philadelphia of the olden time was never more gay than during the winter and spring of the British occupation. Whether because it was useless to undertake great movements in the field, on account of the severe cold of the winter and the deep mud of the spring, or owing to the natural love of ease and pleasure of the British commander, his officers had full time and liberty allowed them to amuse themselves in all those ways which come natural to the youthful and pleasure-seeking mind. Theatricals, balls and parties, with less innocent gaming, revelling, and other dissipations, were their constant occupations; and they went at them with the same amount of energy and spirit which they would have thrown into a campaign. Although many ladies belonging to the prominent Whig families had left the city, a large number remained, and those among the wealthiest and most refined classes of society. Unless the traditions and testimonies that have come down to us are to be entirely disbelieved, these ladies constituted the most brilliant circle in the country. They prided themselves not so much on their beauty—though, if we may credit the French officers, they were the most beautiful women in America—as on their sprightliness and their conversational ability. The ladies of New York, they alleged, had invariably to call in the aid of cards to entertain their visitors; but they depended upon more intellectual means of amusing and delighting their guests.

Thus in a constant round of amusement and gayety, the British officers passed their time, until it was announced, in the spring, that Sir William Howe was to be superseded by Sir Henry Clinton. It might be that this implied a reproof of their winter's idleness; but, whether it did or not, they loved their commander, they had had a glorious time, and they resolved to top off their sport with a display of the grandest and most appropriate character.

So they determined upon the Mischianza—a medley, as the Italian signifies—in honor of their departing Chief, and worthy of him, the ladies and themselves.

Captain André and the Misses Graham had taken their full share in the season's festivities; and as he sat with them one pleasant evening in May, explaining the completeness and novelty of the intended pageant, Isabella turned to him and inquired, in an amused voice:

"And which are you to be, André, a Knight of the Blended Rose, or of the Burning Mountain?"

"I have been chosen as a Knight of the Blended Rose," replied André, with assumed dignity.

"And your brother, the Lieutenant?"

"Oh, he is to be my Squire."

"And your lady?"

"That is just what I am here to ask," said he, turning to Helen.

"What are your ladies to wear?" inquired Helen, archly.

Pemberton, who had just come in, and stood listening, laughed outright.

"Isn't that a woman all over? 'Will you marry me?' said the gentleman. 'What kind of a wedding-dress can

I wear?' said the lady. 'I will not be married at all, if the color does not suit my complexion.'"

"A very sensible woman, I think," commented Helen. "My case, exactly. What are your ladies to wear, Captain André?"

"I'll read it to you—it's all set down," said André, pulling a paper from his pocket—

"'THE LADIES OF THE BLENDED ROSE.

"'A polonaise, or flowing robe of white silk, with a spangled pink sash, and spangled shoes and stockings; a veil spangled and trimmed with silver lace, and a towering headdress of pearls and jewels.'"

"I hate spangles," said Helen, "they make one look like a circus-woman. I hate a towering headdress, it makes my head ache. Get one of the Misses Shippen, that one who doats on you."

"All engaged," replied André, smiling.

"You should have spoken sooner then. Well, there is pretty Miss Redman; she will have you as her knight, or all signs fail."

"Captain Horneck has secured her sweet ladyship."

"Well, there is Peggy Chew; have you tried her also?"

André laughed.

"You know, Miss Helen, that I have not tried, as you call it, anybody. In fact, such was my presumption, that I confidently counted upon you."

"You were very presumptuous indeed. Spangles, and a towering head-dress! No, no, I shall not make a barbarian of myself, even if the Mischianza has to be given up."

"That is foolish, Helen," interposed Isabella; "what serious objection can you possibly have to the costume?

I think it will be very pretty. Do you know what the rival ladies are to wear, André?"

"The same, I believe, except that their white polonaises are to be bound with black, and their sashes are to be black instead of pink."

"Horrible!" exclaimed Helen; "I would not be one of their Knights for the world."

"Well, what am I to do?" said André, ruefully.

"Equip yourself as the Knight of the Sorrowful Countenance, and go without a dame," replied Isabella, laughing.

"And, Helen, you are in earnest, you do not really wish to be one of the Queens of the Fête?" said André earnestly.

"I do not, John."

"Who then shall I choose?"

"The very prettiest girl you can find. I shall not be jealous," she added, in a whisper.

"You suggested Peggy Chew; shall it be she?"

"Yes, a pretty girl, and nice too. If she will accept."

"Of course," said André.

"Of course she will, and be glad of it," said Helen, confidently.

"Do not make Captain André any more conceited than he is," cried Isabella.

André smiled. "I did not ask you, Miss Isabella. You are jealous. Will not you be my beautiful queen of hearts?"

"Not at this late hour; after, how many refusals is it? No, I am engaged to go among the undistinguished crowd. We shall be there, and see how you conduct yourself, Knight of the Burning Rose."

"Awful! Blended Rose, not Burning Rose. Burning Mountain!" exclaimed André, holding up both hands in affected dismay.

"Go and engage Peggy Chew at once, or she will be snapped up also by some other unfortunate Knight," said Helen.

"Why would you not serve as André's lady?" asked Isabella, after they had retired that evening.

"What! and set the whole town to talking? They talk enough about Captain André and myself as it is. Let him wait on Peggy Chew on such a great occasion as this, and it will close their lips for the next month or two."

"You are a very wise little girl, with all your wilfulness, sister mine," said Bella, kissing her, and folding her arms around her. "Sweet, how I love you!"

"Bella, my darling, my precious, I would die for you!" exclaimed Helen, returning her embrace. "These men are going different paths, and we must go with them, but they shall never part these hearts of ours, shall they, Bella, my beautiful, my queenly one?"

"Never, never, never, my beloved, my Peri, my Princess!" cried Bella, returning her passionate kisses and embraces. "Come what may come, their principles and duties and ambitions shall never separate these sister hearts of ours!"

And they lay down to sleep folded in each other's arms.

CHAPTER XVII.

THE MISCHIANZA.

Bright was the scene when to the music gay
Of trump and cymbal swept the fleet away;
Down Delaware's proud breast the gorgeous show,
While cannon thundered, moved sublime and slow;
Flags flew, men shouted, and the ladies smiled,
And with gay sunbeams glad waves wantoned wild.

OH for a pen made from a peacock's plume, whose green aud golden glories might gleam before my eyes, and dazzle all my brain, the while I paint in too brief phrase the splendors of the Mischianza!

For the Mischianza was undoubtedly, and beyond all compare, the finest and most artistic entertainment in the way of a festivity, that ever delighted the eyes of beautiful women and brave men in this prosaic American world.

Philadelphia has had, Boston and New York and Baltimore and all our sister cities have had entertainments, in which it was sought to embody praise and honor of distinguished men—great generals, great statesmen, great artists. But what have they all amounted to?—a feed; or, at best, a feed and a dance; at which wretched and vulgar taste competed with wretched and vulgar ostentation and profusion for the mastery. But the Mischianza was the conception of a nobly-gifted and cultivated soul—one not too old to lament that the days of chivalry were passed, and which was filled with the high-bred refinement of a true cavalier. And in all its principal features was seen the glowing, sportive mind, as in the chief adornments the ready, artistic hand of John André.

It is not our intention to fatigue our readers with a full description of this pageant. That work is already done. But we cannot well avoid a few brief words of outline.

The Mischianza commenced with a regatta. The British fleet lay in a long line the whole length of the city, decked with gay flags, while the vessels of war thundered at appropriate occasions. The flotilla was composed of three galleys, and thirty large flat boats, the latter covered with green cloth, and filled with the ladies and gentlemen of the city, the invited guests. The galleys were reserved for the principal Generals and their suites, accompanied by the most distinguished ladies.

Starting about four in the afternoon from the northern end of the city, the festive squadron floated slowly down, the rowers keeping time to the music, until it reached the southern limit, just below the Old Fort. The houses along the river, the wharves, and the line of transports in the stream, were crowded with admiring spectators.

Arrived at the Old Fort, opposite the then handsome Wharton mansion, the gay company landed, and forming themselves into a procession, marched up through lines of grenadiers and horsemen, to the grassy square prepared for the tournament. Here were two triumphal arches, with pavilions; and under the pavilions ranges of rising seats. The company then took their places—the ladies of the Knights of the Blended Rose and of the Burning Mountain occupying the front seats in each pavilion.

To the sound of distant trumpets rode in two bands of Knights—one dressed in ancient habits of white and red silk, on gray horses; the other in black and orange, their horses jet black. The first were the White Knights of the Blended Rose; the others the Black Knights of the Burning Mountain.

The customary challenges interchanged—the subject of dispute being the superior "wit, beauty and accomplishments" of their respective bands of ladies—the Knights, riding around the lists, made their obeisance to their Dames. Then, after receiving their shields and lances from their respective Squires, they encountered in full career their line of adversaries, and shivered their spears. In a second and third encounter they discharged their pistols; and, in a fourth, fought with their clashing swords.

At length, the two chiefs—Lord Cathcart and Captain Watson of the Guards—spurring forward in the centre, engaged furiously in single combat—until the Marshal of the Field, rushing between them in the name of the Ladies, declared that the Fair Damsels of both bands were perfectly satisfied with these proofs of the devotion of their respective Knights, and commanded them to desist from further combat.

Then the Knights dismounted, and, with their respective Ladies by their sides, headed the procession of the whole company, as they passed under the triumphal arches, and between lines of troops, brilliant with gay colors and streaming flags, into the garden of the Mansion. Thence, ascending a flight of steps, they came into a spacious hall, with its panels painted in imitation of Sienna marble. Here they were served with refreshments.

From this apartment, after a little while, they passed up to a ball-room, with four drawing-rooms, and all painted in pale-blue and rose-pink. Eighty-five mirrors and a large number of wax-lights here lent enchantment to the scene.

The dances—the stately minuet and the cheerful contra-dance, for the quadrille and waltz had not yet come in—continued until ten o'clock, when the doors and windows were thrown open, and a magnificent display of fireworks diversified the entertainment, bouquets of rockets, bursting balloons, Chinese fountains, arches illuminated with rainbow-colored flames, and Fame, spangled with stars, and blowing from her trumpet the words of light, *Tes Lauriers sont Immortels.*

At twelve, large folding doors, hitherto artfully concealed, were suddenly flung wide, and a magnificent saloon, two hundred feet long, and twenty in height, and adorned with fifty large pier-glasses, disclosed to view. A burst of surprise and admiration broke forth from the assembled guests. All was so new, so fresh and artistic, nothing old and stale and common-place. Here were the supper-tables, lighted by innumerable wax-lights and lustres, and laden with all the delicacies that could be procured. Twenty-four black slaves, in Oriental dresses, with silver collars and bracelets, ranged in two lines, stood with bowed heads as General Howe and his brother, the Admiral, led the brilliant company into the saloon.

Supper over, the guests began to depart; though the dancing was kept up until four o'clock in the morning.

Nought occurred to interrupt the festivities. An attack planned by Captain McLane upon the British line of defences, and which was answered by alarm guns from river to river, was represented by the officers to be only a portion of the evening's entertainment. And so the dance went joyfully on. It was a fête of fêtes. And though some may censure the spirit that can thus indulge in gayety and festivity in the midst of war, it must be remembered that the indulgence of strong feeling in any one direction, naturally induces a corresponding indulgence after a time in the direction immediately opposite. It is the effort of nature to maintain the healthy balance and equilibrium of the mind, in other words, to preserve its sanity. This is one great good of amusements and festivities in the usual times of peace, and much less can they be dispensed with in war, unless you mean to allow the necessary and perhaps righteous indignation against the enemy, to sink into a bitter rancour, which shall find vent in acts of unnecessary cruelty and vindictiveness, unworthy of a Christian people, in any cause however just, and toward any foe however barbarous.

CHAPTER XVIII.

AN UNINVITED GUEST.

He was enamored. Ere he touched her hand
His senses reeled within him, as when first
Columbus, gazing, sighted a new world.
She was his Indies, his America,
His missing continent, for want of which
His sphere imperfect was, and lacked the sense
Of fullness and completeness.

We need hardly say that both the Misses Graham were delighted participants in the festivities of the Mischianza. Pemberton escorted them. Devoted Whig as he was, he prided himself upon being neither a fanatic nor a bigot. He could oppose the success of the British arms with all his might, and yet not have an unkind feeling personally toward a single British officer. So far as he knew them to be, like Colonel Musgrave, André, and many others, noble and generous men, just as sincere in their political views as he was in his, he admired and respected them.

As to Sir William Howe, had it not been for his keeping Captain Cunningham in his position of Provost, he would have thought very highly of him. By his own officers and men he was evidently sincerely beloved, and this was greatly in his favor. Pemberton also was sorry to hear of his removal as Commander-in-Chief. He felt a little as Hamilton afterwards did, when Washington communicated to him a plan to capture Sir Henry Clinton. "I am opposed to it," said Hamilton. "We know exactly what Sir Henry is, and what he will be likely to do. We might easily have a worse man—for us—in his place." And the plan was given up.

Sir William's inactivity through the winter certainly was not calculated to make any far-seeing friend of the Colonial cause anxious to have another and, it might be, more active man, put in his place. The new broom might sweep cleaner.

So Pemberton attended the Mischianza, and enjoyed it as much as a person with his artistic perceptions and love of the beautiful would naturally do. Such a sight, enlivened by such crowds of gayly-dressed officers and beautiful women, surely never had been seen in America.

André was engaged the greater part of the time with his chosen lady for the occasion, Miss Chew; and the two soon became the centre of a gay and brilliant circle. The Misses Graham and Pemberton were not of the number however—for Helen seemed determined that evening to let people see that there was nothing between the Captain and herself. She was one of those that hated the shrugs and whispers of a gossipping crowd. It did not suit to have the betrothal declared openly—so she preferred that it should not be surmised.

The three had strolled out upon the lawn to see the fireworks, and as these concluded in a blaze of starry rockets, Helen wandered off alone a little way to one side, into a summer house, and sat down, gazing back upon the fairy scene.

"Good-evening, Miss Helen," said a manly voice; and turning, she saw a gentleman who evidently had come up from the opposite direction. "I thought I should never have an opportunity of speaking to you."

He was apparently rather an elderly man, dressed in a handsome brown suit, and there was something familiar in the tones of his voice, and the glances of his eye. But that light, long hair—certainly she did not know him.

"You have the advantage of me, sir, I am not able to recollect you," said Helen, slightly embarrassed.

"I should know you, anywhere, in any masquerade," replied the stranger, in a low but impressive voice.

Helen's heart throbbed tumultuously. Could it be possible? She bent her eyes earnestly upon the face of the speaker, lit up by the light which shone even at that distance from the ball-room.

"Philip Morris! It cannot be you!" she said in a whisper.

"Yes, but it is. We have no such fun as this at Valley Forge, I can assure you. It is worth coming to see. I never thought to see Fairy land come down in this fashion on old Philadelphia."

"But the risk—the awful risk!"

"Not much more than a battle. Besides," continued he in a passionate tone, "I have not set my eyes on you since that evening I tossed you the rose in Pemberton's porch, nearly six months now. I would rather die than never see you!"

"This is madness!" exclaimed Helen. "You are a rebel, I am an English soldier's daughter, and true to the red cross as steel."

"I care not. I love you."

"I can never love you!"

"Why?"

"You have no right to ask me. It is sufficient to say that I cannot return your love."

"Then I do not care much what becomes of me—after this night. They are going in to supper, I see. May I wait on you for this one time? Captain André, I perceive, is devoted elsewhere."

"You are insane. They will certainly discover you."

"Not for an hour or two. And I care not now what becomes of me. I wish I had half-a-dozen of our men here, and I'd carry off old Howe right from the midst of his adoring red-coats."

"Such a threat is as treasonable for me to hear as for you to utter. Do you not know that if I did my duty, I should immediately summon assistance and have you arrested?"

"Do so. Next to living by you, it would be sweet to die by you. Chatelard never went to the grave, dug by the hands of the queen he madly worshipped, more willingly than I should go to one dug by you."

"Mr. Morris, you will drive me to frenzy. You say you love me—"

"Madly—devotedly!"

"Then how can you give me such keen pain? You must know that I should never forgive myself, if your life were the cost of this reckless passion. You say you love me, why then do you not do as I wish?"

"What is your wish?"

"That you should leave this place, and this city, immediately, and by the way you came."

"I cannot leave the city to-night. Do you not hear the pother that McLane has stirred up?—he has set fire to about a mile of the British abattis."

"We were told that the cannonade was but a part of the programme."

"Pretty good for the managers of the fête. McLane will not like that. He thought to break up the whole affair. But you see I have more courtesy, and, even though uninvited, stepped in to enjoy the party."

"Please now go! Stay: wait a moment. Here comes Mr. Pemberton. Heavens—I fear it is Major Tarleton."

"I was sent by Mr. Pemberton to bring you in to supper, Miss Helen," said Major Tarleton, for he it was, beginning to speak before he reached the summer-house.

"He told me you had strolled off by yourself for a few moments. Ah, beg pardon, I thought you were alone."

"Allow me to introduce you, gentlemen—Mr. Wharton, Major Tarleton"—the gentlemen bowed.

Tarleton cast a quick glance from his keen black eyes upon Philip's face. "I do not remember to have met you before, Mr. Wharton, and yet your face does not look altogether strange to me."

"Probably we have met at some of our mutual friends," replied Philip composedly. "I am almost certain also that I have met you," he added, with a touch of that reckless humor which not even the greatest peril could entirely restrain.

"And your voice, too, sounds familiar," rejoined Tarleton. "I pride myself on never forgetting a face or a voice, Miss Helen."

"And yet you will have to own up that you fail this time," replied Morris, laughing.

"Not yet. Give me half an hour to ransack my memory a little, and I warrant I tell you just when and where we met."

"I'll treat you to a bottle of wine if you do," replied Philip.

During this discussion, Helen could almost have fainted, if fainting would have done any good, and she had been of the fainting kind. To hear Morris thus coolly joking upon a point which involved his life, was as if she were seeing him play with the trigger of a pistol whose muzzle was against his forehead. It almost sickened her. Recovering herself, she said—

"Perhaps, Major Tarleton, you had better tell my sister that I am all safe, and that we will be there in a few minutes. Thanks for your kindness in coming to seek me."

This was too broad a hint for Tarleton to delay a moment. But as he turned, he shot another sharp glance at Morris from beneath his bushy eyebrows, and then a quick gleam of intelligence passed across his dark, swarthy face, not unnoticed by Helen.

"Tarleton suspects you. I saw it in his face. You must not stay in this place a minute longer. Go!"

"Give me a flower out of your bouquet?"

"Here is a cluster of violets. I beg of you to go!"

"Violets! Give me that spring rose out of your bosom. That I can live on awhile."

Helen tore the rose from its fastenings. "Here. Go!"

He took the rose, first covering the hand which extended it with kisses. "Farewell, most fascinating and glorious of women! You are in yourself more splendid than the Mischianza to me."

As he left the back door of the summer-house, Helen sank down upon the bench from which she had risen in her excitement. "I must not go in yet; every minute is a gain," thought she. "Cruel, cruel boy, to tear my heart so, and call it love! Poor fellow, I wish he did not love me. If this comes from saving a man's life, I am sure I'll never try to do it again. I wonder what André would say, could he have seen that stormy shower of kisses? Just as well he did not. Though John is not easily jealous. And he knows I love him as foolishly and wildly as—as Philip Morris loves me."

After waiting some minutes longer, Helen walked to the house.

The first person she met was Major Tarleton. "Where is Mr. Wharton?" he said, with a suspicious look in his eyes, and making an almost involuntary step toward the door.

"Oh, I left him outside. Major, if you will give me your arm, and conduct me to my sister, I shall be greatly obliged to you. I shall never reach her by myself in this crowd."

Tarleton was mollified. He had the greatest admiration for Helen, not only because she was a belle, and admired by other men, but because her gay and dashing spirit embodied his very highest ideal of what was beautiful and charming in a woman. Still he did not altogether forget his suspicions, saying as they made their way through the rooms—

"I know, Miss Helen, who that Mr. Wharton reminded me of—an old Quaker preacher from the country, whom I once met at Mr. Pemberton's."

"Probably his father—or grandfather," said Helen. "Bella, has not Mr. Richard Wharton a father, or grandfather, who is a Quaker preacher, and lives out at a place they call Gwynedd?"

"Yes," replied Bella. But she could not say, for she did not know, that the Mr. Richard Wharton she had in her mind was a very different person from the gentleman of whom Major Tarleton was thinking. In fact, when Helen had been compelled to improvise a name so quickly for Lieutenant Morris, she had used that of this Mr. Wharton, because he certainly did look something like the disguised officer, inasmuch as he also had long sandy hair.

"A little too suspicious again," thought Tarleton to himself. "I really had a notion of looking into that Wharton's identity. I suppose he is off in one of the drinking-rooms."

"What kept you so long, Helen?" questioned Isabella.

"Oh, that Mr. Wharton dropped down upon me—Mr.

Richard Wharton is old enough to be my father, Major—and we had a long talk about this, that and the other."

"I declare, Helen, if you are not the strangest girl. I should not have thought you would care to talk five minutes with Mr. Wharton."

Helen laughed. It was one of her most peculiar charms—a ringing, silvery laugh—which made people always stop their conversation to listen. About once in your lifetime, if you are fortunate, you meet a woman with that silvery, musical laughter. It is a gift—and certainly one of the very rarest.

Helen laughed. "I know it, Sis. I am a strange girl. I astonish myself sometimes. Even Major Tarleton was astonished to-night, as he came up and found me conversing with Mr. Wharton. How blank you looked, Major. You evidently thought you were interrupting a tete-a-tete, a love affair—and with Mr. Wharton!" and Helen laughed again, as if it were the most ridiculous idea in the world.

Helen would soon have lost that silvery laugh, had she often used it thus in insincerity, and as a blind. But certainly she was in no small degree justified in doing it on this occasion. She was afraid that Major Tarleton might talk—speak of her interview with Mr. Wharton as a concealed and mysterious thing; and so she chose to make no secret of it, and place the whole affair in a ridiculous light.

When Helen got a chance in the pauses of the dance, an hour or so afterward, she strolled again upon the lawn with Pemberton.

When well out of hearing of the crowd, she said:

"Arthur, do you know who that Mr. Wharton really was?"

"Why, Mr. Richard Wharton, of course. Though what

a gentleman of his serious tastes is doing here, puzzles me, I confess."

"It was that rebel cousin of yours, Lieutenant Morris," said Helen in a whisper.

"I hope not, he would hardly do such a reckless thing. You are certainly mistaken, Helen."

"I talked with him in that summer-house for at least fifteen minutes by the watch, though it seemed to me an age," replied Helen.

"Phil must be crazy. What could he have come here for?"

"He said to see the Mischianza—and me."

"The reckless, hot-headed fellow! He will do these daring, imprudent things some day once too often, and then perish ingloriously. He tries my patience beyond measure," returned Pemberton in a low but excited tone.

"I wish you would say to him, Arthur—you are his cousin and warm friend, you know—that the admiration he insists on forcing upon me, is not only entirely unreciprocated, but very annoying," said Helen with emotion.

"I have told him as much already; but Phil, though a splendid fellow, is obstinate in certain things beyond all description. He seems to me to have the obstinacy of a whole generation of Morrises concentrated in his single person. Why don't you dash him with cold water yourself?—all women understand how to do that, and none more than you, Helen."

"I have done so—but it only makes him foolish and desperate. He is but a boy, you know."

"Yes, a mere boy—just about a year older than you, Helen," replied Pemberton, smiling.

"But I am a woman, and that makes a great deal of difference. I am sure I feel a great deal older. It is presumptuous in him even to think of me—in that light."

"I don't exactly see that, though. In five years he will be, say five years older, and you will be just what you are now, of course; for a lady never grows any older until she is married."

"It is too grave a subject to make a jest of, Arthur. You know my position with Captain André."

Pemberton had in him a vein of the same reckless humor that distinguished his cousin. "Suppose you ship André —*he* would not be so hard to get rid of," said he, in a serious tone.

Helen took her hand from his arm. "Of course you mean that as a joke, Arthur; but I beg of you, as you respect me, never to jest in that way again. I love John André—more than a thousand Philip Morrises—more than life itself." Helen's eyes shone and her voice trembled with the intensity of her emotion.

"There is no doubt that he will get safely off?" added she, after a pause, for Pemberton had made no reply.

"I think not. Our English friends like good eating, and to have good eating they must encourage the farmers around to come into the city. Phil, doubtless, came in driving a farmer's wagon, and will go out driving one. But take care you do not say anything of this to Captain André."

"Arthur!" There were a host of meanings conveyed in the mode this one word was uttered. It said mainly however—"How meanly you must think of me?"

"I would not betray Mr. Morris to save my life," she added, indignantly.

It was a little perverse in Pemberton, perhaps, but he replied—"And yet it was only yesterday that you justified the hanging of young Hale, and every other rebel spy."

"Oh, that was only a general assertion. If a spy were to flee into my dwelling for safety, I would conceal him if I could, though my own father or husband were on his track. You know I would."

"I believe you would, Helen," rejoined Pemberton; "you, or Isabella either. You are two dear, delightful, splendid, charmingly inconsistent women."

"Consistency! I hate the very name of it!" replied Helen. "I never made so many blunders in my life, as once when I tried, after hearing your famous Dr. Duché, to be consistent for a whole week. Since then, I always act as my heart dictates, and have no trouble, and am—"

"A very bewitching woman!" added Pemberton, interrupting her.

"Nonsense, Arthur—keep all those fine speeches for Bel. And here she comes, to learn what you mean by your long absence."

When Isabella came up with André, at Pemberton's suggestion they changed partners, for he well knew that André, who had scarcely spoken a word with Helen, was anxious to be with her for a little while before the evening closed.

As they strayed from the others, down a garden walk, André said—

"Have I not been good, Helen? I have talked and danced and flirted with a host of belles this evening—with the Misses Chew, and Miss Vining, and the Franks, and the Shippens, and that beautiful, just rising evening star, Miss Willing—and all the time longing to be at your side, my sweet. I think I deserve quite a reward for my self-control and self-sacrifice."

At this moment they were passing behind some tall evergreens, forming a perfect shelter from curious eyes.

Helen stopped a moment, and turned up her face. "Kiss me, John."

"There, three kisses are enough," continued she, blushing and walking on. "We will walk together here just five minutes longer. You have been very good, and stopped the mouths of all the old women—male and female—for at least a month. But you must not undo the good work."

"I do not care what the people say, Helen," exclaimed André, impetuously. "Let them talk: what of it?"

"I hate to be talked about," replied Helen. "Come and see me to-morrow, if you can. Do you not think it was a sacrifice also to me, to have you talking and dancing with the very prettiest girls in Philadelphia, just as if I were nothing to you?"

"You know you are all the world to me," said André, passionately.

"Am I, sweet?"

"Put all the world on one side, and you on the other, and I would abandon all for you."

"I would do more than that for you, John. People call me a wilful, imperious girl. But if there is one of those glorious women who hovered around and petted you to-night, whom you should learn to love more than you love me, I would myself bind the orange blossoms around her brow, and deck her for your bridal. Even if I died the next day—even if I died the next day!"

"It would be just like your generous heart to do it," replied André, with emotion. "But you need not fear, sweet. At any moment this night, it needed but a glance of your eyes to call me to your side. I heard you laugh once—I could tell your laugh among a thousand—and I thought you were having a merry time of it."

"That Miss Willing is very beautiful."

"She is not half so beautiful as you are, my darling; but mere beauty of features is not everything. It is the charm, the fascination which flows from a brilliant intellect and noble soul. Sweet, you amuse me by this doleful strain. You do not seem to know that you have that charm of variety, which not one woman in a thousand possesses. Like the poet pictured the Queen of Egypt,

> 'Age cannot wither you, nor custom stale
> Your infinite variety.'"

"I hope so," said Helen. "I hope I have something to hold you by, John—for I will not hold you by mere force of honor, and it is death to poor me to lose you."

"I never saw you in this mood before, my many-colored opal. My wonder is that so rare a gem as you should be willing to rest upon so plain a bosom as mine. I know well you might have generals and colonels, instead of a simple captain, at your feet, my peerless!"

"You will be a general some day, and I shall help you win the honor," exclaimed Helen proudly.

"Of course," said André, laughing. "Else I could hardly have a glorious funeral in Westminster Abbey, as that Creole witch predicted."

"Please never refer to that. It always makes me shudder," said Helen. "But indeed we are staying out here too long. And, after one more dance—this time with you, my splendid!—we must go home. Isabella was ready an hour ago."

CHAPTER XIX.

THE RATTLESNAKE FLAG.

A stupid fellow this—and yet his blunders
Are oft as good as wiser men's conceits.

One month after the brilliant scenes of the Mischianza, the British army left Philadelphia. Even at that time, the news was in the city that an Alliance, Offensive and Defensive, between France and the American States had been consummated, and that a French fleet and army were being made ready for action.

This altered materially the position of affairs. Military prudence at once dictated the union of the British forces, to enable them to make head against the combined French and American armies. Therefore it was determined that Philadelphia must be abandoned, and the British troops and fleets concentrated at New York.

The British Ministry also assumed a new front. Instead of the submit and be forgiven policy of General Howe, peace at any price, short of Colonial Independence, was offered by the British Commissioners, who had been especially appointed with the view of thus preventing the dismemberment of the Kingdom. The ground taken by André in the conversation with Pemberton which we have recorded, was the ground now of the Ministers and of Parliament. Pride must yield before the danger of the hour. The right of Taxation—everything, if need be—must be given up, in order to preserve the integrity of the British Empire, and to defeat what were considered the selfish and ambitious schemes of Britain's ancient enemy.

There were of course many sad partings when the evacuation took place, for it is useless to deny that the British officers had made themselves, on the whole, popular in

Philadelphia. They had behaved, as a general thing, in a gentlemanly fashion. They had made business brisk in and around the city, by the easy spending of their money —not the Continental paper, which a man was afraid to keep in his pocket over night, lest it should fall fifty per cent. before morning, but the solid gold and silver of the realm. And, besides, many of the officers and men had formed those love-ties, which spurn so often the control of party and race and sect, and which are perhaps more effective than anything else, in holding the various discordant tribes of men in the bonds of a common brotherhood.

André had departed in the suite of General Grey—with many promises of writing and meeting as often as possible. Something was said by Helen of going to New York; but Isabella very naturally did not favor the change, and their guardian, Colonel Musgrave, did not approve of it. There might be, it was thought, an attack upon New York by the allied French and American forces, in which case it would be much better for his wards to be in Philadelphia. There were peculiar advantages also in their being with a lady like Mrs. Pemberton, who felt the affection of a mother for them. Therefore, after commending them to the care of Mrs. Pemberton, and promising to avail himself of every opportunity of corresponding, Colonel Musgrave took a tearful and affectionate parting, and departed with his regiment.

Formed in marching order at sunrise, on a bright morning in June, the British troops marched down below the city, where a large number of boats had been provided, and were rapidly ferried across the Delaware.

It was near ten o'clock, and all of the troops had departed, save a few outposts, which were being rapidly drawn in, when a British lieutenant, at the head of half-a-dozen men, sprang upon the porch of Mrs. Pemberton's mansion, and thundered at the door with the hilt of his sword.

Pemberton opened it in surprise. "What is the matter?" cried he, in amazement.

"You are an infamous traitor!" exclaimed the British officer, in a fury. "You thought we had left the city, did you? But there are enough of us here yet. Here, men, arrest this traitor!"

"What do you mean, are you crazy?" shouted Pemberton, springing back, and seizing an iron bar designed for the door, which leaned up behind it, against the side of the entry.

At this moment Mrs. Pemberton and the young ladies came hastening out, alarmed at the violent voices. Pemberton stood with the bar raised, while the officer had drawn his sword, and the men with their bayonets presented, waited but a word to fall on him.

Pushing in front of her son, Mrs. Pemberton advanced with the air of a queen upon the officer. "What means this? How darest thou make this assault? My friend, General Howe, is not so far off but that he shall hear of this."

"And," exclaimed Isabella, who, with Helen, also had pushed to the front, by Mrs. Pemberton's side, "do you not know who you are insulting? You shall answer to Colonel Musgrave, our guardian, for this."

"What is your name, sir?" asked Helen, with indignant scorn. "Are you drunk, that you thus disgrace the uniform of a British officer?"

The officer had been in a fury, as he sprung upon the porch, but he cooled down now very suddenly. Confronted by three splendid women, whom he knew by common report to be on intimate terms with his superior officers, he did not feel so well assured of the justice of his position.

"I have always supposed, Mrs. Pemberton, that you ere a loyal woman!" said he.

"And I am a loyal woman!" she replied indignantly. "How darest thou call my loyalty in question?"

"Loyal people don't generally fly such flags as that you're flying," said the officer sarcastically.

"Why, what does the man mean, Arthur?" asked Isabella, glancing back at Pemberton.

"Indeed, I don't know," replied he. "I had no idea that any flag was flying. In fact I told Fox positively not to hoist our flag this morning."

"Well, if you will walk out into the street I think you will see that a flag is flying, and a d—d insulting one, too."

Here a soldier came up hastily, and whispered in the ear of his superior. "I don't care," replied he, "I'm bound to see this out."

"Wait a moment," said Pemberton, and he went out into the garden behind the house, preferring that, for evident reasons, to the street. In a short time he came back, half indignant, half laughing, and informed the ladies of what he had seen. Foxey had bettered his instructions. Unknown to Pemberton he had procured somewhere a Continental naval flag, with its warning device of a RATTLESNAKE, and the motto, "DON'T TREAD ON ME," and thinking that the British were all gone, had spread its audacious folds to the breeze. This it was which had, not unnaturally, so deeply excited the anger of the Briton.

"Upon my honor, mother, I knew nothing of the raising of that flag—did not even know it was in the house," said Pemberton.

"It must have been that nigger," suggested one of the soldiers.

"D——n the nigger! He wouldn't have done it, if he had not thought it would please his master," replied the officer shrewdly.

Another soldier came running up. "The rebel troopers will be here in five minutes," cried he, all excitement. "It is just as much as you can do to get off safely."

"You may thank your stars and these ladies," cried the officer, shaking his sword menacingly at Pemberton, "that you don't hang where your feet wouldn't touch the ground, this afternoon."

Pemberton smiled. But Isabella answered haughtily: "And you may thank your stars if you are not dismissed the service before the month is out. Don't you attempt to answer me. Go!"

However the officer might have been tempted in his indignation to delay, his men had no idea of being made prisoners, and were already hastening down the street. With a half-uttered imprecation upon all meddling women, he followed them.

Not a moment too soon for his safety. For ten minutes after, a party of McLane's men, with Lieutenant Morris at their head, came swooping in at a gallop, and halted directly in front of Mrs. Pemberton's house, where they gave three ringing cheers.

"What do they mean, Arthur?" cried Mrs. Pemberton. "I thought they would be more apt to burn us down than to cheer us."

"Oh, they have come straight on to the Rattlesnake Flag," replied Pemberton. "If Foxey came near getting us into one scrape, he has got us very cleverly out of another."

"I do not like it at all—it seems deceitful," rejoined Mrs. Pemberton "Thee must tell Fox to take down that flag as soon as possible. I only tolerated the other one, and I certainly shall not allow this. I shall take an opportunity to explain the whole affair to Philip Morris, the first time he calls."

"That would be very right, mother," replied Pemberton, in the most dutiful manner. "And I think myself it is about time for this flag business to stop. I shall speak to Fox upon the subject."

The Rattlesnake flag waved, however, for several days, sufficiently long to establish a new reputation for the flag-house. The few high in authority who were in the secret, of course manifested no want of respect or sympathy for the Pembertons, while the larger class of Whigs contented themselves with saying that Mrs. Pemberton had just saved her property from confiscation or destruction, to use a Scriptural expression, by the skin of her teeth; and that it was certainly very convenient for the mother to be on one side of the fence, and the son on the other.

FIRST NAVAL FLAGS.

PART II.

CHAPTER I.

ARNOLD THE HERO.

Have I battled through
A host of dangers—periled life and health,
Shattered my fortunes—now to be denied
A few base ducats? Out upon them all!

NEARLY a year had elapsed since the evacuation of Philadelphia by the British forces; a year productive, as it seemed, of very little benefit to the American cause. The Alliance with France had not been attended as yet with those substantial advantages that generally had been anticipated. The failure of the combined attack upon Rhode Island, the result, as it was charged, of the needless and cowardly sailing of the French fleet to Boston, thus leaving the American portion of the expedition to the hazard of capture, had caused deep irritation, not only in the popular mind, but in the army. And the capture of Savannah by the British a few months later, had naturally increased both the irritation and the disappointment.

The continued depreciation of the Continental paper money, also had a very depressing effect. In spite of the most stringent laws to uphold it as a legal tender, it steadily and rapidly decreased in value. In the June of 1778, it took four dollars of paper to purchase one of specie; nine months afterward, it took ten. And the depreciation still went on, almost from day to day.

General Benedict Arnold had been appointed to the

command of Philadelphia, immediately upon the British evacuation. But the extent of his powers was undefined, and he had soon come into conflict, not only with many of the citizens, but with the authorities of Pennsylvania.

Captain André still was in New York, now acting as Aid-de-camp to the British Commander, Sir Henry Clinton. Colonel Musgrave also was in New York. Both had held correspondence with the Misses Graham as often as opportunities were afforded them by the passage of flags of truce between the two armies. If such opportunities did not come very frequently, both Helen and André belonged to that class of lovers who can live a long time on a few words of love, a few cherished tokens. Neither thought for a moment of any failure of affection on either side. They were both extremely admired in their respective circles; and we cannot help thinking that this is a great element of confidence in love. "He loves me, and I am worthy of his love;" she who can say that, is not apt to be jealous. Jealousy is often the result of a conviction that you are overvalued; a fear that the lover will awake from his or her delusion, and see the beloved object as he or she really is. And yet André had once failed in love, when he was younger and less admired; but the nobility of his nature was not easily prone to jealousy, and when he heard occasionally of Helen Graham as a star of the first magnitude in the new circles of Philadelphia, as she had been in the old, and the toast of the French and American officers as she had been before of the British, he felt proud of his beautiful betrothed.

On a fine spring morning in 1779—such days as often come, bringing a taste with them of the balmy sweetness of June—Arthur Pemberton stood in the porch of his mother's mansion, enjoying the brightness and the genial warmth. As he stood there, speaking occasionally to a passing acquaintance, a gentleman in military attire came along. He was a man apparently of about forty years of age, and wore the uniform of a General in the Continental service. He walked with somewhat of a limp, and carried a gold-headed cane to steady his footsteps. Rather above the medium size, and of a muscular and vigorous frame, his face bore the marks of a bold, determined and energetic spirit. But one could see at a glance that he was more than this—that he was also both passionate and overbearing. A man not patient of contradiction or opposition—fiery, impetuous and arrogant—and, therefore, not easily controlled, nor able to harmonize with other men of equal rank. Stopping as he arrived opposite Mrs. Pemberton's, he spoke:

"Good-morning, Mr. Pemberton. A fine day this."

"A very fine day, General; will you not walk in and see the ladies."

"No, I thank you—it is scarcely late enough for that. I am bound up to the Congress. But, as it is rather early, I will sit down on your porch, if you have no objection, and rest for a minute or two."

"Of course. Does your leg pain you much, now?"

"Only at times—in damp and rheumatic weather. But it is stiff, and lags behind the other."

"This is the second time you have been wounded in that leg, I have heard?" said Pemberton, kindly.

"Yes, once at Quebec, and then again at Saratoga. The red-coats seem to have a special spite at that leg. But I cannot complain. I only wondered afterwards at Saratoga, that I got through with my life. It was like going through the big drops of a thunder-storm."

"Well, I hear that you need not have gone into the

fight," replied Pemberton smiling—"that Gates did not urge you to go."

Arnold laughed bitterly. "No, that is true. He sent Armstrong after me to call me back. I tell you, I led him a round. Wherever the fire was hottest, there I spurred—and there followed Armstrong. But after awhile I found a place as hot as hell—and then he stopped following me. They said afterwards I was drunk. They're always lying about me, the scoundrels!"

"It is true then that you had no command?"

"No special command—but, you know, when I was once on the field, I outranked nearly everybody there. And they all seemed glad enough to obey and follow me. God's wrath! in the midst of battle, soldiers know a leader when they see him, though they may lie about him afterwards."

"And where was Gates!"

"Oh, Gates was in his tent, discussing through his spectacles the pros and cons of our dispute with England—arguing it all out with a wounded British officer."

"He wears the chief laurels, however, being the commander," said Pemberton. "You know his friends in Congress, and he has plenty of them, would like to put him in Washington's place. They are perpetually referring to the capture of Burgoyne, and implying that if he had been Commander-in-chief, all the British generals would have been captured by this time."

"They are a set of stupid donkeys," replied Arnold. "Gates did not capture Burgoyne. Schuyler had ploughed and sowed, and Gates came up at the last moment, and reaped the field. It was already yellow with the harvest. Yes, Schuyler planned—Stark first put in the sickle—the murder of Miss McCrea gave us plenty of maddened men

—and I, though I do say it myself, knew how to lead them. Was I not the first man to storm the British works? If not, where did I get this cursed ball in my leg? This may sound like boasting, Pemberton, but they force me to boast. Congress will not do me even simple justice. But you know, of course, how they are hounding me?"

"I am glad to see, General, that their Committee has absolved you from all those charges which were brought against you."

"Compelled to do it, sir—compelled to do it! There was not a tittle of evidence. Satan! some expect a man in face of the enemy to act with the same deliberation and regularity as if he were selling and billing a lot of goods in a merchant's counting-room! But what do you think they are at now—the scoundrels?"

"Indeed I do not know—I thought the whole matter was settled."

"I thought so too, and resigned my command of this city, you know. But now I hear from a friend, that they —that infernal Congress—have made up their minds not to adopt the report of their own Committee of Inquiry, but to order General Washington to subject me to the disgrace of a court martial."

"Oh, I hope not, General," replied Pemberton, for he could scarcely believe it.

"It is so, sir. You may depend upon it. And it is on a par with the treatment I have received from the first. Any other man would have laid down his commission long ago. What does Washington say? He admits himself that it is shameful. Who had done what I had done?—they force me to boast with their infamous injustice—witness the march through the wilderness to Quebec—my men, sir, positively boiling their own shoes to make soup of, such was their hunger; toiling waist-deep up icy rivers; then that fearful siege in a Canada winter before the walls of Quebec—besieging double our own numbers—my wound I count as nothing, compared to all the rest—and then what was my reward?"

"I know it all, general; and I sympathize with you deeply. I cannot understand the action of Congress. But, remember you are not fighting, you did not go through all those fearful perils for your own advancement; but for the Country, and the sacred cause of Freedom!" Pemberton's face glowed with his emotion.

"I know all that," replied Arnold. "Would I have stood this gross injustice so long, had it not been for the great Cause? But every man owes a duty also to himself and to his own self-respect. My motto is—'For myself and for all.' Congress appointed, as you know, five Major Generals, and every one of them was inferior to me in rank. My name was not on the list, though it is a matter of common knowledge that not one of those officers had done and suffered one-half as much for the country as I had. Then, after those other affairs in Connecticut, they voted me a horse, in place of the two shot under me, 'as a token of their approbation.'" Arnold drawled out this last in bitter irony.

"But they also did you some justice. They made you at last a Major General."

"Yes, when for very shame they could no longer refuse to. But they did not undo the wrong, even then; for my late promotion leaves me at the foot of the list, and all the others, my juniors, outrank me."

"I do not support the Congress in this matter, General; but let us be fair to them. You know the reason which was given for your not being appointed in the first place:

that your State already had its share of military honors. I do not myself think it a good reason, but men may honestly differ on such a matter."

"It was *not* their reason," thundered the General, loudly enough to attract the attention of the passers-by; "it was a mere infamous pretence. They were jealous of me, they and their army pets. I had no friends at court. They meant to keep me down, or drive me out of the service. They cannot keep me down, but they may drive me from the service," added he with a fierce oath.

"I trust not, General; I trust you will still cleave to the Stripes and Stars. We cannot spare so dauntless a soldier as you have proved yourself to be."

"Well, I must be going," said Arnold, looking at his watch. "I am bound again to that infernal Congress. You know how I must want money—just on the point of my marriage, too—and yet I cannot get a settlement of my accounts from their committee. I believe they mean to starve me! They will neither accept my accounts, nor reject them. I sometimes almost regret that I ever touched a sword. I should be as rich a man as Bob Morris, and your other magnates who have made a good thing out of the chances of the war, if I had remained in business as they did."

"If Mr. Morris has made money out of his honest ventures, he has also spent it generously and patriotically; you must admit that, General," replied Pemberton, a little warmly.

"Oh, yes, I don't deny that. And I was not finding fault with him for making money. He simply remained in business, and the money flowed into his pockets, as it would into mine, if I had not been so hot-headed, and rushed at the head of my company of State Guards to Boston. Then I should have Congress at my heels, accepting my generous donations with votes of thanks, instead of snarling and biting at me like a pack of mangy curs. But good-bye, Mr. Pemberton—it's a long lane that has no turning;" and the irascible General walked, limping, up the street.

As he left, Lieutenant Morris, who was a frequent visitor to the city since the evacuation, came up from the opposite direction.

"What had the General to say this morning—any new trouble?" inquired he, laughing.

"He is soured to the very dregs," replied Pemberton, seriously. "He is hard to manage, but they do not treat him fairly, Phil."

"I know they do not. No officer in the army would have patiently borne that promotion of five juniors over his head—and he had done more than all of them put together. It puzzled us in the army very much—what did it all mean, Arthur? You are here on the spot, and ought to understand the internal workings of that stupid Congressional machine a little."

"Perhaps I do—a little. But holding their sessions in secret, it is not so easy to find out things even here on the spot, as you may suppose. As to those appointments, many doubtless looked at the matter from the politician's point of view—not from the military. The question was not with them who had shown capacity, and ability to serve the country, but who should partake of the broth. Here was a certain amount of honor and pay—and here were the honorable members' friends in the thirteen States. Now, each State, they held, was entitled to its proportionate share of the broth. To appoint Arnold, would be to give Connecticut more than her proportion—and, if it had not been so, the members from Connecticut had no particular love for Arnold."

"Oh, that is miserable!" exclaimed Philip. "We could hardly believe that, in the army."

"That is one view—the worst one. But there are other men than mere mousing politicians in Congress—there are statesmen and gentlemen—and with them the reason I think was this. Despite all Arnold's capacity and daring, they have no faith in the man. There are always reports floating about of his want of high honor—and even, if it must be said, strict honesty. Even here in Philadelphia, we hear the same things. He will live extravagantly—and he has not the money to pay for it. You know how far an officer's pay, in Continental money, will go to support him?"

"I am not quite certain whether it will buy oats for his horse, or not. Some of the officers say it will; others say it won't—but here is a bill I just now paid, and you can judge a little from it," replied Morris, taking a slip of paper out of his pocket, and reading it:

"Lieut. P. MORRIS

Bot. of W. NICOLL,

1 Pair Boots	$100 00
4 Handkerchiefs—$12	48 00
6 Yards Blue Cloth—$50	300 00
	$448 00

Received payment,

W. NICOLL."

"I don't think an officer's pay could go very far at those rates," said Pemberton, laughing. "You must live on what you all have so much of—glory!"

"But these confounded shopkeepers and bootmakers are such vulgar fellows that they have no proper sense of glory," replied Philip, with a woeful laugh. "Now there's Arnold, if they would only take pay in glory, he has millions of it."

"Yes, it is a sad affair. As you say, he is covered with

glory, and persecuted with debts. Moving in our highest and most expensive circles, engaged to be married to one of the most beautiful women in the city—but who will of course expect to live, as his wife, in the handsome style to which she always has been accustomed—and no money!"

"What! has he no property of his own, and yet living in such an ostentatious and expensive manner?"

"He says that he spent almost the whole of a handsome fortune in that Northern campaign; and brings in a large claim against Congress. The Committee of Accounts will not pass it; evidently doubt its fairness. Arnold storms, for his creditors torment him. Congress will not move. He said just now they meant to starve him, or to force him out of the service; and he implied they might perhaps do the latter."

"It would be a great loss to the country," replied Morris. "He has no equal for dauntless intrepidity, except perhaps it be 'Mad Anthony.' But Arnold has more soldierly ability than Wayne. You have heard how he fought the British flotilla on Lake Champlain? An officer who was there told me that he never saw such fighting. He was outnumbered and beaten, but he would not strike his flag—driving his galleys ashore and setting them on fire, in spite of all Carleton could do. He certainly is a terrible fighter."

"I had not heard so much of that," returned Pemberton, "but I had from an eye-witness an account of his conduct in those two battles near Saratoga. He says Arnold seemed almost crazy with daring, and yet all his orders proved his sanity. He never saw anything like it. The men caught the contagion of his stormy madness, and followed him even up to the muzzles of the British cannon. He shouted, he stormed, he raged like a lion, he plunged into the hottest of the fire, and at last absolutely tried to force his horse into the enemy's entrenchments. In fact, he won Saratoga."

"It seems to me, Arthur, that even the money value of that capture of Burgoyne and his army might be put at a pretty high figure?"

"No doubt about that, but the States are too poor at present to pay for such actions in money, even in Continental money. Arnold and all the rest of you must perforce take your pay in Glory. It cannot be helped, Phil; I am sorry for it, but it cannot be helped."

"I, for one, do not complain," replied Morris. "To be sure I would like to get enough to live decently on. But I am a young man, and unmarried. I have no wife and children starving and freezing at home. Oh, Arthur, if Congress, or the States, could do a little for thousands of the officers and the men who are situated as I have described, it would be both right and politic."

"My efforts shall never be wanting, Phil. You know that of what money I can myself control, I give freely."

"I know you do, Arthur."

"And yet, Phil, so unhappy are the times, that a violent and ignorant party among our citizens, as you may have heard, doubt my patriotism, my devotion to the Cause."

"I came mainly to speak to you about that, but the sight of Arnold turned my thoughts into another channel. Is there any danger of an outbreak?"

"Not against me, or any of the more moderate men. But from what I hear, Lawyer Wilson may be attacked at any moment. The City Troop have been ordered to hold themselves in readiness, and a number of Wilson's friends, myself included, have agreed to aid in the defence of his house if assaulted."

"You may count me in—and McLane," replied the

lieutenant warmly. "Oh that we had our own troop here—would we not sweep these vermin, if they come out of their holes. But why do they make this special tilt at Wilson, he is one of the best lawyers you have."

"You know he defended Roberts and Carlisle, who were convicted of treason."

"But they were convicted, and hung besides. Did not that satisfy them?"

"No. They seem to think that it was even treasonable in a lawyer to defend them, as if it were not a lawyer's business to defend, if need be, the most wretched murderer! But Wilson said, and he really believes besides, that they were not legally guilty of treason."

"I don't agree with him," said Morris. "But we are fighting to make this a free country, and what kind of a free country would that be, where men could not safely differ in opinion?"

"Wilson also defended those merchants who would not conform to the established scale of prices."

"Well, if he has violated the laws, let them punish him according to the laws. But I am opposed to this mob-rule, to the death."

"And I also," said Pemberton. "It is one of our greatest dangers. I hope it will be trodden out at once wherever it shows its snake-like head."

"I must go and tell McLane about this," said Morris, rising, for he had taken a seat on the porch during this conversation.

"Come and take dinner with us, Phil; you know we are always glad to see you."

"I will—or else early in the evening. How is the beautiful Isabella?"

"You mean, I suppose, the adorable Helen?" replied Pemberton, with a smile. "She is as beautiful and bewitching as ever. Phil"—in a low voice—"I am glad to find you are growing more sensible. If you cannot have a woman as your wife, then have her as your friend."

"Arth—old boy," replied Philip, in the same low tone, but his voice quivered with its earnestness, "did you ever know me to give up anything, while there was still the faintest hope? I may alter my plans, but I never alter my purpose. There is no other woman on the wide earth, so far as I am concerned, save Helen Graham."

Pemberton shook his head sadly, as his friend walked slowly away. He had supposed, from the more subdued and sensible manner in which Philip had behaved of late, that he had abandoned all hope of winning Helen. But it seemed that he still loved her with the same intensity as before—and only waited a favorable opportunity to press his suit. Whether Helen had been deceived as well as himself, Pemberton could not tell from her behaviour, which was always exceedingly kind and friendly to Philip.

Our own opinion is that she was not very greatly deceived. Women as keen-witted as Helen, are not apt to be deceived in matters of that character. But she was very much pleased nevertheless with the change in the Lieutenant's manner. She wished him for a friend, if she did not wish him for a lover. What she might have wished, if she had never seen André, it is impossible to say.

CHAPTER II.

A CHARM.

How curious that a few square yards of bunting
Should have so great a charm!

EARLY that evening, Philip came according to promise. But he had scarcely spoken to the family circle, which he found gathered in the parlor, when Foxey came rushing in, wild with terror.

"Oh, Mas' Arth—dey're comin', dey're comin'!" cried he.

"Who is coming, Fox?" asked Mrs. Pemberton, calmly.

"De mob—de wild mob. Dey had a meetin' out Arch Street 'bove Fift. Gen'. Arnol' tried to swade 'em to 'sperse—but dey flung stones at de Gen'ral, and made him run 'way. And now dey're 'bout marchin' down into de town."

Pemberton started up. "I do not think they mean to attack us, mother; but I will wait and see. If they pass us, I shall hurry out through the garden to Wilson's—for probably they are going there. Where are you bound, Philip?"

"Around to the rendezvous of the City Troop.. If we can get a dozen together, I think it will be enough at least to make a diversion. We shall pass here first. Had you not better close up everything in front, Aunt Rachel?"

"What! like convicts, that fear the constable?" exclaimed Mrs. Pemberton, rising majestically from her seat. "Fox, light every lamp and candle in the rooms in the front part of the house. And, girls, I intend going out into the porch to see what these men look like. Will you come out with me? Do not if you think there is any danger."

"Of course, Mrs. Pemberton, we will go with you," replied the two ladies, almost in a breath. "It is the very thing to do, if you apprehend an attack, to meet it at the threshold," said Isabella proudly.

"Yes, as father used to say, always 'face the music.' Let us look these curs in the eye," added Helen haughtily.

Morris looked at Pemberton. It was a glance of interrogation.

"I think the ladies are right, Phil. And bad as mobs are, they cannot get up a mob in Philadelphia, which will harm, or even insult, a woman."

"Then I'm off," said Morris, hastening out of the front door.

By the time Fox had lit up the front rooms, and the ladies had donned their shawls, the noise of the mob could be distinctly heard coming down the street. It was a low, dull roar, as of an approaching tornado.

Mrs. Pemberton and her two aids-de-camp—as Helen laughingly described her sister and herself afterwards—threw wide open the front door, and took their station in the porch, just before the head of the mob reached the house. All the other houses were dark, and tightly closed in front; and the mob, as they came up, were evidently surprised at the festive appearance Mrs. Pemberton's mansion presented, and at the presence of the three ladies on the porch. But they marched along—several hundred silent men, armed with muskets, and dragging two cannon, leading the van; and behind them a noisy, swearing multitude, unarmed save with stones and clubs.

It was evident at once from the passing of the front ranks, that no harm was intended to the Pembertons, unless the breaking of the front windows with stones might be called such. But not a stone was thrown; and when the procession had about half passed, to Mrs. Pemberton's excessive surprise, she saw many eyes cast upward, and then heard a rough voice shout:

"There cheers for the Rattlesnake Flag!" which were given with a will.

"What does it all mean?" said she to Isabella. "Is it possible that old affair is not forgotten yet?"

The young ladies exchanged glances, but said nothing. The roof over the porch prevented them from seeing what was going on above, but they had a strong conviction of what was really transpiring. For Foxey, in his anxiety for the safety of the dwelling and its inmates, had gone up-stairs, and was waving the Rattlesnake Flag as a charm and protection from one of the upper windows.

CHAPTER III.

THE MOB.

> A mob—a riotous, disorderly mob!
> I argue not with men in such a mood,
> Save with the ball and bayonet.

No sooner had Pemberton ascertained that the front ranks of the mob had passed the house, than picking up his hat and cane, he ran rapidly down the garden, and thence to Mr. Wilson's, at the corner of Walnut and Third streets. The mob had not turned into Third street, as he feared, but had gone down to Second, as if to disguise the object they had in view.

At the door of Mr. Wilson's house a number of gentlemen were standing, listening and watching—men of intelligence and high position, who did not choose to see Liberty stricken down in the home of its professed friends. Among the twenty or more thus gathered, were some who held commissions in the Continental army, such as Captains McLane and Campbell, Colonel Grayson and General Mifflin.

Soon they heard the roar of the mob, as it turned up Walnut from Second, and came directly on toward the house. Now the previously silent and armed men began to shout, crying out, "Death to Traitors! Death to all Tories!"

The gentlemen at once retired within the house, and barricaded the doors. The lower windows were closed tight with shutters, but you could see from the street that the second and third story windows were open.

"Bring out that old Tory, Jim Wilson!" shouted one, who appeared to be the leader of the mob. "Bring him out, I say—or your blood be upon your own heads!"

A clear, ringing voice from the house replied—no one ever knew afterwards whose voice it was—"Let all men who love the laws of the land, and would not suffer harm, retire from before this house, which is James Wilson's castle. If they will not, their blood be upon their own heads!"

The words were hardly out of the speaker's mouth, before a shot from some rash hand had entered the second story window whence the voice proceeded. And immediately, like an echo, came the report of one musket from the same window, followed by a shriek from a man who stood near the leader of the rioters, as he threw up his hands, and fell to the ground mortally wounded.

At this, there was a volley from the mob, answered by a return volley from the house. The contest had fairly begun.

"Bring up the cannon!" shouted various voices. But this was not easily done; for the fire of the besieged—and they were good marksmen, and the distance was short—told fearfully upon those who rushed to the ropes of the cannon in response. And soon the middle of the street, within musket reach of the windows, was entirely cleared; the mob clustering in a line on the same side of the street as the house, where it was difficult to aim at them.

But, before many minutes, a party of the rioters, headed by two men with sledge-hammers, made a rush for the door of the dwelling. Here it was impossible for those above to harm them, except by greatly exposing their own persons.

"Thud!—thud!"—went the heavy sledges—soon followed by a sharp crash, as one of the panels of the door was stove in. But the moment the panel gave way, the besieged fired a volley from the entry through the opening, and the two sledgemen staggered back and fell dead on the pavement.

But the contest probably would have gone hard with the defenders of the house, if at this moment a cry of "the horse! the horse!" had not been heard from the rear of the mob; and supposing a whole troop was upon them, the greater part of the rioters—armed men and all—fled in every direction, carrying off their wounded; while up swept, through the dark, like a very small tornado, just nine horsemen. Morris had found these at their quarters, and, hearing the firing, they had concluded to risk an attack, without waiting for any more of their number. As it turned out, these were sufficient; though others, in a short time, came riding in, and the city was put under regular patrol.

Of the defenders of the house—which was called ever afterwards, half in jest and half in earnest, Fort Wilson—one, Captain Campbell, was killed, and several were wounded. Of the rioters, five certainly were killed, and a large number wounded. But of course the number of the latter could never be ascertained—as they had no desire to incur in addition the dangers of a criminal prosecution.

When Pemberton returned home, half-an-hour afterward, he found his mother and the young ladies anxiously awaiting him.

"I am all safe, mother," said he, as he entered the room.

"God be thanked!" exclaimed Mrs. Pemberton, as she put her arms around his neck and kissed him. "And I hope every other mother can say that to-night."

Isabella also came up and kissed him. And then Helen. The excitement and agitation of the moment overpowered their usual ceremonious behavior. It seemed very natural to both of them to do this, and even Mrs. Pemberton, decorous to the last degree, did not open her grave eyes.

Pemberton related what had taken place, a great deal of which they had already surmised from the discharges of musketry, which they had plainly heard.

"Ah, my son," said his mother, "this is what I feared, as the result of throwing off their dutiful allegiance to their King. It is but a step from Rebellion to the Mob."

"Well, we have given King Mob a pretty good lesson to-night," replied Pemberton proudly. "I think it will be a good while before another mob raises its foul head in Philadelphia."

"I hope so," rejoined his mother, shaking her head despondingly; "but this Rebellion began in a mob and, if it succeeds, it will be the triumph of a mob."

"Yes," said Helen, "and then it will die of a mob. Uncle once said that if the King would but withdraw his armies, the Rebellion would fall to pieces of itself."

"I wish he would only try the experiment," replied Pemberton. "Come, Helen, that is a ground we both can meet on."

"I think it is time we were all going to bed, girls," said Mrs. Pemberton. "You must take care of your roses;" and, obedient to her signal, they followed her out of the room. Isabella having to come back again for a moment, however, for her handkerchief—and a good-night kiss.

Pemberton walked the floor for a full hour afterwards. He was a sincere lover of his country, and, in the aid he had given the Rebellion, had no private ends to gratify. Even his ambition was in no wise enlisted in the success of the American cause. The army was not particularly to his taste, even if he had not been debarred from it by his mother's prayers. And for political and civil honors he also cared but little. He valued too highly the precious gifts which generally have to be sacrificed upon the shrine of Ambition, by those who would succeed in her service:

perfect independence of thought, perfect honesty and sincerity of speech and action.

Besides, he was just the opposite of a fanatic and bigot. He always saw his opponent's view of a question quite as clearly as his own. Therefore he could not help laying himself open continually to the suspicions of men of smaller, narrower minds. He was an earnest Whig, but he understood clearly how another man could be an equally earnest, equally honest Tory. And though he was a Whig, he did not blind himself to the force of the arguments that were urged on the opposite side.

Now here was this Mob. How much truth was there in what his mother and Helen had said? Could the country hold together, and establish a great Empire—an Empire without an Emperor—if the armies of the United States should prove successful? They had not been able as yet to adopt the Articles of Confederation, although reported two years previously—and even these Articles were lacking in those powers necessary to the very existence of a government. No tax could be laid, or money appropriated, without the consent of nine out of the thirteen States. What could such a Confederation, even if agreed upon, amount to?

Then again, what would this one-sided French doctrine of Equality—unbalanced by the equally true doctrine of Inequality—lead to? Mob Law? Perhaps; though the natural instinct of self-preservation in the Community, might be relied upon to meet and check that.

But, carrying out the idea of Equality, and coupling with it the kindred doctrine of the absolute right of the Majority to rule—where would that lead? Where could it lead, but to the making the ignorant and uncultivated classes the real and legal rulers of the land, who would hold that they had the right to decide all questions, political, moral and religious; and that by their decision, the wiser and more cultivated classes should abide. It was a dark picture of a future, when men of ability and culture—the natural and God-given leaders of the nation—should be thrust aside from all places of trust and power, to make room for a set of unprincipled Demagogues, who would flatter the people, crying *Vox Populi vox Dei*, as his flatterers cried out to King Herod, careless that the same result would follow, and this many-headed Herod also be eaten to death by worms.

Still, he saw nothing else to be done, than to go forward. Not exultingly, like many, but still earnestly and hopefully. Giving what influence he had to the adoption of such energetic measures as were absolutely necessary to the success of the war, while he also gave his influence to the support of those great principles of Individual Freedom, without the establishment of which, the success of the States would neither be conducive to their own progress in civilization, nor to that of the world at large.

And having come to this conclusion, Pemberton looked at his watch, saw that it was an hour later than his usual bed-time, dismissed the subject from his mind, and occupying its place with the more agreeable thought of Isabella Graham, retired to his room, and to rest.

CHAPTER IV.

THE SPY.

> "This concurrence,
> This opportunity, is in our favor,
> And all advantages in war are lawful;
> We take what offers without questioning."—*Wallenstein.*

It was several weeks after the events related in our last chapter, when a young woman called one morning at Mrs. Pemberton's, and asked to see Miss Helen Graham for a few minutes at the door. Helen went out, and inquired as to her business.

"If you are Miss Hilen Graham," said the young woman, "Mrs. Malone wished me to stop and inquire whether your leddyship wanted any things washed yet this week?"

The woman spoke with a slight Irish accent, but was apparently a native of the colony.

"I have a few handkerchiefs and collars for her," replied Helen. "Come up-stairs with me, and I will give them to you."

The woman followed Helen up into her room—closing the door of the chamber after her as she entered; and Helen soon made up a small bundle, and handed it to her.

As the woman took the bundle, she handed Helen, in return, a small sealed note, the familiar handwriting of whose address caused a glow to spread instantly over her features.

"I will wait a moment," said the woman, with a half smile, turning delicately away, and gazing out of the window.

The note ran thus:—

"MY SWEETEST AND DEAREST—

"You may trust the bearer of this, who is called Captain Fanny, implicitly. She has a message for you. I am not able, for it would not be wise, to write much relative to our private affairs—for this letter may perhaps be read by strangers. I am very well, however—and hope you will be able to assure me, in return, that the dearest girl in the world is as well as she is beautiful. Believe me ever and eternally your own A."

"Who gave you this?" said Helen, after thrusting the note into her bosom—looking attentively into the woman's face.

"Captain Andry"—in a low voice.

"The note you gave me speaks of a Captain Fanny."

"I am her."

"A captain?"

"They call me captain," replied the woman, laughing. "I care not."

"Are you a spy?" whispered Helen, while her face whitened.

"I am a spy," returned the woman carelessly. "Anything to aid a good cause, your leddyship knows."

"You have a message for me?"

"I have. Will your leddyship lock the door?"

Helen did so—and from a pocket under her skirt, the woman produced a medium-sized pistol. Helen saw it was primed, and ready for use. Her visitor then by a considerable exertion of strength, unscrewed the barrel about the middle, and took from it a long slug. This also unscrewed, and disclosed a cavity which was filled with a roll of thin paper, closely written in a very small but clear handwriting.

"You see," said the woman, "if I am taken, or fear

being taken, if I can only git a chance to discharge my pistol, they may search me after that as much as they plase."

Helen took the paper. "Take a seat," said she, "till I have time to glance over it."

While Helen is glancing over her note, let us say a word or two relative to her visitor. In the first place, Captain Fanny—though Helen did not know it, and never knew it—was not a woman, but a man. Francis Malone was one of those curious beings, who delight in disguises, merely for the sake of the disguise and the deception. As he was rather under the usual size, and slightly though strongly made, with a frame tough and elastic as whalebone, and as he also was naturally almost destitute of a beard, his most frequent disguise was that of a woman.

He was well-looking, with blue eyes and sandy hair, and was thus enabled to personate not only a woman, but a young and pretty one. Many were the flirtations which he had indulged in when thus disguised, and great was the help which his feminine attire afforded him in his frequent journeys between the British and the Continental camps. A perfect mimic, and able to imitate the feminine voice and characteristics as one to the manner born, Fanny Malone—or Captain Fanny, as the supposed woman was frequently termed—was a universal favorite. She even stood high among the rude soldiery of both camps, for, as may be surmised, however she might flirt, her virtue was above suspicion.

But not only did she deceive the soldiers, Captain Fanny also deceived the generals. All thought to the last that she was a woman. Washington, Sir William Howe, Sir Henry Clinton, and their respective officers attached to the secret service, were all deceived in this respect. And there is no doubt that André was also. For Fanny never forgot herself—and her acting was perfect.

But even more curious still, Captain Fanny deceived both parties as to her integrity. She professed the utmost loyalty to one side, the most devoted patriotism to the other; but the truth was, she served and betrayed both alike, except as personal preferences sometimes influenced her actions.

In fact, Francis Malone was one of those men who cared nothing for the principles involved in the contest. He did not care a particle which army succeeded. His only preference was that the war should go on; for he liked the business of a spy in itself, and he found it very profitable. The States might be poor, but Washington never thought of offering him Continental money. The British generals had plenty of gold, and they paid liberally. He evidently thought the whole contest a stupendous joke; and he fooled each party to the top of his humor.

But how could he do this? By never betraying any great secret of either party, and by conveying to each respectively a large amount of second-rate and yet useful information. It required adroitness; he gloried in possessing it. It required an infinite amount of plausible lying; he had not the least regard for veracity. And any one who has had experience of such a natural liar, knows that it is almost impossible to convict a man of falsehood, who never scruples to utter not only the first lie, but one hundred more, if necessary, to substantiate that first.

Every case has its exceptions. Francis Malone had his. He had no comprehension of great principles; but he had a keen sense of gratitude. In certain cases where an important favor had been done him, the Captain was the soul of truth and honor. He would not deceive nor betray his benefactor, while he would serve him to the utmost of his power. This was Captain Fanny's sound point amid so much rottenness, if we may call that rottenness which, from the Captain's point of view, was merely harmless and profitable joking with a pack of lunatics, who had gone crazy to the point of fighting, upon a question of no earthly consequence whatever.

When Helen had finished the reading of this second and more important letter, she placed it carefully in a small drawer, under lock and key, and turned again to her visitor.

"I am told that you can be trusted with perfect confidence?"

"It is so. I shall niver betray Captain Andry. Or the Cause," added she.

"Have you known Captain André long?"

"No; only a short time."

"I thought you spoke as if you knew him well." Helen was not in the least suspicious, but something in the tone with which André's name had been mentioned, had caught her ear as implying a certain warmth of feeling.

"Captain Andry once did us a great favor; and I niver forgit favors. Did you ever hear him tell of a boy he saved from Captain Cunningham's clutches?"

"The boy who was captured with a party of rebel soldiers?"

"The same boy. He was my brither, my leddy. I, nor none of us, will ever forgit it. Niver!"

Helen's face lightened. "I feel we may trust you entirely, my good girl," said she.

"To the black death!" replied Captain Fanny earnestly.

"I cannot answer this letter at once. Suppose you bring home those articles in three or four days. Ask to see me. Could I find you at the washerwoman's, if I wanted you?"

"Yes. I'm boarding there. Ask for Mr. Malone, ef I don't come to the door."

"Mr. Malone?"

"Yes; I dress up like a man ginerally in Philadelfy."

"It must be very unpleasant to you."

"Yes, it is rather onpleasant, but I'm used to it. I think, my leddy, when you see me, you'll own I am a pretty nate-looking boy."

"I think you would be very good-looking—for a man; for you are really quite a pretty girl."

Captain Fanny laughed—"So the soldiers often tell me."

"You should be very careful how you trust yourself about the camps," said Helen gravely, with a world of warning and caution in her tones.

"I am, my leddy, very careful indeed. We poor girls haven't much but our repitation, and when that's gone, there's nothing lift," and the girl put a corner of her check apron to her face, to hide, as Helen thought, her modest blushes—but really to conceal her smiling, for the whole scene was perfectly delightful to Captain Fanny.

Fanny then took up the bundle, and making a very excellent curtsey indeed as she left the room, took her way down stairs, and out of the house.

Helen watched at the head of the stairs, until she heard the front door close upon her visitor, and then returned to her room. Locking the door, and unlocking the drawer, she took from it André's letter. But before she set herself to giving it another and more careful perusal, she took the first note from her bosom, and having read and re-read that, and pressed it again and again to her lips, in a fashion not uncommon with very impassioned lovers, she placed it in a box, sweetly scented, among a number of others which evidently were written in the same graceful hand.

The other and longer letter, which she then sat down to consider, read as follows:—

"Light of my eyes, will you pardon me for writing you a mere business letter? But it is in a case of the utmost importance to the good cause. We are in some perplexity, and I thought perhaps you could aid us. Sir H. C. has recently received several anonymous letters from P.— and he is very anxious to know who is the writer. All the signs point to one man. You remember the name of that girl you told me you disliked so at Bethlehem. If he is the man, he is worth winning back to his allegiance. He may become perhaps a second General Monk, and put an end to this unhappy war between brethren. Monk was made Duke of Albemarle. The man, or men, who can restore peace and union to the Kingdom, shall surely not miss of their reward. The Colonies shall have a Parliament like England, including a House of Lords, men ennobled for their services to the King; and a Viceroy, with kingly state. You need not hesitate to name these rewards, if he is the man—nor he to name them in confidence to others. At the first great success of the King's arms, this plan will be announced. Everything will be granted to the Colonies but Independence. Everything must be done to keep the Kingdom united, and to defeat Roman Catholic France, the great foe of England and the Protestant faith.

"Sweet, you know I am ambitious—but it is not for myself alone—it is for you also, my peerless one! Perhaps I may yet take my seat in an American House of Lords, and be able to place a coronet on your beautiful brow. What is life, without some great aim? Of course we may fail—but life is dignified and ennobled, even if Fame and Station are not won.

"I know you will as gladly aid in the work, as take your part in the reward—and enjoy the reward the more, because you have thus aided in achieving it.

"I would not expose you to danger, but there can be no risk for you, if you are prudent—and, at the very worst, there is only the risk of your being sent into our lines, where you would find a hearty welcome from all loyal souls—to say nothing of my private longing to see you.

"As to the rightfulness of a man's coming back to his allegiance, who can doubt it? General Charles Lee went over from the King's service to the rebels, on condition that they should make up the loss of his commission to him; and their Congress did it, and made him next highest to Washington. If a loyal man can thus become a rebel, how much more rightfully can a repentant rebel become loyal! These and other considerations, will doubtless occur to your own quick wit—as also the way in which you had better approach the man. If it is the one I suppose, in writing me call him Vasa. Answer by the bearer as soon as convenient. Use no more names in writing than are absolutely necessary—though our precautions against discovery are I think admirable. Your loving A.

"Burn this letter as soon as you have carefully read it. Of course speak of it to no one. Be wise as a serpent, as you are innocent as a dove. Again farewell, sweetest and dearest!"

Three times did Helen peruse this letter, until every line and word were fully impressed upon her memory. Then ordering a light to be brought up, which she was in the habit of doing, for sealing-wax was then commonly used in sealing letters, and she had several correspondents among her old school-mates in various parts of the country, she committed the hazardous epistle to the flames.

This done, Helen sat down to think. The mission entrusted to her was not entirely pleasant, for it involved secrecy and finesse, and her natural disposition was so frank and open, that anything that savored of concealment was distasteful to her. But not for a moment did she hesitate on that account. Neither did a thought of there being anything wrong in the trust confided to her, take definite shape in her mind. She accepted it just in the light that her lover had presented it: a repentant man was anxious to return to his duty, a distracted kingdom was to be reunited on liberal terms, the sacred cause of Protestantism was to be maintained against its ancient enemy. That in aiding and encouraging a repentant rebel to return to his duty to his King, she would be acting a dishonorable part, was an idea that never even entered her mind. There might be some risk in doing so, as she might thus incur the enmity of bad or misguided men, but Danger went often in this world hand in hand with Duty.

Then she should be aiding her lover in his plans, his duties, his ambitions; and her eyes kindled, and her cheeks glowed. This consideration would have swept away any small conscientious obstacles, if such there were. And, besides, she had her own ambition. She would rather, of course, marry John André, plain captain though he was, than a King's son; but still she fully sympathized with his craving for distinction and glory. That thirst for Fame which is "the *last* infirmity of noble minds," she was not above, for him, however little comparatively she cherished it for herself. To see him take that high place to which his natural make and qualities entitled him, and she by his side, a coronet, perhaps, as he had said, encircling her brow, this would be worth toiling and striving for indeed! The narrow walls of Helen's chamber, as she thus mused, expanded into a palace, the plain Quaker furniture changed into costly mirrors, and silken curtains, and paintings and statues, and through lofty colonnades she moved in queenly attire, and her name was Helen André!

"Why, Helen, where have you been all this while? Dinner is almost ready. I thought you were out, and have been sitting in the parlor waiting for you to come in."

Helen came back to her ordinary life with a start, as Isabella entered and thus accosted her. "I have been building castles in Spain, Sis. Pleasant work, is it not?"

"I think it quite excusable in your circumstances, pretty one," replied her sister lovingly. "I wish this hateful war were over, if only for your sake, *ma belle Helene*. But, come, let us go down to dinner."

Helen was rather absent-minded the remainder of that day. One question that she put to Pemberton may show us, however, where her straying thoughts were.

"Arthur, was not General Lee an officer in the British service, before he took up arms under the Colonies, against the King?"

"He was."

"Did not Congress agree to compensate him for his pecuniary loss in making the change?"

"They did."

"Was it honorable in him and them?"

"What's up now?" said Pemberton smiling. "I have not heard you talk so much politics for six months."

"I am not talking politics, Arthur; I am simply asking for information."

"Well, if you mean to ask whether I consider Lee acted honorably in coming over to us, I answer, that I do not suppose the mere fact of entering into the King's service binds a man forever after, so that he can never again have a mind and judgment of his own. Lee thought the mother country wrong, and he preferred to fight on the side of the Colonies. Therefore he resigned his commission, gave up his half-pay, and was paid in return thirty thousand dollars, and made second in command in the Continental army. It strikes me that it was all plain sailing."

"Yes—but it seems he really lost nothing by the transaction."

"I, myself," said Pemberton, "would have liked the look of the thing better, if he had made no stipulations with Congress; but this, after all, perhaps, is a mere matter of taste."

"Did not the British officers call him a traitor?"

"Yes—but that charge would not hold. For, when they had him a prisoner, they forbore to press it. You see, Helen, the point was this—he resigned his commission and gave up his pay, before taking service with us. If he had not, I would not have given much for his life."

"I think that shows the scrupulous care with which the King's officers discriminate in all cases involving military honor," said Helen. "And this was a case in which a loyal gentleman had become a rebel."

"It certainly was a proof of the good sense of the British officers, Helen. And I think this is a ground that we can both unite on. You know I dislike to differ with you, *ma belle Helene.*"

"And I with you, Arthur. I don't know what I would not give, if you only thought in this matter as I do. And there is Bella, too"—and Helen put her handkerchief to her eyes, for she indeed felt very sadly about it at times.

"No matter, Helen, sweet," said Isabella, passing her arm around her and kissing her; "all will come right, some time. And if we do not see alike in this matter, that is no reason why Arthur and I should not love you and John better than anybody else in the wide world."

And Helen returned the warm, sisterly kiss, and was quieted for the time, if not entirely comforted.

CHAPTER V.

HELEN AND ARNOLD.

Fair lady, you are bold; and, by Saint Judas,
You need be bold as she who slew Marat,
To come on such an errand.

In a room on the first floor of his handsome house in Market Street, the same room in which Isabella had obtained the pass from Sir William Howe—and which had been elegantly fitted up for his office and library—sat General Benedict Arnold.

Affairs had not improved with General Arnold since his conversation with Mr. Pemberton. Congress had done as he had been forewarned—had refused to adopt the favorable report of its own investigating committee, and had directed the Commander-in-Chief to institute a Court Martial. Arnold's marriage, however, already arranged for, had gone on. The beautiful and charming Margaret Shippen, a daughter of one of the best families in the State, had become his wife. That he loved her with all the ardor of his passionate nature, there is no reason to doubt. And she loved and admired him—partly for himself, and partly for his high position and his military fame. The brave to the end of time will always be admired by the fair.

Arnold had rented one of the largest and handsomest houses in the city, had married a wife accustomed from her earliest years to luxury and expense, and was now living on intimate terms with the highest and most extravagant circles of the metropolis.

And he had no money, save his little stipend of pay, and the uncertain profits of various mercantile speculations, which it was scarcely consistent with his military position to have anything to do with.

It seemed in the very nature of the man to live showily and extravagantly, as if he would dazzle the eyes of men with his prodigality, as he had dazzled their imaginations with his dauntless and almost superhuman courage.

But he had no money.

Bills and impatient creditors came pouring in upon him. He put them off with stories of his large claims upon Congress, which when settled would afford him the means of freeing himself from debt. But Congress turned a deaf ear to his constant importunities—would not even take any definite action upon his claims.

As Arnold sat this day in his study, and mused upon these things, his thoughts, for a newly-made bridegroom, were dismal enough.

"Was it for this he had exposed his life on countless occasions—stormed the barriers of Quebec, fought his galleys on the lake, faced the leaden storms and very whirlwind of war at Bemis's Heights? Granting that he had been careless in his accounts, had made entries perhaps not entirely justifiable—he had given also of his own services with a careless and lavish hand. Similar services often had been recompensed by kings, with the gifts of titles and large estates—but Congress haggled over a few paltry thousands, in the sum which was due him."

And then his thoughts reverted to those promotions of

others over his head, which always inflamed his proud spirit to the utmost. St. Clair—what had St. Clair done? Stirling—what had he done? that they should be preferred before him. What had any of them done, to entitle them to stand even upon his level?

A gentle tap was heard at the door. "Come in!" he cried, without rising from his seat.

The door opened. "I called to see Mrs. Arnold, General, and finding she was not in, concluded to wait for her a little while. The servant said you were in the library, and I had the unpardonable assurance, you see, to beard the lion in his den."

It was Helen Graham that spoke, and at the sight of her, the General sprang up, and gallantly handed her to a chair. Helen had been one of the bridesmaids at the wedding, being on quite familiar terms with Miss Shippen.

"My dear Miss Helen, I am delighted to see you," said Arnold. "It was like you to drop in upon me here, and cheer me up a little."

"Cheer you up!" replied Helen, opening her eyes as if wonder-stricken. "What treason to love and the honeymoon!"

"Ah, Miss Helen, you ladies think that love is all. But here am I, a disabled soldier, which is bad enough—awaiting a Court Martial, not from the red-coats, which would be very natural, one would think, considering the injury I have done them, but from my own ungrateful countrymen."

Arnold's face flushed—he could not talk calmly upon this subject even to a lady, nor avoid talking upon it.

"Perhaps if you had been serving the King, instead of the Colonies, you would have experienced different treatment," rejoined Helen.

"I have heard that you were a little of a Tory, Miss Helen."

"If you mean by a Tory, a loyal woman, I am all a Tory, General. And I only regret that so brave a man as you are is not also on the right side."

"I suppose it would be a good deal better for me financially, if I were," replied the General bitterly. "I do not think any government on earth, with the exception of this Rump Congress, would have the meanness to treat a faithful soldier as I have been treated."

"Why then do you submit to it?" asked Helen, lowering her voice. "You know how a Rump Parliament was adroitly overturned by a man not so brave and not more influential than you. Why do you not give peace to this distracted country, preserve the Kingdom, and win for yourself the most glorious name on this American Continent? I ask you why?"

Arnold gazed intently at her for a moment without replying. He seemed to feel that the conversation had entered upon dangerous ground. He knew what in his madness he had already done, and he knew not whether this was a simple, natural conversation, or a lure. If the latter, who was the fowler, and on which side of the contest did he stand?

Opening a drawer in the table by his side, he took from it a large, horseman's pistol. Then he fixed his eyes sternly on his visitor, and said in a cold, ominous voice:

"About a year ago, Miss Helen Graham, a man dared to talk to me, as you are talking now. Do you know the answer I made him? I said not a word. But I took out this pistol, cocked it as I do now, and levelled it directly at his forehead."

As Arnold said this he levelled the pistol at the smooth white brow of the woman before him. Helen's cheek paled, and her heart beat as if it must be heard, but she blenched not a hair's breadth from the line of the barrel, and her face assumed that firm, undaunted look which men of her race had worn in the stormy centuries before, in battle and on the scaffold.

Still holding the pistol thus pointed, and with his finger playing near the trigger, Arnold continued sternly:

"He soon understood that hint, and slunk from the room like a cowed spaniel."

"Indeed!" said Helen scornfully. "But he must have been of some common strain, and not a Graham. I really think I can see the ball in that pistol," and she leaned forward, and put one of her eyes to the terrible muzzle.

Arnold uncocked the weapon, and laid it deliberately back in the drawer. "Whatever else you may be, Miss Helen, at least you are no coward."

"Nor tattler either, if I am a woman. I remember well a story my father once told in my hearing. He said that when General Monk was meditating his great project—'honest George Monk,' he said the soldiers called him—his brother came to see him with a message from the King. 'Have you spoken to any one else on this subject?' inquired Monk. 'Only,' replied his brother, 'to your chaplain, in whom I know you have the greatest faith.' Monk said nothing, but it was enough; he listened no further to what his brother had to say, but changed the conversation to unimportant matters. That anecdote I shall never forget. If I had a message for the King, I should not prate about it even to his most trusted counsellor."

Arnold seemed lost in thought for a few moments. Then he said abruptly:

"Show me your papers."

"I have no papers. I have burned them, to avoid all risk—as I was ordered."

"Why should I trust you?"

"Because, in the first place, as you see, I am no coward."

"Good, so far; I hate cowards!"

"Secondly, because I am Helen Graham. And, thirdly," and her voice sunk to a whisper—while maiden modesty caused it to quiver as fear could not—"because I am the betrothed of Captain André."

"Enough!" said Arnold, drawing a deep breath. "I will not say as yet what I will, or what I will not do. I must take time to consider. That I am not pleased with the way things are going, every one may know. That this Congress is but little better than the Rump Parliament, many of our best officers do not hesitate to say. That the French Alliance is a deception and a snare, the whole country is beginning to believe. What a perfect farce that attack on Rhode Island was! The French are fools on land, and cowards at sea. But how to mend all this?—that is the question. If Congress should come to its senses, and resolve to do me justice, I should hate to kick out of the traces. But I will not serve men who seem to consider my most important services as worth no recompense. Such men are neither fit nor able to govern. It is my nature to seek the high rewards of life—and I will have them! If not from one set of men, then from another. But I heard the front door close just now—Mrs. Arnold must have come home."

The door of the library opened, and a very handsome woman entered—Tarleton said afterward, when she went to England, that she was the handsomest woman in England.

"And so, General, you are having a nice, cosey time with Miss Helen, are you?" cried Mrs. Arnold, in a lively tone. "I must say that I admire your taste."

"Yes, it is universally admitted now, Margery, that I have an admirable taste in women. Where have you been, Sweet?"

"Out shopping; buying a lot of trumpery, as you gentlemen say. You look rosy, Miss Helen. Has the General been complimenting you? Do not believe him—he is, like all military men, a sad deceiver."

"Oh, he has been very far from employing his time so pleasantly—to me—as that. We have had quite a serious talk, have we not, general?"

"Never had a more serious one in my life," replied Arnold.

"What! it is getting serious already, is it?" exclaimed the gay young bride. "Ah! General, I thought you promised me never to flirt any more."

"I don't know that I ever promised you anything of the kind, Margery," replied he, half smiling, half serious. "I think there was no necessity of my making such a promise. But as for you, my Bird of Paradise, what security have I that your heart will not fly away some day, and leave me forsaken and disconsolate?"

"Now, hear the General, Helen! You would not think from the way he talks, that half the young ladies in Philly were dying for him—and when I carried off the prize, could have stabbed me with their knitting needles."

And so the happy bride rattled on, until Helen, saying that she had stayed too long already, bade adieu, and took her departure.

And Helen never walked with a prouder and more queenly step than she did that day. She had done something, she thought, for a good cause; and more, she had done what it would please her lover well to hear. There could be little doubt but that Arnold was the author of those letters. If he were not, he was almost ready to enter into such a correspondence. Nothing but such a change in the action of Congress as was not at all probable, would prevent him, in case the Colonial cause grew no brighter, from gradually settling down upon the loyal side. And he might begin and inspire a defection as momentous in its results as that of General Monk, in the great contest between Charles the Second and the Long Parliament.

Of course I am picturing both Helen and André—and Arnold also—as they were, and in the light of their own feelings and convictions. I am not representing Helen as feeling upbraidings of conscience on account of her efforts to overthrow a cause which she believed to be unjust and wrong—simply because she felt no such upbraidings of conscience. On the contrary, she felt precisely as a young lady on the American side would have felt, who thought she could aid in bringing over to her own party some influential British general. Even were that general Sir Henry Clinton himself, and the result most disastrous to the royal arms, and he be rendering himself liable to the charge of treason, it is not to be supposed that she would suffer very greatly in her conscience on that account. In truth, it is probable that in such a very supposable case, the young "rebel" lady in question would rejoice even in proportion to the mischief she was able to work the enemy—and that her countrymen would hold her forever afterwards in high esteem, instead of in detestation.

In all such cases, everything depends upon the point of view. From Helen and André's point of view, the whole proceeding looked glorious and honorable. Arnold was a brand to be snatched from the rebel burning. And the result was to be Peace and the lasting Union of the British

Empire—on terms entirely satisfactory and honorable to the Colonies.

Of course, there was another side to the question—a very weighty and powerful, and, as it proved, the decisive side—but our concern is not with that, just at present.

CHAPTER VI.

CAPTAIN FANNY AGAIN.

> I serve both sides, and, serving both, am true
> To both, or neither, as it suits my mind.
> Enough for me to leave no careless clue
> That would betray me, floating in the wind.

HELEN had her reply, which was very adroitly and cautiously worded, so as not to compromise any one if it should fall into the wrong hands, fully prepared by the time Captain Fanny brought back her articles from the washerwoman. Fortunately, too, Isabella was out, Helen having been indisposed (to go out), in anticipation of this visit, for several days. She led the seeming young woman again up into her chamber, and locked the door, while Fanny took out the pistol, and inserted the little but important roll of tissue paper in the cavity of the leaden slug.

"Suppose they suspect you, and take the pistol from you?"

"I shall be on the look-out for the likes of that," replied Fanny. "There is no great harm done by shooting, you know, so you hit nobody. And a woman, besides, my leddy, is not expected sure to aim very straight." Fanny laughed, as if the bad shooting of the female sex was rather amusing to her.

"I don't know about that. I warrant I could hit you every time at twenty paces," said Helen, who, as is the fashion of high-spirited women, was never much disposed to hear her sex in any way disparaged.

"And sure I'm not the woman who'd let you try it," rejoined Fanny, "if they do call me Captain."

"That is a curious name for a woman, especially one so young and good-looking as you are," said Helen.

"Thanks, my leddy; but it's you who are the beautiful crathure. They call me Captain because—who is that?"

Pemberton's voice was heard in the entry. He was evidently going up to his room in company with another gentleman.

"Do you remember, Arth, that visit you had from a Quaker preacher?" said a loud voice, plainly heard through the door, followed by hearty laughter from both.

"It is Mr. Pemberton and Lieutenant Morris," said Helen in a low voice.

"I thought so. The Liftinant would know me at a glance. He must not see me here—neither him nor McLane. I will come either as a man or as an old woman, next time. Will you know me?"

"I think so."

"They have gone into the opposite room, I heard the door shut," said Fanny in a whisper. "Plaze look out, and see if the coast is clare."

Helen opened the door quietly; the loud conversation, accompanied with louder laughter, still continued in the opposite room. Helen beckoned to Fanny to come. But the two had just reached the head of the stairs, having closed the door behind them, when the door of Pemberton's chamber was opened quickly, and Morris came out, walking as if in a hurry.

"Beg your pardon, Miss Helen, Arthur said you had gone out," cried Philip, as he nearly ran against her. "But I am delighted to see you. Why, is that you, Fanny? What odd chance brought you here?" added he, evidently in very great surprise.

"And so you have a personal acquaintance with my washerwoman's servant?" said Helen, covering her confusion as best she might.

"Yes, Fanny and I are old acquaintances—are we not, Fanny?" returned Morris, gazing in perplexity from one to the other.

"Why, what is going on outside here?" cried Pemberton, opening the door of his room, which Morris had closed behind him. "I thought you had gone out with Bella, Helen?"

"But you see I have not," answered Helen, a little sharply. "Or else it is my wraith."

Fanny had not spoken; but now she said, "I have a little message for Mr. Morris, Miss Hilen; have you any objection to my giving it to him?"

"Not the least," replied Helen with dignity, as she swept back into her room.

Morris smiled. "Come in here, Captain," said he, opening the door of Pemberton's room again. "We can then sit down and talk at our leisure."

"I suppose you are rather surprised to see me here, Liftinant?" said Fanny, after they had entered.

"Well, rather!"

"I'm sure I could aisily explain matters," continued Fanny, with an almost imperceptible glance at Pemberton.

"I suppose you can," replied Morris. "Do not mind my friend Pemberton here, he is just as reliable as I am."

'I brought the beautiful leddy,'' said Fanny smiling, ''a letter from her lover in New York.''

Philip winced. ''From whom?''

''Captain Andry,'' said Fanny in a whisper. ''It's a mighty good thing to do, for it gives me the best of rasons to go back'ards and for'ards. An' it puts me in the way of picking up news. Did Captain McLane tell you what I told him—how the red-coats feared that the Spaniards would soon join us and the Frenchmen?''

''Yes, McLane told me. When do you go back to New York?''

''In a few days. I'm waitin' for Miss Hilen's letter to her swateheart. Will I bring it to you to rade before I go?''

''No!'' exclaimed Morris peremptorily, his face paling.

''I thought ye might be amused with it. His was mighty divarting readin'.''

''There is no need of my seeing the correspondence, Arthur—is there?'' said Morris, as if on second thought he was questioning what his duty as a Continental officer required.

''Not a particle, I think,'' replied Pemberton. ''Helen is not acquainted with any suspicious characters—and she could not tell André anything if she would, more than any common spy could pick up. Besides, lovers generally have more interesting matters than public affairs to write about.''

Morris leaned his head on his hand. All the life and spirit of half an hour before had gone out of him. He had half hoped that in André's absence Helen would gradually forget him; but here was proof that the love between the two was burning as warmly as ever. He gave a deep sigh.

''It would be very unpleasant to me, Arthur, to interfere in the least with Miss Helen's correspondence—and I shall have nothing to do with it. I shall leave it entirely to you. It is not a case that I can even trust myself to deal with. If you think there is any doubt as to its propriety, please consult McLane or Harry Lee. I am very sorry indeed that it has been my bad luck to know anything about it. I must go now, good-bye. Take care of yourself, Fanny." And Philip walked slowly out of the room—feeling ten years older than when he entered the house that morning.

"I will go also, if your honor has nothing further to say to me," said Fanny rising. "Shall I bring you the letters as I git them?"

"No—not unless I send you word to that effect. I suppose Captain McLane knows where you can be found?"

"Yes, the Captain always knows that. Good-mornin', your honor."

As Fanny went out, she carefully closed the door after her, and then tapped gently at the door of Helen's chamber. A low voice said, "Come in."

Fanny entered, closing this door also carefully behind her. Helen was seated on the opposite side of the room, gazing steadily out of the window.

"Miss Hilen."

"Well—have you betrayed me—and him?"

"I shall niver betray him—excipt to save him," replied Fanny in a very low but very earnest voice.

"What did you tell them?"

"I was forced to give them the shell, my leddy, in order to save the karnel."

"What did you tell them?"

"I told them, my leddy, I was carrying love-letters between you and the Captain."

"What else did you tell them?"

"Nothing."

"You read that letter you brought me—I mean the one in the pistol?"

"I did."

"You betrayed the substance of that letter?"

"Niver!" replied Fanny in an emphatic whisper.

Helen turned around, and looked her visitor straight in the eyes. "Do you mean to tell me," said she in a low but stern voice, "that you did not betray what was in that letter? Look me in the eyes, girl—and answer!"

Fanny looked her straight in the eyes. "By the blessed Virgin, the Holy Mother of God, and by God himself, I swear I did not!"

Helen walked to her jewel case, and took out a gold cross, set with pearls. "By this crucifix, on which the Saviour suffered, gemmed with these pearls, which are the tears of Mary, you swear it?"

"On that crucifix, wet with the tears of Mary, I swear it!" and Fanny reverently touched with her lips the cross.

"Enough. I believe you. A young girl like you could not perjure herself, and consign her soul to everlasting flames. But how is it you know Mr. Morris so well?"

"He thinks, my leddy, that I am a ribel spy. But I only use the ribels. Faith! I kin turn them round my finger."

"They will detect you some day."

"Perhaps. But I don't think they'll harm a woman very much, my leddy, if they do."

"You say that you had to tell them I was getting letters from Captain André."

"How could I hilp it? They knew that something was going on."

"It is not pleasant—but I suppose that must be borne.

And it may prevent suspicion of more serious matters. Fanny, you will not show that letter I have given you, on any pretence whatever? I would rather die than have you do it."

"And I would rather die than do it," replied Fanny vehemently. "Did I not tell you that Captain Andry had saved my brither from that horrid prison? And that I niver forgit a favor?—niver! Besides, my leddy—but perhaps you would not like to hear it."

"Tell me—what is it?"

"I am a poor young girl," said Fanny, and she absolutely seemed to blush—"and Captain Andry is a noble gintleman—and your lover—and may you be happy thegither in the long years to come. But I cannot spake it," said Fanny, hanging down her head.

"Go on, my good girl," said Helen, her curiosity now thoroughly excited.

"I was only goin' to say, my leddy—that as we see a star, sometimes, so bright and gran' above us, that we pick it out for our star, though we know the star cares naught for us—no, never hears or thinks of us poor mortals—so mysilf, a poor but honest girl, my leddy, gazes up at and almost worships one bright, gran' man! It cannot harm him—nor me—leddy. And do you think I would ever betray him?"

"My poor, good girl!" said Helen, sadly; "take this cross, and wear it, for his sake, and for mine."

"May the good heaven bless you," replied Fanny, hanging the cross by its ribbon around her neck, and concealing it in her bosom. "And now, if you will plaze write me a show letter, in case they should want to see what you have sint to the captain, I'll go."

"A good idea that, Fanny," said Helen. "And I will make it strong," thought she to herself, "so that if Mr.

Morris insists upon reading it, much pleasure may he derive from it."

When the letter was written and sealed—"strong" indeed in expressions of attachment, but without address or signature, save the single letter H.—Fanny concealed it in a twinkle about her person, manifesting considerable sleight of hand; and then bidding a respectful adieu, she quietly opened the door, and succeeded this time in descending the stairs and leaving the house, without interruption.

When Fanny got out into the street, she walked along in a very composed manner until she had reached a more unfrequented part of the town. Then she began to smile, and finally almost to shake with suppressed laughter. The whole affair had delighted Francis Malone—whom we have spoken of in the feminine gender, in accordance with his assumed name and character—as much as anything of the kind that had happened in the course of the war. It was just such occurrences as these, that lent to his occupation as a spy such zest and flavor. The last scene especially, in which he had gone out of his way to represent himself as enamored of Captain André, seemed to him one of the most felicitous strokes he had ever made.

"I clinched it then," said the captain to himself. "She'll never doubt me after that. It was jist the thing to go down with a woman;" and the captain laughed this time outright, so heartily that if any one had been near, he certainly would have thought him a little crazy. "She wouldn't have been quite satisfied with the truth, that Captain Andry did save little Barney from the jail—bless his ginerous heart for it!—and so I tipped her somethin' more in her woman's way. Oh, if I could only tell it—it's most too good to kape."

So Captain Fanny went home to her, or his, lodgings, in high good humor; while Helen sat in her chamber, till her sister came in, musing over all that had passed. Fanny's fervid admiration for André did not seem to her woman's heart at all wonderful—and perhaps if Fanny had really been a woman, it would have been neither curious nor improbable. As it was, it did a great deal to strengthen Helen's trust in Fanny's reliability. Helen was a keen-witted woman, and yet she had more faith in the sentimental falsehood that had been told her, than in the other true but more prosaic statements. She was right however in her reliance on Fanny's integrity, if she was wrong in crediting one of the principal reasons given for it.

As to the divulging of the fact that she was corresponding with André, she cared little that either Pemberton or Philip knew it. She had detected in the latter some growing germs of hope, and she was not sorry, both for his sake and her own, that they should be thus rudely crushed. She liked Morris very much, and now perhaps he would be satisfied to be to her as a loving friend and brother.

As to Pemberton, he knew through her sister of their engagement—for Bella never could keep anything long from Pemberton—and therefore would not wonder that André should seek to correspond with her. And both Pemberton and Morris could be depended upon to keep her secret from the outside world. So Helen came to the conclusion that things were not going on so far very badly, after all—and her countenance was quite serene and placid when she met Pemberton an hour or two after at the dinner table. Of course, neither of them—then or afterwards—made any allusion to what had occurred.

CHAPTER VII.

ARNOLD THE TRAITOR.

What am I doing worse
Than did famed Cæsar at the Rubicon,
When he the legions led against his country,
The which his country had deliver'd to him?
Give me his luck, *that other thing* I'll bear.—*Wallenstein.*

In the same library where the interview had taken place between Helen and General Arnold, the latter was again seated. He was writing a letter to a lady in Boston. It read as follows:

"About three months ago, I was informed that my late worthy friend, General Warren, who was killed at Bunker Hill, left his affairs unsettled; and that, after paying his debts, a very small matter, if anything, would remain for the education of his children, who, to my great surprise, I find have been entirely neglected by the State. Permit me to beg your continuing care of the daughter, and that you will at present take charge of the education of the son. I make no doubt that his relations will consent that he shall be under your care. My intention is to use my interest with Congress to provide for the family. If they decline it, I make no doubt of a handsome collection by private subscription. At all events, I will provide for them in a manner suitable to their birth, and the grateful sentiments I shall ever feel for the memory of my friend. I have sent to you by Mr. Hancock five hundred dollars for the present. I wish you to have Richard clothed handsomely, and sent to the best school in Boston. Any expense you are at, please call on me for, and it shall be paid with thanks. Yours, very respectfully,

"BENEDICT ARNOLD."

Having sealed the letter, and addressed it to Miss Mercy Scollay, of Boston, Massachusetts, Arnold leaned back in his chair. "It seems rather amusing for a man like me" —such was the tenor of his thoughts—"who can hardly find money enough to pay for his marketing and clothes, to be playing the benefactor, but I cannot let poor Warren's children suffer. Massachusetts, Republic-like, may forget her own gallant son; but I, his friend, cannot forget him; he, the chivalrous and gentle! Poor, noble Warren!"

The door of the library was opened, and a servant ushered in Mr. Pemberton.

"Good morning, Mr. Pemberton. Take a seat. I was just thinking about you, and how you came on with the collections."

"Not very well, General, I am sorry to say," replied Pemberton, taking a seat. "I drew up a paper as you suggested, and headed it with my own name for a hundred dollars, but beyond one or two little contributions, scarcely worth the going after, I have done nothing."

"That is strange," rejoined Arnold. "They all know that Dr. Warren behaved most gallantly, and was the life of the Cause in Boston for years."

"All admit that, but some say that it is the business of Massachusetts to care for his children, others say Congress should do it."

"And in the meantime, I suppose, his children must go naked. It is a mean piece of business, Mr. Pemberton."

"Others say they have given, and given, for one thing and another—this day for some one of their own citizens, then again in aid of the soldiers—until their funds and patience are alike exhausted. Besides, the Ball in honor of the French Alliance is to take place soon, and the subscription papers are out for that."

"D——n the French Alliance!" exclaimed Arnold fiercely. "I hate the French! When I was a boy I pulled trigger on one of them, because he had the impudence to come courting my sister Hannah. You'd have laughed to see him streaking out the window. I should think the cowardice or treachery those French monkeys showed at Newport, would be enough for men with a grain of common sense in their heads."

"I think you are unjust to our Allies, General," replied Pemberton earnestly; "the storm off Rhode Island was a bad one, as is shown by the fact that the English fleet also had to put back to New York."

"Yes, they might well do it, for their end was attained. And then to think of D'Estaing's impertinence, in putting out that proclamation to the French Canadians, to return to their allegiance to the French King. That shows which way the French ideas are drifting. But for my part, if we *must* have a foreign master, I would rather have old England, badly as she has acted, a hundred times over, than those slippery, frog-eating Frenchmen."

"It was, of course, an unwise and ill-considered step in D'Estaing—and the folly of it has no doubt been by this time represented to the government at Paris—but still, General, the French Alliance is a great thing for us. The British might be in this city now, but for that."

"Well, I have no great objection to it. But I think it more sensible to wait until the French really do something worthy all their display of ships and men, before getting up balls in their honor, with the money that should recompense our own brave soldiers."

"Have you sounded Congress relative to a pension for the Warrens?"

"Somewhat, and I think they will do something, or at least they say they will—though they are great liars, between you and me. They promise that the children shall have a Major General's half-pay, dating from the time of the Doctor's death."

"I thought they could not refuse."

"No—it wasn't likely they'd refuse. But they have a way of never doing things, that amounts to about the same thing. It's not very different whether you starve your dog to death, or knock him on the head at once."

"How about your own claims, General?"

"They are trying the starving plan on me. I have enemies in Congress, sir. I see them clearly through the grass, but the weather is too cold for them to bite. But they keep up a constant hissing, sir—a constant hissing. This Court Martial is their work, and it pleases them all the better that the exigencies of the service prevent its being held. Of course I shall be acquitted when it is held—but until that time I am under a cloud. My enemies know this—Reed and the rest of them."

"So far as I for one have had influence, General, I have used it in your favor," said Pemberton. "I think you are occasionally too impulsive and rash both in speech and action—you will pardon me, I know, for speaking frankly—but I would have had Congress overlook all these little things, in consideration of the great services you have performed to the country."

Arnold held out his hand. "Thank you, Mr. Pemberton, both for what you have done in my behalf, and for your frank speech just now. I know you have been my true friend, and I shall never forget it. As for me, I am as God made me. If I were not impulsive and rash, I never should have led that expedition to Quebec, or aided in bagging proud Burgoyne."

"I know well," replied Pemberton, "that men's highest virtues and their greatest errors are often curiously connected together—seeming to grow often out of the same root."

"Mine do, I am sure," replied Arnold. "Mr. Pemberton, if ever in the future I do that which you think worthy of blame, pray judge me as leniently as you can. Will you not?"

"I will," replied Pemberton. "It is one of my principles of action, to think as charitably as I can of all men and their deeds; and of you whom I have known so well, and admired so much, I shall always think most charitably."

"Thank you!"

"As to this matter of the Warren subscription," continued Pemberton, "I think there is no use in doing anything further at present. I will let you have the sum I have myself subscribed, at any time you wish it; and will do more as it is needed."

Shaking hands, Pemberton left the room, accompanied to the door by Arnold. The latter then returned to the library, and resumed his interrupted musings.

"Was it likely the Colonies could succeed? If they did, would France be in fact their master, as well as ally? Was even Independence desirable, if England would abandon her odious pretensions, and grant them self-government in all local affairs? And as to himself—which was the best for him? Was there any prospect of further honors and of wealth, if he adhered still to the colonies, and they were triumphant? Would they not come out of the struggle terribly exhausted—utterly poverty-stricken? And how then was he to live in a manner becoming his position—and his wife's position?

"If he should imitate in some degree the role of Monk, and be able to throw the game into the King's hand—what then? Would he be Viceroy, with corresponding dignities and estates? Duke of Connecticut perhaps? Or, if not Viceroy, at least one of the American House of Peers? How his young wife would adorn a Court! And himself—he felt in his soul the power to rule. He could not court the populace—he was too much of the Coriolanus mould for that—but he could accept a position from the King, and prove that he was as able to rule as to fight.

"But to imitate the example of Monk, required a Monk's opportunities. He had no command. In order to play a great part, he must have a separate command—and time to win over his officers and soldiers.

"The hour too must be well chosen. An auspicious moment, when his defection would almost decide the contest. It was evident that there were a great many things to think of, a great deal to mature and to plan, before such a step could be taken.

"If he succeeded—all would be well. Success, and such great success, would gild anything. But suppose he should fail? Then he would be a traitor and an outlaw. Even if he succeeded, of course his old friends in the army would look upon him as a traitor, but that could be borne, for the shrill cry of the disaffected few would be drowned in the loud applause of a whole nation.

"But if he should fail, and England fail, and the Colonies come out triumphant? It was well to look everything honestly in the face. Then he should stand as a double-dyed traitor—and even England would not love the unsuccessful traitor, while the World, which always looks at men and things through the eyes of the victors, would confirm the verdict.

"And if he did not escape, he should be ignobly hung!

"But that is nothing!" exclaimed he in a proud tone, his dark thoughts at last finding vent in words. "When I was a boy, and bathed beside the huge and dripping wheel of the old mill, I feared not to clasp my arms around it, and let it swing me high into the air, although I knew it would plunge me soon again beneath the cold, deep water. The round of that was certain—a certain rise, a certain fall. Here rise and fall are both uncertain; but not for fear of the cold plunge, from which no soul emerges, shall I hesitate. Whatever else God made me, he made me no coward. I have offered death my hand too often, to care that he should take it, sooner or later, now. Failure I fear, and poverty, and men's scorn; but not death—no, not death!"

CHAPTER VIII.

A NEW SCHEME.

If doublet and hose do make a man,
Then this is a he, deny who can.

ONE day, soon after breakfast, a sealed note was brought in to Helen. It had been left at the door, and read as follows—though the writing was not remarkably legible:

"*Private.*—Will Miss Hilen plaze come and see me this morning? FANNY."

Helen knew where her washerwoman lived, having been there once when she engaged her services. There was no reason why she should not go, and making an excuse of some necessary shopping, which she could do on the way, she arrayed herself and started forth.

Mrs. Malone, the washerwoman, lived in South street, the southern line of the city, not far from the theatre, which had been erected just outside of the city limits, on account of its being prohibited by the very good and somewhat narrow-minded people of that day, as an ungodly and wicked institution.

When Helen arrived at Mrs. Malone's, she found that lady—a very honest and decent woman, by the way—hanging out some clothes to dry in the yard attached to the dwelling; and, upon asking if a young woman by the name of Fanny boarded with her, was, with a smile, politely requested to walk into the house, where she would find her.

But, upon entering, much to Helen's surprise, the only occupant of the room was a young man, who started up briskly and came toward her.

"I wished to see a young woman by the name of Fanny," said Helen.

"I thought your leddyship said you would know me agin when you saw me," replied a voice which Helen immediately recognized.

"Why Fanny, is this indeed you?" exclaimed Helen, gazing at the figure in astonishment.

"The very same, may it please your leddyship. You see," added he—or she—smiling, "I am Captain Francis Malone now, and perhaps it would come aisier to you to call me Captain."

"But you certainly are a man," said Helen, looking at the Captain dubiously. And surely nineteen persons out of twenty would have come at once to the same conclusion. Not taller than Helen herself, but lithe, elastic, muscular, clothed in a homespun coat and breeches, such as were commonly worn by the poorer classes at that day, with the hair combed back, and tied with eelskin into a long queue, Captain Fanny really presented the appearance of quite a bright-looking and well-made young man.

"I think, my leddy, I am pretty well got up," said the Captain. "I have padded out my shoulders you see, and tied up my hair, and, were it not for my voice, I think I might be called a pretty dacent young fellow."

"Yes, your voice is rather feminine," rejoined Helen doubtfully; "and still I think I have heard men whose voices were no more masculine than yours is."

"I'm delighted to hear it," exclaimed the Captain, "the voice is my only wake place."

"Have you been to New York?"

"Yes, and got there and back safely, as usual. He is looking splindid"—with a passing attempt at a sigh, which did not suit the present attire as well as the female one. "Half the young gals in New York are dead in love with him, his sarvant told me."

Helen laughed. "Did you bring anything for me?"

"Yes, your leddyship, I have a letter in my little steel safety-box up stairs. Will you walk up; it's more private there?"

Helen glanced at the masculine-looking figure. "No, I think not. Bring it down here; these windows are curtained, I see."

"Yes; and my auntie 'll give us notice of any one's coming. I will bring it down to your leddyship."

The Captain soon reappeared with a small roll, which Helen concealed in a little pocket she had made in the bosom of her dress. "I will read it at home, and bring you my answer as soon as possible," said she, preparing to depart.

"One word before you go, Miss Hilen. I don't know whether the Major speaks of a little project—"

"The Major?"

"Bless my soul, and you had not heard it? Mr. Andry's been promoted—and I'll warrant you he'll not stay long a Major even—why, he's Sir Henry's right-hand man. Iverybody says that."

"That is good news," said Helen quietly—but her eyes shone with an added lustre. Another step upward had been taken.

"But I interrupted you."

"I was goin' to say, that perhaps the Major has not told you in the letter, of a little plan that's on foot. We're going to try to bag the rebel Chafe," said the Captain in a whisper, as if the very walls might carry the news abroad.

"What, Washington?"

"Yes," said he, in the same cautious tone. "When the great Ball comes off. It's to be at Bush Hill, you know, and they say he'll be there. There's a dozen of us engaged. Half are to be sarvints—the other half outside with the horses. We would push for the head of Chesapeake, where there'll be a vessel waiting. All is fixed but one thing."

"What is that?" queried Helen, almost breathless with the boldness of the proposed exploit.

"All depinds upon his going out into the gardin', away from the house. We want some lady to hilp us—and you are the best one we can think of."

"I!" replied Helen. "How could I help you, even if I would?"

"You are the handsomest, and the most bewitchin', and the most captivatin' leddy in the city," said the Captain, in his most insinuating voice. "Iverybody says that."

"I am not acquainted with General Washington," replied Helen, coldly, and rather haughtily.

"But you could git an introduction to him."

"Doubtful. And I would not care to, for such a purpose."

"Thin, it must all be given up—and the war must go on—and the ribels perhaps beat us after all. That one nate stroke might save thousands of poor fellows' lives!" exclaimed Captain Fanny, pathetically.

Helen thought a moment. Perhaps there was something in her lover's letter about this.

"Tell those that are planning this desperate scheme, that I will think it over, and give them my answer in a few days. If they can find, however, some other lady to aid them, I should greatly prefer it."

"I am sartin, my leddy, that when you come to think of it, you will help us," said the Captain. "The Ginral shall not be hurt at all, at all, no more than Ginral Lee was, or Ginral Priscott. And it'll end the war. And you'll do it all, my leddy."

Helen left the house, walking up the street as if in a brown study, and the captain went up to his room. "She will do it, I'm sure, if the major tills her to," said he musingly. "An' it's a splindid stroke—even better than that plan I got up with the ribels to carry off Sir Hinry—and which they gave up, because they were fearsome they'd git a worse man in his place. But it 'll stop the war, sure. And I'm almost timpted to blow on them. That would spile my business so. I would if the major was not in it. But you must stick up for your friends, captain—and besides, I swore to be true to the major, on this pretty cross"—and the captain took out the cross from his bosom, and kissed it devoutly. "But it 'll be great fun. That Ball will be worse than a cannon-ball, if it carries off Washington. But they must not hurt him—for he's every inch of him, and he's over six feet, a true gintleman."

And in this way, Captain Malone considered the subject of the proposed abduction, pro and con, from his point of view; which was different probably from the point of view of any other man or woman in the country.

CHAPTER IX.

SHALL I DO IT?

O noble errors! how ye gem the dark,
And prove that even in hell a God is there!

WHEN Helen found herself once more in the privacy of her own room, and secured from intrusion by the locking of the door, she took out her lover's letter. She was very anxious to see the business portion of its contents, and yet, woman-like, she perused again and again the many endearing expressions with which it opened, and then glanced over to the close, to see with what sweet words it ended, before entering upon a continuous perusal. We need not quote the letter entire, but shall simply give a brief summary of the, to us, more important contents.

André thanked her, in the name of his general, for the important aid she had afforded them thus far in the matter of "Vasa." A note addressed to Gustavus, and signed John Anderson, was also inclosed, to be placed in "Vasa's" hands, with a request for a reply through the same channel. Then the plan of abduction at the coming ball was referred to, and shown to be feasible, if the general could only be found strolling in some distant part of the grounds. Helen was not directly asked to take part in the affair, but it was suggested that if some loyal lady would persuade the American commander into a promenade in the garden, during the latter part of the festivities, she would aid in the most important manner the loyal cause, and be entitled to the warmest thanks of the King and nation. As to the effect of such a capture, it could hardly be over-estimated. No man could take Washington's place. Even if the loss of his military talents could be supplied, the loss of his high and disinterested character could not be. And strict orders should be given that he was not to be injured in any event. Neither should he be punished in any way for his share in the rebellion. The King was ready to grant a complete Amnesty at the first decisive moment—and the Americans should have all they wanted, except Independence. They should have a Viceroy; and if Washington would be that Viceroy, he should be made Duke of Mount Vernon, and installed at once. It therefore was not to injure any one, but to save the further shedding of blood, and end the war at a blow, that this plan had been arranged with the warm encouragement of Sir Henry Clinton.

Such was the purport of André's letter. And Helen's brain almost reeled after reading it. She had a right noble and generous nature. Naturally open and sincere, she hated everything that even looked like duplicity. And yet she was evidently regarded as the most available person to take a principal part in a scheme involving treachery and deceit. Granting that all was fair in war, and that she was a loyal woman, while Washington was a rebel, she *was* a woman, and therefore outside of the contention and risks of arms—claiming immunity from the sacrifices and losses of the war, because she was a woman. What right had these men, with their rough feelings and consciences, to plan a part for her—a high-bred, truthful woman? Why did not John André shield her from this entirely—as it was evident from the tone of his letter, he had done in part; the superior power behind him urging him on. She would not—would not—do it!

But then came the revulsion, which every one feels who weighs a great decision. The plan fails—the war goes on. Perhaps her own guardian, her own lover falls in the next fight—a battle which never would have been fought, but for her delicate scruples. The thought was madness.

Why should she pretend to be wiser or better than these high-toned, honorable men? Was not Washington himself continually engaged in trying to deceive the royal officers, by false letters, false reports, false movements, by deceptions and lies of all kinds, acted and spoken? Would he not plan in the same way, the abduction of Clinton—and, if it succeeded, and through some fair woman's wiles, would not the whole rebel land ring with her praises?

Helen walked up and down the room in the agony of her emotions—first swaying to one side of the question, then to the other.

At last her eyes fell upon a small velvet-bound volume lying upon the bureau. It was the Bible. And, as many a poor, benighted mortal had done before her—forgetful of what the Scripture itself says, that "no prophecy of Scripture is of any private interpretation"—she said to herself: "I will open the Bible three times. It shall decide my course. Good Father, guide me!" Shutting her eyes, and groping with her hands, she opened the Book. Her eyes unclosed, and she saw where she had opened.

It was the book of Judith—and Judith was standing by the bed of Holofernes, whom she had deceived, with the drawn sword in her hand.

Helen drew a deep breath. She turned away her head for a minute's space, and again she opened the sacred volume.

It was the book of Esther, and Mordecai was saying to the Queen:—"If thou holdest thy peace at this time, thou and thy father's house shall be destroyed!"

"Twice out of three times," she said in a low voice solemnly; "but I will try yet once more."

Again she opened the book. It was at the story of Deborah, and this was the verse her eyes first fell on—

"And I will draw unto thee * * the captain of Jabin's army, * * and I will deliver him into thine hand."

Helen was not unusually superstitious, but there often flows a current of superstition in the depths of the strongest and sanest minds. She had appealed to the Scriptures, and, as she thought, had been answered Her decision, therefore was made. What she was called upon to do, was not so treacherous and cruel a part as Judith's, and yet Judith had come down in praise through the long generations, because she had forgotten the woman in the patriot. Nor even so cruel as Esther's, for no man was to perish through her agency; on the contrary, he was to be elevated, if he would, to the highest honor in the land. But it seemed clear to her now that this deed was chosen for her—was her destiny. She was to act a principal part in the last scene of the drama, which should end the war, and prevent the dismemberment of the Empire. And, if successful, her name would go down on the pages of history, as that of one worthy to rank with Judith and Esther and Deborah.

Helen had probably never heard the maxim, "when the time has come for action, stop thinking;" but it was in her brave and resolute nature to do this, through the force of its own instincts. And, having once determined on her course, she washed all traces of emotion from her tell-tale face, smoothed her luxuriant silken hair, and went down calmly into the parlor to wait for dinner.

Isabella and Arthur were there before her, both too much interested in their own affairs, to ask many questions of what she had been doing. Lovers are not apt to ask many questions—not wishing to answer any in return. And the lives of these two lovers were flowing on in the most placid, but most delightful current. It was a long June day with them. They were so happy, that there is absolutely nothing to tell of them. Even lovers' quarrels were things of which they did not dream. For they both happened not only to be most noble and generous, but very reasonable people. Talking or reading together, and even sitting at times without conversation, Arthur reading, or playing his flute, Isabella sewing, or knitting, or playing the *harpsichord—for the piano, the enlarged and improved harpsichord, was not yet in common use—they enjoyed the blissful present as not many lovers, in this imperfect world, are able to do.

"We were just talking of going to the Ball," said Arthur, after a few minutes. "I also bought a ticket for you, Helen; will you go?"

"Who will be there—a lot of Froggies?"

"Yes, if you call them that; though I think you will speak more respectfully of the French, when you know them better. But a number of our own officers will also be there; and, most probably, Washington himself."

"I should like to see Washington, I confess; that is if I could have a little conversation with him; if just for one thing, to find out why you and Mr. Morris go off in such a blaze of rockets whenever his name is mentioned."

"Well, if you will go," said Pemberton, "I will try and give you an introduction. Of course you will be one of the handsomest women at the Ball, and Washington, no doubt, knows a pretty woman when he sees her."

"Thank your lordship!" said Helen, with a courtesy. "Your own perceptions of the beautiful need very little

*There is an amusing account of pretty Nelly Custis practising at the harpsichord in 1794: "playing and crying, crying and playing, for four or five hours at a time;" Mrs. Washington, her grandmother, who was a rigid disciplinarian, holding her steadfastly to her task. Her harpsichord cost one thousand dollars. It had double rows of keys, and looked like a small piano. The harpsichord was in general use as late as that time, although the piano was invented in Germany about forty or fifty years before.

more cultivation. But I think I know one gentleman—and he a rebel officer too—who could improve even on your compliment."

"Very probably," replied Arthur.

"I could do that myself," said Isabella, "for if Helen will only do due honor to her charms in her dress, I'll wager that she will be the most beautiful woman there—and by long odds, the most fascinating."

"Oh, you sweet little Sis," cried Helen, throwing her arms around her; "you know well that the most beautiful woman at the Ball will be Bella Graham. What do you say, Arthur?"

"I agree with you perfectly, *ma belle Helene.*"

"Arthur is such an impartial judge," said Bella, smiling serenely. "But wait till Lieutenant Morris comes in."

"If I go, I mean to dress like a Queen," said Helen. "So that when people ask, who is that? they may get the answer, that is one of the Mischianza ladies. Yes, and I'll copy the Mischianza dress too, for the fun of the thing—except, of course, those horrid spangles."

"All right," said Pemberton. "A woman as pretty as you are, can do anything. Besides we do not war upon women."

"And yet a woman's hand has often turned the scale of Destiny," exclaimed Helen proudly. "Joan of Arc, and Esther, and Judith, and Semiramis—"

"Oh, those terrible creatures!" commented Isabella.

"Names," continued Helen, "that have come down to us, and will go down to the latest generation, in proof of what the soul and hand of a woman is able to perform."

"Why, Helen, you look quite the heroine, with that commanding eye and brow," cried Pemberton, laughing. "I shall be careful to lock up all the loose nails and hammers about the house, lest you treat some of us rebels, as that model heroine, Jael, treated Sisera."

"For shame, Arthur, how can you talk so!" said Isabella reprovingly, as Helen sat down in a little of a collapse. The idea of Jael, with her cruel nail, was not pleasant to her.

"Will Washington really be there?" queried Isabella.

"There is very little doubt of it," replied Pemberton.

"He certainly is a very handsome man," continued Isabella. "He looks the great man, if any one ever looked it."

"He looks it, and is it!" exclaimed Pemberton enthusiastically. "Why, Bella, I positively believe, in real, sober earnest, that he alone upholds our great Cause. I tremble sometimes to think how everything hangs on that one man's life. A chance ball, and where are we?"

"There are no chance balls!" replied Isabella, fervently. "I am happy in the faith that all is ordered by the Wise Supreme; and that while Washington has his great work to do, no Indian's sure aim, no Ferguson's matchless rifle, will be able to take him off."

Helen listened attentively—her whole form was agitated with her emotion, though as she took no direct part in the conversation, her sister and Pemberton did not perceive it.

"It would almost seem to be as you say," rejoined Pemberton. "Lee was captured, as the result of a piece of recklessness, and, as some of us think, just at the right time. He might have superseded Washington, and lost us everything. Washington committed precisely the same fault when down near the head of Elk, and came off safely. If he had been captured, like Lee, I tremble to think of the result."

Helen broke in: "If Washington then should be captured, it seems to me to follow from what you say, that it would be a proof that Providence thought the proper time had come to allow the Royal cause to prevail."

"I confess it would almost seem so to me," replied Isabella, faithfully holding on to the line of her argument.

"I don't know about that," said Pemberton with a laugh; "that is a kind of application of our doctrine, that I for one, I must say, would not be quite ready for. I should be for fighting it out, I am afraid, to the bitter end, trusting that Providence was still working in our favor, though in some mysterious way."

"Arthur, I do not think you really have any faith," said Helen gravely. "Isabella has faith, and I can understand her; but I do not like people who carry water on both shoulders in religious matters, as you do."

"For my part," replied Pemberton laughing, "I think it a very sensible thing to carry water on both shoulders; when one shoulder gets tired or dislocated, you can then turn to the other. But I think I heard the dinner-bell just now. Allow me to wait on you out, fair ladies."

CHAPTER X.

THE BALL.

"This was the noblest Roman of them all"—
A Christian Roman! drawing forth his life
From Palestine and Rome! and lacking this,
Or lacking that, had been of lesser height,
Less fit to guide and mould the infant State.

THE evening of the Ball had arrived. The old Manor house of the Penn Family, at Bush Hill—then a short distance beyond the suburbs of the city—was untenanted, save by an aged negro couple whose business it was to keep the house and grounds in some kind of order, and was chosen as the scene of the festivities. A number of French officers had come on to Philadelphia to pay their respects to Congress—taking advantage of the curious inactivity which characterized the campaign of 1779; and as the Philadelphia of that time, notwithstanding the mixture of the Quaker element in society, was greatly devoted to pleasure-seeking, this Ball had been devised as a means of showing them honor, and promoting the good feeling between the two nations.

Washington also had arrived, and would be present. The Commander-in-chief did not altogether approve of the mirth and feasting which was so much the order of the day in the Quaker city, but he was very anxious that every kindness and all due respect should be shown to the French officers. Especially was he anxious that it should be done at this time, when the unfortunate affair of Rhode Island still rankled in the popular mind, and tended to reawaken those feelings of dislike and contempt for the French, which had grown up through the animosities of many centuries.

There was a large and gay party assembled at the

manor-house of Springettsbury that evening. The mansion itself was brilliantly illuminated with wax candles and lustres, and adorned with mirrors and paintings and statues, and the intermingled flags of France and the United States; while the extensive grounds attached to the house, with their gravel walks and evergreen arbors and wilderness of shade, including thick groves of cedars and catalpas, were lighted up with Chinese lanterns for the enjoyment of promenaders. Nearly a hundred French and American officers were present, and a still larger number of civilians, including members of the Continental Congress, and other gentlemen of high political and social repute. As we have said, Washington also was present, the centre of admiring and venerating eyes.

Helen had come, as she had planned, but not in the Mischianza attire. When rallied by Pemberton for the abandonment of that significant costume, she had simply replied that she was a woman, and had her privilege of changing her mind. But it was evident that to whatever reason the change was due, Helen had done wisely so far as the elegance of her dress was concerned. In truth, as Judith arrayed herself in her finest apparel when she went forth to captivate Holofernes, and Esther to ask her favor of Ahasuerus the King, so Helen resolved to spare no pains to increase the effect of her own surpassing charms. She was attired in a beautiful pale-green silk—of a shade nearly resembling that which we of this day have seen reproduced under the title of "*eau de Nil*"—fitting closely to her shapely form and trailing behind her, but cut low, and disclosing the faultless contour of her dazzling white neck. Her white arms also were uncovered from just below the shoulder—save as all were hidden by an overdress of costly lace, which covered but only partially concealed her virgin beauty. Around her neck she wore a carcanet of pearls, with a cross attached to it, and hanging low upon her bosom. And pearls were also entwined in her gold-brown hair, which was worn somewhat high, after the fashion of the time, but unpowdered, and braided like a coronet around her classically shaped head. And from her small, beautiful ears also depended pearls.

The festivities commenced with a dance in honor of the Alliance between the two countries. Pemberton and Isabella took part in this. It was a double Quadrille—which dance the French officers had brought over with them, and which was just beginning to take the place of the more ceremonious Minuet. Four of the eight gentlemen were arrayed in the French, and four in the American military uniform; while four of the ladies wore blue, with American flowers in their hair, and four white, with green scarfs, and artificial *fleurs-de-lis*. The American officers dancing with the ladies that represented the French, and the French officers dancing with the ladies in blue.

As the company crowded to the sides of the room to make space for the dancers, Helen found herself, very little to her own surprise, but apparently very unpremeditatedly, quite close to Washington. She was surrounded, as was apt to be the case, by quite a company of admirers, and this, together with her liveliness and wonderful beauty of face and form, evidently attracted the notice of the General. Helen was in splendid spirits. Never had she shone more brilliantly than on this evening. That her excitement was not entirely natural, did not detract from its power. She was intoxicated with the excitement of her bold design—for she had agreed to act the part which had been planned for her, if she possibly could.

Soon the Alliance Quadrille was over, and the couples engaged in it mingled with the rest of the company. And then Helen felt a touch on her arm, and turned to see Pemberton and Washington standing at her side.

"Allow me to present to your Excellency, Miss Helen Graham," said Pemberton. Helen made a deep curtsey.

"Shall I have the pleasure of dancing with you, Miss Helen?" said Washington; "I see they are waiting for me to lead off."

Helen signified her assent, and putting her gloved hand in the large, masculine one extended toward her, was led to the head of the principal set.

Helen was so excited that she could scarcely trust herself to speak. It seemed hardly regular. His Excellency, many evidently thought, should have begun with Mrs. President Reed, and danced with some twenty other dowagers before ever thinking of the young ladies. But it was not a clear case of fascination and wilfulness. Washington revered the proprieties, although they were intolerably irksome to him at times. But, strictly speaking, this was not a ball in his honor—it was in honor of the French—and he merely attended as a private gentleman; therefore he was entitled to exercise the freedom of a private gentleman.

He was not apt to make a mistake in etiquette, and he had fully considered all this before he came to the ball. Therefore he felt at liberty to conform to his own inclinations. As for dancing itself, he liked dancing with a good partner: and when he got a good partner, he was not particularly anxious to change. He had danced three hours at a time with Mrs. General Green, as it was not at all unusual in those days for a gentleman to dance the whole evening with one partner. In fact, in some parts of the country, it was esteemed almost a slight to the lady to leave her before all the dances were over.

Helen gradually regained her composure as she went

through the short, dignified steps of the stately minuet with the General, and soon was quite ready to take advantage of the pauses of the dance, to keep up an animated conversation. They talked of the new dance—the quadrille—of the weather, and of all those various topics which well-bred gentlemen and ladies use to keep up the shuttlecock of conversation on such occasions. Then, after half-an-hour or so, Helen requested to be led to a seat, saying, with an arch smile:

"I want to get home safely this evening, General—and if I monopolize you too long, some of these beautiful ladies will never forgive me."

Washington smiled. "How adroitly you young ladies can manage things. Now I know there is some young gentleman around, who wonders how long I am going to take advantage of my position to appropriate you."

"That *might* be true, your Excellency—and does justice to your penetration—but it happens to be otherwise. There is not one young gentleman in the room for whom I care, in the way you allude to, a silver button."

"Then I shall claim your hand for another dance before the evening is over, for I have quite taken a fancy to you, Miss Helen."

"Thank you," said Helen, inclining her beautiful head; "you do me much honor. And I shall be greatly pleased to dance with your Excellency again, toward the close of the evening. You will not forget it?"

"I never forget engagements," replied Washington smiling. "Now I will leave you and see if I really am so popular among the young ladies as you say. Who is that standing talking with Mr. Pemberton?"

"That is my sister Isabella. Is she not beautiful?" exclaimed Helen in her enthusiasm for her sister. "She will be delighted to dance with you. It will 'do her proud,' as the school girls used to say at Bethlehem."

"I think she looks very much like you—only with a difference. She looks graver, and less—less—"

"Volatile and giddy; thank you, General."

"Impulsive, was the word I was seeking. Do not forget that dance." And Washington walked, in his stately way, over to her sister.

"Well, what do you think of the General?" asked Pemberton, coming up to her, as Washington led Isabella to a place in a new set.

"I wish you would take a seat by me here on this lounge, Arthur, and keep off everybody. I don't feel like conversing with any one just now, I've got a bad headache."

"I am very sorry, indeed. Can I not get something—"

"What a foolish man! I mean the figurative headache, which ladies get when they do not wish to be bothered."

"Oh," said Pemberton, smiling. "I feel very much flattered indeed. But I suppose our apparent tete-a-tete will keep others off, and your bad headache will keep me off, and so you will be unmolested in the very midst of society. I am glad you have a beautiful sister, not subject to bad headaches, at least when I am about."

Helen made no answer. Her eyes were following Washington and Isabella through the stately dance—or rather Washington, for she did not even see her sister. He was certainly a grand figure. Attired in a complete suit of black velvet, with the exception of the pearl-colored waistcoat, and with a dress sword at his side, he was the most stately and dignified man that Helen had ever seen.

And she liked him. His face was calm, grand, serene—and when he smiled, it lighted up with a most beautiful and benignant expression. And he also evidently liked her—would perhaps have danced with her all the evening, had she been willing to allow it.

Helen was in no mood just then for sportive conversation. The thought of what she had agreed to perform—and what she still meant to perform—had grown in one short hour very unpleasant to her. Judith had persevered to the tragic end, and without the least womanish shrinking of heart; but would she if Holofernes had resembled Washington?

This man doubtless was engaged in a bad cause, but, like Arthur, and Morris, and so many others whom she personally knew, he was honest and sincere to the very core. It was not pleasant, however right and expedient, to carry out such a design as she had agreed to aid, when such a man was the object.

But yet this awful war—and its possible consequences to those she loved best. She saw now how it was that this one stately figure, like a Doric column, held up the entire edifice of the Rebellion. He once removed, and the whole evil structure would come down. And it was for his good also, as for the good of all—that of the Colonies, and that of the whole Empire.

Her brain seemed to reel under these conflicting pleadings of the mind and heart. But she must not disappoint her friends—she must not disappoint her lover—she must persevere in her purpose.

They were handing around some refreshments. "Please get me a glass of water," said Helen to Pemberton. "I cannot drink wine just now."

Pemberton left her, and at that moment one of the negro waiters came up to her with a cake tray. He was slightly made, and of a tolerably dark color, though with none of the usual African features. As Helen took a cake out of a basket of silver filagree work, he said in a low voice—"Do not forgit. We shall have all ready by twilve."

Helen started. She recognized the voice at once as that of Captain Fanny. He moved on as Pemberton came back with some water. No one, who was not suspecting, could have detected the captain under his negro disguise. It gave Helen a startling sense of the reality of the conspiracy, which was very unpleasant to her.

Isabella's coming up broke the charmed circle of the apparent tete-a-tete; and the two sisters—the acknowledged queens of the Ball—were thenceforward surrounded by a gay crowd of gentlemen. Helen welcomed it as a relief from her confused thoughts. She altered her determination, and drank glass after glass of wine; she danced with gentleman after gentleman, even with two of the French officers—she smiled, and sighed, and almost flirted—and was to the height the charming, fascinating, bewildering being that nature so often sends into the world to set men wild and crazy.

As the company came out of the supper-room, and prepared to resume dancing, Washington again came to her. "Are you ready for that dance yet, Miss Helen?"

"I have danced and danced till I am almost tired of dancing, and should prove, I fear, a sorry partner. Would not your Excellency prefer a stroll out in the grounds, where we could get a little fresh air this warm evening?"

Washington immediately offered his arm. "I think I should enjoy that myself much better than the dancing," replied he.

They walked off together, leaving a disconsolate group of beaux behind them.

"You seem to have had a merry time of it this evening,

Miss Helen," said Washington, looking down upon her benignantly.

"Yes—too merry! I think I should enjoy a little sober and sensible conversation for a change. I am not always so absolutely frivolous, General."

"If I am not greatly mistaken in my judgment, you are not a *mere* woman of society, Miss Helen. There is a depth of tone in your voice, which no mere worldling's voice ever has. And these are times to call out the deepest emotions, both of men and women."

"Oh would that this cruel and unhappy war were over!" exclaimed Helen, almost passionately. "You must hate war, General—any one can see that in your face. Why then not agree to a peace?"

"I do—to use your own strong expression, my child—*hate* war," replied Washington. "And gladly would I aid in making peace. But the road to Peace, I am sorry to say, lies just now through the smoke and carnage of the battle-field."

"I do not see it so; I do not see it so," replied Helen, with animation. "I know from what the British Commissioners said to me and to others when they were in the city last year, that England is ready to grant every demand of the Colonies."

"Except one!" said Washington with brevity.

"I suppose your Excellency means Independence—but that was not one of the original demands."

"No. But the war has opened our eyes to its necessity. It has awakened those who thought themselves only children, to the proud consciousness that they are really men, and that the parental rule should of right cease. If we were to agree to resume our allegiance, in the course of a few years the struggle for Independence would force itself upon us. It is the part of wisdom, as it seems to me, to persevere, especially as the French and Spanish alliances make our success, if we do not grow faint-hearted, absolutely certain."

They had been walking up and down, at first, amid or near a score of other couples; but Helen had purposely directed their course toward the outer paths of the grounds. Now they were near the extreme limit, where, amid a small grove of cedar trees, an arbor had been placed, with a couple of seats, and a small table between them. Helen knew the place by description well, it was the very spot agreed upon, being not only close to the rear entrance, but in the most shaded and secluded portion of the grounds.

"I feel tired," said she; "shall we sit down a moment?"

They took seats, with the little table between them.

"You spoke, General, of the French Alliance," said Helen, resuming the conversation. "I, for one, cannot forget for how many centuries France and Spain have been our almost natural enemies, and the enemies of the Protestant cause. Has the King of France grown to love Republicanism of late, that he has joined the Colonies, or is it not rather the old hatred against England and Protestantism flashing out, according to the wise maxim, 'Divide and conquer'?"

"I do not suppose that the King of France acts from very philanthropic motives," replied Washington smiling; "but when a man is struggling in the water, he is not generally very curious as to the motives of the man who is trying to help him out. The good service is the same."

"And having helped him out, what if he says, 'now do as I bid you, or I will throw you in again?'"

"If that time should ever come, certainly he would be even then in a better position than before, for he would be at least on his feet, and on the land."

"This French Alliance seems to me positively wicked," continued Helen earnestly. "Providence cannot smile on it. Your Excellency has heard, doubtless, of that accident, as some call it, at the dinner given by Monsieur Gerard to the French officers, last week?"

"I heard a brief allusion to it. What was it?"

"The lightning struck the house, in the midst of their festivities, melted the very silver spoons and plates they were using, stunned half the company, and killed one of the French officers outright. Should not that be a warning?" said Helen excitedly.

"Yes, my dear child, I think it should be. I think Monsieur Gerard should profit by living in the same city with your wise Dr. Franklin, and have a lightning-rod put up before any further damage is done," replied Washington with a grave smile.

"Do you not believe then, General, that Providence interferes in the affairs of this world?"

"Of course I do. But you will find it, my dear girl, impossible to regulate your conduct by omens. For instance, this is one; but then, as you doubtless know, another stroke of lightning melted the crown on Christ Church steeple. And the falling snow deadened the noise of our surprise of Colonel Rahl at Trenton; and the coming up of a sharp frost aided us to escape from Cornwallis at Assunpink Creek, and to fall upon his rear at Princeton. Therefore, you see, the omens are by no means all on one side."

"The Rev. Mr. Tennent, a very good man, as Mrs. Pemberton once told me, was struck by lightning in the streets of Philadelphia, and was not injured in the least. Not even the smell of fire was upon his garments, though the silver buckles at his knees and on his shoes were melted," rejoined Helen.

"And many a bad man doubtless also has been struck, and received no damage; while numberless good men and women, and innocent children, have been killed."

"I cannot help believing there is something in these things, these natural or Divine interpositions," said Helen, thoughtfully.

"Why, my dear girl," said Washington, smiling kindly on her, "if I had attended to my premonitions, I should not have been here to-night."

Helen started, and gazed eagerly into his face.

"All day," continued Washington, "I have felt an unaccountable depression, an omen, some might think, of impending evil. But should I stay away from this ball, and say that I was frightened by an omen? My duty lay just here, and that should be enough for any man. I did do one thing, I brought along my Guard, as a prudential measure, which, perhaps, I should not otherwise have done."

"I think you ought to have attended to your feelings—as Mrs. Pemberton, who is a Quaker, would say—and have stayed away."

"What! and missed making your acquaintance, Miss Helen? Why, I am not so old but that I would run a little risk to have a nice talk with a charming woman. Of course I cannot talk much with men. I must keep up my dignity with that presuming sex."

Helen glanced at her watch. It was half-past eleven. Twelve was the appointed hour, but they might think it expedient to anticipate it. And she had not yet positively determined what she would do. Could she betray, even for his own good, this noble man, who evidently liked her, and would trust her to the utmost.

"General," she continued, "one thing more I should like to say. Of course it is a woman's idea, but I think it could be realized. I should like to see the Colonies have their just rights. I should like to see them united, with their own American Parliament, composed of a House of Commons and a House of Peers. I should like to see a Viceroy of native birth, some man of commanding appearance, talents and character, who should be ennobled, hold his office for life, and represent the King. And I should like that man to be George Washington."

For the first time Washington's eyes gazed keenly upon the beautiful woman before him, as if he half suspected she spoke the words of others. But he recovered his equanimity in a moment, and said simply, with a pleasant smile:

"My dear Miss Helen, how little you understand me. Putting aside the question of Republicanism, I have positively no desire for such honors as you speak of. What little ambition I had once, has been completely dissipated by my experience during the last three years. To be in a high position is to have one's motives constantly impugned, to have the wisest actions misconstrued, and be the constant prey of anxiety and care. Did I not think it my duty to serve my country in the position where she has placed me, I would resign my present rank to-morrow. You spoke of Peace! How gladly shall I welcome it, and return to the calm pursuits and pleasures of private life. Viceroy of America! Such a position would have no charms for me. I long for rest, not for power and splendor. Give me a homespun dress rather than purple robes."

Helen gazed up into his face with admiration not unmingled with awe. This man was too kingly to covet the crown of a king. He was the Roman Cincinnatus come back to earth. She started as she heard a tread, but it was simply a servant bearing a silver waiter, with some ices and wine upon it. It was Captain Fanny. He set down the waiter on the table between them, and poured out two glasses of the wine. As he poured the wine, he caught Helen's eye for a moment, and shook his head, as if signifying that she was not to drink it.

"Marse Cadwal'der said, gib his compl'mens, an' say dat wine was de werry best old Madeery he eber tasted."

"Tell him I am very much obliged to him for remembering me," said Washington.

Helen sat a moment as if stupefied. The whole concerted plan flashed before her. She was to possess herself of Washington's sword—for so powerful a man might not easily be mastered, even if approached from behind. And it was evident that to make assurance doubly sure, this wine had been sent—drugged, doubtless, with laudanum, or some other powerful narcotic. Washington spoke to her, but she made no reply. She heard his voice, but she did not comprehend his words. She sat gazing out before her, as if her eyes were fascinated by some horrible object.

Receiving no answer, Washington put out his hand and took up one of the glasses of wine. But before he had time to put it to his lips, Helen sprang forward wildly—overturning the table with its contents, that went crashing upon the ground, and striking the wine-glass from his hand—shrieking, "a snake! a snake!"

Washington started to his feet, put his left arm around her, and with his right, after vainly looking about for a meaner weapon, drew his sword.

"Is it gone? is it gone?" cried Helen, breathlessly. "Oh, let us not stay here a moment longer; let us hurry to the house."

"Are you certain you saw a snake?" asked Washington, as they made their way toward the mansion.

"Oh, I am so frightened," said Helen. "I was never frightened at a snake before. But it was horrible, horrible, horrible!"

A number of persons had heard the shriek, and they now gathered around the General and Helen inquiringly.

"Miss Helen thought she saw a snake," said Washington, with a smile. "Why, what is the matter?" exclaimed he, as he felt Helen's weight begin to drag on his arm, and, looking around, saw she was sinking to the ground.

Helen had fainted. The terrible excitement of an evening passed under such circumstances, and culminating in the drugged liquor and her change of purpose, had proved too much for her highly sensitive organization.

Washington was possessed of immense strength, and disregarding all offers of assistance, he took the fainting girl up in his arms as if she had been a child, carried her into the house and laid her upon a sofa. Then, directing the anxious crowd to stand back and give her air, while Isabella, who had hastened up, unloosed her clothing, he calmly took a seat on a chair near her.

In a few minutes Helen began to revive. She partly opened her eyes, as if to see who was near her, and seeing Washington, feebly put out one of her arms, and laid her hand in his. But, as she recovered consciousness more completely, she seemed to recollect where she was and the proprieties, and gently withdrew it.

"I am sorry the snake gave you such a fright, my dear child?" said Washington tenderly.

"Snake!" cried Isabella, opening her large eyes even wider; "Helen doesn't care for snakes. She once killed a rattlesnake in the woods near Bethlehem, while all the other girls ran screaming away."

"This was a very large snake," said Helen, in feeble

accents. "And it had no rattles either. It was a mean, miserable, horrible anaconda!"

"I think we had better get Helen home as soon as we can," said Isabella to Pemberton; "she is evidently quite unwell, and wandering in her mind."

And so the carriage was ordered, and, supported between Pemberton and Washington himself, Helen was taken to it, and put in; his Excellency bidding her good-bye in the most affectionate manner, and telling Pemberton to be sure and let him hear the next day how she was.

As the carriage drove off, Washington turned to the officer of his Guard, which latter lounged about near their horses, some ten or twelve picked men.

"Any strangers around here to-night?" asked the General.

"Not very many. A couple of wagon-loads of rather rough-looking fellows from the country, and some people I judge living in the outskirts of the city; all come to see the show, they said."

"What has become of the countrymen?"

"They drove off, a while ago, laughing and swearing; something seems to have amused some of them and irritated the others, very much."

"Get your men ready; I shall leave in a short time," replied Washington, and re-entered the house.

As he leaned back in his carriage, and rode home, soon after, Washington was cold and silent, replying briefly to President Reed, who rode with him, as if desirous of being left free to commune with his own thoughts. He suspected something of the true state of the case, and that he had possibly escaped a snare; but he was not a man given to hasty conclusions on slight premises, and he knew how apt the imagination is to run away with the judgment. "In any event, she repented at the last, and the danger is now all over,'' was the unexpressed conclusion to which he arrived; and though the subject frequently recurred to his mind in the course of the night, his return to camp the next day, and the important duties which there awaited him, soon crowded all further recollection of it, and all thoughts of Helen Graham—except at distant intervals—from his mind. What the fate of America would have been, had this bold scheme to capture him succeeded, we think hardly admits of a question. There was no other man who could have held in check the discordant factions, united all in one vigorous opposition to the British rule, and by the force and grasp of his unequalled judgment preserved the armies of the infant Republic in the hour of weakness, and led them in the hour of promise to ultimate and enduring triumph.

BANNER OF WASHINGTON'S LIFE GUARD.

CHAPTER XI.

RUNNING THE GAUNTLET.

Men are my counters, and I play the game
With red or blue. My winnings are the same
If red king conquer, or blue sweep the board;
All goes to make my triumph and my hoard.

WHEN Helen came down to breakfast the next morning, she looked as well and as blooming as ever. She expected an avalanche of questions from Pemberton, but it was not possible to avoid it, and therefore she thought she might as well meet the onset at once, and have it over. Scarcely had she and Isabella taken their seats, than Arthur began.

"I am delighted to see you looking so well again, Miss Helen. I feared last night that you were about having an attack of some serious illness."

"I feel pretty well again, Arthur, thank you," replied Helen. "Do you think it will rain to-day? It is very cloudy."

"It does look lowering. I should not be surprised if it rained cats and dogs, or even snakes," added he, smiling.

Helen had managed up-stairs to avoid an explanation with her sister, but now Isabella broke in:

"Of all ridiculous things, Helen, the idea that you should faint at seeing a snake! I would not believe it, unless—unless—"

"The snake were to tell you so," added Arthur, now laughing outright.

"I don't see, Bella, why I should not have the privilege of fainting at the sight of a snake—a very big one—"

"A perfect anaconda, with horns," interrupted Pemberton.

"Just the same as other young ladies," continued Helen demurely, finishing her sentence.

"Nonsense, Helen, how can you be so absurd!" exclaimed her sister, a little impatiently.

"Shall I tell you what I overheard a young lady say?" asked Pemberton.

"I have not the least wish to hear any of the idle gossip of a ball-room," replied Helen, with dignity.

"She said she did not believe you had seen any snake; that you had been trying to attract the General's attention all the evening, and simply fainted, in order to have him carry you in his arms into the house."

Helen straightened herself up indignantly. "If that young lady will tell me that to my face, I will box her ears for her," exclaimed she, her eyes flashing.

"That would never do, Helen; every one then would be certain that you had not fainted at the mere sight of a snake."

"Arthur, there is no use in teasing Helen any more," said Isabella appealingly. "She is too sensible a girl to faint for nothing; and if she does not choose to tell us, why I, for one, am very well content to know nothing about it."

Helen was sitting next to her sister, and at these words she put one arm around her, and leaned over and kissed her. "Bella, you are a perfect woman," she said fondly, "and I'm only sorry there is not a man in the world who even begins to be worthy of you."

"That is so!" said Mrs. Pemberton heartily, who had been employed in pouring out the coffee and chocolate.

"My own opinion also, to a notch," added Pemberton.

"And Isabella is perfectly right as to your teasing Helen, Arthur," continued Mrs. Pemberton.

"No doubt you are right, mother," replied Arthur

laughing. "But I really believe myself, that Helen was decidedly smitten with Washington, and he with her; and if he were a younger man, and there was no Mrs. Washington—and plenty of snakes—there is no telling what might happen." Arthur seemed to enjoy the matter hugely.

"I was very much pleased with General Washington, indeed," said Helen, with dignity. "I thought him one of the grandest and noblest men I had ever seen, and I felt honored that he seemed to like me."

"Oh, my! what are we coming to?" cried Pemberton. "Such a good Tory as you used to be, Helen, and he the very head and chief of Rebels. What would Captain André say?"

"Captain! Major, if you please," replied Helen, proudly.

"Major, indeed! why who told you that, Helen?" asked Pemberton.

"A little bird brought me the news."

"Are you certain it was not the snake? Well, I am very glad to hear it; but what would the gallant Major say, to hear you talk thus of the chief of the Rebels?"

"I regret very much indeed that General Washington is a rebel," said Helen.

"And so do I," joined in Mrs. Pemberton.

"But rebel as he is," continued Helen, "mistaken as he is in that one great respect, I should be false to myself, if I did not confess the very highest respect and admiration for him. And if John André knew him, I am sure he would say the same."

"I will not tease you any more after that, Helen," said Pemberton; "I really have not the heart to do it. Only admire Washington, and you may faint at all the snakes at Springettsbury; all of which I expect could be put into a good-sized thimble."

The conversation here diverged in another direction, and Helen, having run the gauntlet, was allowed to rest in peace. Those who know what most family gauntlets are, may think she got off very easily. But not every Helen has a sister like Isabella, to speak the right, sisterly word at the right time for her. Oh, ye brave and kindly hearts that read this, will you not oftener imitate Isabella; and interpose your shield when some unfortunate sister or brother is running the family gauntlet?

Breakfast over, Helen felt that she must try to see Captain Fanny. No arrangement had been made for such a meeting, but she had little doubt she would find her at Mrs. Malone's, as usual; and as the lowering clouds had lightened, and gave every indication of breaking away, she donned her street attire, and leaving the house by the garden, proceeded down to South street.

Mrs. Malone was, as before, in front of the house. She did not receive Helen with her usual good-humored smile and salutation, but appeared to eye her rather suspiciously. To her question if Fanny were at home, she answered in the negative—but said that Fanny's mother, who had come to town for a few days, was inside, and perhaps could tell her how soon she would be in.

As Helen entered, she saw the old lady in question sitting by the fire, as if its heat were pleasant to her aged frame, though the morning was rather warm than otherwise. She seemed a much older woman than Mrs. Malone—the thin gray locks straggling out from under her white cap, while her form was bent, and she moved feebly and as if with pain.

"Will Fanny soon be in?" inquired Helen.

"And is it you, me swate, that is Miss Hilen Gra'me?" asked the old woman.

"I am Helen Graham."

"Will, me swate, Fanny lift a missage for ye. She wants to know, me swate, be you playin' her true, or be ye playin' her false?"

"How dare she tell you to ask me such a question as that?" replied Helen, indignantly.

"Don't get angry now, me swate," said the old woman, in a thin, tremulous voice; "but, after the last night, Fanny says she's afeard of you. An' she wint off, list you should sind a file of sogers for her this mornin'."

"She is not in the least danger," answered Helen, her sincerity expressing itself in every tone and feature; "I am not in the habit of betraying people. Tell her that she might be sure of that, after last night."

"I will till her at wunst—for sure an' I b'lave she's jist up-stairs, my swate," said the old woman; and she rose from her seat, and made her way up the stairs, with rather more agility than Helen had thought possible in one apparently so infirm and decrepid.

Some time elapsed, and as Helen heard only one person moving about in the room above, and no murmured conversation, she began to wonder at the delay, and question whether Fanny really were in the house. But at length a step was heard on the stairs, and Fanny herself came tripping down, attired as she was when Helen had first seen her.

"And so you were afraid I had betrayed you, Fanny?" cried Helen, in a half-chiding, half-reproachful tone.

"It is best to be on the safe side, my leddy—and you broke your promise to the party."

"There was nothing said about drugging, Fanny. I could not sit still and see so noble a man poisoned like a rat."

"He is a very strong man, my leddy—and would give half a dozen of the boys a dale of trouble to manage," replied Fanny. And then as if with a sudden thought she added—"besides, my leddy, you were mistaken, that wine was jist as good, innocent wine as Ave ever gave to Adam in Aden."

"What did you mean, then, by that look of warning you gave me?"

"Bless your heart, my leddy, I gave you no look of warnin'—I only looked to say it was time for your leddyship to git hold of the Ginral's sword," and Fanny gazed straight into Helen's eyes, with that look of perfect innocence which some unwise people say that guilt cannot counterfeit.

Helen of course believed that Fanny was lying to her, but she saw no use in trying to make Fanny admit it. She had had sufficient experience of that kind of people, to know that it would be labor wasted. So she simply said,

"Did any one recognize you in your negro disguise, Fanny?"

"Niver a one of them," replied Fanny, laughing. "Oh, but it was capital divarsion. Half a dozen of them officers knew me—and the Ginral himself—but not one of them had ever seen me as a man, to say nothing of a nagur."

"When I met you here that day, dressed up like a man, I was not quite certain for a little while myself, whether you were a man or a woman. But I see now that you are really one of my own quick-witted sex."

"Yes, indade, an' I should scorn to be anything else," cried Fanny, with quite a show of feminine dignity.

"I suppose however, you find your masculine garb at times a great convenience as well as safeguard."

"Yes, my leddy, and that is the only raison that could

induce me to wear it. It half breaks my heart at times— my modesty is so shocked, my leddy."

"I should think it would be," replied Helen sympathizingly. "Do you go soon to New York again?"

"In two or three days, my leddy. What shall I tell them about the plan's failing?"

"Tell them I found that I was not the right stuff to make a Judith of. But I will write to—to him, and tell him myself all about it. I'll bring the letter to-morrow or next day."

"I don't think, mysilf, you're the right stuff to make a Judy of," said Fanny with emphasis. "And yit it was a splendiferous plan. But then it would o' made an ind of the war, and that would been bad."

"Bad!" exclaimed Helen.

"I only mane it would put an ind to a great dale of fun," said Fanny thoughtfully.

"It is the kind of fun I should like to put an end to," replied Helen earnestly, rising to leave.

"Yes, my leddy, no doubt you are right. It's a terrible state of affairs; men killin' and slaughterin' each other, jist like so many hogs," rejoined the easily converted Fanny.

It was as much as the Captain could do, to restrain his mirth until Helen had got beyond hearing distance, after her departure. As he rehearsed in memory her feminine expressions of sympathy, he was delighted beyond measure. If it had been a man, or a woman of his own social rank, whom he had thus egregiously deceived, he would not have been so vastly delighted, but Miss Helen Graham, whom every one knew to be renowned as much for her wit as for her beauty, a woman of women, to have passed himself off on her first as an old, and then again as a young woman, in the course of a single hour, this was a feather in the

Captain's cap indeed, of which he was proud beyond measure.

As to the failure of the plan to capture Washington, he cared very little about it; for it had, as we have shown, from his point of view, its bad as well as its good side. Why Helen had acted as she had, now that it was evident she had not gone over to the enemy, puzzled the Captain not a little. It might be that she had taken a sudden fancy to Washington—women often did such things. Or she might really have seen a snake, and been scared out of her senses by it—the bravest of women were such cowards. But, whatever was the explanation, it made, as we have said, but little difference to the Captain. He had been paid well, and had got through scot-free, and that was enough for him. What now was to be the next game on the table? Another plan to capture Washington, or one on the other side to bag Sir Henry Clinton? It mattered but little to the Captain what it was, so it did not touch Major André, and one or two others on the British side, and about as many on the American. Whichever party succeeded, he meant to win. The war was a piece of nonsense all around, like a fight at Donnybrook Fair. But it was capital sport for all that, and afforded great room for the display of the Captain's peculiar genius—including his theatrical ability, his readiness at lying, and his almost perfect impartiality between the contending parties. In the Captain's view, although he never had read Shakspeare, the world was but a stage,

"And all the men and women merely players."

CHAPTER XII.

PLANNING TREASON.

"Whate'er is human, to the human being
Do I allow—and to the vehement
And striving spirit readily I pardon
The excess of action. * * * *
But not to the traitor can I yield a pardon."
—*Max in Wallenstein.*

THROUGH Helen's instrumentality, as we have said, a direct correspondence had been opened between Major André and General Arnold. So far, however, nothing very important had come of it. Arnold, it was evident, hesitated to pass the Rubicon. The correspondence was secret, and under feigned names, and he might withdraw from it at any time. And even if he had decided upon imitating the example of General Monk, he was not at present in a situation to do so.

It is not a slight matter, even for a man naturally bold and unscrupulous, to desert the cause to which he has attached himself, and the friends to whom he is bound by ties of affection and gratitude, and become a villain and a traitor in their sight. And Arnold was not utterly unscrupulous. His motto, which he had attached to the sign which he hung out, when as a young man he commenced the business of a druggist at New Haven, was *Sibi Totique*, and the meaning he evidently attached to it was, *For himself* AND *for all.* He was, perhaps, for himself first, but he would rather also be for all. If he had to choose between his own claims and the claims of his country, which would he prefer above the other? That was not an entirely easy question to answer—for he had exposed his own life, none more often, in his country's service; and even in the midst of his great pecuniary difficulties had assumed and regularly paid the expense of educating Gen. Warren's children.

Arnold, like most men of great force and ability, was too much of an enigma to be deciphered at a breath.

But his debts were pressing. He could see no way out of his pecuniary troubles.

One way—not the most honorable, and yet not the most dishonorable—had suggested itself. And it had failed.

He had applied to the French Minister in Philadelphia, had stated his great need, and requested a loan, and had been politely but firmly refused.

He had not said to the French Minister, "the borrower is servant to the lender;" but the French Minister had replied—though in kindly terms, for he was a great admirer of Arnold—as if he had said it, and had declined to accept his servitude.

It had galled Arnold to the quick. His thoughts reverted again with added impetus to the British offers. If successful—a title, money, high position. But he must dignify these desirable things, even to himself, by the plea of true and real patriotism.

The country was exhausted. Agriculture was depressed. There was no trade. The Continental money still depreciated month by month—"faster than a fast horse could trot," was a common saying. Thousands of professed patriots were ready to throw up their hats and welcome the restoration of the royal rule—especially if coupled with a substantial abandonment of the obnoxious British claims. All that was needed to inaugurate a rebellion against the rebellion was some decisive success of the British arms.

If that could be attained without bloodshed—as Monk's triumph was attained—all the better; by far the better.

And so a plan gradually evolved itself in the dark depths of his determined and sagacious mind. He could not have a separate command in the field—it was not possible. But the Hudson river divided the Middle and Southern States from the peculiarly rebellious East. The strong Fortress of West Point—the Gibraltar of America—dominated the Hudson river, and the roads by which the Eastern and the Middle States were united. Could he not obtain the command of West Point—allow himself, by a well-planned arrangement, to be surprised, and yield up the fort with its defenders, and its stores of military material, without bloodshed? If a proper time were chosen, this might also involve the peaceable surrender of a portion of the allied French and American army.

On the heels of such a blow, which would naturally dishearten the most ardent patriot, let the British commander offer the most liberal and generous terms—a full pardon to all, and everything, in fact, except independence. Then he, Arnold, could come out in a manifesto to his countrymen, urging them, as the part of true wisdom, to accept the British offers; himself, for one, accepting them. Other officers, with whom he should have made interest, would follow suit; the Continental troops would desert; the rebellion rapidly melt away; and in one month's time, perhaps, the French army be forced to capitulate, and the British rule be fully re-established.

If the affair were well managed and successful, he might possibly be suspected by a few, but they would be careful to conceal their suspicions. What rewards should be heaped upon his head by the British Ministry, would be naturally accounted for by his being the first officer of high rank to abandon the American cause, and to renew his allegiance. Washington would, of course, be made Viceroy, if he did not hold out too long, and were willing to accept the position. But he would not accept it—any one well acquainted with his character could foretell that. Who, then, more likely to be made Viceroy than the man who had planned the whole movement, and brought it, by his daring and sagacious course, to a triumphant issue?

So Arnold reasoned—and almost grasped in his imagination at times, a King's delegated sceptre.

His need of money, his ambition, his love for his young wife, all tempted him. His hatred of Congress, his Court Martial, his fierce anger at the apparent contempt manifested for him and his services, all urged him on. What held him back? Honor—faithfulness to his friends, and especially to Washington, who had always been a friend in his hour of trouble—the natural dislike of a brave man to change side—the fear of possible failure, and of the utter contempt in which he would then be held, especially if his countrymen ultimately succeeded in the contest—all these considerations held him to the narrow path of duty.

Why was it the path of Duty? Had not Arnold a right to change his mind, and act in accordance with that change? If any British officer had become convinced that the cause of the Colonies was right and just, would it have been wrong in him to desert the British flag, and fight thereafter under the American banner? Had not General Charles Lee done this with the universal acclaim of the most honorable men in the Colonies?

We answer that General Arnold had a perfect right to change his mind, and to act in accordance with his new convictions. But, before moving a step, he should have resigned his commission in the Continental Army. Honor required that he should be "off with the old love, before he was on with the new." When his resignation had been accepted, he was once more a free man—and had the same right to join the British forces as Beverly Robinson and thousands of others, whose persons were always held sacred when captured by their offended countrymen.

But all men hate a Traitor. Even those that love and profit by the Treason, can hardly avoid hating the Traitor. For, even if the cause be good which his treason serves, he injures another and far greater cause—the common trust and faith of man in man—so deeply, that the evil done to universal man far transcends the little benefit that he may confer upon a few. For without that common faith and trust, how shall human society be held together? Even a band of robbers cannot exist without it. And how shall communities and kingdoms exist, and make treaties of peace and commerce with each other, if treason be not considered one of the greatest crimes that man can commit against man? Human nature instinctively revolts from it, as from a violation of one of nature's most sacred laws—a spiritual law of gravitation and human cohesion.

But it is one of the many curious contradictions—generally more apparent than real—which meet us in life, that while all men agree in this, they also generally agree that it is perfectly allowable to profit by treason done to an avowed enemy. Just as even an honorable man, if a military commander, hesitates not to deceive the foe by false reports, cunningly devised letters, insidious actions, so he also profits by the use of spies, and even by the perjuries of traitors, if he can. Washington was one of the most honorable of men, but he never scrupled to use all these means; though no treason to the British, on anything like so large a scale as that of Arnold's, ever offered itself to his acceptance. If it had, there is little doubt that however much he might have despised the traitor, he would have felt it his duty to accept the treason. In fact, the employment of spies involves nearly the same principle.

Each party in the Revolution, as in all wars, hung a spy when caught, almost on sight, and without compunction—and each party employed spies by the score, if not by the hundreds. What a curious inconsistency! to hang men for that which you are daily hiring other men to perform, and which you are honoring some, like Captain Hale, for doing!

But, as we have said, these contradictions which we find in life—and even more especially in the concentrated life of war—are more apparent than real. In war the two parties agree, as it were, to deceive each other, to a certain extent. Each General deceives his opponent by false pretences of various kinds—this is lawful; it is in accordance with the rules of the game. He may even ask to treat for a surrender, his real object being not to surrender at all, but merely to gain time. But when he deals directly with the enemy, he must adhere strictly to his plighted word. He says it is my right to employ spies. It is your privilege to shoot or hang them, if you can. If I can seduce any of your officers from his duty, I shall certainly do so. Of course you will hang him, if you find him out. But when I say in so many words to you, that I will agree to a certain thing, be it a truce, a capitulation, a guarantee, of safety, or whatever it may be, then I will hold to my word, though the earth quake and the heavens fall. And this is the rock of Trust in the midst of the false and treacherous waves of war. And the falseness, and treachery, and lying, and deceit, are in a manner justified, for they are mutually understood to be allowable in this terrible and deadly game.

PART III.

CHAPTER I.

A CHANGE OF SCENE.

If so thou playest with edged tools, beware
Sharp edge and treacherous point.

THE Autumn season of 1780 had come, and the trees along the magnificent Hudson were beginning to array themselves in their yellow and crimson robes, when two gentlemen sat conversing in the private office attached to the headquarters of the British Commander, in the city of New York.

The war was still undetermined. The British forces had apparently succeeded in reducing to subjection the Carolinas and Georgia. Gates had been defeated at Camden, and the laurels awarded to him, but not fairly won, at Saratoga, stripped from his brow; though the gallantry of the regular troops from Delaware and Maryland, led by the brave but unfortunate De Kalb, had maintained the honor of the Continental arms. The allied French and American forces had also made a second failure, their attack on Savannah being repulsed; one portion of the French fleet soon afterwards setting sail for home, and the other for the West Indies.

Affairs were not looking bright for the States. Their army was small, and they had no money but the Continental currency, the depreciation of which had become fearful. Seventy dollars now in paper would go no further than one in silver. And when it is considered that not only provisions and all the munitions of war were to be purchased with such a currency, but that the troops were to be paid with it at its legal value, it is wonderful how the first could be obtained at all, and how the army could be kept together. It required four months' pay of a private to buy a bushel of wheat, and a common laborer could earn four times the pay of an officer. Of course those officers who had not private means, could not keep up an appearance suitable to their rank; and cases were not unfrequent when officers would live on bread and cheese, rather than take their share of meat from their men's scanty allowance.

That mutiny and desertion in such a state of affairs should become common, is not to be wondered at. That a large proportion of the community should become disheartened, and ready for peace on any terms, is what might naturally have been expected. Who can wonder that Washington should write at that time to those who had his confidence—"The prospect is gloomy. The storm threatens. Now is the decisive moment. I have almost ceased to hope."

There was a probability of France and Spain becoming discouraged, laying the blame of the repeated failures of the allied arms on the Colonies, and making a separate peace with England. New York had been menaced by a combined attack, but the arrival of Sir George Rodney's fleet had given the British again the superiority at sea, and the attack was postponed.

At this juncture, a great success on one side or the other, might virtually decide the contest. For if the States were exhausted, England was tired and disheartened by the stubborn resistance she had met with. She had found foemen worthy of her steel—chips off her own tough British block—and the boast that a few thousand British regulars could march through America from one end to the other, was riddled by the guns that tore the ranks of the adventurous Burgoyne.

All these facts, and the exact situation of affairs, were well understood by the two gentlemen to whom we have alluded; for one of them was our old acquaintance, Captain André—now however Major, and Adjutant-General of the British army—while the other was his commander, as well as patron and friend, Sir Henry Clinton.

"You have everything prepared for your trip, Major, I suppose?" asked Sir Henry, a short and rather corpulent man, with a round face and prominent nose—not a handsome man, by any means, though his countenance indicated the possession of much kindness and amiability.

"Yes, Sir Henry; I am ready to start by to-morrow, early."

"I am almost disposed to forbid it, even at this last moment," said his Commander. "Were it not for Arnold's almost peremptory demand that you, or some other officer of his own mensuration, should meet him personally to arrange matters, I would forbid it. It not only involves danger to you, but may provoke suspicion and inquiry."

"I beg that your Excellency will not think of the danger to me," returned André proudly. "I am a soldier, and prepared to take the risks of a soldier's life, in the way of my duty."

"One thing must be understood, however, fully and clearly," replied his General. "There is to be no going into the enemy's lines, no assuming of a disguise, no carrying of important papers. You know how careful I was as to this last, in Commissary Clark's case."

"There shall be nothing of the kind Sir Henry. He is to meet me on board the Vulture. If he does not come, I shall agree to no arrangement involving the risk of being considered a spy. I know too well the temper of the Colonists to give them a chance of retaliating for Captain Hale."

"Retaliating for Hale! Why, Major, do you not know that they have hung not only Lieutenant Palmer, but at least seven others, since Hale's execution? I was greatly pleased the other day when Washington asked me to spare that last spy we caught, as I hope it will put an end to all these barbarous hangings. I thank God that I have not put a single man to death in that way, since I have had command of his Majesty's forces."

"I did not know, I will confess, Sir Henry, that the record of humanity in that respect stood so largely in our favor. For my part, it seems rather inconsistent to hang spies, at the same time that we employ so many. I can conceive how a perfectly honorable man could act as a spy, and I suppose both Hale and Palmer were such—but still I have not much liking for that branch of the soldier's profession."

"Well, my dear boy, take care you keep out of it. But if we have made no mistake in our man, what excuse can he possibly give the rebels for meeting either you or Robinson on board the Vulture? It will certainly cause suspicion."

"I admit the risk of that, Sir Henry."

"He will find, when he thinks longer upon it, that it will not do. He will probably propose some other place of meeting. Now, Major, I repeat it again, go neither within their lines nor put off your uniform. You know there is a possibility that he really means to betray us at the last moment, instead of the rebels."

"I think not, Sir Henry, But of course there is a possibility of it. For that reason I am the more anxious to meet him, and judge for myself of the honesty of the man.

If I am entrapped, that will amount to but little—but to have a large detachment of the army entrapped, would be, at this critical moment, a very serious matter indeed."

"Yes, Major, I see that you must go. And if, when you meet him, you could manage to get something in his handwriting that would seriously compromise him with the rebels, I should not fear so much his backing-out at the last moment."

"I will try to do so," replied André.

"Of course you will arrange with him the plan of attack, so that resistance shall be almost impossible. And if we could manage to surround the Fortress while Washington was there, and capture him also, I think it would finish the war at a blow."

"If Washington is not there, Arnold might send to him for reinforcements. Knowing the value of West Point, he would probably head them himself; and then if the post should be surrendered just before he arrived, and the proper dispositions made by your Excellency, he might be surrounded and taken prisoner with his whole detachment. This certainly would end the war."

"Major, you shall be made Brigadier, at least, when that happens," said Clinton warmly.

"Thank you, Sir Henry. I will not say that I am not ambitious—because I am. But I will say that I am perfectly willing to leave all such questions to your generosity, and that of my King and Country. So far, you have rewarded me beyond my deserts—and I am truly grateful. But what shall I say to Arnold? One great object of his in meeting me, no doubt, is the settling of his reward, beyond all after cavil. In fact, he hinted in one of his letters, that the ready money would be very acceptable."

"No—no—I am too old a bird to run the risk of being caught with chaff," replied Sir Henry. "He must be content with the word of a British officer. That is the reason he so strongly urged that you should come, Major. See what it is to have a reputation!" And the General smiled kindly on his favorite Aid-de-camp.

"What am I empowered to offer him?" continued André.

"Offer him £30,000 in case of success, and an equal rank with his present one in the British army. And if the result is, as we trust, the overthrow of the rebellion, tell him that his services shall be duly considered in the appointment of the new officers for the Colonies. As to the general plan of Pacification proposed, you already understand that fully. The Colonies shall have everything they have hitherto contended for."

"I infer there are other officers who will follow his lead, what of them?"

"They shall be rewarded in proportion to the extent of their services. I leave all this to your discretion, Major. There probably will not be time to communicate with me. Consult with Colonel Robinson, if you can; he is a gentleman of very solid judgment."

"I think I understand your Excellency's wishes and views fully, but I will confer with Colonel Robinson whenever I can. I trust to bring the whole affair to a satisfactory issue."

"And take care of yourself, my dear Major. Do not put yourself into the lion's mouth. He is terribly excited and ferocious just now. What time do you start?"

"Early in the morning. And I will now bid your Excellency good evening, as I have a number of matters to arrange before retiring."

"Stay. Give me your arm around to Colonel Williams's. I promised him to call in at his dinner party, and stay a little while with them."

Leaving headquarters, Sir Henry and André proceeded a few blocks to the quarters of Colonel Williams, at the ancient bowerie or country-seat of Jacobus Kip. They found there a brilliant assemblage of officers, enjoying themselves with conversation and speeches and songs and wine, who hailed the entrance of their Commander with great applause, and conducted him to a seat reserved for him at the head of the table. André remained for a few minutes, interchanging salutations with his many friends, and then turned to leave. Instantly there was a loud outcry all around him, remonstrating against his departure.

"You are not going, Major?" cried his host. "Really we cannot permit it; can we, gentlemen?"

"No, no, no!" rang from all sides.

"No such shirking as that!"

"Stand to your colors, Major!"

"Face the music!"

"Drink to your lady-love!"

"Order him to maintain his position at all hazards, Sir Henry!"

"Hip, Hip, Hurrah!"

André turned smilingly from one to another of the lively circle. Then, when room was given for a word, he said pleasantly, "Thank you all, gentlemen; but I have some important business to attend to this evening, and, much to my regret, will have to be excused."

"Then sing us a song before you go," cried a voice. And "a song from Major André! a song from Major André!" rang around the table.

"What shall it be, gentlemen?"

"Sing us Wolfe's chanson, Major, to begin with," said Colonel Williams. This was the little song attributed to General Wolfe, and sung by him on the eve of the battle in which he died—that desperate struggle on the Heights of Abraham.

"I do not fancy it entirely," replied André, "but I'll obey orders"—and so saying, he sang in a rich, mellow voice as follows:—

> "Why, soldiers, why
> Should we be melancholy, boys?
> Why, soldiers, why,
> Whose business 'tis to die!
> Whose business 'tis to die!
> For should the next campaign
> Send us to Him who made us, boys,
> We're free from pain;
> We're free from pain!
> But should we here remain,
> A bottle and kind landlady
> Makes all well again!
> Makes all well again!"

Tumultuous applause followed the song—in the midst of which André would fain have escaped from the room. But the gay revellers around him would not permit it, detaining him with rough but kindly hands, "One more song they must have," they said, "and then he might go in peace."

"Give us something of your own composition this time, Major," cried Colonel Williams.

"The very idea."

"Good for you, Colonel."

"One of your own songs, Major,"

"Do be quiet, gentlemen."

Again André sang—and evidently with more care and greater warmth of feeling:—

I

> Oh, soldier, how
> Canst thou be gay?
> A day, an hour;
> Thou, like the flower,
> Shalt pass away.

A ball's sharp crush,
A bayonet's push,
  A sword-cut sore:
Thy name at call,
Or banquet hall,
  Is heard no more!
  Is heard no more!

II

Oh, lady fair,
Oh, lady fair,
  My fears are still;
I cannot die,
Beneath God's sky,
  Against God's will.

From mast and crag,
Our red-cross flag
  Still streams on high.
Let that float free,
O'er land and sea,
  E'en though I die!
  E'en though I die!

Amid the wild applause which followed his song, and this time unopposed, save by warm hand-claspings, André left the room.

"There goes the most popular young officer in the army, Sir Henry," said Colonel Williams.

"Yes, and justly so. The Major is a second Bayard, '*sans peur et sans reproche*,'" replied Clinton. "I love him almost as my own son.'

CHAPTER II.

THE MIDNIGHT CONFERENCE.

Now, by the shade of Hecate, you have chosen
A fitting spot for such an ominous deed;
Come, Midnight, hide our presence with thy pall,
And make Life mute as Death!

It was about eleven o'clock at night, on the 21st of September, 1780, when General Benedict Arnold mounted his horse at the White House, the residence of Mr. Joshua Smith, to ride down to the foot of Long Clove, where he had at last arranged to give Major André a meeting. It was a dark but calm and beautiful night, the stars-shining with even unusual brilliancy; and the General, attended by a negro servant, rode as composedly along, as if he were going simply on a common journey, and not to one of those momentous interviews which affect for good or evil the destiny of great nations. That Arnold's spirit was as composed as his manner, we should not feel at liberty to say. The risk was too great, the stake at issue too important, to render such a state of inward quiet probable. But he was a man of iron nerves, and had fully determined to brave the peril, and stand the hazard of the die. With such a man—one who was emphatically a man of action—a state of composure in the midst of the most desperate enterprises is possible, which men of a more thoughtful and intellectual cast can never-hope to attain.

And so Arnold rode deliberately on through the night, along the river road, and over the rugged hills, and through the deep valleys and ravines which lined the lonely Hudson, until he came near the appointed rendezvous at the foot of Long Clove mountain. Leaving his horse here in the road with the servant, with directions to await his return, he made his way to the bank of the river, at the spot where he judged the coming boat would land. Before long, gazing intently from the close shelter of a thicket toward the middle of the river, he discerned through the dark a still darker object approaching—though with very little noise, for the oars had been discreetly muffled—and retired at once to the concealment of a group of fir trees.

As the bow of the boat grated against the bank, two gentlemen sprung out. As the latter of the two leaped on the shore, he stumbled over a stone or a root, not visible in the darkness.

"A bad omen that, Mr. Anderson," said the first.

"Oh, no, Mr. Smith; it means that I shall soon regain possession of my property," replied the second lightly.

"I think you will find the General in the shadow of those firs," said Mr. Smith in a whisper. "Shall I attend you?"

"Thank you, but there is not the least occasion for it," replied the other, in the same cautious tone, walking forward.

When he reached the firs—which were not more than forty or fifty yards distant, though barely visible in the obscurity of the night—he beheld what seemed the figure of a man in the deepest portion of the shade. Advancing toward it, he uttered but one word in a questioning tone:

"Gustavus?"

"I am he. You are Major André."

"General, I am very happy to make your acquaintance. It has taken us a good while to get together."

"Yes. I could not come on board the Vulture; it would arouse suspicion."

"We are not within your lines here?"

"No. You are perfectly safe."

"I have no objection to taking a fair risk; but there are some risks I do not choose to take."

"I am taking every risk," replied Arnold, with some bitterness in his voice.

"We are ready to repay you for it."

"I care not mainly for that," was the reply. Was Arnold in earnest, or was this the opiate plea which he administered to an unquiet conscience? "I wish to be fully assured that the Colonies, if conquered, shall have all their just rights.

"I am fully authorized to assure you that they shall. Why, we have been offering these assurances openly for the last year."

"Everything but Independence?"

"Everything but Independence."

"And a full pardon to all who, even at the last moment, shall submit?"

"A full pardon—even to Washington himself."

"Then with what do you propose to repay me for my risk and my services in this matter?"

"What do you propose to do?" asked André.

"To deliver up West Point, with its garrison, and its munitions of war, and its large store of supplies. In other words, to throw that mighty Fortress into your side of the scales, and determine at one blow, even without a blow, the whole contest."

"Without a blow?"

"Yes; I can so arrange my forces that you shall be able to reach with a picked corps a point which commands Fort Putnam, which is the key of our works. Once there, you will be as completely master as Burgoyne was when he reached the top of Sugar Hill, at Ticonderoga. One ravine left unguarded, or too slightly guarded, and West Point is yours."

"But is there not a heavy chain or boom across the river? Our friends tell us so. How are we to pass that?"

"I have sent one of the main links to be repaired. The chain is now merely tied together, and will yield to the slightest shock."

"You said, if I understand you, General, that we could take the Fort without loss of life?"

"With little—or perhaps none. I will not expose the lives of my soldiers. Besides, I mean this thing to be kept quiet; so that while my generalship may be called in question, none shall doubt my good faith. This is necessary to the after workings of my scheme."

"How do you propose to follow up the surrender?"

"Sir Henry Clinton must immediately issue a proclamation, offering the most liberal terms—such as you just mentioned—to the Colonies, if they will lay down their arms; and a free pardon to all who will embrace those terms. I will immediately accept them, and persuade as many other officers as I can to join me in so doing."

"Are any other officers concerned with you in this proposed West Point transfer?"

"Not one. It would be dangerous even to entrust another with the secret. But, if things go as I have planned, I believe there are many that will soon join me, especially if I can offer them some ready money. Hundreds of them are without a dollar, even a worthless paper dollar, in their hungry purses—and the wives and children of many are suffering for the common necessaries of life. It is time the whole ridiculous nonsense was exploded."

"We should like to capture Washington also," said André, in a still more cautious tone than that in which the conversation had so far been held.

"No. I will not do it. He has always been a good friend to me—in spite of that cursed Congress."

"We mean him no harm," replied André. "We mean only to decide the war, at once and forever."

"I will not hear to it. I will not see a hair of his head injured," said Arnold peremptorily.

"So far from injuring a hair of his head, I am convinced that it would rest entirely with himself whether a Viceroy's coronet should not repose there. We do not mean to do things by halves, General, if we are triumphant. We shall never give those Frenchmen another opportunity."

Curious heart of man! Arnold had revolted from arranging to deliver up his Commander and his friend; and now the hint of André's that Washington might be Viceroy if he pleased, only made him more determined that it should not be done. For if Washington were not made Viceroy, whose claims would be superior to his own?

"No," said he; "I will not agree to it. Whatever else I may be, no man shall say that I am ungrateful. I owe no gratitude to Congress—it and my country owe me gratitude. But to Washington I owe a debt that I shall never repay with what he would consider the grossest perfidy."

"Of course, General, you must judge for yourself in such a matter," said André, courteously. "I am merely suggesting these things as a British officer, not as a private gentleman."

"And, for all this, what shall be my reward?" asked Arnold. "I mean to restore a Continent to England—what does she mean to give me in return!"

"Your greatest reward, General, you must find in the approbation of your own conscience," replied André; "in the proud consciousness that you have laid the wrathful and destructive demon of war, brought peace and prosperity to thousands of distracted homes, restored concord between quarrelling kindred, and reunited a mighty Empire, the bulwark of the Protestant Faith. No mere money can pay you for all this, General."

"Very true. But a little money nevertheless would be very acceptable to me, as it is apt to be even to British generals and majors."

"Undoubtedly," replied André. "And England is always generous to those who serve her. She is no penurious mistress."

"I should like to serve a mistress of that kind, as a change. Congress is a mean enough master, God knows."

"I suppose they are poor men, and pay poorly," said André.

"They are mean men, and pay meanly," replied Arnold with bitterness.

"Too—hoo—oo—oo—oo—" quavered an owl from the branches of one of the firs, as if in delight, or mockery, it was hard to say which.

André started at first, but then gave a low laugh. "It is the bird of wisdom," said he, "come to assist at our conference."

"Wisdom! the wisdom which looks wise as Solomon, but all the time only means mice. We've plenty of these solemn owls among us, especially in Congress, Major. But to come back to business. What may I expect? You know as well as I do what my risk is. If I am discovered, and fail, a rope from a branch like that"—pointing to one just above them—"and curses and maledictions, perhaps forever. That is even worse than the rope to a man as ambitious as I am. I will not run this terrible risk for nothing. I mean to be paid well, or give up the whole affair."

"To-hoo-oo-oo-oo," again hooted the owl derisively, now amid the branches of an adjacent tree.

"D—n that infernal bird!" exclaimed Arnold, in a suppressed voice, and feeling about with his foot for a loose stone.

"What would you consider fair payment, General?" questioned André.

"Fifty thousand pounds, and the same rank in the British army that I hold in our own."

"I cannot do it. I was instructed to offer you twenty-five thousand. The equality of rank we would agree to."

"Then we might as well separate. I will not take twenty-five thousand," rejoined Arnold.

André was about to reply, when he saw through the darkness a form coming toward them. It was Mr. Smith.

"Gentlemen," said he, "had you not better adjourn to my house, and finish your conference there? The men are tired and sleepy, and my ague is coming on with this chilly dampness."

"No; I must go back to the Vulture to-night," replied André firmly.

"I do not see how you can do that," replied Smith. "The men are tired; you know the boat is a very large and heavy one. Besides, they say the Vulture is to be cannonaded at daybreak—".

"How is that?" said André quickly, turning to Arnold.

"It's only some of Livingston's cursed folly. He applied to me for two of my heavy guns, but I did not choose to strip the Fort; and so he intends blazing away, it seems, with his four pounder."

"The men will have plenty of time to go and return before the cannonade," said André; "besides they have their passes."

"I have urged all that upon them," rejoined Smith; "but they obstinately refuse to go."

"I think, Mr. Anderson," urged Arnold, "that, on the

whole, the better plan will be to ride over to Mr. Smith's. If you do not, we may require a second meeting to arrange those affairs, and I do not see that it will be possible for me to give you another."

'When would I return?" said André, seeing the force of Arnold's plea, and unwilling to let so important a negotiation fall to the ground.

"You could return to-morrow night," replied Arnold. "If the Vulture is forced to shift her position, the boatmen would have further to row you, that would be all; and, if need be, my passes would take you to Dobb's Ferry."

"I suppose it is the best we can do," commented André dubiously.

"Of course it is," replied Arnold. "Mr. Smith, you can return home in the boat; Mr. Anderson will accompany me on the horse my servant rode."

As Mr. Smith hurried away, evidently very glad to escape any further detention, Arnold said: "Even if you accepted my offer, I see not how I could explain the defences of our works to you here in this confounded darkness. At Mr. Smith's I have all our engineer's plans—and it would be very important that whoever leads the attacking party should understand the details thoroughly."

"I suppose what must be must be," replied André, good humoredly. "How far off is this house of Mr. Smith's?"

"Oh, not so very far. Come this way; I have a couple of horses that will take us there in a twinkling."

Arrived at the spot where the horses had been left, they mounted, Arnold giving the negro a five-dollar note, "to buy a dram with," to comfort him for having to walk home.

"I never carry anything less than five-dollar notes in

my pocket," said Arnold, laughing sardonically. "You can't buy even a glass of grog for less than that, with this cursed shinbone currency."

André made no reply. Their road lay through the woods, which made the night seem darker than before, and it required some care to ride safely.

"To-hoo-oo-oo-oo."

"D——n that owl—if it is not following us!" exclaimed Arnold. "If it were not for the noise, I'd send a pistol bullet at it."

"To-hoo-oo-oo-oo."

"It is not very pleasant music to ride by, but I suppose we must submit to it," said André good-humoredly.

They had ridden several miles, and André was beginning to wonder why they did not reach Mr. Smith's abode, when suddenly he found himself in the midst of a little hamlet, and then the hoarse "who goes there?" of a sentinel broke upon his ear.

André's first thought was, "I am betrayed," and his heart sunk within him; but Arnold's immediate reply, "Friends," and his utterance of the countersign, "Congress," reassured him. Then, the immediate danger over, he grew very indignant. As soon as it was prudent to speak, he rode up to Arnold's side.

"Did you not understand me, General, that I would not go within your lines? That was my express stipulation with you."

"You have your uniform on, under that surtout, have you not?" replied Arnold sternly.

"Of course I have; and this is my usual watch-coat."

"Then what does it matter? You are just as safe within our lines as outside. They could not do more than make a prisoner of you, and they would do that as soon at Long Clove as here."

"There is more danger here, though."

"I did not suppose a British soldier cared for a little danger, more or less," scoffed Arnold.

"Neither do I. But I have a point of delicacy in my share of this business, and that constrained me to insist that the negotiation should take place outside of your lines."

"If you had so much delicacy of feeling, you should have kept out of the business altogether," exclaimed Arnold savagely. "To me such boyish scruples seem nonsense, in view of what you are asking me to do for the King and the Empire."

There was great force in what Arnold said, as André could but own. His position was delicacy itself compared to Arnold's; so much so, that it even seemed insulting to dwell upon the subject. But yet the affair left an uneasy feeling in his mind. It was evident that he was dealing with a man naturally and boldly unscrupulous; and therefore who might deceive one side as well as the other.

As André rode on silently, thinking of all this, he felt the importance of obtaining some security in Arnold's handwriting that might hold him to his word. Everything so far, of a direct character, was in a disguised hand, and under his assumed name. Else the British forces might find West Point only a decoy, and themselves with a strong Fortress in their front, and the whole Continental army in their rear. If they were tricked, they should at least be able to show that they had acted upon reasonable assurances of good faith.

A traitor's mere word, it was evident, could not be wholly relied upon. If it could, he would not be a traitor. Even treason to a bad cause, seemed to involve this conclusion. See, Arnold had broken faith with him at the very start. It was a small matter, some might say, but where a single acorn falls there is an oak. André, as he reflected thus, grew fearful—not so much for himself, as for the army and the royal cause.

"Major," said Arnold, after a time, and in a frank and friendly tone, "I am sorry for what has happened. In fact, I forgot all about that outpost being at Haverstraw, until we had allowed Smith to leave us, and it was too late to reconsider our determination. I am myself as rash as—as I am cautious; but in your place, would think it safer, to hold our conference in the privacy of a house, than in such an exposed spot as that we met in. Why, what with the midnight and the darkness, and the river plainings, and that accursed owl, it seemed just like a haunt of conspirators."

"Perhaps you are right," returned André, a little coldly. "But how much farther have we to ride?"

"We are almost there. You will see the white walls even through this darkness before many minutes. Ah, here we are!" And, turning into a little inclosure, Arnold pulled up at the door of a medium-sized house, evidently belonging to a gentleman of considerable means and pretensions.

Dismounting, they walked into a well-lighted room, being greeted only by a negro servant, the master of the house not having yet arrived, and his family all being absent on a visit adroitly planned for this occasion.

"Take a glass of wine, Mr. Anderson!" said Arnold, walking up to the sideboard, and pouring out a glass from one of the decanters which stood there. "It will warm you up a little. The Hudson is a grand river, but I should like it better if it were not so good a place for agues. Poor Smith—did you see how he was shaking?"

Andre took the wine, and then Arnold swallowed three or four glasses in rapid succession. It needed something powerful to brace up his iron nerves. "Now, if Mr. Smith's cook will dish us up something smoking for breakfast, we can go up-stairs, and finish our conference."

Talking upon indifferent subjects, they awaited their host's arrival. When he came, they all sat down and partook of breakfast, and, that over, it being broad daylight by this time, Arnold and André retired to one of the upper chambers, where they could plot and plan unseen and undisturbed.

CHAPTER III.

THE PRICE OF TREASON.

> We want security,
> That we shall not expend our men and money
> All to no purpose.—*Wallenstein.*

BEFORE sitting down to breakfast, as mentioned in our last chapter, the noise of the cannonade opened upon the Vulture, had broken upon the ears of the party at the White House, as Mr. Smith's residence was usually called. And from one of the windows of the second story room in which Arnold and André were now seated, they had watched the progress of the cannonade, until they saw the Vulture weigh her anchor, and sail down the river out of the reach of her enemy's fire. Then they had seated themselves before a table covered with drawings and papers, and resumed their conference at the point where they had been interrupted at Long Clove.

"General," said Andre, "the terms you mentioned are inadmissible. I will give you at once the limit of my powers—and then you must accept or reject, as you think best. I am authorized to offer you at the highest, Thirty Thousand pounds, payable within ten days after the surrender of the Fortress. This is the very best I am authorized to do."

There was sincerity in every lineament of André's face as he spoke; and Arnold, though grown habitually distrustful—perhaps he had always been so—knew at once that what he said was the exact truth.

"I will accept your offer, Major—though the sum is, in my opinion, just Fifteen Thousand pounds too small. It being understood of course, that I accept simply because you are not authorized to go higher; and reserve my right to petition the King for the additional sum, to be granted or not, at his good pleasure."

"I can see no objection to that," replied André.

"As life is uncertain, Major, and men's memories treacherous, you would oblige me by giving me that promise in writing," continued Arnold.

"I would willingly do so, but it would be rather a dangerous document to have about you, General—especially if they should suspect and search you."

"I shall be satisfied with an indirect voucher, in your own natural hand," said Arnold, handing him a pen and a sheet of paper. "Write as I dictate:—

"I promise to pay for the Robinson estate, if restored, Thirty Thousand pounds sterling. Mr. Gustavus to have the same Agency as heretofore."

"It is written," said André with a smile. "Now how shall I sign it?"

"Sign it, John Anderson, Agent."

"It will do," said Arnold, also smiling. "It is not a first-class voucher, but it is the best I can trust my pocket and neck with."

"Now," continued Arnold, "as we have that little matter settled, let me instruct you fully in my plans. Here is Duportail's plans of all the forts; he is a Frenchman, but a capital engineer, you must admit. You see this dot at Fort Putnam—that is a breach through which a section could march abreast; it is closed just now with a few loose boards. Here is the place where you land—and here your path. Once at this spot in strength, and Fort Putnam is yours—that taken, all is taken. You will have no difficulty in finding guides, I suppose."

"Not the least—we have scores of refugees in New York from this region; and they are more earnest, and far more bitter in their loyalty, than even the royal troops themselves."

"And here," added Arnold, "are six important papers: 'Estimates of our forces,' 'Remarks on the Works,' 'Major Bauman's account of the ordnance on the different forts, batteries,' &c., nearly all in my handwriting, you see. You might take a summary of these, detailed as so many barrels of sugar, with remarks on the condition of the merchandize, which would refresh your memory when referred to."

"I think I had better take the papers themselves," said André. This was the opportunity he had been waiting for—something in Arnold's own writing that would hold him, as much as anything could, to his bargain.

"If these were discovered on you they would betray all," replied Arnold.

"I must risk that. There is little danger between here and the river; and on the river I shall hold them in my hand, tied up with a stone, so that I can sink them at once if necessary."

"We have had good luck so far, but I am afraid this is tempting Providence," rejoined Arnold, who, like most men, good or bad, evidently considered the success of his schemes a sure sign that Providence had favored them.

"This one risk we must run!" exclaimed André in a resolute tone. "As you said, a little danger, more or less, is not of much consequence."

"Well, be it so!" replied Arnold gloomily. Was it that he really feared the danger, or realized that a withdrawal from his treason was no longer possible to him?

"And now," said André, "let me go carefully over all these plans. I shall probably lead the attack myself, and am anxious not only that it should succeed, but that, if possible, not a single life should be sacrificed."

We need not repeat the numerous questions and answers which ensued, before the British officer felt himself completely master of the details of the proposed movement. The very guns and other signals to announce the British progress were agreed upon. When within three miles of the place, two British officers in American uniforms were to ride up at full gallop to Arnold's headquarters, receive his final words, and hasten back to the English commander. Never, perhaps, was a treasonable plot more ably elaborated. But "the stars in their courses fought against Sisera!"

WEST POINT IN 1780.

CHAPTER IV.

A PERILOUS JOURNEY.

I carry with me England and her fortunes—
Give me, you saints, a safe delivery!

It was all arranged; and Arnold had gathered up his charts and plans, and taken his departure. At his earnest solicitation, André had secreted the six important papers which he had resolved to keep as a guarantee of the traitor's good faith, placing them between the soles of his feet and his stockings. And now, the British officer, somewhat fatigued from the want of sleep on the previous night, awaited the coming of the darkness to be conveyed back to the Vulture.

He passed a miserable day, as may be supposed. There he was, in the enemy's lines, liable at any moment to capture. Through his chamber window he could see the Vulture, which had resumed her former position. The vessel was lying between three and four miles off, down the wide river, almost at this place a bay in its magnitude, evidently awaiting his coming. Oh that he had the wings of a bird, that he might fly on board, and be once more in safety!

About the middle of the afternoon, his host appeared, and disquieted him still further. Mr. Smith alleged that it would be impossible to get him back the same way he had come. The boatmen had been frightened by the cannonade, and obstinately refused to go. He himself was suffering from an ague brought on by the last night's exposure, and it would be as much as his life was worth to venture again on the water. And to these were added the other excuses, reasonable and unreasonable, which a weak man who has obstinately made up his mind not to do a certain thing, always has on hand.

André was indignant—he demanded to see the boatmen himself; but they had gone off somewhere—at least Smith so alleged. He was in fact at the mercy of that gentleman, and must do as he said, or get back the best way he could without him.

"Well," said André, at length, bitterly, "what do you propose, Mr. Smith?"

"To cross the river at the Ferry this evening, and go by land," replied that gentleman complacently.

"What! in this dress?" exclaimed André, glancing at his British uniform. "I should be arrested at the Ferry, as certainly as I reached there."

"I have provided for all that," replied his host. "The General gave me a pass both for myself and Mr. John Anderson to White Plains, and I have in the closet here a coat and hat which will fit you famously."

"Do you know what a risk I should expose myself to by assuming that disguise?" questioned André sternly.

"Oh, there is no danger, Mr. Anderson—not a particle. If you meet the Americans, you have General Arnold's pass; if you meet the British, all they can do is to take you where you want to go. I am not a soldier, as you are—and doubtless a brave one—but even I should not be afraid to take a little risk like that."

"I will not do it!" said André resolutely.

"What will you do then, Captain?" asked Smith, venturing a guess at the rank of his guest; for André's uniform did not denote his precise rank. "I promised the General that I would see you safely back; but of course that depended upon your following my instructions. If you will not do as I wish, of course my door is open, and you can take any other course you prefer. Only do not hold me responsible for the consequences."

Smith evidently did not know to whom he was talking

—evidently had no idea of the importance of the business his visitor was intrusted with. Arnold, it was clear, had not taken him into his confidence. If Arnold had not, it would not do for him, André, to do it. And yet how could he overrule him, and bring him to his senses, without exposing more than Arnold, who knew him, evidently thought safe. Never was man more puzzled.

If he assumed the disguise, he was acting in the very face of his General's instructions—exposing himself in case of capture to the most fearful and dangerous suspicions—putting himself, even if not captured, in a false position, from which his inmost soul recoiled.

But, on the other hand, if he refused to act in accordance with his host's counsel, what should he do? In his uniform, he could not stir out of his room in the daytime without danger—and where, in the night, could he find a boat to put him on board the Vulture? Debating these things in his mind, he walked up and down the room in a turmoil of indecision and indignation.

His host awaited his decision with ill-concealed impatience. At last he said, "You do not seem to be aware, Captain, that while you remain in that uniform, you are not only in constant danger of bringing yourself into trouble, but also of compromising me. Suppose a party of Lee's dragoons should ride up and discover you—do you think they would let me go scot-free?"

"You might have a little trouble, but General Arnold would see you through harmless."

"General Arnold, I reckon, wouldn't thank you or me for stirring up this matter."

"I can see no good reason why you should not put me on board the Vulture this evening, as originally planned," rejoined André.

Smith made a gesture of impatience. "Well, I will

tell you," said he. "The men will not go. They went the first time, as I did, because we were willing to put ourselves into a little danger to oblige Colonel Robinson, who you know used to be a great man in these parts. But when they found that it was not the Colonel after all, but you, a perfect stranger, they thought they had been a little tricked. Now there is more danger than then, since that four-pounder is down there; and they know that any boat that did not show a flag, especially in the night, would be fired at just as soon as seen. 'If the General wants you put on board,' they say, 'let him send his own barge, with a flag, and put you there.' Now, what answer can I make to all this?"

"I am not in the habit of giving reasons to my men for what I order them to do," replied André haughtily.

"Yes, yes, that will do very well in the army," rejoined Smith. "But these men, though tenants of mine, have a will of their own. If it were not that they hate the war, and wish it were all over, one way or the other—they don't care much which—they would not have gone in the first place."

"If you'll find me a skiff, I'll put myself on board."

"I should not know where to go to find one. The river guards appropriated every one of them long ago."

There seemed nothing else to do than to act in accordance with his host's suggestion. "I suppose I must do as you think best," at last said André, "but it is the most despicable thing that I ever was forced to do in the whole course of my life, and I would not do it now, were not the safety of others involved with my own."

"You take it too seriously, Captain," returned Smith lightly. "One red coat is just as good as another—and better too in this case."

So saying, he opened the closet, and produced a coat

of a dark crimson, garnished with gold lace, a common dress for a gentleman at that period—but somewhat faded and threadbare from use. A well-worn beaver hat also was brought forth. André took them and substituted these for his military coat and hat; the remainder of his dress, nankin waistcoat and small-clothes, with handsome white-topped boots, was allowed to go unaltered. Then, putting over all his well-worn watch-coat, with its heavy cape, and buttoning it closely about his neck, to conceal, as it were, even from himself his hateful disguise, he announced that he was ready.

It took a little time to get the horses saddled, so that it was almost twilight before they set out, being accompanied by a negro servant. They crossed King's Ferry about twilight, Smith stopping to chat and drink with the American officers on the other or eastern side of the river, while André and the servant rode slowly onward.

Between eight and nine o'clock they came across an American patrol, under Captain Boyd, who demanded their errand. Smith showed their passes, and declared aside to the captain, that they were on their way to obtain intelligence for Arnold.

Boyd said that the road before them was infested with Cow-boys, as the predatory bands of Tories on the neutral ground between the two armies were called, and that it would be madness to go further that night.

André would have pressed on, but Smith thought it safer or less suspicious to take Captain Boyd's advice, so they sought the dwelling of a neighboring Scotchman, who cheerfully offered to give them a night's lodging. So far they had come safely.

CHAPTER V.

FOR THE THIRD TIME.

We are such stuff
As dreams are made of.
Shakspeare.

Drawing off his heavy military boots, and divesting himself of his surtout and his coat, André was prepared for the night's slumbers. But before extinguishing the tallow-candle with which their host had provided them, André turned his back to his companion, and drew out a little miniature from where it hung, attached to a blue ribbon, beneath the linen of his bosom. It was a very striking likeness of Helen Graham, painted from memory by his own hand. Such had been the excitement and deep interest of the last twenty-four hours, that, devoted lover as he was, he had not even thought of his beautiful mistress, much less looked upon her likeness. The important negotiations entrusted to him, his embarrassing personal position, involving not only his own safety, but that of others, and the success or failure of a deeply-planned scheme, pregnant with momentous results, had banished all softer thoughts from his mind. But now, nothing was necessary to be thought or done for his General and his King, and the power of habit asserted itself—first, his brief but earnest prayer, then a glance at the pictured face of his betrothed.

André thought that he slept the sounder and sweeter for both these things—and that if he dreamed, he was more certain to be transported in imagination to the side of his lady, to hear the rich music of her voice, to be thrilled by the tender glances of her brilliant and beautiful eyes. Doubtless it usually was so. But the charm this night did not work—seemed overpowered by some baleful and malignant influence.

He lay for some time wakeful and watchful. It appeared impossible for him to compose his mind so that he could sleep. And when at length his senses settled into unconsciousness, his thoughts still heaved and surged like the waves after, or before, a terrible storm.

And then at last he dreamed—the dream of his life! For the third time—that dream which he had related at the pleasant dinner-table of Mrs. Pemberton, the evening of the adventure on the Wissahickon. He was riding—alone. He came to the brow of a gentle declivity. All around seemed familiar to him. He rode on. There was the gigantic poplar, with its immense branches, gnarled and twisted, descending at places to the earth, and then rising again. Suddenly a man in British uniform stepped forth, with presented musket. "Halt!"

The loudness of this command seemed to awaken him. "It is curious," thought he. "That old dream. The third time. Well, I am glad the fellow was in British uniform," with a smile, as he composed himself once more to slumber.

Again he dreamed. This time it was different—but more fearful. It was the Sibyl's prediction—but clothed apparently with the reality of life. Acted out bodily and mentally—not to be distinguished for the time from reality—all palpable, painful, tumultuous, terrible! There was the gallows. There he stood—felt himself to be standing. He mounted the wagon, his hands were bound, the noose was placed around his neck. He awoke with a cry of horror, that aroused his slumbering companion.

"What's the matter, Captain?"

"I beg your pardon. I had a horrible nightmare, and cried out."

"Oh, that's all," said Mr. Smith, turning over, and settling himself to his slumbers.

André wiped the cold sweat from his brow. "I know not what is the matter with me to-night," thought he. "That was a fearful dream—that Witch's horrible scene over again. It may mean nothing—probably does mean nothing. But—whatever it mean—it cannot mean anything that I, an officer and a gentleman, cannot meet bravely and firmly endure. Especially if Westminster Abbey come after all"—and he smiled a proud smile.

Still no settled, peaceful slumber. All wild, heaving, tumultuous—though nothing further shaped and definite. With the first faint dawn of morning André wakened, and was eager to leave his bed, and go out into the cheerful day.

CHAPTER VI.

ON THE WAY.

Our glories float between the earth and heaven,
Like clouds which seem pavilions of the sun,
And are the playthings of the casual wind.

—Bulwer's Richelieu.

As André opened the front door of the farm-house, and stepped out into the porch, the first faint amber light of morning was beginning to illuminate the perfectly clear horizon. Glorious in the East, above the dawn, still shone the Morning Star—Lucifer the Magnificent! And as the British officer stood and watched the gradual coming of the day, he felt—poet and artist as he was—that fervor of admiration, which almost has a tinge of remorse at its own inadequacy fully to realize or express the mingled sublimity and beauty which it beholds. It is the homage which the Finite pays to the Infinite. That deep feeling of "I cannot paint thee, cannot even express, or fully understand thee! I see thou art sublimely beautiful—but I mourn that I cannot contain thee! And now thou art passing from my view—and if thou didst not thus pass, thou wouldst become as common and tame to me as common day, with all its wondrous beauty, variety, and grandeur. Thus the Infinite which I cannot grasp, grows Finite to me with use and custom. Therefore pass away, oh, glorious sunrise—pass away, with thy amber and green and blue and crimson and gold—lest thou, too, become to me prosaic and commonplace!"

Thus thought André, as so many poetical minds had thought before him, since first the day-spring lighted up the East, since first the day-death faded in glory in the West. Thought, also, of how the sun goes rolling on, accompanied by those two triumphal arches of sunrise and sunset, never failing him for a moment, only shifting their places of abode—the constant attendants and evidences of his glory, the splendidly attired heralds that announce the coming and proclaim the departure of the sovereign Lord of Earth.

And as André stood there in the early freshness of the morning, the cool breezes seemed also to blow through his brain, and dispel the gloomy visions of the night. The weight which had seemed to be resting upon his mind when he had awakened, had already passed away, and even the memory of it seemed obscure and faded. It is curious what slaves we are to darkness and the night. The fear that appals at midnight—which causes the heart to sink and the pulse to throb—loses its terror in the clear, full light of morning. Why is it that darkness, and even candle-light, make such cowards of us all?

Rousing their negro attendant, André directed him to saddle the horses; and the moment Mr. Smith came down they mounted, and were soon, as they deemed, entirely out of reach of the American patrols. This fact, combined with the fineness of the day, and the exhilaration of riding, made André feel like another man. Such was his exuberance of spirit that it overflowed even toward Mr. Smith, who ever afterward declared that he had never met with a more delightful companion—so full of pleasant conversation was he; while the charm of his mere presence was a constant delight.

They were now in the Neutral Ground, and the grass-grown and deserted roads, the gates torn from their hinges, the crops that frequently lay ungathered and rotten, and the absence both of men and cattle from the fields, all united in proclaiming the hapless condition to which the war had reduced the garden county of Westchester. For who would till when he knew that in all probability the fruits of his toil would be wrested from him? But although these evidences of the rapine of man could deface, they could not destroy the beauty of the landscape. For the woods were in the first flush of Autumn, and the country through which they passed picturesque beyond description. From every eminence André gazed with fresh delight upon the glorious hills of the Highlands, looking harmonious and mystical in their misty robes of blue, and thought, these truly are the Delectable mountains. Gazing at them he forgot for the time his disguise, the perils of his position, the great war which convulsed the land, and thought only of the glory of this wonderful earth, so passing all description.

But he was suddenly recalled to sublunary things, by seeing another traveller approaching. This horseman wore a cloak, so that it was difficult to decide whether he was or was not a civilian; but, as he came near, André saw at a glance that the face of the traveller was familiar to him. So he resolutely kept his head turned to one side, until the stranger was nearly abreast of them; and, as they passed each other wiped his eyes with his handkerchief, thus almost concealing his face from view. The horseman gazed earnestly at him, but passed on with a brief salutation and without apparent recognition. André drew a deep breath. He saw that it was Lieutenant Morris, but whether the latter had recognized him also, he could not certainly know, though he felt tolerably confident from the Lieutenant's manner that he had not.

After riding a few miles further, Mr. Smith proposed that they should halt at a wayside cottage which they were approaching, and see if they could not get their horses fed, as well as some breakfast for themselves. Its mistress agreed to supply their wants, though she told them with a sad countenance that she had been visited during the night by a party of marauders—"either Skinners or Cow-boys," she knew not which—and plundered of all she possessed, save some corn-meal and hay, and a single cow. With the meal, however, she soon prepared them a dish of that New World porridge, which she called *soupaan*, but which the Pennsylvanians call mush, and the New Englanders hasty pudding; and which, when eaten with milk or with molasses, or as a certain distinguished personage prefers it, with both, is one of the most nutritious, wholesome and pleasant dishes for a hungry man that the wide world affords.

André and his companion ate it with that hearty relish which a ride in the brisk morning air is apt to create. It was an old acquaintance of André's, for he had often eaten it when a prisoner at Lancaster among the Pennsylvania Dutch.

At the conclusion of their repast, Mr. Smith announced to the English officer his intention of letting him take the rest of his way alone. He had agreed with General Arnold, if they went by land, to see André safely to White Plains. But, for some reason or other—perhaps because he thought it useless, perhaps because he wished to be rid of the company of a man who was evidently far other than he seemed—he did not perform his promise. If he had, what might not have been the result? André might have gone safely under Smith's guidance, for they almost certainly would have taken the direct road to White Plains, or, if they had not, would probably have gone unchallenged, for Smith was personally known through all that part of the country.

But Smith did as he did. Was it merely chance? Is there any such thing as chance in the course of great events, even if there be in the course of small ones? Who can answer?

If it were not in the order of Providence that this plot should succeed, why was it not nipped at an earlier stage? A mere shadow of suspicion thrown across the mind of Washington, the result of some casual conversation with Greene or Lafayette—both of whom disliked Arnold, and who had themselves the warmest confidence of their Chief—and the command of West Point would have been entrusted to another, while Arnold would have disappeared from the further scenes of the war.

Or, if the plot was to be allowed to come to a head, and have its open failure and its victim, why was the guilty Arnold allowed to escape almost so miraculously, and the comparatively innocent André be caught in the toils, and offered up as a scapegoat to the vengeance of a justly incensed army and people?

If Providence did not interfere, how was it that the plot was so curiously and marvellously brought to naught? If Providence did interfere, why was it that the toils were drawn around André, the gentle and generous and accomplished, the poet and the artist, while Arnold, who betrayed the trust of his commander, the confidence of his friend and benefactor, and the cause of which he had been one of the most determined champions, was allowed to brush aside the net which was rapidly closing around him, make his escape to the enemy, and afterwards dare with impunity all the hazards of active war?

We can ask, but we cannot answer these questions. They lie among the inscrutable facts of life and history. Our intuitions cry out against the supposition that Chance and not an Overruling Power directs the issue of great events; but why that Power seems to act at some times, and not at others—and often apparently in a manner so inconsistent with itself—baffles our best reason and judgment to decide.

But we anticipate. And why not? Nature anticipates. Before the bursting of the storm, you hear the sad wailing of the wind. Before the earthquake, you feel the shudder of the anguished globe. And as we approach the saddest scene of our story, the wind seems to wail and the earth to shudder with an anguish that rolls down the years, through the long course of almost a century.

CHAPTER VII.

THE ARREST OF ANDRE.

So fall my visioned splendors to the earth!
And all our schemes, so grand and absolute,
Melt like a bubble, touched by some child's hand.
Out upon Life—we are the jest and sport
Of every breeze that blows!

BEFORE parting after breakfast, Mr. Smith explained particularly to the British officer the route he should take; though it seemed impossible, as he said, to go astray, so long as he kept in a southerly direction. After crossing the Croton river, a mile or so distant, he could either keep on due south to White Plains, or take the road which bore off toward the West, and which would soon bring him to the river road, which ran down to New York along the Hudson.

"I shall take the latter then," said André at once.

"Perhaps it is the best for you, Mr. Anderson, though if I were going, I should take the other. You may meet Cow-boys along that route."

"And Skinners on the other. I prefer to meet the Cow-boys."

"Neither are very desirable acquaintances," replied Mr. Smith laughing; "but of the two, perhaps the Cow-boys would treat you best. Of course, if you do meet the Skinners, you had better show your pass. The Cow-boys, I am afraid, would think rather less of you for showing it."

"I think you counsel wisely."

"I believe I have now given you all the necessary directions. I wish you a safe and pleasant journey, Mr. Anderson. Remember me to my brother, the Chief Justice, when you meet him in New York."

"I will, certainly. And I wish you also a safe and pleasant trip home again, Mr. Smith. Tell the General when you see him, that you left me nearly through, and all safe."

And they parted. Mr. Smith and his servant returning the way they came; not recrossing the river however, but keeping straight on to Arnold's headquarters.

André rode south, crossing the Croton, and then took the turn which led to the river. An hour or so, and he was on the river road. It was a beautiful ride—hills, valleys, and continual glimpses of the Hudson on his right—and yet his mood had changed, he knew not why, and he felt uneasy and disquieted. He had entered under the cloud; but he knew it not.

As he rode on and on, the gloomy visions of the previous night seemed to gather within him. All without was sunshine, save where dense woods and deep ravines made a darkness as of twilight; but his heart was heavy, and his mind was covered as with a funeral pall. Suddenly he pulled up his horse on the top of a stony hill, and looked around and before him.

The scene was strangely familiar. He seemed to recognize every surrounding object—even to a huge moss-grown rock, with a young sapling apparently splitting it asunder. He touched his horse with the whip, and slowly descended the hill, gazing intently about him. It came to him with the rapidity and intensity of lightning; it was the scene of his three dreams. For a moment he felt so unnerved that he feared he should tumble from his horse.

Then he drew in his breath and summoned up his courage, as is the way with a man not only physically but spiritually brave. The feet of his horse were now clattering on the logs of the little bridge that lay across the stream, in the depths of the ravine. And before him, on the right of the road, was the immense Poplar tree, which he now saw for the fourth time, with its huge contorted branches.

"Now for the soldier with his levelled musket," was his sudden thought; and, at the moment, a man sprang into the road before him, and with his gun pointed at his breast, cried sternly—

"Halt!"

The well-known military attire and word recalled the British officer to himself.

He pulled up his horse, and took a rapid glance at the man, whom he now saw was not alone, but had two comrades. He was a tall, lusty fellow, and wore a faded British uniform. It was evident he was either a British soldier or a Cow-boy.

"My boys," said André, "you must not delay me. I see you belong to our party."

"Which party?" asked the one who wore the uniform, and was evidently the master-spirit, and whose name was Paulding.

"Why, the lower party, the loyal party, of course."

"You look as if you belonged to our party, by the direction you came from," said Paulding, with an oath.

"I do, nevertheless, my boys. I am a British officer, on urgent business; and if you are true friends of the royal cause, you will not delay me."

"I say, Paulding," cried another of the men, "he looks like a British officer, in them ere riggings, doesn't he? Officers generally wear rigimentals where I come from."

The three laughed jeeringly.

"To prove to you I am what I say, look at this watch," said André, producing a gold repeater. "The gentlemen up in this part of the country do not usually carry gold watches, do they?"

"And even if you were a British officer," exclaimed Paulding, "blamed little we'd care. We belong to the other side, Mr. Officer."

André's heart gave a great leap. Had he committed himself too soon? This man, like himself, might be in disguise. Then he laughed lightly.

"All's fair in war, my boys," said he. "A man must do anything to get along. The truth is, I am travelling on public business by General Arnold's directions; I'd have shown you my pass at first, but for that dirty red-coat. You'll see this is all right," and he handed them the pass from General Arnold.

"What's the blamed thing say, Paulding?"

"It's d—d bad writing—as most writing is," replied Paulding, investigating the pass with as much intentness as if it had been written in Chinese or Hindoo—"but I make out it says 'Pass' and 'White Plains,' and 'B. Arnold' at the tail of it—but whether this is the gentleman that the General orders us to pass, the Lord only knows, I don't."

"I bleeve he's a rascally trader, with lots of money, going down to New York to buy and smuggle out dry goods and groceries," said the one of the party who had not spoken, and who was named Van Wart.

"Yes, probably one of them fellers that makes us poor country folks pay ten prices for our rum and sugar," chimed in Williams.

"Let's search him," exclaimed Paulding, "and find out what he is. If he's one of them blasted speculators, he has plenty of money somewheres about him."

"Yes, I say sarch him; we'll find something that 'll tell whether he's an officer or a speckilator," cried Williams.

"Hands off there!" exclaimed André indignantly, wresting himself from the rough hands that Williams had laid upon him. "How dare you presume on such a thing in the face of this pass? If you attempt it, I warn you you'll have to answer to General Arnold, who is not a man to be trifled with."

"D—n General Arnold!" cried Paulding. "The law of the Neutral Ground is the law of the strongest."

"I shouldn't wonder," said Van Wart, "if General Arnold was consarned with this feller; he's always up to some speckilation or other to make money. A friend of mine who came from Philadelphy, told me he was all the time at it down there, until the people hated him like pisen."

"Well," said Paulding, "if he is one of Arnold's cronies, we'll take a share too. It's not fair the General should be making all the money. The law of New York says that any good Whig may capture and confiscate all supplies intended for the enemy; and if this gentleman is going to New York with a lot of money, it is our duty as good Whigs to confiscate it, and put it to better uses. Isn't that so, boys?"

Van Wart and Williams swore with many an oath that

that was good law; not only Neutral Ground law, but good law anywhere.

"Now, sir," continued Paulding, addressing André, "we give you your choice. You may either come out of the road, and into the bushes with us, and allow yourself to be peaceably searched, or you may make a row, and force us to do it by main strength. It don't make much matter to us which you do; there are three of us, and either of us as strong as you are; but it may make a good deal of difference to you."

"Supposing you do not find that large sum of money, will you be satisfied, and let me go on my way?"

"Well, yes; I think we may say yes, boys," replied Paulding.

"It is a bargain, then," said André, somewhat relieved. "Here is my purse, containing a few sovereigns, and here are my two watches;" for in accordance with a common custom of the fine gentlemen of the time, André then wore two watches, a gold and a silver one; "these are all the valuables you will find upon me."

The whole party then moved off from the road, to a spot under the gigantic Tulip Tree, where some bushes and the low bending branches of the tree concealed them from the view of any traveller who should pass by.

As André took off his coat and vest, he handed them to his captors for examination.

They found nothing, though they felt the garments very carefully all over, to ascertain whether anything was concealed between the cloth and the lining, even ripping the lining open at several places.

"What is this?" said Van Wart, giving a pull at the ribbon to which the miniature of Helen was attached.

André pulled out the miniature. "My boys, I ask as a special favor, that I be allowed to retain this. It would not be of much value to you; it is of the greatest value to me."

A smile passed over the faces of his captors—but they examined the miniature with no small degree of interest.

"A d—d beautiful lady that, Mister!" exclaimed Paulding. "Boys, we won't touch that. We've got sisters and sweethearts ourselves, and be she sister or sweetheart, and it's none of our business which she is, we don't confiscate things of that sort."

"No, he'd have to be a blamed mean man that 'd take that from you," cried Williams.

"Thank you!" said André, while his face lighted up. "May both sisters and sweethearts smile on you for this!"

After this little incident, there was a touch of softness in the language and manners of his captors, that they had not manifested before. But they resolutely went on with their search.

Still, they found nothing. At last they came to his boots. "Sit down, sir, on that stump, we must pull off your boots now," said Paulding.

"My boys, you might as well have believed me at first. I have got no more money about me. There is no money in my boots, how could I carry money there?"

"We mean to be sure of it," replied Paulding. "While you are talking, we could see for ourselves."

The boots were drawn off; Van Wart put his hands down as far as he could, but could feel nothing. "I should like to have a pair of boots like those," said he admiringly.

"What would you do with them, Van?" cried Paulding, with a laugh; "wear them on your hands, or give them to Betsy, to see if she could get them on?"

They all glanced down at their huge cowhide shoes, with a loud laugh. The boots were so small that they absolutely were not worth stealing; though a good pair of boots was a very precious article among the country people of that day.

"Try his stockings," said Williams.

Paulding knelt down and passed his hand across his feet.

"By the Lord, here it is!" exclaimed he, feeling a package under the sole of one of André's feet.

"I knew we'd find it!" cried Van Wart, excitedly. "Bank of England notes, I'll bet!"

"My boys," said André, while his face blanched, "you are mistaken. That is not money. It is simply some private correspondence of mine."

"Oh, get out!" cried Williams, feeling under the other foot. "Here's some more, boys. I'll warrant this 'll pay better than even those cattle dealers we were watching for."

André knew it was useless to say more.

Paulding soon had the papers in his hand. "No money, after all!" said he blankly.

"No money!" repeated the others disconsolately.

"I told you so, my boys," said André. "You will oblige me by handing those papers back to me."

Paulding was engaged however in slowly spelling out to himself the contents of one of the papers.

"This seems to be all about West Point," said he, evidently puzzled. "Fort Putnam—stone—wan-ting great re-pairs—wall on east side broke down! Good God, boys, he's a spy!"

"A spy!" cried both the others excitedly—and gazing on André as if they expected to see something very unusual manifest itself in his appearance.

"Nonsense!" exclaimed André, putting on a brave face, though he felt in all its awful intensity, the peril of his situation. "I told you that I was on the public business, under General Arnold's orders. You said I was not —and that I had lots of money for speculating with. You wished to search me, and agreed if you did not find the money, to let me go without further trouble. It has all come out just as I said. Now I ask you to do as you promised."

"Yes," said Paulding, "and so we would, if we hadn't found those papers."

"What difference does that make?"

"See here, Mister—we're poor men. We live here on this Neutral Ground. There's no use working—our crops are all trodden down or stolen. Everything we had to live on, has been taken from us. We must live. It's no great harm to pluck a Tory, 'specially if he's just been taking cattle down to New York. The law says we may confiscate the cattle if we can catch them, and we'd just as lieve confiscate the hard money after the cattle's sold. But, you see, we are good, true Whigs with it all—and if you are a spy, and it looks confoundedly like it, we're not going to let you get off to New York with all that about West Point in your stockings."

"No—that's a horse of another color," cried Van Wart.

"And a durned black color at that!" exclaimed Williams.

"And so you are such good Whigs, that though I show you the pass of your own General, ordering you to let me go on to White Plains, because I am on public business by his direction, you choose to think you know better than he does, and interfere with his wise plans."

"Let's see that pass again," said Paulding.

André had resumed his attire, and now took the pass from his waistcoat pocket, and handed it to him.

After spelling at it for awhile, Paulding said—"This pass says, 'Permit Mr. John Anderson to pass.' How do we know you're Mr. Anderson?"

"Because I have the pass."

"You said at first you were a British officer."

"I thought you were Cow-boys then—that red coat misled me."

"Blast the coat. But when I was a prisoner the other day down in New York, I made the exchange in order to get off. It's the second time I've been in that stinking, lousy jail of theirs. They can put me in, but they can't keep me in—curse them!"

"Yes, and when he said he was an officer, he seemed in good, hearty earnest too," said Williams to Paulding.

"Well, sir," continued Paulding, "I'm sorry if you're one of General Arnold's men—but you'll have to go with us to Colonel Jameson at North Castle. If he says you're all right, it won't delay you very long; and if he says you're a spy, why you'll have to hang, that's all. And I should be confoundedly sorry for the last, even if you're not a very old acquaintance."

"But my business is of such an important character, that it will not admit of even a couple of hours' longer delay," said André earnestly. "You have already seriously incommoded me."

"Can't help it!" replied Paulding resolutely; "you've got to go. So get on your horse."

"What will you take to let me alone, and molest me no further? I had better pay you something, than allow the public business to suffer."

"What will you give?" asked Van Wart.

"I'll give you a hundred guineas."

"We won't do it," said Williams.

"I'll give you five hundred guineas."

"How can you? You say you have no money."

"You can accompany me to King's Bridge, and I will stay there with you until I can send into the city for the money."

"Yes," said Van Wart, "and do as that other officer did the other day. He paid the money, and then had the fellars sent to the Sugar House Jail and flogged. This was giving them a devilish sight more than they'd bargained for."

"It will not do," cried Paulding sternly. "You must go to North Castle."

"I will give you a thousand golden guineas," cried André, despairingly, "and pledge you my honor as a gentleman, that you shall leave King's Bridge unharmed and unmolested."

They were poor men, and the sum seemed an immense one in their eyes. They hesitated; it was evident the temptation was a very strong one.

"No!" at length exclaimed Paulding fiercely. "Not if you would make it ten thousand! I tell you, my boys, we've struck something mighty important, to be worth such a big price. I don't understand it," turning to Addré, "but I'm more determined now than ever to take you in. D—n it, I'd shoot my best friend, if he stood in the way! Am I not right, boys?"

"It's a big sum of money—but we're true Whigs, and he must go in," replied Williams.

"And I say so too," said Van Wart. "Though if I thought he was a mere common spy, and 't would do no harm to the cause, I'd go for taking the money. I bleeve he'd pay it."

"So do I," said Paulding. "But suppose West Point should be taken, and this gentleman be the man that had done it, how would we feel?"

"Durned cheap!" said Van Wart.

"Come, sir!" said Paulding to André, in a stern voice. "We have made up our minds. Mount your horse. It'll only take a couple of hours or so to get to North Castle. Then if you are not a spy, you can explain matters to Colonel Jameson, who is a true gentleman, and he will let you off, and you won't have to pay a sixpence either, besides getting your purse and watches back again."

There was nothing more to be said or done. André mounted his horse. Their party was soon increased by the arrival of three or four others, who had been off in another direction. And with one of his captors grasping his bridle, and the others walking on either side, he was conducted along the roads and across the fields, by the most unfrequented ways, to North Castle.

It was a dismal ride, for although André did not apprehend any very serious results to himself, the whole subtly planned scheme would evidently now be brought to light. The first thing to be done, was to get word of his arrest to Arnold, in order that the American General might make his escape. Possibly, Arnold might liberate him also. Though that was doubtful. It all turned upon the character of Colonel Jameson. If he were naturally unsuspicious, the avalanche might be held back, until both Arnold and himself were out of danger.

But however this might be, all his bright anticipations of an immediate and successful issue to the war, based upon the triumph of treason, were dissipated forever. All the glory of having achieved this important and probably decisive stroke, had faded away from his brow. In its stead, rested upon his forehead the stigma of being a spy, which, however undeserved he might consider it, his disguise, and the valuable papers found in his possession, naturally tended to fasten upon him. A sad, sad ride it was to André. Was it strange that he thought at times of his three-fold dream, so curiously fulfilled, and of that other dream, the same as the prediction of the Sibyl, with its awful ending?

CHAPTER VIII.

BREAKING THE NEWS.

He was not born to shame:
Upon his brow shame is ashamed to sit;
For 'tis a throne where honor may be crowned
Sole monarch of the universal earth.—*Shakspeare.*

It was toward the close of the fourth day after the capture of André, that a horseman rode up to the door of the Pemberton mansion in Philadelphia. Both horse and man looked dusty and weary, as if from the effects of a long ride. Dismounting and fastening the weary animal to the hitching-post, the traveller mounted the steps, and knocked at the door. Very soon Foxey made his appearance.

"Is your master in, Foxey?"

"Bress my soul, Cap'n Morris, is dat you? Ob course Mas' Arth's in. Walk back to de libary, won't you?"

Captain Morris—he had been captain now for some time—stepped hastily forward into the library, just glancing into the parlors as he passed, and, as he entered the room, closed the door after him.

"Why, Phil—glad to see you," exclaimed Pemberton, springing from his chair with extended hand. "But what makes you look so solemn?" continued he, noticing the serious countenance of his friend. "The army been defeated?"

"The army is all right; but I bring sad news, Arthur. Major André is a prisoner."

"Not wounded, I hope."

"No, not in the least."

"Well, that is not so bad. He is out of harm's way—where he can neither hurt us, nor get hurt himself. And when he obtains his parole, we shall have, I trust, the pleasure of his society for awhile."

"Ah—would he were only a prisoner!" rejoined Morris, excitedly. "But Arnold has turned traitor—would have delivered up West Point. André plotted the whole affair with him—assumed a disguise to get back, and was arrested in his disguise near Tarrytown."

"Arnold a traitor! It is not possible!" exclaimed Pemberton.

"Would to God it were not! But he has fled to the enemy. The army is furious. André was captured in disguise; and papers discovered on him which divulged the whole infamous plot. He was arrested as a spy—he is to be tried as a spy—and if something be not done, and that speedily, he will meet the death of a spy."

Pemberton flung himself upon the sofa, and covered his face with his hands. It was terrible—all terrible! Arnold's treason—André's danger. For he loved John André beyond the love of a brother.

"Merciful God!" at length he said. "And how can we tell Helen?"

The tears came into Morris's eyes. "That has been worrying me all my long ride," he said. "Arthur, rather than she should suffer as she will, I would cheerfully die in André's place."

"But he must not die!" exclaimed Pemberton, starting up. "What were the facts—did he enter our lines in disguise?"

"No, I learn not. He says he entered our lines in his own uniform, and unknowingly—he having expressly stipulated with Arnold that they should meet outside. But Arnold deceived him—he might have known that a traitor could not be trusted—false to one, false to all! Then, once inside, and unable to get back the way he came, at Arnold's request he assumed his disguise. He flings back with scorn the charge that he is a spy."

"I would believe John André against the world," exclaimed Pemberton. "We must save him! I will return with you at once to Tappan."

"We will do what we can," replied Morris gloomily; "but I fear all our efforts will be in vain. The army, as I said, is furious—from the General-in-Chief down. They all demand a sacrifice. You have seen Washington set his lips together; then he looks stern and implacable as Nemesis. André has laid himself open by his change of dress to the charge of being a spy; and nothing, I fear, can save him!"

"Arnold is gone?"

"Yes, safe in New York. If he were in our hands, André could be saved. Of course Clinton will not deliver him up, even to save so great a favorite as André."

"Of course not!" replied Pemberton. "André himself would be the first to spurn such a proposition."

They sat for awhile in silence.

"I suppose it might as well be done first as last, Phil."

"Yes—but I would tenfold rather storm a battery," replied Morris. "Where are the ladies?"

"In the parlor, I suppose. Let us go to them."

"You must do all the talking, Pemberton. I know I shall break down, at one look of Helen's face. Ah me!"

They entered the parlor. The two ladies were seated by a table—Helen reading, Isabella sewing.

"Why, Captain Morris!" exclaimed the latter as he entered. "I am very glad indeed to see you."

Helen looked a smiling welcome, and extended her hand.

Morris shook hands, said a few words, and then took a seat a little to one side.

Helen looked surprised—his manner was so different from usual.

Then Pemberton spoke. His voice trembled a little, in spite of him.

"Helen, my sweet sister, that is to be—I have often heard you say that you belong to a race that never feared the face of Death, on the battle field or on the scaffold. Can you meet as patiently and bravely the stern, sad face of Sorrow?"

Before he had half finished his sentence, the girl was gazing from one to the other of the young men with an eager, questioning look, as if she would read their very souls. Then, as Pemberton paused, she exclaimed passionately:—

"What is it? Who is it? Is Colonel Musgrave—"

"I have heard no bad news of the Colonel," replied Pemberton. "Calm yourself, my dear Helen—be calm, I implore you!"

"Is *he* dead?" moaned Helen, in a low, quivering voice.

"He is not—but he is a prisoner."

"And wounded?"

"No, he is not wounded!"

She drew a deep breath.

"But why do you look so solemn? To be a prisoner and unhurt is not so sad. He was a prisoner before. Tell me, Philip—you tell me. Quickly! Quickly!"

Poor Morris brushed the tears from his eyes with his

hand. He looked at Pemberton. The latter nodded, as if it were better told at once now.

"Major André is accused of being a spy," faltered Morris.

"I deny it! It is a foul calumny! He is no spy!" cried Helen impetuously—her mood changing into one of intense indignation. "What does he say?"

"He also denies it."

"I knew so! I knew so! What do they mean by making so false a charge, Arthur?"

"When he was arrested he was in disguise. He admits that he assumed his disguise within our lines. He had planned the surrender of West Point with General Arnold. Arnold has escaped to New York; but André was taken, with the fatal papers upon him. The army is greatly incensed. His position is very perilous indeed."

"With Arnold!" faltered Helen. She well understood now the whole affair. She herself had aided in the beginning of the perilous game, which threatened to prove so disastrous at its close. She leaned her head upon her hand and wept bitterly.

"We shall do all we can to save him, Miss Helen. Do not give up hope," said Morris, taking a seat near her.

"You are very good, Philip. I know you will."

"When do you start for the army, Arthur?" said Isabella, who had been so far a silent but attentive and sympathizing listener. "Of course Helen and I will go with you."

"To-morrow morning. There is no time for delay. You can endure a two or three days' ride on horseback?"

"I think so; if Mrs. Stephens could come all the way from Boston with her infant in her arms."

"We will all go together then."

"Helen and I will retire, if you will excuse us, gentlemen, to make our arrangements. We shall be ready at any hour you fix. Good evening, Captain; I suppose you will return with us?"

"I design doing so. Good-night, Miss Graham; good-night, Miss Helen."

"Good-night, Philip," said Helen, stopping before him for a moment. "I shall never forget your kindness in this dark hour."

"Phil, we must save him!" said Pemberton earnestly, after the ladies had left the room.

"I will do all I can, as you know, Arthur; but I have not the least hope. I have heard the army talk. Every man, from the highest to the lowest, says, 'Death!'"

"How is he guarded?"

"There is no hope there. Two of our best officers are constantly with him, day and night; and six sentries guard the passage and the doors. Besides, there will be, I fear, no time to do anything. Not more than three or four days."

"What, so soon? Is this great haste not unusual?"

"Not in the case of spies, you know. They are often executed on the spot. And the officers consider this a painful duty, and one that the longer it is put off, becomes the more painful."

"Then, indeed, we must be moving," said Pemberton. "I shall see Washington at once. And then André. Whatever may be the result, I shall stand by him to the last. Oh, Phil, John André, Englishman as he is, is the very noblest, sweetest man I ever knew. I shall not easily get over it, if they harm him."

"He is a grand fellow, no doubt. And I would risk my life to save him," replied Morris. "But, ah, Pemberton, it is mainly because I love Helen Graham. Is it not true love, Arthur, which serves the object of its affection, even by serving, if necessary, a successful rival? But for me there is no other woman in the wide world. I told you that two years ago, and I say the same thing now."

"You are a noble fellow, Phil—and only too much of a true and devoted lover. But I must see that your horse has been stabled, and order Aunt Dinah to get some supper for you. You will, of course, stay with us to-night. For we must be off bright and early to-morrow.

CHAPTER IX.

PEMBERTON AND WASHINGTON.

I know my duty. Though it makes me weep
Hot tears of blood, that duty will I do.
Down, foolish heart! this is no place for thee.

It took three days of hard riding, a considerable portion of it over mountain roads, before our party reached the vicinity of the American camp at Tappan. Captain Morris obtained lodgings for them at a comfortable farm-house a couple of miles from the camp, where the ladies were received with great kindness by an honest Dutch farmer named Jansen, and his substantial wife. The ladies were greatly exhausted, not so much by the ride itself as by the excitement of their emotions. Sorrow which is without hope, is very hard to bear. And neither Pemberton nor Morris felt at liberty to encourage any hopeful anticipations. In truth, they did not feel absolutely certain that they should find André alive. And the true state of their feelings, although not expressed in words, insensibly communicated itself to their sensitive companions. So that Helen, notwithstanding her undeniable courage and high spirit, seemed almost as much dead as alive, when, near the close of a pleasant Saturday afternoon, Morris assisted her from her horse, and into the sitting-room of the farm-house.

All Pemberton could learn from the farmer was that a Court of Officers had been sitting the previous day, to try André; but what the verdict was, Mr. Jansen did not certainly know, though he had heard it was "guilty." The first part of this information Pemberton thought best to communicate at once to the sisters. And then he announced his intention of riding over to Tappan, to hear what the verdict really was, and, if necessary, to see the Commander-in-Chief, as also to procure a permit for all of them to visit André.

Helen beckoned him to her, as he was about following Morris from the room. "You will see him, I know, before you return," she said, in a low voice. "Tell him from me that I never loved him more than now—never! That I know he has acted in all things like a noble man and true gentleman. That I believe in him fully. And that, were it well to do so, I should glory in sharing his prison with him. Tell him this—and as much more as you can find words to express. Tell him I am his always—utterly; for this world, and forever!"

She sank back on the farmer's rude lounge, overcome with the violence of her emotions.

Before Pemberton and Captain Morris reached the village of Tappan, they met an officer, an acquaintance of the latter, who informed them briefly of the true position of affairs. The Court had been held—composed of all the General Officers with the exception of Wayne and Irving. No witnesses had been examined. André had made a plain, unvarnished statement of all that had taken place.

And, basing their verdict upon that statement, and the laws of war, he had been unanimously declared a spy, and worthy of death. The sentence had been approved that very day—and the next day, Sunday, October 1st, at 5 P. M., been appointed for the execution.

Pemberton's cheek blanched, and his heart sank within him. "So soon!" he exclaimed.

"The sooner the better," replied the officer gloomily. "It *must* be done; and yet we are all learning to love the prisoner. The longer we leave it, the harder our duty grows."

"There is no hope then but in Washington!" exclaimed Pemberton bitterly; "when a man's very virtues are made a reason for hastening his fate."

"Shall I go in with you?" asked Morris, when they reached the stone farm-house where Washington had his headquarters.

"There is no time to lose," replied Pemberton. "I will see the General alone, if you will see the principal officers, and try to get a paper signed by some of them, asking for a reversal of the sentence, or at least a respite."

"I will do all I can, but do not be surprised if I get no signers," rejoined Morris, as he left him. "I will meet you at your quarters this evening."

Having dismounted, and sent in his name, Pemberton was invited to enter the little room used by Washington as his reception chamber. The Chief was alone, and rising, cordially welcomed his visitor, inquiring almost immediately as to the health of the Misses Graham.

"They are not very well, though very near here now," replied Pemberton. Then, noticing the surprise expressed in the face of his listener, he added, "General, probably you do not know that Miss Helen Graham is betrothed to

Major André. It is a secret from the world, but I may trust it to your ear."

A change passed over Washington's face. "God pity her!" said he, with deep emotion.

"Yes; if your Excellency will not take pity upon her," replied Pemberton.

"What can I do?" said Washington, in a sad but resolute voice. "He has been tried by the highest Court I could summon. My Generals say unanimously that he is guilty of being a spy, and must suffer death. They speak the voice of the whole army, the whole country. How could I set their decision at naught, even if I would? I have had to tell Colonel Hamilton this, over and over. He does not dispute it, but still pleads for mercy. Mercy that I have neither the power nor the right to grant."

Pemberton had been told that Washington was a cold, stern man—had himself partly believed it. He acknowledged to himself now how false the charge was; for the man before him was evidently full of emotion; his face glowing, his voice, though low and even, impassioned. But Pemberton had determined beforehand to save his friend if he possibly could, and to admit nothing, however reasonable, that told against him. For once he was determined to be fanatical and one-sided in his reasoning and his purpose.

"If your Excellency will pardon me," said Pemberton, "it seems to me, and to Miss Graham, that everything depends on your decision. Whatever your officers may say, the ultimate decision must rest with you. If you say live, the army will approve, and recognize in your voice that sentiment of Mercy which is so natural to you."

"And is nothing then to be done, sir, to satisfy our outraged sense of Justice?" replied Washington. "Justice has its claims as well as Mercy. Is Treason—the most infamous Treason—to be plotted in our midst, and those engaged in it to go unpunished, as if it were merely some little peccadillo of which they had been guilty?" As he spoke thus, Washington's face assumed that cold and somewhat severe expression which usually sat upon it in moments of trial and danger.

"I am not able to perceive," rejoined Pemberton warmly, "that Major André has done anything more than I would have done in Philadelphia, had Sir William Howe, or any of his officers, proposed to play a similar game with the British, that Arnold has played with us. And I think your Excellency's sense of justice will pardon me for adding, that if I had done so, your Excellency would have applauded instead of rebuking my conduct."

"I do not deny it, Mr. Pemberton. But you will remember that I told you expressly, that, while I regarded your services in Philadelphia as of the highest value to the Country and the Cause—"

"'And such as a high-minded gentleman might perform;' pardon me for interrupting your Excellency."

"And such as a high-minded gentleman might perform," replied Washington, emphatically, "still that if you were discovered, it might be impossible for me to save you. It is often not only blameless, but noble to act the spy; I trust I would, if there were sufficient reason, imitate King Alfred, and, to save my country, penetrate the camp of the invader myself; but not the less does the rule of war say, Death to all spies! Major André has come within the rule."

"Begging your Excellency's pardon, I do not think so. I have learned from Captain Morris that he assumed his disguise under General Arnold's orders, after he had been brought into our lines against his request."

"He who deals with a Traitor, must beware of Treason.

The old proverb says, 'Who sups with the Devil should have a long spoon.' André took the risk, and has lost. He must pay the penalty—unless—"

"Unless what?" asked Pemberton, seeing that the General hesitated.

A gloom as of night gathered over Washington's face. He rose from his seat. It was evident to Pemberton that he was about to witness one of those tremendous bursts of indignation of which he had been told—and which were more startling on account of their infrequency. It was almost a relief when it came—the clenched and menacing right hand and extended arm giving force to the words—

"Unless we can catch that infamous Traitor, that lying and perjured wretch, Benedict Arnold—and hang him as high as Haman, in André's place. If I can once lay hold of him"—letting his massive hand fall upon Pemberton's shoulder, and giving it involuntarily a grasp that left the marks of his fingers in black and blue for days afterwards —"I'll make him an example to devils and to men!"

"I devoutly trust we may take him," said Pemberton, after a pause, in which the General had resumed his seat. "He is a Traitor, and richly deserves death. But André is an honorable, high-toned man. It will not punish Arnold to injure him."

"Whom now can I trust? Whom now can I trust?" mournfully exclaimed Washington, dejection mingling with his indignation. "Do you not see, sir, that this treason of Arnold's, throws suspicion upon everybody? I appointed Arnold—the perjured wretch—to the command of West Point—and you know, Mr. Pemberton, being behind the scenes, what some very influential people in your good city think and have said of me. What will they say now?"

"I know it well; but I also know that your Excellency has never stooped to play at their intriguing game; and that you have met secret malice with open and honest argument and wise and merciful action."

"I care not for myself," continued Washington; "but they wound the great Cause through me. I and my officers must not only be guiltless, we must be unsuspected. Add the suspicion of Treason to the other influences which are now engendering strife and disunion among us, and the country is lost. I should like to oblige you, Mr. Pemberton, but the welfare of the Cause will not allow it. This great Crime will have its Victim. Missing Arnold, it clutches André. I fully appreciate and sympathize with your devotion to your friend, but it is needless to prolong this conversation. My resolution is unalterable."

"And this, then, is the answer I am to take to Helen Graham," exclaimed Pemberton bitterly. "Pray God it does not kill her too. She will insist, I know, upon seeing your Excellency herself, and begging for Mercy upon her knees. What shall I tell her?"

A groan burst from Washington's breast. "I cannot, cannot see her! I am but a man, Mr. Pemberton, a weak man, simply trying my best to do what is right. Why should I be exposed to such a weight of agony? My answer must still be the same. I beg you spare me such an hour of torture!"

"Your Excellency will at least favor me with a pass for myself and my friends to visit the prisoner?"

Washington sat down at a table and wrote a pass. "This will admit you to-morrow morning. It is too late to-night."

"I must bid your Excellency good evening," said Pemberton coldly, taking the pass.

Washington held out his hand. "We are still friends,

are we not?" said he, while his face resumed that benevolent expression which was usual with him when in the presence of his military family.

"We are still friends," replied Pemberton, taking his extended hand; "though you have denied mercy to the very dearest friend I have on earth." And he walked gloomily from the room.

CHAPTER X.

CRUSHED BY THE BLOW.

Life thou dost strain too hard upon this heart.
It must have rest—or break!

OUTSIDE the door, Pemberton met Captain Morris, who had ascertained he was still within, and was awaiting him in the twilight.

"I need not ask you what success you have had?" said Morris, with a glance at his friend's sorrowful face.

"He is as immovable as these granite hills," replied Pemberton. "Have you had any better success?"

"I cannot get a single name; though Colonel Hamilton says he will sign, if I can obtain enough others to give the paper any weight. And yet they all express the utmost admiration and sympathy for André."

"Cursed be their admiration and their sympathy, if they will not move a hand to save him!" exclaimed Pemberton indignantly. "What excuse have they for their cruel coldness?"

"They all give the same reason—the crime is so great that there must be a victim. Hamilton says the army feels as the Romans did when that great gulf opened in the Forum, and the Augurs averred it would not close until something most precious had been flung down into it. Arnold's treason, he says, has opened the hideous gulf; and either Arnold or André must die, to prove that the Army is true and faithful, and thus close the chasm up again. The very fact that André is the valuable man he is, and so great a favorite with Clinton, renders, in their view, his sacrifice the more imperative."

By this time the young men had remounted, and were on their way to the farm-house.

"What shall we say to Helen!" said Pemberton, in a voice full of emotion.

Morris made no reply—save to wipe his eyes with his handkerchief. And they rode on in silence.

As they neared the house, Morris said: "You got a permit, I suppose?"

"Yes, for to-morrow."

Dismounting they fastened their horses. The light was shining out from the already opened door, where Isabella was standing.

She held up one hand with a warning gesture. "Speak low," she said, "if you have bad tidings."

"Is anything the matter with Helen?" asked Pemberton.

"I fear a great deal. She was awaiting your return, all excitement and eagerness, about an hour ago, when a neighboring farmer came along, and called out to Mr. Jansen that 'the spy had been sentenced to be hung to-morrow at five o'clock.' Helen gave a great shriek, and fell to the floor. Mrs. Jansen and myself got her into a back room, and into bed; and she has lain there since, seemingly unconscious of all around her." Isabella spoke in a whisper, but rapidly, and with great emotion—frequently turning her head and listening. "I left her for a few minutes, hearing you coming. Oh, merciful God—

what makes you look so sad? Why don't you deny it?—It cannot be true! Speak, I say—or I too shall go mad."

Pemberton took a step forward, and passed his arm around the waist of his betrothed. "My precious darling!" said he soothingly. "Do not fail your sister at this awful time. If you give way, who shall comfort her?" With words like these, and with gentle caressings, he sought to soothe and sustain her. And it was soon evident not without effect. For Isabella's manner, after a great flood of tears, became more composed, and it was evident that the first force of the dreadful blow had spent itself. Then she said,

"I must now go back, and see how Helen is."

But as she turned toward the door of the room, it opened, and a tall white figure came in. It was Helen, in her night-dress, and with one of the sheets of the bed folded like a shawl across her shoulders, and hanging draped around her.

"Good evening, gentlemen; I am glad to see you. Where's the Major? Fie, fie, to be so late; and on his wedding night, too!"

"Why, Helen," cried Isabella, in an agonized voice, springing to her, "do come back to your room, my dear sister." And she took her by the arm, and would have led her back.

"Isabella, I am surprised at you! You forget yourself, to act thus before our friends," exclaimed Helen, drawing herself up with great dignity. "Mr. Pemberton, you must excuse her. Ah, you have come to dance at my wedding, Philip? That's a good boy." Here she broke out into one of her childhood's songs:

"'The frog he would a wooing go,
With a string strang molly mitty kimo;
Whether his mother would let him or no,
With a string strang molly mitty kimo.

Kimo nero gilto karo,
Kimo nero kimo,
With a string strang a parawinkle
Marabone aringtang,
Aringtang a molly mitty kimo.'

"What makes you look so serious, gentlemen? Is it such a solemn thing to get married!" Here she gave a wild laugh; that mad laughter which is so dreadful to hear. "But," with a sudden change of expression, "perhaps you think the bridegroom will not come? Hark!" holding up her finger. "Why doesn't he come? Why doesn't he come?"—here her voice mounted almost to a shriek—"ah, I know, I know, I heard them say"—here she paused and seemed to be trying to recollect something—"oh, I remember—they said he could not come—because he was—to be hung!" and, with a fearful shriek, that tore the hearts of her listeners, Helen again relapsed into unconsciousness, and would have fallen to the floor, had not Isabella and the young men—who sprung forward—sustained her in their arms.

"It will not do to leave her a moment, Arthur," said Isabella, when the unconscious girl had been placed again in her bed. "And, as I would wish to have the command of all my strength, please bring me no more news—unless, of course, you can bring us good news. I would rather have everything hereafter a great blank—and think of nothing but Helen. She will need all my care, if we would preserve her life and her mind. I do wish the physician that I sent for would come."

She had hardly finished speaking, before the physician—one of the medical gentlemen attached to the army—was shown into the room. He pronounced it an attack of brain fever, naturally enough brought on by the terrible circumstances of the case, with which they felt bound to acquaint him. If Helen had, however, as she seemed to have, and as Isabella said she had, a strong and vigorous constitution, he thought with careful nursing, and the utmost quiet, she might ultimately recover her full health both of mind and body. The case however was evidently a very serious one, and, under the most favorable circumstances, would confine her to her room for weeks, if not for months. He prescribed certain quieting medicines, recommended the constant application of cloths wet with cold water to her head, and said that if she was not better by the next day, her heavy hair would have to be cut off.

We may simply add here, that she did seem rather better the next day, though still lying apparently unconscious; but the beautiful light-brown hair, which had shone like threads of gold in the sunshine, to the graceful movements of her imperial head, no longer existed. That one night of sorrow and suffering had changed the glossy gold into a lustrous silver.

CHAPTER XI.

PEMBERTN AND ANDRE.

What I did, I did in honor,
Led by the impartial conduct of my soul.—*Shakspeare.*

THE next day Pemberton rode over to see Major André. Presenting his pass at the front door, where several sentinels were stationed, he was conducted along an entry where a sentinel also paced, to the door of the room, where another sentry kept guard. Every precaution seemed to have been taken to prevent an escape.

In the room itself, two officers of approved vigilance and fidelity were constantly posted, with strict orders not to leave the prisoner, by day or by night, even for a moment.

André, dressed in the rich uniform of a British officer, was seated at a table conversing with his guards, as Pemberton entered. Recognizing his friend, he sprang to his feet with an exclamation.

"Dear Arthur—I am so glad to see you!" cried he, flinging his arms around Pemberton's neck, while tears came into his fine eyes. And Pemberton responded with equal fervor.

Then after introducing Pemberton to the American officers, who drew back with delicacy to the other end of the room, the friends seated themselves.

Several sheets of paper lay on the table, and André smilingly pointed out to Arthur two drawings he had been making with pen and ink for the amusement of his guards. One was a likeness of himself, as he sat then at the table—an excellent likeness, though executed without the aid of a mirror. The other was more humorous, being a picture of himself shortly after his arrest, and while being escorted by his rough captors to the American post at North Castle.

"A man must do something at a moment like this, to keep his thoughts employed," said he, with a slight shudder. "But you know what I am longing to hear. How does Helen bear this cruel stroke?"

"She is in God's mercy lying so ill as to be unconscious of anything," replied Pemberton solemnly. Then he narrated to André how they all had journeyed to Tappan to see him, and how the excitement and sorrow had thrown Helen into a dangerous illness—omitting, of course, the more painful features of the story.

André leaned his head upon his hand and said nothing for a time, though his countenance, as Pemberton caught glimpses of it occasionally, was convulsed with grief. Then he seemed to master his feelings with a strong effort, and he said quietly;

"Perhaps it is best—perhaps it is best! It would unman me—it would kill her—to meet thus, and part! You see this miniature"—taking it from his bosom—"it is the work of my own hand, and I think a good likeness, although painted from memory. I wish to have it next my heart so long as I live; then take it, and give it to her when she can bear to see it, and tell her, Arthur," here his voice broke down and he paused for a few moments—"tell her that I loved her to the last, and that my greatest regret in dying is that I have so clouded with my fate her young and glorious life."

"She told me to tell you," replied Pemberton—"it was yesterday, before her attack of illness, and she thought I should see you at once—that she never loved you more than now. That she loved you utterly, and knew that, in all you had done, you had acted like the noble gentleman and true man you always were."

"God bless her noble heart!" responded André. "It takes half the bitterness of death away to have her say that. Tell her, when she recovers, that I said this, and tell her, also, that I know I have done nothing of which an honorable man and a British soldier need be ashamed. Do you think I have, my dear friend?"

"I do not. I have told Washington himself so, and have urged every plea I could in your favor. But with no effect. They all respect and pity you, John; but they all think that policy demands your sacrifice. I see no hope," added Pemberton, in an agonized voice.

"I gave up all hope when the Court-Martial made its unanimous decision." said André, in a voice which did not even falter. "I saw it in their faces that I should have to die, to prove that they were true to their country—that Arnold's defection began and ended with himself. Well, so be it! I am prepared to die like a man. But I would wish, also, to die like a soldier. Do you think, Arthur, that Washington can refuse this last request?" and he opened a drawer and took out a sheet of paper. "Here is a copy of a petition I have just forwarded." Pemberton took it and read as follows:

"SIR: Buoyed above the terror of death by the consciousness of a life devoted to honorable pursuits and stained with no action that can give me remorse, I trust that the request I make to your Excellency, at this serious period, and which is to soften my last moments, will not be rejected.

"Sympathy toward a soldier will surely induce your Excellency and a military tribunal to adapt the mode of my death to the feelings of a man of honor. Let me hope, sir, that if aught in my character impresses you with esteem toward me, if aught in my misfortunes marks me the victim of policy, and not of resentment, I shall experience the operation of those feelings in your heart, by being informed that I am not to die on a gibbet.

"I have the honor to be your Excellency's most obedient and most humble servant,* JOHN ANDRE,

"Adjutant-General to the British army."

"Have you had any reply to this?" asked Pemberton, with deep emotion.

"Not as yet. There has scarcely been time. Is it properly worded?"

"It could not be better. It reads like the man and

---

* N. P. Willis has beautifully paraphrased this letter to Washington, as follows:

"It is not the fear of death
  That damps my brow;
It is not for another breath
  I ask thee now;
I can die with a lip unstirred
  And a quiet heart—
Let but this prayer be heard
  Ere I depart.

"I can give up my mother's look—
  My sister's kiss;
I can think of love—yet brook
  A death like this!
I can give up the young fame
  I burned to win;
All—but the spotless name
  I glory in.

"Thine is the power to give,
  Thine to deny,
Joy for the hour I live,
  Calmness to die.
By all the brave should cherish,
  By my dying breath,
I ask that I may perish
  By a soldier's death."

gentleman you are. They must be cruel indeed, to deny your request. But they will not deny it. No policy surely can dictate that."

"It will be, I confess, a cruel blow to me if they deny this poor last petition," rejoined André, with deep feeling. "But whatever may be the result, I trust I shall be able to meet it with the composure of a man and the courage of a soldier. It is crime alone that can make any punishment ignominious and shameful; and if I know my own heart, my great object in this affair was to put an end to this unhappy civil war, and to prevent the further shedding of blood. I admit that I was ambitious—but, as I am a true man, Arthur, the motives I have given you were my leading motives."

"You had a right to be ambitious, John," said Pemberton, gazing with sorrowful eyes of admiration upon the noble countenance of his friend—"you, so accomplished, so gifted! You had the same right to be ambitious as a young eagle has to use its wings."

"Alas," replied André, with a sudden revulsion of feeling, "here is the end of all my ambitious dreams! I have reached the age of twenty-nine, and am a Major, and Adjutant-General of the British army. It is little, Arthur, to what I had hoped to attain, before the last page of my history should be turned, and Finis written below it. If I had succeeded—I should have touched those steps which lead up to the highest honors. I should have ended the war. I should have pacified and fully satisfied every reasonable man among your countrymen. I should have preserved this immense Continent to the British Empire and the Protestant Faith. But one false step, one foolish word, undid it all."

André paused, and seemed lost in his reflections.

Pemberton made no reply. He could not argue against

a man on the threshold of the grave—although the officers of the guard, who caught snatches of the conversation, gazed at times curiously at him.

André observed them not however, or cared not for them and their thoughts. In a few moments he resumed.

"I suppose it was to be so however. It is difficult to think that it was a mere chance, which a little more caution might have averted. You know the dream, Arthur, that I told you about, the evening after our Wissahickon adventure. And the Fortune-Teller's vision. One has come true. The other doubtless will come true this day. What of Westminster Abbey? Will that come true, too?"

"I have no doubt of it," Pemberton felt himself almost impelled to reply. He could not himself analyze the impelling force. Perhaps it was the mere humane wish to comfort his friend. "I have no doubt that when they hear at home of your sad fate, your name will be enrolled at Westminster among the noblest and bravest of England."

"Think you so?" exclaimed André, the cloud of grief upon his face lightening—"then I have not failed utterly, after all. I might have died in battle any day, and the annals of my country scarcely have known that such a man as John André ever existed."

"You have written your name upon the enduring marble of your country's history, you may depend upon that," rejoined Pemberton, with proud sympathy.

The door opened, and a young officer entered. It was Colonel Hamilton.

He had been André's best friend since his capture, and was well known to Pemberton.

"You are reprieved till noon to-morrow, Major," said he, after shaking hands with both of them, but without any manifestation of pleasure in his face.

"What does it mean?" questioned André.

"Sir Henry Clinton has deputed General Robertson to meet General Greene and make certain representations relative to the case, and the true state of the facts. Of course, courtesy to Sir Henry required the reprieve."

"I am very much obliged to Sir Henry for his kindness," replied André, with emotion. "He has always acted toward me more like a father and a friend than a general. But of course it will amount to nothing," looking at Hamilton.

"It will amount to nothing. It is a mere formality on our part," replied Hamilton gloomily. "Though some of the officers think—I do not—that Sir Henry is ready, as a last resort, to offer in exchange for you that traitor, Arnold."

"Never—never—never!" cried André impetuously, springing to his feet. "To save his own son, his own father, Sir Henry would never do that! Not if Arnold himself were to propose it."

"Of course not," said Hamilton. "I merely told you what many think. But as to Arnold, the story goes, 'to give the devil his due,' that he really has proposed it to Sir Henry."

"It is a nobler act than I should have given him credit for," replied André, in whose mind, as our readers know, Arnold's conduct had not left the most favorable impression, "but, of course, Sir Henry would not hear of it, and I would not hear of it."

"I do not know that the story is true," said Hamilton. "It is merely rumor."

"It is not entirely unlike Arnold's daring recklessness," said Pemberton. "He once told me that he scarcely knew what fear was."

"I believe that," rejoined Hamilton. "I saw him receive the Major's note, telling him that the game was up, and go on with his breakfast, crunching some dry toast, just as coolly as if nothing had happened. Then he made an apology and left the table, and soon after was thundering down on horseback to the landing, thence into his barge, and with his pistol in his hand, down the Hudson to the Vulture. He must have been in the ship by the time I started on horseback to intercept him at King's Ferry."

"What do you suppose he would have done if you had been in time?" queried Pemberton.

"Pushed through, if he could, in spite of us. If the worst came, blown his own brains out."

"Colonel, to change the subject," said André, "has any decision been come to, relative to that last request I made to you?"

"I believe it is still under consideration," replied Hamilton. "I can assure you, Major, it shall not fail from want of any urging of mine."

"I should think it would not require any great amount of urging, to gallant men and soldiers," rejoined André, a little coldly and haughtily.

Hamilton rose to withdraw. "I will no longer interrupt your conversation, gentlemen. Anything I can do for either of you, shall be most cheerfully done, I assure you."

When Hamilton had closed the door, André said—
"That man is a true gentleman, Arthur. And more, he seems to me the ablest man I have yet met among your leaders. I have not seen Washington—he appears to avoid me."

"Washington is a man to whom the supreme thing is his duty to his country. He means to be as just and impartial as eternal Fate. He is afraid, I judge, to see you;

lest seeing you, his sympathy should cloud his judgment."

André smiled. "Your friendship makes you too complimentary by half, Arthur. From what I have heard of your great leader, I am not the sun that could thaw in the least such a perfect statue—of ice."

"Indeed, you wrong him, John. If you knew him as I do, you would do him justice. But I had intended to ask whether there was any way in which I could be of service to you."

"In no other way than by giving me as much of your company as possible. Even to the very last," added André, with a deep breath. "I shall go more cheerfully to the gallows—or whatever it be—if I can see your dear, loving eyes as I go. You will not fear to witness what I shall not fear to bear?"

Pemberton wrung his friend's hand. "I am not certain that mine will not be the harder task; but I will stand by you, John, to the end."

"I knew you would, friend of my heart!" exclaimed André, while the tears filled his eyes and fell upon the hand of Pemberton. "And it seems to me, as you and I sit here, the truest of friends, though arrayed under different banners, that it typifies what, in some way, in the inscrutable providence of God, shall take place hereafter. That the time shall come when the great fact of our being created kindred shall prevail over all this foolish contention and bitterness; and America and England be joined once more, in heart and soul, if not in political bonds, like two generous and loving brothers."

"God grant that it may be so!" exclaimed Pemberton with enthusiasm. "Blood is indeed thicker than water!"

Nothing was said for a time, then André caught up the

pen, and made a rapid sketch. "Do you recognize the scene?" asked he when it was completed.

"It looks like the Hudson, but I do not recognize the place."

"It is the Hudson, as I saw it that wretched day from the chamber of Smith's house. That is intended for the Vulture. You see how wide the river is there, it is almost a bay. It is a magnificent view, I can assure you; but it was a very sad one that day to me. So near safety, and so impossible to reach it. I tell you, Arthur, it was like looking over the walls into Paradise."

"May I keep it?"

"Of course. I drew it on purpose for you and for Isabella. You said she was well. She is one of the very noblest women I ever knew. Remember me to her, as to the dearest loved of sisters. I had hoped to dance with Helen at your wedding—and then have you dance at ours. Ah me! Ah me! 'Man is like the flower of the grass, that to-day is, and to-morrow is cast into the oven.' But there is a kind Father, that rules all and controls all—and without whom not a sparrow falls to the ground. In this belief, which my mother taught me, Arthur, I shall die content—yes, content!

"I have written to my poor mother, and to my sisters and brothers," added André after a pause. "It will be a sad blow to them."

"Your will—is it made?"

"I fortunately drew it up before leaving New York, and I have written to Captain Boissier about the disposal of my effects. Yes, I think everything is done."

After some further desultory conversation, Pemberton left, promising to call in again in the afternoon.

CHAPTER XII.

CAPTAIN FANNY'S PLAN.

Give me but breathing time, I'll rescue him,
Though forty thousand sentries stood on guard,
With Argus at their head.

As Pemberton was riding homeward slowly, he observed a solitary female figure standing beneath a tree on the side of the road. Absorbed in his unhappy thoughts, and supposing that it was merely some country maiden, he would have ridden on, had not the girl accosted him with a "Good-mornin' to ye, Mr. Pimberton."

"Why, is that you, Captain Fanny?" exclaimed he in surprise. "What brings you up into this part of the country?"

"The same that brings you, Mr. Pimberton."

"Ah!"

"The Major did my brither a great sarvice once, yer honor. And you remimber how I carried love-letters betwixt him and Miss Hilin—the magnificent crathure!—And now they say he must be hung!" the tears that came into Fanny's eyes proved her earnestness.

"I would give everything I have in the world to prevent it, Fanny—but I can do nothing."

"That is jist what I wanted to see yer honor about. They say he is to die this avening."

"It has been put off until to-morrow at noon."

"'Twill not do. It's not long enough, yer honor. Get us a week—only one week, yer honor—and we can save him."

"I will try," said Pemberton, turning his horse's head; "but I have no faith that I can obtain one day's further delay. You say if you had a week, you could save him; would your plan endanger any man's life?"

"No man's life—but his—and mine. And had he not better die, in a bold push for fradom, than stay there and be hung up like a dog?"

"I will try then what I can do," said Pemberton. "Have you anything more to say to me than this?"

"Nothing, yer honor. Get me the week—jist one little week. For the sake of the blessed and merciful Virgin, jist one week—and I will answer for the rest, in spite of their sax sentinels and two officers."

As Pemberton rode back toward headquarters, he questioned within himself as to Captain Fanny's competency to perform her promise. But he had heard Morris speak with so much admiration of Fanny's courage and capacity, in a conversation suggested by the unexpected rencontre between the two at his mother's house, that he did not feel disposed to omit anything which offered even a possible chance for his friend's deliverance. If she failed, matters could not be made worse.

Some may think that Pemberton in this matter was not acting a very patriotic part. Probably they are correct. But I am not depicting a model patriot, but only a fallible man, who possessed in a strong degree the feelings of a man. He did what I am narrating—and must be judged by the record. That he was not ashamed of what he did, was proven by his frequent declarations after the war, when talking over the matter with his friends, that if he could have aided in André's escape, he would certainly have done so. And he always further took the ground, in opposition to the nearly unanimous sentiments of those friends, that the execution of André was not called for either by considerations of justice or of sound policy. So much, in explanation and partial vindication of Pemberton's course. Though probably, after all, he was governed in what he did, more by feeling than by reason.

When he arrived at Washington's headquarters, he found the General surrounded by a number of his principal officers. As there was no time to be lost, he made known, as soon as possible, the purport of his visit, pleading earnestly just for one week's delay—one little week.

"If you could give any good reason for such a delay, Mr. Pemberton," replied Washington, "I would grant it. But as all the facts have now been considered, and our decision is irrevocable, it would simply be inflicting a week of torture upon the prisoner, to grant your request. Do you not think so, General?"

General Greene, a large, portly man, in whose judgment his Chief had great confidence, nodded his head emphatically.

"It would be unwise, I think, in every respect. It would be cruelty to the prisoner, cruelty to us whose unpleasant duty it is to be his guards and executioners, and would bring down upon us a fresh load of threats, remonstrances and Commissioners from Clinton. To the country it would look like an evidence of weakness—perhaps of fear. When the act is once done, then Clinton will have to reconcile himself to it—for as yet he has made no positive threats of retaliation which he will feel bound in honor to adhere to. I therefore give my judgment"—looking around the circle of officers—"decidedly against another day's postponement."

A unanimous burst of assent from the officers followed the close of Greene's remarks.

"You have your answer, Mr. Pemberton," said Washington, kindly but firmly; "there is but one opinion upon the subject."

Pemberton bowed respectfully but coldly, and, making no reply, left the room.

Fanny was awaiting his coming at the same spot.

"It is as I said; I can do nothing. Not a day will they grant him."

"The murtherin' spalpeens!" exclaimed Fanny fiercely. "Thin all is over! Good day, yer honor"—and Fanny wiped the tears from her eyes.

"How would you have saved him?" asked Pemberton, checking his horse, which he had touched with the spur.

"Good strong brandy, and plinty of goold sover'ins, and a line in a peach to the Major, and a fury of a fire at midnight, and two good horses, and the Vulture down the river; it could ha' been done, yer honor. Besides, some of the sentries already think it a divil of a shame to hang such a swate jintleman—'specially two, who were in the troop of Baylor's rigiment that the Major saved 'gainst orders, at the night masseker at this very place."

Captain Fanny's face lighted up in thinking of the bold scheme. "But it's all over now; there's no time to save him!" added Fanny, with a deep sigh.

And Pemberton again touched his horse with the spur, and rode back to the farm-house.

CHAPTER XIII.

THE DEATH OF ANDRÉ.

There was glory on his forehead,
 There was lustre in his eye,
And he never walked to battle
 More proudly than to die.—*Aytoun's Montrose.*

THE hour of noon had been appointed for Major André's execution. André rose from his bed at his usual hour, and after partaking of breakfast—which was supplied him as had been the custom, from Washington's own table—began to make his preparations for the solemn scene. His servant Laune had arrived from New York some days before with a supply of clothing; and André this morning shaved and dressed himself with even more than his usual care. He wore the rich scarlet uniform, faced with green, of a British officer; though without the customary sash and sword.

When Pemberton entered about eleven o'clock, he thought he had never seen a more splendid face and figure. The face was of a deadly paleness—the brow especially showing like a clear pale marble beneath the clustering masses of raven hair. The features appeared even more refined and intellectual than was their wont; and the beautiful expression which sat upon them, and shone forth from his deep and melancholy eyes, was such as naturally takes captive the hearts of men, and fills with devoted enthusiasm the souls of women.

"He is the handsomest man I ever saw!" exclaimed one of the officers in attendance, to Pemberton; "and the most gentle and winning."

"I am glad you have come in good time, Arthur," said André with a serene composure. "You see I mean to die in the dress of a British officer. How is Helen this morning?"

"She is still lying unconscious—but we think she is rather better."

"Thank God! Do not forget what I told you about the miniature. What a sad ending to her happy dream! But I must not think any more of that—save to feel that her proud eyes are upon me, to see that I blench not nor tremble in this closing hour."

Pemberton's heart was ready to burst, but he knew his duty to his friend too well to allow his sorrowful feelings to master him for a moment.

"To the brave, true soul, John, all that men can do is nothing. The heart right, and the conscience clear, as yours are, my friend, and we can say well-met to death, without a shudder."

"Are you ready, Major?" said one of the officers.

"I am ready," replied André proudly.

As André emerged from the prison into the free, fresh air, he took a deep breath, and gazed up into the beautiful blue sky above him, hazy and golden with the glory he so much loved of an October day. He walked arm-in-arm between the two officers, Pemberton walking near him. A captain's command of thirty or forty men marched immediately around them, and André glanced expressively to Pemberton when he saw these, for he thought they were the firing party, and that his last request had been granted.

An outer guard of five hundred men also attended, at the head of which rode nearly all the principal officers of the army, with the exception of Washington and his staff, who from a feeling of delicacy remained in-doors. Large crowds of the soldiery, and of the citizens from the surrounding country, also were present.

As André passed on, he retained his composure in a wonderful degree—nodding and speaking pleasantly to those officers with whom he was acquainted; especially to those who had constituted the court-martial.

The gallows had been erected on the summit of an eminence that commanded a wide view of the surrounding country. It was also in full view of Washington's headquarters; but the doors and shutters of the latter were closed, not a soul was to be seen, save the usual sentinels pacing in front of the house.

As the mournful procession turned from the high road into the meadow, André first saw the gallows. He suddenly recoiled, and paused for a moment.

"I thought you meant to spare me this indignity!" he exclaimed, almost passionately.

"We have simply to obey our orders," replied one of the officers.

"Gentlemen, you are making a great mistake," cried Pemberton to a couple of higher officers, who were riding near.

"If we are, we are doing it honestly, and because we think it our duty," replied one of them.

André moved on. "I must drink the cup to the dregs, it seems," he said with deep emotion. "But it will soon be over." The pleasant smile, however, had vanished from his face. It was evident that what he thought a needless indignity, cut sharper than the sentence of death itself.

The gallows was simply a rude but lofty gibbet, with a wagon drawn under it. Inside the wagon was a roughly-made coffin, painted black. As André stood near the wagon, awaiting some brief preparations, his agony seemed almost more than he could bear; his throat sinking and swelling as though convulsed, while he rolled a pebble to and fro under one of his feet. Laune, his servant, totally overcome, burst out into loud weepings and lamentations. This seemed to rouse and restore his master, who turned to him, and uttered some cheering and comforting words. All around there were solemn faces, and many were even in tears.

At a word from one of the officers, André flung his arms round Pemberton's neck and kissed him, and sprang lightly but with evident loathing into the baggage-wagon, standing upon the coffin. Then he looked around him—upon his executioner, with his blackened face; upon the saddened soldiery and the mournful crowd; upon the glorious landscape, resplendent with the hues of Autumn, and melting gradually away into the hazy distance. Then the old, proud look came back into his face—and he seemed more like a hero, mounted in the car of triumph, and prepared to receive the acclamations of his followers, than a man about to suffer a shameful death.

The executioner approached him, but he waved him away with a grand disdain, and tossing his hat to the ground, removed his stock, opened wide his shirt-collar, and taking the noose, adjusted it himself properly about his neck. On his face was a proud disgust as he did this—as if he said without useless words, "You have the power; and though you use your power meanly, I am man and soldier enough to submit to it!" Then he bound his handkerchief over his eyes.

The order of execution was read loudly and impressively by Adjutant-General Scammel. At its conclusion, Colonel Scammel informed the prisoner that he might speak, if he had anything to say.

Lifting the bandage from his eyes, and gazing around once more, as if that last look of earth and sun and sky and human faces was sweet indeed, André said in a proud, clear voice :—

"Bear witness, gentlemen, that I die in the service of my country, as becomes a British officer and a brave man."

The hangman now drew near with a piece of cord to bind his arms; but, recoiling from his snaky touch, André swept his hand aside, and drawing another handkerchief from his pocket, allowed his elbows to be loosely fastened behind his back. Then he said in a firm voice—"I am ready!"

Almost at the word, the wagon was rolled swiftly away, and, with a terrible jerk and shock, the noble soul of John André was severed from the beautiful frame with which the Creator had clothed it.

And there was a solemn stillness through all the multitude gathered around, broken only by the sound of weeping. For all felt that this was no common man; and that he had done nothing worthy of death. Only that it was necessary that he should die for the good of their country.

PART IV.

FIVE YEARS AFTER.

O thou that sendest out the men,
To rule by land and sea,
Strong mother of a Lion line,
Be proud of those strong sons of thine,
Who wrench'd their rights from thee.—*Tennyson.*

NEARLY five years had passed since the death of Major André. The war was over. The "Triumph"—appropriate name—had arrived at Philadelphia, bringing letters from Lafayette to the President of Congress, informing him that a Treaty of Peace had been signed at Paris. And on the 19th of April, 1783—precisely eight years after the opening of the conflict at Lexington—Washington proclaimed the Cessation of Hostilities in the General Orders to his faithful Army.

The war therefore had been over for more than two years. In fact it had really been over since the surrender of Cornwallis in the Autumn of 1781. That, and Greene's successes in the Carolinas, had turned the scales against the British. As we have said before, both parties were tired out, and a great reverse to either was enough to settle the contest against the loser.

Helen Graham did not die—though she lay at the point of death for many weeks, and did not recover sufficiently to return to Philadelphia, until the ensuing Spring.

We have said that she did not die, but we feel like amending the expression. The beautiful, serene lady, with shining masses of silvery hair, who came back to Philadelphia, could hardly be called the Helen Graham that is known to our readers. That was an ardent, impulsive, proud, passionate, and wayward girl—this was a quiet, composed, and unexcitable, though also, in her different way, lovely woman. There seemed to be a mystery in the change, which puzzled all her friends—her sister more than all. It was as if she had been transformed—or else that she had lost some portion of her original essence and spirit, in those cruel days of pain, and that the remaining and quieter elements of her character had crystallized into a new form, which shone with a milder radiance.

At the declaration of peace, Pemberton and Isabella had been married, with the full approbation of Colonel Musgrave, who after attending the wedding, had sailed with his regiment for England. They were still living with Mrs. Pemberton as before, and Helen, as a matter of course, resided with them.

Captain Morris, upon the cessation of hostilities, had entered into a partnership with Pemberton, for the carrying on of a mercantile business in Philadelphia. He was the active business man of the firm; Pemberton furnishing the greater part of the capital, but devoting a good deal of his time to his favorite studies. The times were happily "slower" then than now, and it did not need that a man should give himself entirely up to his business—body, soul and spirit—or else run a great risk of becoming a bankrupt. That fierceness of competition, which spares neither the man himself, nor his dearest friends—which immolates whatever stands in its way, unhesitatingly and unscrupulously, on the shrine of Mammon, and then takes its seat on Sunday, in the high places of the Church, and even perhaps "runs" a church of its own—had not yet become one of the distinguishing features of our American city life. Men were then industrious in their business, and being also moderate in their desires, and economical in their expenditures, had time to think of something else than the mere adding of dollar to dollar.

Captain Morris was a frequent, a very frequent visitor of the Pembertons. The hospitable mansion of his friend, with its pleasant grounds, extending to the line of Dock creek, was a pleasant place for any one to visit. And knowing the whole family so well, and moreover being a cousin, the gallant captain always felt perfectly at home. He was not there perhaps every evening—but his visits were certainly oftener than every other evening; and he walked in as naturally, and hung up his hat, without asking for any one in particular, as we all probably have enjoyed doing at some happy period of our lives, when fortune for a time has smiled propitiously upon us, and placed us in relation to some delightful family on a footing of the most intimate friendship.

Helen always received him with the greatest cordiality on such occasions—but in her serene and composed way, and without the least embarrassment. If the outside world said, and Arthur and Isabella thought, that Philip was still as enamoured as ever, Helen never seemed to know or care. She treated him with the kindness and familiarity which she would have shown to a brother; and either remembering and respecting her sad past, or else calmed and quieted by her sisterly manner, Morris never breathed a word—scarcely gave a look—which would convey the impression that he felt still the old, determined passion.

Other suitors, and avowed ones, however, Helen had had, and some that would persist in their suit, notwithstanding the intimations of her manner, until they received in words the fatal negative. One of them, a Colonel Avery, only a few days before the time of which we are speaking, had opened his heart to Morris, as to a friend of both parties, and asked him whether he thought it would be safe to venture a proposal. Morris felt the awkwardness of his own position, but replied:

"'Faint heart never won fair lady,' you know, Colonel. I must confess I think your chance is a doubtful one; but you cannot be more than refused—and that in the sweetest and most ladylike manner."

What the issue had been, or whether the Colonel had really put the matter to the test, Morris did not know—but during the whole of the next week, he never met the Colonel at the Pemberton mansion.

This was June. And on a beautiful sunny afternoon, the next Sunday but one after the counsel given to the Colonel, Helen and himself had strolled out into the grounds, and taken a seat on a shaded bench near the outer line of the garden. Ah, for the ravages of time! Where that bench stood, is now neither garden, nor lofty buttonwoods, nor visible creek. There the money-changer, high-priest of Mammon, sits and arranges his subtle plans; and all around, the "bulls" and "bears"—more savage than those of the fields and the wilderness—toss and tear each other.

At a pause of the conversation, Morris looked up and said, "I have not seen Colonel Avery here lately."

"No," replied Helen, while a slight glow came into her usually clear, white cheeks, "I believe he has started on a trip Northward."

"He asked my advice about a week ago, upon a certain matter, and I told him that 'Faint heart never won fair lady,'" continued Morris, with a smile.

The glow deepened a little upon Helen's face. "You did wrong, my friend. You ought to have known that my days of love were over."

"I suppose I ought," rejoined Morris, a little bitterly; "but, you see, it is a hard lesson for me to learn."

Helen turned her eyes full upon his face. "The girl perished that you loved, Philip; and it was well, for she could never have returned your love." She spoke in the kindest and gentlest of voices.

"The girl that I loved did not perish; and the woman I love still lives, as beautiful and precious to me, this day, as ever!" exclaimed Morris passionately, but rather avoiding the mild blue eyes bent serenely upon him.

"Oh, Philip, my poor boy!" she said, with more emotion than she had hitherto shown, "such warm love as yours deserves true love in return. Philip, I am not capable of loving. All that was so fervent and passionate in my nature, went out from me that awful day. I am a marvel now to myself. I picked up an old letter not long since—one written, but not sent, for want of a messenger—and read it all over. It sounded so strangely to me! I said to myself—can I be the Helen Graham whose name is signed to those burning words? I do not think I could write such a letter now—to any one, not even to him, should he come back again to life. No, Philip, Helen Graham—all that was glorious and precious about her—is dead? This is the mere case which held the finer spirit."

"I know you are greatly changed, Helen. How could it be otherwise?" replied Morris, in tones that quivered with the excess of his emotion, now breaking forth anew after those years of constant repression. "But you are still to me the Helen Graham to whom I declared my boyish passion at the Mischianza. Or, if not the same Helen, an even nobler and more seraphic one. It is you, as you are, Helen, whom I love, and I shall never love any other woman."

"Poor, foolish boy!" rejoined Helen, as she pityingly smoothed with her white hand the hair over his forehead, apparently unconscious how he thrilled beneath her cool, calm touch. "And would you, Philip, marry a woman who says she does not love you—one who, as she is now, could not love any one?"

"I would marry you, Helen—this moment. I love you, and, as you know, always have loved you. I have love enough for both, Helen."

"If I thought it would be right—and that it would be acting fairly toward you," and Helen paused. She was evidently considering the matter. There was no embarrassment in her voice, and her calm, affectionate eyes did not avoid the ardent glances of the passionate soul which looked out of the eyes of her companion.

"Oh, Helen, my only love, say yes, and make me happy!" whispered Morris, in the delirium of his unexpected bliss. "I know you love me more than any other man in this wide world. If not, why have you refused those others?"

"Of course, Philip, I should not think for a moment of marrying any living man but you," replied Helen, in a composed but affectionate tone. "I always did like you greatly, Philip. And if I marry you, it will be because I like you, and value your happiness so much—and because you are so foolish as to think so highly of me. But, if I do marry you, Philip, and you get tired of me, and think you have made a great mistake, I shall not blame you in the least, my friend."

"If I do, just take one of my pistols and blow my silly brains out," exclaimed Morris, in high rapture. "Oh, Helen, my pearl of great price, you cannot imagine how happy you have made me!" And Morris, for the first time in his life, put his arm around the woman he had always loved so madly, and kissed her ripe red lips.

A rather deeper tint came upon Helen's cheeks, but she not only allowed, but returned the kiss. Then she said:

"One thing I can promise you, Philip; that I will be a faithful and affectionate wife to you—careful of you and your interests in all things. If I cannot love you, as you deserve to be loved, I can at least honor and obey as well and I think a little better, than almost any other woman you would be apt to meet." Helen said this in a low, sweet, earnest tone that was enchanting to Morris, whatever it might have been to a more exacting lover.

"I know you will make a perfect wife—for you are a perfect woman!" exclaimed he, devotedly, looking upon her with rapture, as if from the heights of Paradise. "I always said I intended to marry you, Helen, from the first day I saw you, when you saved my life at Germantown—you, and no one else—and in spite of all obstacles—and now, you see, my words are coming true."

Helen smiled sweetly, and rising they took their way back to the house. And there was such a triumphant expression on Philip's face when they entered the parlor, and such a soft, sweet look in Helen's eyes, that Isabella shot a meaning glance over to her husband, and then rose and kissed her sister on both cheeks.

"Philip has been asking me to do a very foolish thing," she said, in answer, with a smile.

"I am glad that you consented, Helen," replied Isabella. "There is no other man in the world I would like to give you to—and Philip could not be happy with any other woman. He will wear you like a wondrous pearl, *ma belle Helene.*"

And so Helen and Philip, in the course of the ensuing Autumn, were married. At Helen's request it was a very quiet wedding, and Morris, man like, cared but little, now he had secured the bride he wished, whether the marriage knot was tied in the presence of ten or of ten thousand beholders. Helen was dressed beautifully but not showily—and she smilingly said when they came to arrange her hair, that it was already powdered.

But never had a more beautiful bride given away her hand in marriage, even in her own city of fair women. And the shining coils of her silvery hair were not the smallest of her charms—they seemed so in harmony with the fair white cheeks, and the serene brow, while they added depth and lustre to the calm violet eyes.

As for Morris, he looked the very image of what a bridegroom should be—full of life and ardor, and all glowing with the fervor of manhood's love. This was the day of days for him—and he felt every inch of him a king; for was he not to wed his Queen?

And these two, as also Pemberton and Isabella, lived thenceforth a happy life—till death did them part—in our own goodly city of Philadelphia. And they had sons and daughters, to rise up and call them blessed. And Morris never regretted that he had married where he was not deeply loved—for, as he had said, he had love enough for both. And in the serene and beautiful woman who was a perpetual fountain of sweetness to all around her, he recognized what was to him the very highest ideal of a perfect womanhood.

Pemberton also was fully satisfied—for he too had found his ideal woman. A nobler woman than Isabella Pemberton never drew the breath of life. As compared with her sister, she was now the more impassioned of the two. And such was necessary to satisfy the heart of Pemberton, who, in one sense, had not enough love for both. He pleased Isabella the better because he had not. She was a glorious creature; and Pemberton, as he was, with his deficiencies as well as his superiorities, filled her eye. She would not have altered him, nor he her, one jot or tittle. Even when their years increased, and Time began to make his changes, they would not have had it otherwise. Such as theirs are the marriages which are made in Heaven!

CONCLUSION.

It only remains to add a few lines of information and elucidation, and then we shall conclude this little history.

The Sibyl's prediction as to Westminster Abbey came true. When the sad news of Major André's death reached England, the greatest sorrow and sympathy were manifested. The latter found expression in many ways. The King instantly ordered a thousand guineas from the privy purse to be given to André's mother, and an annual pension of £300 to be settled on her for life, and afterwards to be paid to her children. And a Baronetcy was conferred upon his brother, Captain William Lewis André, of the 26th Regiment, and upon his heirs male forever.

In addition to the above substantial proofs of a nation's sympathy, a stately cenotaph was erected, and now stands in Westminster Abbey. It is of statuary marble, and on a panel is to be read the following inscription: "Sacred to the memory of Major John André, who, raised by his merits, at an early period of his life, to the rank of Adjutant-General of the British Forces in America, and employed in an important but hazardous enterprise, fell a sacrifice to his zeal for his King and Country, on the 2d of October, 1780, aged twenty-nine, universally beloved and esteemed by the army in which he served, and lamented even by his foes. His gracious Sovereign, King George III., has caused this monument to be erected."

Forty-one years afterwards, the remains of John André, including a few locks of the once beautiful hair, were disinterred by the order of the Duke of York, at the suggestion of Mr. Buchanan, the British consul, from the lonely grave at Tappan, and placed in a costly sarcophagus, hung with black and crimson, for rêmoval to England. Amid the deep sympathy of his former foes, all that remained of the once glorious face and form was gathered tenderly together, and the faces of men grew sad, as they thought over the old story, and fair women sent garlands to decorate the bier. And thus, with all honor, and due solemnity, the bones of one of England's most accomplished and chivalric sons were borne home, and deposited near his monument, in that shrine sacred to the memory of her departed greatness and glory.

But though the prediction thus came true, apparently in all its features, as to André, it evidently failed, so far as it went—at least in details—as to Helen. It is not our part to account for this, but only to state the fact.

As to Madame Dumont herself, she left America soon after the war, and sailed for Europe. In Paris she found a wider field for her art, and a more congenial atmosphere. There, under another name, she startled thousands, and even titled personages and crowned heads, with the marvellous magnetism of her presence, and the wonderful accuracy of many of her predictions.

It may be that some of our readers feel an interest in knowing what became of Captain Fanny. The reckless Captain, under the name and in the masculine dress of Captain Francis Malone, took no small share of glory to himself for the part which he—and his twin-sister Fanny, he said—had taken in obtaining information for the American commanders during the war. Fanny, he alleged, had died about the conclusion of hostilities. Of course, there really had been no such twin-sister; but it answered the Captain's purposes to invent a personage of this character, who could bear some suspicions and inquiries that might perhaps be a little troublesome to himself.

Helen was deceived entirely, and for all her life, by this adroit imposture. Captain Fanny and Captain Francis were, to her mind, two persons; and she was well pleased, as the Captain intended she should be, in thinking this.

As the years went on, the Captain became a famous politician—caring no more, however, for the "great principles" which divided parties, than he had formerly cared for those which divided rebel and tory. In truth, it seemed to him the very height of the ridiculous, that the same men who had once been banded together as rebels, should afterwards be nearly as bitter against each other as they had been against the common foe. This was a standing joke with the Captain, whenever it was safe to utter it; and confirmed him in his opinion of the utter folly of having any principles at all, save those which added to the holder's comforts. The Captain therefore was first an ardent Federalist, and afterwards an equally ardent Anti-Federalist—never getting on the losing side, except when he made a mistake; and having a most wonderful sagacity, the result of his perfect coolness, as to the current of the popular opinion. So the Captain, on the strength of his many patriotic services during the war, and his apparent devotion to the winning side, became first a Justice of the Peace, then a member of the City Councils, and finally a Representative in the State Legislature. That was about as high as such a man could get in those aristocratic times; but if he had lived now-a-days, he doubtless would have gone on until he became a member of Congress, a Governor, and possibly a Senator of the United States.

A few words more—relative to Benedict Arnold, and we must conclude. Arnold did not obtain the high rewards for which he had bargained, and doubtless would have received in case of his success. He was made however a Brigadier General in the British service, and received besides the sum of seven thousand pounds.

Small pay this, however, for the curses heaped upon him by his indignant countrymen. His name became a word of loathing to them. Probably no man was ever more bitterly and generally hated by the country which gave him birth. Secret plans were set on foot to entrap him. And orders were given, in case of his capture, to hang him at once, and without a trial; orders which would have been rigorously and eagerly followed.

The knowledge of these things, or the failure of his great schemes, acting on the natural sternness and severity of his character, made him fierce and cruel. He headed predatory expeditions against his old friends, and ravaged the coast even of his native State with fire and sword. Thousands would have delighted to shoot him, and yet, while exposing himself on these adventures, he seemed to bear a charmed life. Neither secret wile nor open warfare touched him.

He went to England, and was received with honor by the King, as a repentant subject, who had done the State some service, and would have done it more. But the contempt which follows Treason—especially when it is allied with Failure—attended him, more or less, shouting or whispering its detestation, wherever his footsteps trod. Perhaps he derived some consolation amid the bitterness which thus always accompanied him, from the steadfast affection of his young and lovely wife, who seems to have been kept in entire ignorance of his projected treason, but who joined him afterwards in New York, and while he lived, continued faithful to him and to his fortunes.

Tradition tells—we know not how truly—a story like this. When the last days of Arnold approached, the enfeebled but still stern old man seemed to grow restless and unquiet, as if he missed something that was dear to his heart. At length, on the last day of his eventful and stormy life, when the final hour seemed to be drawing near, he bade them bring him the old and faded blue-and-buff uniform which he had worn when a Major General in the

Continental service. Smiling grimly when he saw it, he dragged himself from his bed, and mustered up strength sufficient to array his wasted frame in the old, rejected garb. There he was again, a Major General of his country, with the blade which he had so effectively wielded in her cause on so many hard-fought fields, girded once more by his side. Drawing himself up for a moment to his full height, the dying General forgot his treason, and waving his sword in his hand, as he so often had waved it in the heat of battle, he shouted, "*On, my brave fellows!*" and fell at full length, dead, on the couch before him. If this tradition be true, it may mingle with the memories of his early and heroic services, and lead a forgiving country to drop a tear even over the follies and the crime of Benedict Arnold.

MONUMENT TO MAJOR ANDRE IN WESTMINSTER ABBEY.

Tricotrin. The Story of a Waif and Stray. By "OUIDA," author of "Under Two Flags," etc. With Portrait of the Author from an Engraving on Steel. 12mo. Cloth. $2.

"The story is full of vivacity and of thrilling interest."—*Pittsburgh Gazette.*

"Tricotrin is a work of absolute power, some truth and deep interest." —*N. Y. Day Book.*

"The book abounds in beautiful sentiment, expressed in a concentrated, compact style which cannot fail to be attractive and will be read with pleasure in every household."—*San Francisco Times.*

Granville de Vigne; or, Held in Bondage. A Tale of the Day. By "OUIDA," author of "Idalia," "Tricotrin," etc. 12mo. Cloth. $2.

"This is one of the most powerful and spicy works of fiction which the present century, so prolific in light literature, has produced."

Strathmore; or, Wrought by His Own Hand. A Novel. By "OUIDA," author of "Granville de Vigne," etc. 12mo. Cloth. $2.

"It is a romance of the intense school, but it is written with more power, fluency and brilliancy than the works of Miss Braddon and Mrs. Wood, while its scenes and characters are taken from high life."—*Boston Transcript.*

Chandos. A Novel. By "Ouida," author of "Strathmore," "Idalia," etc. 12mo. Cloth. $2.

"Those who have read these two last named brilliant works of fiction (Granville de Vigne and Strathmore) will be sure to read *Chandos.* It is characterized by the same gorgeous coloring of style and somewhat exaggerated portraiture of scenes and characters, but it is a story of surprising power and interest."—*Pittsburgh Evening Chronicle.*

Under Two Flags. A Story of the Household and the Desert. By "OUIDA," author of "Tricotrin," "Granville de Vigne," etc. 12mo. Cloth. $2.

"No one will be able to resist its fascination who once begins its perusal."—*Phila. Evening Bulletin.*

"This is probably the most popular work of Ouida. It is enough of itself to establish her fame as one of the most eloquent and graphic writers of fiction now living."—*Chicago Journal of Commerce.*

Puck. His Vicissitudes, Adventures, Observations, Conclusions, Friendship and Philosophies. By "OUIDA," author of "Strathmore," "Idalia," "Tricotrin," etc. 12mo. Fine cloth. $2.

"Its quaintness will provoke laughter, while the interest in the central character is kept up unabated."—*Albany Journal.*

"It sustains the widely-spread popularity of the author."—*Pittsburgh Gazette.*

The Old Mam'selle's Secret. From the German of E. Marlitt, author of "Gold Elsie," etc. By Mrs. A. L. WISTER. Sixth edition. 12mo. Cloth. $1.50.

"A more charming story, and one, which, having once commenced, it seemed more difficult to leave, we have not met with for many a day."—*The Round Table.*

"Is one of the most intense, concentrated, compact novels of the day. . . . And the work has the minute fidelity of the author of 'The Initials,' the dramatic unity of Reade and the graphic power of George Eliot."—*Columbus (O.) Journal.*

Gold Elsie. From the German of E. Marlitt, author of "The Old Mam'selle's Secret," etc. By Mrs. A. L. WISTER. Fifth edition. 12mo. Cloth. $1.50.

"A charming book. It absorbs your attention from the title-page to the end."—*The Home Circle.*

"A charming story charmingly told."—*Baltimore Gazette.*

Countess Gisela. From the German of E. Marlitt, author of "Gold Elsie," etc. By Mrs. A. L. WISTER. Third edition. 12mo. Cloth. $1.50.

"There is more dramatic power in this than in any of the stories by the same author that we have read."—*N. O. Times.*

"It is a story that arouses the interest of the reader from the outset."—*Pittsburgh Gazette.*

"The best work by this author."—*Philadelphia Telegraph.*

Over Yonder. From the German of E. Marlitt, author of "Countess Gisela," etc. Third edition. With a full-page Illustration. 8vo. Paper cover. 30 cents.

"'Over Yonder' is a charming novelette. The admirers of 'Old Mam'selle's Secret' will give it a glad reception, while those who are ignorant of the merits of this author will find in it a pleasant introduction to the works of a gifted writer."—*Daily Sentinel.*

The Little Moorland Princess. From the German of E. Marlitt, author of "The Old Mam'selle's Secret," "Gold Elsie," etc. By Mrs. A. L. WISTER. Fourth edition. 12mo. Fine cloth. $1.75.

"By far the best foreign romance of the season."—*Philadelphia Press.*

"It is a great luxury to give one's self up to its balmy influence."—*Chicago Evening Journal.*

Magdalena. From the German of E. Marlitt, author of "Countess Gisela," etc. And THE LONELY ONES ("The Solitaries"). From the German of Paul Heyse. With two Illustrations. 8vo. Paper cover. 35 cents.

"We know of no way in which a leisure hour may be more pleasantly whiled away than by a perusal of either of these tales."—*Indianapolis Sentinel.*

www.ingramcontent.com/pod-product-compliance
Lightning Source LLC
LaVergne TN
LVHW020113110826
845151LV00001B/149

* 9 7 8 1 4 2 5 5 4 2 9 9 3 *